THE LAST WITNESS

Richard Montgomery

PublishAmerica
Baltimore

© 2011 by Richard Montgomery
All rights reserved. No part of this book may be reproduced, stored in a retrieval system or transmitted in any form or by any means without the prior written permission of the publishers, except by a reviewer who may quote brief passages in a review to be printed in a newspaper, magazine or journal.

First printing

This is a work of fiction. Names, characters, places, and incidents either are the product of the author's imagination or are used fictitiously. Any resemblance to actual persons, living or dead, events, or locales is entirely coincidental.

PublishAmerica has allowed this work to remain exactly as the author intended, verbatim, without editorial input.

Hardcover 978-1-4560-4979-9
Softcover 978-1-4560-4980-5
PUBLISHED BY PUBLISHAMERICA, LLLP
www.publishamerica.com
Baltimore

Printed in the United States of America

Dedicated to the memory of my Father-in-Law,
Robert Lee Payne…a good man!

Acknowledgements

I want to thank Jim Hinkle, Sally Guillily, Lynn Futral, Karen Custer, Nancy Grandoff, Marty Higgins, Gary Lavelle and Angel Pala who took the time to read a draft of the book, provide valuable comments and encouragement.

I especially want to thank my daughter, Casey (Montgomery) Bushey, who was the inspiration for the character Brooke, and most of all for her enthusiasm and untiring effort to edit both the draft and final manuscript.

And finally, there aren't enough words to express my love and appreciation for my wife, Cheryl, who has put up with me and my adventures for over forty years.

Chapter One
New Mexico
October 18, 2009
Sunday
0300 hours

Sixty miles east of Albuquerque, New Mexico, a dark blue 2009 Ford Crown Victoria turned north on highway 285. It was a cool October night, the moon was full, and the three men in the car had remained mostly silent on this second night of their journey. They traveled only at night. The inside of the car reeked of stale cigar smoke, garlic and the unmistakable aroma of failed deodorant. By now they had exhausted all of their stories even the small talk. The driver, Luis Escobar, was in his late fifties. He was a well-built man at five feet eleven inches. He had immigrated to America on the Mariel Boat Lift thanks to President Jimmy Carter. The right seat passenger was Mickey "Little Mickey" McGuire. Little Mickey had grown up in Glens Falls, New York. He was the quiet one. He was the third of nine children born to Sean and Erin McGuire. The rear seat passenger was Dominic "Dom" Corsetti. His parents had immigrated from Sigonella, Sicily just after the Second World War. His dad, Elvio, had fought against the Americans at Palermo.

About twenty miles south of Cline Corners the car passed a small white cross adorned with a bouquet of flowers that had long since died and were begging to be replaced. Luis commented that the cross probably marked the spot where someone had lost a loved one in an accident. Dom quickly spoke up and said that since he hadn't seen a car in the past hundred miles or so that the cross probably marked the spot where somebody, "must have got hit by a fucking buffalo." Mickey shook his head as Luis turned slightly and accused Dom of being a real sentimental guy.

Mickey asked Luis to pull over so he "could take a leak."

"Good idea," said Dom, "I was beginning to think you guys didn't have bladders."

All three were in the process of watering the cholla cactus when Mickey zipped up, turned to walk away, reached into his coat, drew a small 22-caliber pistol and without hesitation turned and shot Dominic in the back of the head. The bullet ricocheted around Dominic's skull. He dropped like a dead bull. Luis glanced back showing no emotion whatsoever as he looked down at Dominic. Dominic's hands and feet twitched in rebellion for a few seconds then stopped forever. Luis finished his business and zipped up as the silence returned to the desert terrain. The smell of cordite was in the air. Mickey shut his eyes, tilted his head back and took a deep breath. He liked the way it smelled. Both men picked up Dom's limp body and carried it nearly fifty yards from the highway. The body left little drops of blood and urine along the way. They dumped what was left of him into a four-foot grave that had already been prepared. A small T-handle shovel stood at attention on top of the dirt pile. It cast an eerie cross-like shadow into the final resting place of Dominic Corsetti. Both men were winded. Mickey bent forward with his hands on his knees and took several deep breaths. He straightened up, threw the maskened-taped pistol on top of the still warm body, looked over at Luis and without a word spoken between them, proceeded to fill in the grave. Forty minutes later, Luis and Mickey were on their way to Dallas. The cross and dead flowers were gone.

Chapter Two
Chesapeake, Virginia
October 18, 2010
Monday
1030 Hours

One year and one day later...

October was always an interesting time of year in the Tidewater area. Although it wasn't the last month of the hurricane season, if Virginia were going to get a hurricane, it would probably hit in late September or early October. However, this October the weather was ideal. There were no hurricanes in sight. There were no *easterly waves* coming off the west coast of Africa, and none were expected. The jet stream had dropped down and was heading due east over the top of Virginia Beach at over two hundred miles per hour. If a hurricane did form in the Atlantic Basin it would have a hard time making landfall in southeastern Virginia. The weather was cooling down, the golfing was great and the lake fishing was at its best. It was a good time of year to catch a citation largemouth.

This Monday morning represented a major milestone for Richard B. Morgan. He had just received a call from his lawyer informing him that the Spectrum Corporation had just delivered all of the final closing documents for Rick and his partners to sign. Matrix Inc. had sold. The deal was firm and the closing was scheduled for Friday morning at ten o'clock. Rick had mixed emotions. The past fourteen years had gone by like the...proverbial bullet. Matrix had been fun and very lucrative. The company had grown to over eighty employees supporting numerous government contracts involving information technology, weapons systems acquisition and Rick's specialty, covert operations. However, the time to sell was ripe. The partnership had been strained for the past two years. The senior partner was having serious health problems, and Rick and his younger partner hadn't had a civil conversation in months. The Spectrum Group's offer was just too good to pass up. As he put down the phone, he leaned back in his chair and looked out of his second story office window just in time to see a large flock of Canadian geese flying in right echelon. They had begun landing in the vacant lot next door. They would probably spend the afternoon grazing on the newly planted seed. Their life was so simple—fly, eat, poop, sleep and propagate—and not necessarily in that order. Another phone call interrupted his amusement with the landing pattern.

"Rick, Carl Peterson is on line two."

"Thanks Linda." He would miss Linda. She was the ideal executive assistant. She never let him forget anything. She hardly ever made a mistake, and if she did she was the one who caught it.

Rick and Carl Peterson had known each other for over forty years... forty-six to be exact. Both had been recruited on the same day in one of the little wooden shacks that lined the back perimeter of the University of Miami campus. They were built during the Second World War. The majority of the little white buildings were now used by a select group of professors to house their special projects. To this day, Rick can still visualize the recruiters... both in their kaki trousers and white cotton short-sleeved shirts. They both had crew cuts, were quite fit, well tanned and had firm handshakes. Their paths would cross many times over the years.

"Carl, good afternoon. How are you doing?"

"Very well, thank you, and how about you?"

"I couldn't be...better."

The slight hesitation in Rick's voice was not convincing.

"I was wondering if you have had enough time to consider my offer?"

"Your timing couldn't be any better. As of Friday I will be unemployed."

"So...do I take that as a yes?"

Rick hesitated slightly before answering, although he had already made up his mind.

"You may indeed," he said firmly.

"Great, I was hoping you would accept. Have you said anything to Lynn?"

Carl's deference for Lynn's approval was genuine. He had gained a lot of respect for Lynn, although, down deep inside he *knew* that the feeling wasn't mutual.

"Not yet."

"Will she be okay with your decision?"

"I'm sure that after a week or two she will be happy to hear that I have something else to do other than bother her all day. You know Carl, women *like* their space."

"That's what I have been told. Rick, I am looking forward to seeing you. How long has it been this time?"

"I believe the last time was during the Southern Command proposal."

"SOUTHCOM…ah yes, I believe you're right."

"I really thought we had a good shot at that one."

"Well so did I. However, as with many of these things, it turned out that the proposal was wired for a company out of Miami. I probably should have listened to my intelligence people. They told me it would be a waste of time and resources. However, I thought we had *resumes* that couldn't be beaten. We did get some very valuable exposure in DC."

"That we did," said Rick knowing that he could account for six million dollars in contracts as a direct result of their *losing* proposal.

"Rick—when will you be available?"

"Soon Carl I…I need a little time off. It has been a long process preparing for the sale. Lynn wants to head down to Florida after the closing. I certainly owe it to her. She has always been there for me…or, should I say…put up with my *little* escapes into the world of business and finance. Plus, I really do need to get back in shape."

"You…back in shape? I can't imagine *you* ever being out of shape."

"I could be in better shape," said Rick as he looked down at a slight paunch.

"Take your time my friend. There is no rush. The job will be here when you're ready."

"Thanks Carl. I'll be in touch."

Six months of preparing all the due diligence documents had been mentally exhausting. Rick really did need the time off. Fortunately, he had always been able to stay in relatively good condition. He came from good genes. He looked much younger than his age, and at six feet he carried his two hundred and ten pounds quite well. He still had a thirty-six inch waist, sixteen inch biceps and could easily bench press two hundred and fifty pounds. Not bad for a guy who was eligible for Social Security. However, for the past fourteen years, he had little opportunity to workout on a regular basis. He played racquetball only occasionally…just enough that he never seemed to get over the soreness. Lately, the arthritis that had taken up residence in his knees was winning the battle of time. It was getting more difficult to go up and down the stairs. Down was particularly difficult. He had just finished a series of shots that provided some relief, but he knew it was only temporary and just a matter of time before he would finally give in and have both knees replaced. He wanted to do it while he was still relatively young and healthy. He was determined to do both knees at the same time. However, right now he was looking forward to *semi—retirement*, lying on the beach and working out at Gold's Gym. He would have to pass on the long walks on the beach with Lynn. He knew that getting in good shape wasn't difficult. Getting in great shape required commitment, dedication and time. Time was finally on his side.

Rick slid back into his high-back leather chair. Life had been going by at a pace that he hadn't been able to control. It seemed to be going by much faster as he got older…and it was, indeed, going by much faster. He picked up the cup of black coffee that occupied a prominent position on the right side of his desk. It had been cold for well over an hour. The Matrix logo had faded from years of microwaving. His cup was special. It was the first cup purchased by Matrix Inc., and no matter what its condition, it would remain with him forever. He got up and glanced out the window. By now the geese were in full dine mode. Two alert sentries provided watch. He walked down the hall to the small gedunk, rinsed his cup and poured a full cup of hot black coffee that had been brewing for most of the morning. It had a velvet texture, was strong for most, but just right for an old salt.

He returned to his office and slowly sat down in the chair being careful not to spill a drop. As he settled back it finally hit Rick that this was the last Monday he would ever be a part of Matrix Inc. He felt like he was selling his baby…it wasn't a good feeling. He felt a slight twinge in his stomach. He held the cup tightly in both hands and moved it close to his chin. He slowly swiveled the chair around, his eyes roamed the office décor. Most everything that was there was there for a purpose. Rick's office was a working office, with the exception of his *I love me* wall. The wall got his attention. He got up, coffee cup in hand and looked at each of the plaques that represented nearly forty years of government-related service. The only one he would keep was not on the wall. It couldn't be displayed. The others would end up in a box in the attic only to be thrown away someday. It reminded him of Dr. James Dopson's comment that, "all trophies end up in the garbage". So sad. His mind wandered back to a time long ago in Miami, Florida. A time when he would run in full combat gear in the tidal plain north of Tahiti Beach. He and Carl Peterson would make the run in the early morning through the marsh at low tide, just before the bikini-clad joggers awkwardly stumbled through the mud and reeds. At most the water would be six to eight inches deep. There were numerous tidal pools and dry spots. The tidal pools were brimming with little creatures waiting for the tide to return. They had no idea where they were, or how they got there. Their whole purpose now was to avoid the great blue herons that instinctively knew when the tide was out…where the food was! He and Carl had made the run enough times to know where the more solid ground was located. They both would look ahead, instinctively picking their course across the marsh trying to repeat the previous day's run. The tide had a way of making every run a new adventure. Every once in a while Rick's boot would sink into a soft area. It would sink in up to his ankle. He would pull it out with a loud sucking sound and continue on without losing a step. Nothing would slow down the young Richard B. Morgan. Each time they made the run, they would add more weight to the weight belt that was secured tightly around their waists. Sometimes Rick would vary the weight. Other times he would put weight in the rucksack he carried on his back. The daily routine was competitive. Neither Rick nor Carl wanted to lose the morning jaunt. Both men had built the strength and stamina needed to prepare them well for the covert missions into Cuba, Nicaragua, Guatemala and Bolivia. The only guys that could even attempt to stay up with them were their *comrades*, the ones that put their lives on the line, trusted one another for their very being. Rick was one of the youngest recruits. It was a long time ago, but it was only yesterday in his mind.

Rick took a swallow of the strong black coffee. Actually, he only liked the first cup in the morning. The rest were a physical pause… something to do while thinking, or to give the impression of thinking. He leaned back in the chair, his eyes resting on the bookcase that was full of three-ring binders containing Matrix's winning government proposals. Fourteen years ago there was only one…and that one was in his briefcase. The binders reminded him of the look on Lynn's face when he broke the news to her that he was starting his own company. They were having dinner when he broke the news.

"I quit my job today."

At first he didn't think that Lynn had heard him. She *had* heard him. Women hear everything.

"You what?" she said with a look of surprise.

"I quit my job," replied Rick as he cut a piece of steak.

"You quit your job today?"

"No, technically, I quit it last night."

"Oh…funny. So when were you going to tell me?"

"I was going to tell you…soon," said Rick as he put the fork into his mouth.

"And why would you quit just after you got a nice promotion and a healthy raise?"

"I have started my own business."

Rick immediately raised his hands in a gesture of surrender and shrugged his shoulders slightly.

"And before you say anything, I already have my first Delivery Order."

"So…basically you are still working?" said Lynn. A slight look of relief crossed her face.

"Still working!"

Lynn squinted a little bit as she was in the process of digesting what Rick had just told her. Rick continued to eat as if nothing had changed, having full confidence in his decision. He knew it was always tougher on the wife. The husband retires and the wife ends up with twice the husband and half the money. Still squinting, Lynn lifted her wine glass and responded just as he knew she would.

"You know…you're nuts!"

Rick smiled without looking up. That was fourteen years ago. Rick would be unemployed—temporarily—for the first time in forty-six years.

Chapter Three
Washington, DC
US Marshal's Office
October 19, 2010
Tuesday
1645 Hours

The phone startled Ben. He was deep in thought. He stared at it with contempt for several seconds before snatching the receiver from its cradle. He never did like talking on the phone, especially late in the day. Late in the day was never good. This day would prove to be no exception.

"Anderson," he said in a firm clear voice.

"Hey Ben, Dobson here. Have you heard about Spanelli?"

"Yeah Charlie, I just got word about a half hour ago. Frankly, I'm not surprised."

"How the hell did they find him so soon?" I heard that Lou Mallory's team was the best."

"Charlie, Lou's team *is* the best. *Lou Mallory* is the best, but nothing is ever a guaranteed sure thing. You of all people should know that. It appears that we greatly underestimated how badly someone wanted this guy dead."

"You don't think there was a leak from inside do you?"

"No I don't. At least I certainly hope there wasn't, but who knows seems like everybody has a guy on the inside these days. Charlie, money and fear are great motivators."

"Hell Ben, I was really looking forward to this one. I really need to get back in the game."

Charlie Dobson was new to the Witness Protection Program. Spanelli was going to be his first project. Charlie went into the US Marshals right out of college. He had been assigned to a joint task force team.

He stood out as a field agent and was due for a promotion when he and his partner were gunned down during a stakeout in San Diego, California. Charlie had sustained life-threatening injuries that kept him hospitalized for nearly three months. It had been touch and go for quite a while. But Charlie Dobson was young. He was tough, and to the amazement of several attending physicians, he was able to walk out of the hospital and back into service. However, his spinal injuries had left him with a considerable amount of numbness in his left leg and a slight limp. From a physical standpoint, his field days were over, but he wanted to remain a Deputy Marshal…in any capacity. He was assigned to Ben's team in support of the Witness Protection Program.

"Yeah, I was too, although, I do believe Spanelli would have been a real pain in the ass."

Down deep inside Ben shared Charlie's disappointment. Both men had worked many hours setting up the program, getting everything in place, making all the necessary contacts and setting the stage. A lot of up front work had already been accomplished prior to Spanelli's appearance before the Grand Jury.

"Ben, I don't think this was one of your typical up close and personal hits."

"It doesn't seem to be."

"Have you heard anything from the guys downtown?"

"From what I have been told so far, the kill has all the earmarks of a military-trained sniper."

"Military sniper? Kind of makes you wonder who was really behind the hit."

"Charlie, no matter who is responsible it is out of our hands, and it really doesn't matter to Spanelli. He's stone cold. Some medical examiner is probably weighing what's left of his brain as we speak."

"Yeah, you're right Ben."

"He's not our concern anymore. Charlie, look at it this way, we'll be first in line for the next one."

"Ben, I had no sympathy for this guy one way or the other. I just hate that we have wasted so much of our time and the team's time."

Neither man spoke for several seconds. Charlie Dobson was right. A lot of pre—planning had gone into this project. For that matter, a lot of planning goes into every project. However, Spanelli was a special case. So special that the Attorney General wanted daily updates. It didn't matter how much Spanelli was talking; the Attorney General needed him to say the same things in front of the Grand Jury. Charlie had worked especially hard setting up the procedures required to ensure witness protection. Ben broke the silence with a change of subject.

"How are Marcie and the kids?"

"They're doing very well, thank you. Are we still on for Sunday?"

"That we are. Everything is set. I'm looking forward to a relaxing afternoon, a very large porterhouse steak, baked potato, green beans and watching the Skins beat the living hell out of the Bears."

"It may not be too relaxing, Marcie is a big-time Bears fan."

"I didn't know that. How long has she been a Bears fan?"

"Forever. She was born in Chicago."

Ben wasn't really listening to Charlie. His mind was still on Spanelli.

"Charlie, it has been a long couple of months. Too bad it had to end this way. But as they say, it *is* what it *is*. Listen, I need to make a couple of quick calls. Carol and I are looking forward to seeing you guys. By the way, it's your turn to bring the beer."

Anderson hung up the phone and reached for the file on Spanelli. He had spent several weeks getting everything lined up. The Attorney General was looking forward to putting this guy on the stand. He was the biggest catch since "Sammy the Bull". Ben had scheduled the plastic surgeon, dentist, real estate agent, speech therapist, and all the usual players. He was looking forward to putting Spanelli behind him and getting on with the next project. Ben knew that everyone was after Spanelli. Spanelli had been a driver for Anthony "The Weasel" Carbone. He knew everything about the Carbone family business, their contacts, the skeletons in the closet, skeletons that would be in the closet, politicians on the take, dirty cops, dirty lawyers, Spanelli knew it all. He had been Carbone's right hand man for nearly twenty-two Years. Carbone would have trusted him with his *enlightened* sixteen year-old daughter…the one with all the tattoos. Spanelli was an insider. But now he was in custody and singing like a bird. The feds couldn't stop him talking. They just needed him to say the same things in front of the Grand Jury—where it really counted. Carbone knew that Spanelli had become a loose cannon. Spanelli was spilling the beans on everything and everybody. Ben knew it was going to be a difficult task providing around the clock protection. No place was safe, not even the basement in the Federal Court House. Ben got up from his desk and went down the hall to the small kitchen just off the conference room. He made a fresh pot of coffee. Most of the agents and office personnel didn't drink much coffee after two in the afternoon, but Ben could drink coffee right up until he went to bed. Caffeine never seemed to have any adverse effect on him. As he waited for the coffee to brew he remembered a statistic that he had just read that morning. The article mentioned that since the inception of the Witness Protection Program, more than 7,000 witnesses had entered the program and been given new identities, and over 9,000 family members were also in the Program. They all entered the program believing that they would be safe. None of them realized how vulnerable they really were. How ironic. Spanelli was a case in point. Ben's first call was to Lou Mallory. Mallory was the agent in charge of protecting Spanelli. Mallory's tone signaled that he knew this call was coming. He wasn't looking forward to it. Mallory was frustrated…really frustrated!

"Yeah…Mallory," he answered in a gruff voice aggravated by too many years of non-filtered cigarettes.

"Lou, Ben Anderson here."

"Hey Ben, I was expecting to hear from you."

"I just heard about Spanelli. What the *hell* happened down there?"

Ben really didn't want to play boss with Lou, but his emphasis on the word "hell" clearly defined the chain of command, and put Lou on the defensive.

"Ben, you know how long I have been doing this job?" responded Lou, his voice rising.

Lou Mallory was a well-seasoned agent. He had been with the Witness Protection Program forever. He was obviously upset and immediately took an offensive posture. Ben had been around for a long time also. He knew how to play that game.

"I guess not long enough. What part of *Witness Protection* do you or your team not understand?"

"Hey, fuck you, I have been doing this since you were"

Ben interrupted him; he knew that Lou was the best. Lou Mallory was a legend. He had never lost a witness in over thirty years on the job. Lou knew how to cover his tracks, move from house to house day or night, never leaving a trail. Blending in. That is why he was selected to cover Spanelli. The US Marshals knew that there were several contracts out on Spanelli. Hell, there were always contracts out on the witnesses. Ben really liked Lou and didn't want a confrontation. Besides, no matter what, the damage was done. Nothing was going to bring Spanelli back from the fiery pit of hell.

"Calm down Lou, I was just surprised that someone figured out so soon where you guys were."

"Ben, this guy pissed off the world. Everybody was after him. The Philadelphia guys, judges, dirty cops; I wouldn't be a bit surprised if the Catholic Church wasn't after him. Hell, I wanted to shoot the son-of-a-bitch myself."

"I know you did your best to protect him. This was a tough assignment. Any thoughts on how they found you, who found you, what went wrong?"

"Yeah I got some thoughts. Ben, you are not going to believe this. My new, fresh out of the academy, I-know-it-all computer-wiz-kid partner, Lawrence Stein, orders a pizza with Spanelli's favorite topping."

Lou's inflection on the kid's name gave Ben an image of Lou's partner *Lawrence* sitting in a far corner with a large pointed hat on his head.

"Favorite topping?"

"Yeah favorite topping! Pizza with olives and pineapple. Who the hell do you know orders pizza with olives and pineapple? I guess this Gomba always made the same order. Didn't take a whole lot of detective work to find out where we were. Obviously, somebody had a line on all the pizza parlors, and when the order went in bingo, Spanelli was dead meat."

Ben was having a hard time imagining eating pizza with olives and pineapple.

"Guess they don't cover that in school."

"Ben, you can't teach street smarts. What the hell was Stein thinking? I guess I should have paid more attention to what the kid was doing."

"I hear Spanelli got it just outside the safe house door. Did you guys see or hear anything?"

"Hell no, we didn't see anything. We didn't see it coming. The only thing I heard sounded like a pumpkin being hit with a sledgehammer. Neither Stein nor I heard the shot. We had just exited the row house. We were walking down the steps. Stein was in front of Spanelli, and I was behind. The next thing I know Spanelli is down. The bullet entered Spanelli just below the left eye and blew out the back of his skull all over my pants. He never knew what hit him. Hell, I was lucky that I didn't take the rest of the bullet. It ended up in the lower part of the door. I don't even know how far away the shooter was. He could have been a quarter of a mile away for all I know. This guy was good... real good."

"How is Stein taking all this?"

"Okay I guess he's new. First time he's seen the real thing in the flesh. I gave him my pants and told him to enter *that* into his bullshit computer!"

The vision of Lou taking off his pants and handing them to agent Stein brought a slight smile to Ben's face. Hopefully Lou had waited until they were alone, but knowing Lou, he probably took them off right there on the stairs.

"The kid can certainly learn a lot from you. Take it easy on him, Lou. Don't blame yourself. This was a really tough assignment. Sorry, but you know I had to make this call. Talk with you later."

Ben hung up the phone. There were too many people interested in seeing Spanelli dead. In fact, Ben was amazed that he had lasted this long. Less connected guys got "whacked" for a lot less and usually before they started talking or making any deals. Ben knew that there would be another one. There always was another one. He finished his coffee, picked up his cell phone and started to make a call to Phoenix Arizona. As he was dialing he realized that he wasn't in the mood to discuss the Spanelli case any more. He could call Phoenix later in the week.

Chapter Four
Miami, Florida
October 21, 2010
Thursday
0830 Hours

Manny Dominguez slowed down as he approached Alhambra Circle. He had been driving around killing time. He checked his watch. It was nearly eight thirty. The morning commute was just about over. He checked the rearview mirror for the blue Ford Mustang. He had seen the car several times on South Dixie Highway, then on Ponce de Leon Boulevard. He suspected that it was following him. But, as he was looking in the rear view mirror, he saw the Mustang turn into the University of Miami. Maybe he was getting paranoid; it was probably just a couple of students. Many of them drove Mustangs, but this one was a little too plain for a student, especially one that could afford to go to "Suntan U". Those spoiled little rich kids from the north always drove fancy cars. Manny continued to check his rear view mirror. He was suspicious by nature. In his business it paid to be suspicious of everything. Manny was always aware of his surroundings; what was behind him, and in front of him. He had to be. It wasn't long before he noticed that a pale green Buick seemed to be keeping pace with him. The Buick was tucked in behind a F-150 three cars back. It could have passed the truck but it didn't. Manny made a few random turns; the Buick followed and then turned south on 57th Avenue. About two minutes later he noticed the blue Mustang again. Someone was tag teaming him. Most likely it was the DEA. Manny mused to himself that these *maricones* watched too much TV. They couldn't follow a fifth grader without being noticed. It must be the *little red wagon* they drove. He stopped in front of a small stucco house on Blue Bird Road and honked the horn twice. He waited several minutes and honked again. He was getting a little impatient when his cousin Danny Ochoa finally stepped through the doorway. Danny was buttoning up his shirt. He looked around, and then walked briskly to the car. He jumped into the passenger side, gave Manny an, "I just got laid and it was great!" look, and motioned for him to drive on.

"Danny…one of these days daddy is going to come home early and you're going to get your ass shot off."

"You drive, I'll worry about my ass," snapped Danny. "Have you heard from Paco?"

"Yeah, the shipment is coming in on a freighter out of Monrovia. It is already off the coast. Just waiting for high tide and the harbor pilot. Should be docking in about three hours."

"What about Customs?"

"Paco said he took care of it. Nobody is going to hassle us. Besides, our little diversion off the coast has them all jumping through hoops."

"What did it cost us this time?"

"A hundred thousand."

"A hundred thousand? Ay coño…that's twice what we paid last month. What's going on? What does Paco think?" asked Danny.

"Paco thinks that Agent Trombley is getting too greedy. He doesn't trust him anymore."

"What do you think? Do you trust Trombley?"

Manny checked the rearview mirror and look at his side view mirror then over at Danny.

"I agree with Paco."

"Maybe it's time we find ourselves a new Customs agent," responded Danny.

Manny hadn't trusted Trombley for quite some time. Trombley was getting too big for his britches. He was buying too many *toys*…toys that would attract attention.

"Danny, I have another Customs agent in mind. The guy is heavy into the horses and is into his bookie for eighty-five thousand. I bet he'll jump at an opportunity to work with us, and for a lot less than a hundred K."

"Set it up. How did the truck turn out?"

"It looks so much like a FedEx truck we'll have people wanting us to take their packages."

"Oh great! That's just what we need—fucking people running up to a truck hauling a container full of cocaine."

"Danny, I'm just kidding, nobody is going to run up to the truck."

"But, what if they do? What do you say to them? Manny, we don't want anyone to become suspicious. We don't need to make stupid mistakes."

"Don't worry, Ernesto is driving the truck. He used to work for FedEx. He knows what to say to them. Besides it is a container hauler. Nobody is going to run up to container hauler."

"What about the rest of the guys? Are they in place?" asked Danny.

"Manuel and Guillermo will be at the warehouse. They will help unload the stuff when the truck arrives. Jose will be helping Ernesto with the pickup at the pier. Should be routine."

"Manny, look at me, nothing…*nothing* is routine. Remember that! Nothing is routine. This is our biggest shipment ever. We got twenty million of our own money on the line. These mooks on the street will pay two hundred fifty for an *eight ball*; we'll make thirty million in profit. So it *isn't* routine. It's never routine. You forget about Murphy's Law?"

"Who the hell is Murphy?"

"Hell, I don't know, but he always gets blamed for fuck-ups."

Danny Ochoa was a rough character. He had grown up running the numbers in little Havana for his uncle. He was only twelve years old when he was busted for selling pot. His uncle wasn't too happy with him, but Danny was blood. One day he would inherit Raul Ochoa's business, and all of his *other* businesses as well. He was being groomed to take over the family business. His uncle had a long talk with him following the arrest. Danny was never arrested again.

Manny made a left turn onto South Dixie highway. The blue Mustang made the same turn. It was a few cars back.

"Danny, we're being followed, it's the blue Mustang a couple of cars back."

Danny lowered the passenger seat visor and pretended to be combing his hair. He adjusted the visor just enough to see the Mustang. There were two people in the car.

"Looks like Agent Smalley and that skinny shit who talks with a lisp. Where the hell do they find these guys. They're both fucking useless."

As Danny continued his fake grooming, Manny reached into his jacket pocket and pulled out a *montecristo* from a silver cigar holder. He offered it to Danny. Danny waived him off. Manny put it back into his pocket. He wouldn't smoke unless Danny did.

"Manny, as long as they are following us they're out of action. Let's have some fun with these *maricones* and head out to Liberty City. Let's see if they can make it through there in one piece with their *unmarked* DEA surveillance vehicle."

Chapter Five
Port of Miami
October 21, 2010
Thursday
1030 Hours

The Chief Port Pilot met the Morning Star at the Sea Buoy. The seas were forecast to be three to five feet. The forecast was correct. The wind was from the southeast, the result of a Bermuda High that had lingered off the coast for several days. The pilot boat moved in harmony alongside the big ship. Captain Mike Bitiscomb prepared to grab the rope ladder. He had made this jump hundreds of times before. However, he was never complacent. The jump was never routine. As the two vessels danced in harmony across the Atlantic, Captain Bitiscomb reached out, took hold of the ladder and as both vessels rose together, he made his move. He took extra precaution climbing the one hundred foot rope ladder to the deck. This was his eighteenth year as the Chief Port Pilot. He was in great shape and wouldn't trade his job for anything. He loved it. He was met by the First Mate whose handshake represented many years of hard work at sea. The First Mate escorted him to the bridge. At 1030 hours Captain Bitiscomb took the Conn.

At the very moment Captain Bitiscomb took control of the Morning Star, Ernesto Garcia and Jose Mendoza were presenting their IDs at the Port of Miami Security gate. Ernesto's container truck was inspected, and he was given directions to the container staging area where he would later sign for and receive the container of goods from Egypt.

A fifteen-knot tailing wind helped push the Morning Star into the Port of Miami. Captain Bitiscomb skillfully maneuvered the ship past the shoals and into the inland waterway where numerous small boats and jet skiers jousted willingly with the big ship. Don Quixote was alive and well…and riding a jet ski. Captain Bitiscomb, with the help of two tugboats, had the ship tied alongside the pier at 1130 hours. The ship's manifest listed containers from China, Egypt, Greece and Italy. Most of the containers were filled with toys from China to be delivered just in time for Christmas. As the last lines were being secured, the longshoreman commenced unlashing the container rods. As soon as they had unlashed a couple of rows, the quay-side cranes began transferring "cans" to the utility tractor rig (UTR) trucks. The longshoremen deftly moved across the top of the containers being ever vigilant of the quay-side cranes. They leaned over the edge, and unhooked the last of the rods. One slip, a momentary lapse of attention, and there would be another fatality at the Port of Miami. At 1345 the longshoremen unlashed the final row of the nearly 4000 containers that were aboard the Morning Star. The quay-side cranes continued to move in a robotic pace as they methodically transferred "cans" to the UTR trucks, which, in turn, transferred them to the staging yards.

At 1620 one of the quay-side cranes transferred a dull brown container with Egyptian marking to a UTR truck. The UTR truck hauled the container to the southern most staging area where a FedEx truck was parked close by. The lettering on the container indicated that it was of Egyptian origin. The ship's manifest would later say that the container housed artifacts for the Chicago Museum of Natural History. Ernesto Garcia and Jose Mendoza were in the truck. Ernesto got out of the truck and motioned to the crane operator, indicating that the brown container was for him. The crane operator hoisted the container from the UTR truck and deftly transferred it to the FedEx truck. The process was very impressive, and it was quick. As Ernesto was checking the rigging, one of the Custom's agents came over and introduced himself as Agent Joseph Healy. Healy was middle-aged, had a close-cut haircut, and was quite obviously out of shape. He would have a hard time zipping up his blue Customs jacket. In fact, he had never zipped up the jacket. He presented his ID to Ernesto. Ernesto gave it an "I don't give a shit" look and handed it back to Agent Healy with a per functionary nod of approval.

"I'm Agent Healy. Are you the driver?"

Ernesto responded non-chalantly.

"I am, may I help you?"

"Let me see your Delivery Order."

Ernesto went back to the cab and returned with a tri-fold metal clipboard. He fumbled through several documents, lifted two metal tabs and presented the Delivery Order to Agent Healy. It was the typical FedEx Delivery Order containing information regarding the shipment, point of origin, item numbers, description and final destination. Attached to the Delivery Order was a copy of a letter from the Chicago Museum of Natural History. The letter confirmed that FedEx would be transferring the identified items for further shipment to Chicago. The letter was written on the Chicago Museum of Natural History's letterhead. All the documents appeared to be in order. In fact…all were very good forgeries. The Custom's agent took the Delivery Order and walked over to his vehicle where he had a laptop plugged into the cigarette lighter. His laptop was connected via satellite to the Customs Service Network. He made several keystrokes, gazed at the screen for a moment or two, and then made a few more keystrokes. After several minutes he returned, handed the Delivery Order to Ernesto and proceeded to examine the seal on the container's door.

"May I go now Agent Healy? I am on a very tight schedule. I have a crew waiting at the airport to load the contents onto one of our planes."

"Yes, but before you do I need to speak with the museum's representative. Is he here or at the airport?"

The question obviously caught Ernesto off guard. Agent Healy could sense the change in Ernesto's demeanor; little beads of sweat began forming on Ernesto's forehead. He was obviously very uncomfortable. He wasn't expecting any questions; money had exchanged hands. Agent Healy already knew the answer to the question, but was stalling for more time.

"I I don't know where *he* is. He certainly isn't with me. I was given this Delivery Order and told to pick up the cargo and deliver it to our facility at the Miami International Airport. That's all I know."

"I must talk with him first," responded Agent Healy.

Agent Healy had a serious look on his face. Ernesto was obviously confused by the request. He certainly did not want to get into a confrontation with Healy. He pulled a cell phone from his belt and opened its cover.

"I will call my office. They must know something about this shipment that I don't know."

"Go right ahead," responded Agent Healy with a wry smile.

Jose, showing no emotion, lit a cigarette and leaned against the side of the FedEx truck. He was muttering something under his breath, but Agent Healy couldn't make out what he said. Ernesto dialed Paco Ramirez. Paco recognized the caller ID. He was expecting to hear from Ernesto. He also expected to hear that everything was going well and on schedule.

"Hola Ernesto, que pasa?"

Ernesto pretended to be talking to the FedEx office dispatcher.

"Yes, this is Ernesto Garcia. I am at the Port of Miami. I was supposed to pick up a shipment for transfer to the Chicago Museum of Natural History. The Customs agent wants to speak with the museum's representative. I know nothing about this. Who do I need to talk to? What should I do? Can you help me?"

"Ernesto, can *he* hear you?"

"Yes, that is correct."

"Who is this guy, what is his name?"

Ernesto turned to the Customs Agent. It is Healy correct?

Agent Healy nodded in the affirmative.

"I am here with Agent Healy. He needs to speak with the museum's representative before we can leave. I think he expected the museum representative to be here with me."

"Ernesto, something is wrong. I don't know this agent Healy. Trombley is our inside man. Tell him that your office will contact the museum and call you back as soon as possible. I will give you the number of the FedEx office where Luis Sanchez works. He is one of our guys. He can stall this guy. In the meantime I will call you back and request that you make another pickup. You can unhook the cab. You need to get out of there. Ask him for his cell phone number."

"They want your cell phone number."

Agent Healy went along with the charade.

"Area code 305-555-1213," he responded.

Ernesto passed the number to Paco. As he was putting the phone on his belt he noticed three black Chevrolet SUVs going behind a row of containers in the staging area about fifty yards west of his location. He pretended not to notice them. The windows were heavily tinted. Probably DEA. Ernesto turned to Agent Healy.

"My office is going to call the museum. They will call you back. They will also provide the number of the FedEx office and the person handling this order."

Ernesto's phone interrupted his conversation. He answered the phone.

"Ernesto Garcia."

Ernesto paused as if listening to directions from the FedEx dispatcher.

"Yes, I guess we have time. Give me the location. Okay."

Ernesto wrote down the fake directions and turned to Agent Healy.

"The FedEx dispatcher wants Jose and me to help load a truck on pier four while we wait."

As Ernesto was talking, two DEA agents had slipped into position about thirty feet to the left of the FedEx truck. Ernesto saw them out of the corner of his eye. They crouched behind a stack of containers with Chinese markings. Two more agents were in position on top of a small building just north of the truck. Both agents had sniper rifles trained on Ernesto and Jose. The snipers had a clear view of the suspects. Two more agents were in the open approaching from the right. Ernesto quickly assessed his situation. He and Jose were surrounded. Although he had been an Army Ranger, he was not prepared for a confrontation. He and Jose hadn't brought weapons. They couldn't carry weapons through the port security check. They hadn't expected or planned for this turn of events. He knew that his only chance was the river. Jose would have to fend for himself. Agent Healy raised his hand to signal the DEA agents to come in. In a firm loud voice he declared,

"Stay where you are. You are surrounded. You are both under arrest!"

Without hesitation, Ernesto bolted toward the edge of the pier. Agent Healy yelled for him to stop. As he jumped, two quick shots penetrated the afternoon stillness. Ernesto disappeared into the inland waterway.

Paco Ramirez had been sitting in his car about three miles from the pier where the Morning Star was docked. He had planned to follow the FedEx truck to their warehouse. When he hung up he paused to consider the situation. He knew that the operation had been compromised. He couldn't call Trombley. He needed to get Ernesto and Jose out of there. They would have to sacrifice the shipment. Danny Ochoa was not going to be a happy camper. Paco started his car. Before he could move, two black SUVs blocked him from the front, and a Miami Dade police car blocked his rear exit. The agents leaped from their vehicles with weapons in hand.

"Get out of the car! Get out of the car and lie face down on the pavement! Do it now. GET OUT OF THE CAR!"

Paco glanced at the Glock 380 resting on his console. It was loaded and he had two extra clips, but he was severely outnumbered. There was nowhere to go. He rolled down the window of his Mercedes 420.

"I'm coming out, I'm unarmed, don't shoot—don't shoot! I'm unarmed! I'm getting out of the car."

Paco got out of the car and laid face down on the cement—arms out stretched. The agents swarmed over him like ants on a dried piece of fruit. They ground his head so hard into the cement that it left little pockmarks on his face. Some began to bleed. They pulled his arms behind his back and handcuffed him. Paco Ramirez was taken into DEA custody.

Chapter Six
Port of Miami
October 21, 2010
Thursday
1630 Hours

Ernesto had grown up in Miami. He could swim like a fish. His training as an Army Ranger had prepared him quite well for escape and evasion. He was the only Ranger in his class that had escaped during POW training in the jungles of Panama. He had long, lean muscles, a washboard stomach, and was in great shape. His daily routine included a three-mile run, two hundred pushups, five hundred sit-ups and ten one-arm chin-ups—with each arm. He was able to hold his breath for two and one half minutes, and he knew how to use the water to his advantage. Agent Healy ran to the edge of the pier.

"Shit! Shit! Was he hit? Can anybody confirm that he was hit? Frank, did you hit him?"

Frank Caputo was still on the roof. His rifle was now trained on the side of the truck where Jose stood with his hands in the air. Jose was nervous. He was looking in all directions.

"I'm sure I hit him, Joe. I'll check the camera, but I'm sure I hit him."

Frank Caputo was an Army-trained sniper who had twenty-three confirmed kills in Afghanistan. He could hit a moving target at fifteen hundred yards in high wind with a fifty-caliber sniper's rifle. He never missed. However, Agent Joe Healy didn't want to take any chances. He was a seasoned field agent and had been a US Customs agent for twenty-two years. Unfortunately, he hadn't had enough time to put this operation together. Trombley had been a tough nut to crack. Agent Healy had only learned about the operation early that morning. The fact that he was able to organize the task force on such short notice was a tribute to his tactical ability. He pointed to Agent Ray Kilgore.

"Ray, get the Miami Port Police searching right away. Alert the Coast Guard. I want this guy, or his dead body, found by sundown."

Agent Kilgore already had his phone in hand. He never said a word, gave a partial salute with his right hand and immediately began punching numbers on his phone.

Ernesto had stayed very close to the pier. He was indeed hit. One of the bullets hit him as he dove into the water. It hit him on the left side passing through his shirt. Although a glancing blow, the impact snapped his head back. The bullet left a large burning gash several inches long from mid back to the top of his left shoulder. It was deep enough to leave a small blood trail in the water. Ernesto could feel the sting from the salt water. The tide was beginning to move out. He knew that the harbor patrol would concentrate their search in the direction of tidal flow. His only chance of escape was to move against the tide and try to find a good hiding place until dark.

Paco Ramirez didn't say a word as he was driven in the back seat of one of the Customs SUVs. Ironically, it was an SUV that had been seized by Customs several months earlier; one that Paco was familiar with, one that he had ridden in many times before. He recognized the cigar burn on the dashboard where Manny Dominguez had spit out his cigar after spilling a hot latte in his lap. Now he had been seized, he was a US Customs acquisition.

Danny Ochoa was seated at a little round table in the corner of a sidewalk café in Coconut Grove. From his vantage point he had a clear view of the street, sidewalk and the building across the street. He sipped an espresso and gave a slight smile, complemented by a head tilt and salute to a couple of young coeds sitting a couple of tables away. They giggled and gave toothy grins in return. He was old enough to be their father, but that didn't bother him. He had been with girls even younger than these. He checked his watch, then folded the Thursday addition of the Miami Herald and placed it neatly on his lap. He hadn't heard from Manny. He was becoming a bit concerned. Should have heard from him by now. He checked his cell phone. Just then a waiter approached and handed him a portable house phone.

"Hola?" he said his face giving away to a quizzical expression.

"Hefe," said the caller on the other end of the line.

Danny immediately recognized Manny's voice. Manny sounded out of breath.

"Where the hell have you been? You with some puta? Are you getting laid on my time?" Danny shouted not caring who heard him.

"No! No! Danny I got bad news. Everything went to hell! Somehow Customs and DEA got wind of the shipment. Jose is in custody. Shit Danny, it looks like the DEA guys shot Ernesto as he was jumping off the pier. They haven't found him yet. They got boats, the Coast Guard and every swinging dick in Miami looking for him."

"What about Paco?" Asked Danny his voice under control.

"I haven't heard a word from Paco either. I tried to call him but his phone went directly into voice mail. For all I know, they got him too. DEA probably has him downtown Miami."

There was silence on the line. Danny was obviously assessing the situation. Manny could hear him breathing deeply. He knew not to interrupt.

"Manny, get Silverman to find out where they got him."

"I'll call him. What about Jose?"

"Manny, he's just a slug, he don't know anything."

There was a slight pause in the conversation. Manny didn't really want to say the next few words. He knew how Danny would react.

"Danny…we lost the shipment," he said in a sheepish voice.

"Don't worry about the shipment."

Manny wasn't sure that he had heard Danny correctly.

"Did you say…don't worry about the shipment? Are you fucking kidding me?"

"Manny, we didn't loose the shipment. Everything went as I planned. It's already in the warehouse, being cut as we speak."

Before Manny could say anything Danny continued.

"Those DEA maricones are going to be real surprised when they open the container from Egypt. They will have a hard time making a drug case on a load of fake artifacts."

There was dead silence on the line for several seconds before Manny responded. Manny's tone signaled his total confusion.

"Danny, what the hell are you talking about? What fucking artifacts?"

"Manny, the real shipment came in by air from Mexico City. It came in under—shall we say—*diplomatic immunity*, although our friend the diplomat didn't know he was a flying mule."

It was now becoming very clear to Manny. It really pissed him off that Danny didn't take him into his confidence.

"You prick…you never told me. Did Paco know about this?"

"Paco knew. He set it up with Luis Sanchez. Manny, I didn't want you to know."

Manny had always considered himself to be Danny's closest ally.

"You know you can trust me!"

"What you don't know won't hurt you. I cannot afford to *lose* you."

Manny didn't like being kept in the dark. However, he knew that Danny was shrewd, and that he had been suspicious of Agent Trombley for a long time.

"So…if Paco knew, why the hell then did Ernesto try to escape?"

"Manny, Ernesto didn't know either. I told Paco not to tell him."

"But…why? Ernesto would give his life for you," responded Manny.

"I needed Ernesto to appear uneasy if Customs or the DEA guys showed up. I figured if he looked scared or confused they would be more apt to buy his story. They would believe that they were making a good bust. I hate losing him. But Paco, on the other hand, is another story. I didn't expect him to get caught. He knows—too much! Way too much!"

If Manny was Danny's right hand man, Paco was his left. Paco knew everything about Danny's operation, the key players, sources, distribution points, money laundering, corrupt officials, the list went on and on. Paco could sink Danny; he could sink them all.

"Manny, we got to get Paco back one way or the other."

Manny knew exactly what Danny meant by the *one way or the other*. He, Paco and Danny went back a long way. He didn't think that Paco would talk, but he knew that Danny couldn't, and wouldn't, take any chances. Friends are friends and business is business, and Danny was all business. He was tough, he was calculating, and he was Hefe!

"Manny, call Silverman. By now the DEA guys have had enough time to process Paco. I'm sure they'll delay as long as possible, but Silverman has contacts. Get him to start snooping around. Maybe he can get Paco out on bail, or at the very least, find out where the hell they're holding him."

Chapter Seven
Scottsdale, Arizona
October 21, 2010
Thursday
1530 Hours

Ben's second call concerning Spanelli was to Taylor Reese. Taylor owned one of the largest land-developing firms in the southwest. Taylor was a Connecticut born *Yankee* who wanted to be a cowboy ever since he was a kid and became a Dallas Cowboy fan. Walt Garrison was his hero. He loved cowboy boots, cowboy hats, turquoise bracelets, big rings, booze and wild women. He found them all in Arizona. He had come from money, he still had a lot of money, he enjoyed making money, and more than anything, he loved to gamble. His only office was located in Scottsdale. On this particular afternoon he had just received word that one of his contracts involving a super mall had been ratified. He finished calculating his share of the commission and was very pleased with the six-figure number that came up on the LED display. It brought a wide smile to his face. He sat back in his rickety wooded swivel chair, lifted his leg and rested a snakeskin cowboy boot on the corner of his desk. His desk was covered in newspapers, contracts that he was still working on and several Dallas Cowboy magazines. One of the magazines was opened to a section featuring a voluptuous dark haired cheerleader that had enough silicone in her body to fill the entire memory chip requirements for the Department of Homeland Security's mainframe computer. She was young enough to be his daughter. There was a lot of light blue smoke in the air emanating from the cheap cigar he was chomping on when Ben called. Taylor smoked because all cowboys smoked. He had no idea what it took to make a good cigar, or how long it took to make a really good cigar. The White Owl was good enough for him. He looked at the caller ID.

He swung his leg from the desk, rolled the cigar to the left side of his mouth and picked up the phone with his right hand. He was genuinely happy to hear from Ben Anderson.

"Ben, how the hell are you?" he answered in a booming voice.

"Health-wise Taylor, I feel great. But, from a business standpoint, the market is down."

"I thought the market was on the rebound. Hell, I am about to close a large mall deal, and I sold three properties last week. One, by the way, for you—or should I say, for us."

"Taylor, that is the main reason for my call. That one you will need to put on hold. Spanelli was killed, or more accurately, he was hit outside one of our safe houses. Happened just the other day."

"No kidding, who killed him?"

"It has all the earmarks of a mob hit. I just wanted to let you know that I might get a call from the Department. With the current budget crunch, I wouldn't be a bit surprised if they put a hold on the deal and asked for the money back. I might be able to convince them to keep the house for our next witness. Either way, I'll let you know what they decide."

"That's no problem. What if I get a chance to sell the house?"

"Then, by all means, you should sell it."

"Okay. When you coming out this way?"

"Probably for Easter. Carol is itching to see her family, and I could certainly use a vacation. I would love to play some golf at TPC."

"Well, you know that I'm a member."

Taylor enjoyed the membership crowd. Even though he was well qualified from a wealth standpoint, he would never be accepted into the Phoenix social elite. He was a Yankee foremost, and not only that; they considered him to be a rube. As far as they were concerned he had inherited the bulk of his estate from a father that had *earned* every cent of Taylor's fortune *the old fashioned way*. Taylor continued:

"Been playing twice a week. Since the course is on the PGA tour, it gets a lot of action. You just need to give me a little advance notice, so I can get us a tee time. They'll probably hook us up with another twosome. Is that okay with you?

"That's fine, I just need to get out of DC and into the fresh air."

"Ben, we can do the male bonding thing."

"Yeah…the bonding thing. Speaking of bonding, are you still dating that little hot tamale? What was her name?"

"Rosita. Her name was Rosita."

"Was?"

"Ben, she got arrested for selling pot. Can you believe that shit? With all the money I was giving her and she's dealing pot…then, come to find out she's an *illegal* alien! I really miss her. I miss her scrambled eggs and hot pepper breakfasts. I miss her big brown eyes, hot lips, and most of all, I miss her tight little *illegal* ass. You know Ben, it's better when it's *illegal*."

Ben laughed.

"You're a trip Taylor. I'll let you know about the house. Keep in touch."

"So long Ben, don't forget to let me know when you're coming."

The deal that Ben had with Taylor Reese was simple and brilliant. Taylor was a land developer. Actually, he was a really good land developer. He probably could have done it without his daddy's money. He had built several large housing complexes throughout Arizona and the southern part of New Mexico. Several years prior, Ben had met Taylor at a Giant's Fantasy Camp in Scottsdale Arizona. Taylor was a natural born athlete. He was six foot two and weighed two hundred and five pounds. He loved football and baseball, and living in Arizona, he was also an avid San Francisco Giants fan. Ben could care less about baseball, but Carol had given him the Fantasy Camp vacation as a birthday present. She had ulterior motives; she wanted Ben to buy some property in Phoenix so that she could be close to her parents. So he went along. What the hell, he would get to meet some great old-time ball players. He and Taylor had ended up on the same team. For whatever reason, they hit it off right from the beginning. One night Ben and Taylor went out for a couple of beers at one of the local body exchanges. The conversation circled the globe and finally came around to the US Marshals and Ben's job in support of the Witness Protection Program. Ben gave a short overview of his responsibilities, what he did, and how the program worked. Taylor immediately saw a way to make a quick buck. Then again, Taylor always saw a way to make a quick buck. He measured everything in dollars. He had convinced himself a long time ago that the only *big* thing women were interested in was the size of his checking account. Taylor Reese was the ultimate salesman. After a couple more beers the conversation came around to the *what-ifs* and *hypothetical situations*. Taylor presented a simple scenario where he could mark up a house and sell it to the US Marshals in support of the program. He and Ben could split the additional profit—sixty-forty. They continued to enjoy the music and ordered another round of beers. Ben upped the ante a bit by offering the same scenario, but with a slight twist…no witness shows up to occupy the house. Taylor was curious.

"So…where is the witness?" he asked as he took a healthy swallow of beer.

"Let's just say that he is…unavailable."

"And what about the US Marshals? Do they still think he is in the house?"

"Something like that," responded Ben as he looked around the room.

They both tipped their bottles; Taylor re-lit his White Owl and flashed a tell-me-more smile.

"So…we get to split the whole cost of the house," said Ben. He added a muffled, "sixty-forty."

"Not only that, we could sell it again," added Taylor.

They did a beer bottle salute punctuated by a half-drunken laugh. What a deal.

"Taylor, tell me, how the hell can you hide a house?"

"What do you mean?"

"Let's say, hypothetically of course, that the US Marshals need a house for a witness. They buy a house from you. They pay you cash. They *own* the house."

"Wait a minute Ben. Do they own the house, or does the witness own the house?"

"Well, actually the house is purchased under the witness's new name. That way it is much harder to trace the home through the Freedom of Information Act."

"You mean someone could actually FOIA that kind of information?" said Taylor.

"A person could get that information if the house remained the property of the US Marshals and the documents weren't redacted properly."

"Unbelievable. So what you are telling me is that the house belongs to the witness. All the paperwork is in his, or her, new name?"

"That is correct. And, not only that, the purchase is made with non-tax money."

"So, where does the money come from?"

"Taylor, you're going to love this. It comes from the sale of properties confiscated from drug busts."

"Holy shit Ben! So what you have is a program financed from non-taxed income that nobody really gives a crap about?"

"That is right my friend," responded Ben as he took another drink.

"What happens to the witness after he has done his testifying and has moved into the house under his new identity?"

"Well, if we have done our job right, he becomes invisible in his newly acquired life."

"What about the US Marshals? Do you guys still provide protection?"

"We do…from a distance."

"How long does the government keep providing funds for his support?"

"When the witness lets us know that he is self-sufficient, we are done with him. From that point on we really don't give a damn what happens to him."

They finished their beers and signaled for two more. A large-bosomed cowgirl, at the far end of the bar, seemed to be noticing Taylor. Ben mentioned it to Taylor. He signaled the bartender and told him to give her another one of whatever she was drinking. Taylor saluted her with his bottle. She acknowledged, but he wasn't distracted for very long.

"Ben this is an ideal setup. The witness buys a house from me with drug proceeds. He owns the house. He starts a new life. Then somewhere down the road he lets you guys know that he is self-sufficient. At that point, the US marshals are done with him. He's on his own, correct?"

"Not only that. Since our hypothetical guy is one of my projects, I'm the guy he notifies."

"You're shitting me. This is getting even better. Now if I understand *your other scenario*, you're saying that, *for whatever reason,* and I really don't want to know the reason, the witness never shows up."

"Right, he doesn't show up."

"But won't the US Marshals know that he didn't show up?"

"Again…only if I tell them."

"So, not only will they think he is in the new house, but they will also be funding him until *he* reports that he is self-sufficient. Is that right?"

"That's right."

"This is really too good to be true. Who the hell designed the program? So all's we need is someone to collect the mail and let them know when our *missing* guy has a job, and when he is self-sufficient."

"Right again."

"I suppose that someone in your organization would need to see the paperwork?"

"Taylor, I would be the someone taking care of the paperwork. Our *missing witness* could sell the house and really disappear for good. In fact, if he sold the house before getting a job, there would be no need for fake paperwork saying that he was self-sufficient. No threat. Besides, we'd get a double hit on the property! Just hypothetically…of course."

"*Of course,*" responded Taylor as he tipped bottles with Ben.

A wry smile crossed Taylor's face. Both men enjoyed the music for several minutes. Ben ordered two more beers. The cowgirl at the end of the bar had two more drinks in front of her. Taylor had some competition. He looked over in her direction. She smiled. It looked like he was still in first place. The country western singer was doing a pretty good impersonation of George Strait's *All My Ex's Live in Texas*. There were several couples dancing the two-step enjoying the music almost as much as they were enjoying each other. Ben actually liked the place. There was sawdust mixed with peanut shells on the floor. Everybody wore cowboy boots except Ben. This was down home, the easy life, no worries, just cheek-to-cheek…and, more importantly, miles from DC. He should have just enjoyed the beer and music, but he was making a shady deal. He had been there before. What was he thinking? He hardly knew Taylor. Taylor broke the silence.

"You know Ben, if you had an accountant on the inside, it would be much easier. It could work…I mean it could *really* work!"

Ben looked at Taylor. He was sober—very sober.

"I know just the guy."

Taylor smiled and they both finished their beers. The plan was hatched before the impersonator had sung, *that's why I hang my hat in Tennessee,* for the last time.

Chapter Eight
Miami, Florida
October 21, 2010
Thursday
1900 Hours

Ernesto moved very slowly through the water. He had been in the water nearly two hours and was beginning to feel its effects. He was cold and hungry. He purposely stayed outboard of the ships in the shadows. He knew that most of the attention and bright lights would be directed pier-side. There were a few small boats in the channel. The inland waterway was stirring from a slight evening breeze that camouflaged the ripples from his motion. It was dark close to the ships. The smell of oil was more predominant close to the ships. He could see the searchlights from the Miami Port Police and Harbor Patrol boats scanning the pier and water for him—or his body. They were looking right where he thought they would look. His wound had stopped bleeding. It didn't hurt nearly as much as the occasional sting from the hundreds of dying jellyfish that populated the inland waterway this time of year. It was getting late. The quay-side cranes were still in the process of transferring containers to and from the ships. The Port of Miami worked twenty-four/seven; they never stopped. As he looked around, he noticed that there wasn't any action around one of the ships about fifty yards from his position. In the dim light he could see that there was a Jacobs ladder hanging over the side going down to a scaffold. There were ropes hanging down from the scaffold. Two of the ropes reached the water's level. Fortunately, no one was working on the side of the ship. Ernesto was sure that he could make it to the deck without being seen. He believed that the crew would be on liberty, and there were probably three crewmembers on watch, if that many. Since the Port of Miami was known for its security, he assumed that the *watch* personnel would be on the bridge sucking down a couple of beers. Ernesto continued to move slowly through the water. There were several fishermen in johnboats fishing around the ships and casting toward the pier. The last thing he needed was to end up on the end of a fishing lure. Ernesto moved in behind a large container ship that was being unloaded. The lights were bright, but he was able to move amongst the shadows until the parade of johnboats went by.

He remembered the last time he was in the water under similar circumstances. It was during POW training in Panama. It was his class's final test. Half his class was interred in the Army's POW training camp. The mission for the other half of the class was to attempt to rescue them. The Army Intelligence community ran the Army POW training camp. The Intel guys were notoriously brutal to Rangers. Ernesto happened to be in the group that was split off as POWs. He was the senior officer. The Intel team was extremely rough with him. They were determined to break him. During one of the interrogations, an over zealous Intel officer broke Ernesto's collarbone. One of the rules as a POW is to *never* raise your hands above shoulder level. If you did, you were fair game. Ernesto was not good at obeying the rules. Even with a broken collarbone he overpowered the interrogation trio. With his good arm, he broke the Intel officer's nose knocking him unconscious. He took down one of the interrogators with a *crescent kick* to the head. The other interrogator didn't move. To him it had always been a game. He was frozen in place. Ernesto knocked him out with the chair. He then escaped from the camp. During his escape and evasion he had ended up in a swamp. As the Intel search team approached, he slipped into the water. Just before the team reached the water he slowly slid beneath the surface not making a ripple. The water was a chocolate brown and covered in milfoil. Ernesto didn't move. He could hear the Intel team above talking about what they were going to do to him when they caught him. This was no longer a training situation. After two minutes, he rose to the surface. The *posse* had moved on. He knew to lie low and wait. About thirty minutes later he saw one of his classmates, a young coal miner named Roscoe Tanner. Tanner was from Charleston, West Virginia. Roscoe didn't see Ernesto. When he came close, Ernesto pulled him to the ground and placed his hand over Roscoe's mouth and indicated to him to be quiet. Roscoe led Ernesto back to the rescue group. Once they saw what had happened to Ernesto they were on a *new* mission. Not only did they rescue their fellow classmates, but also in the process, they bulldozed the Army's POW camp to the ground. The team graduated with honors. The Army was not happy with Second Lieutenant Ernesto Garcia. He was almost court marshaled, but the Army chose not to be embarrassed by the evidence.

He waited a couple of minutes and then swam back to the outboard side of the ship toward the ropes. Although his hands were cold and stiff, he was able to muster enough strength to pull himself up to the scaffold. He laid flat on the scaffold while regaining his strength. The Jacob's ladder was a lot friendlier. Ernesto climbed up the Jacobs ladder to the deck of the Sea Rover. The flag on the stack indicated that the ship was of Liberian registration. He laid low for a few moments until he was certain that no one was on deck. He easily found the crew's berthing compartment and was dressed in dry clothes in less than five minutes. There were three ID cards attached by little metal clips to a wire stretched between two of the lockers. He selected one that bared a slight resemblance. He memorized the information. It was passable. Ernesto slipped out of the crew quarters and slowly moved toward the bridge. He could see the flicker of a television. He had guessed right, the watch team was on the bridge, but he needed to be sure that *all of them* were on the bridge. He moved cautiously across the deck, staying in the shadows, being careful not to be seen. He waited in the dark next to one of the starboard lifeboats. If there were a roving patrol Ernesto would see him within a couple of minutes. He waited—no patrol. As he expected, they were all watching the tube. Besides, there was no cargo on the ship to protect. He slipped out from behind the lifeboat and worked his way toward the aft brow. No one was there. The brow had three small lights illuminating the way to shore. Ernesto walked off the brow as if he were a crewmember. No one questioned him. The longshoremen were busy loading empty containers on several ships, including the Morning Star. He joined several other sailors that appeared to be going on liberty, and walked through the gate unchallenged. Five minutes later he was in a cab heading down Port Boulevard. The cab dropped Ernesto off at Monty's Crab house. He paid for the fare with a slightly wet twenty, telling the cabbie to "keep the change". Ernesto went into Monty's, ordered the 'all-you-can-eat' Stone crab and two Modellos. He finished the first Modello without taking a breath. He picked up the other one, went to the pay phone and dialed Manny Dominguez.

"Hola."

"Manny, it's me, Ernesto."

"Ernesto! Ernesto, where the hell are you? Are you okay?"

"I'm okay."

"We have been worried sick. We heard that you were shot by the DEA guys."

"Manny, I'm okay. It was just a flesh wound. Sorry we lost the shipment. What about Jose?"

"He's been arrested…Paco too."

"What the hell happened? I thought we were clear with Customs. Shit Manny, there were Customs and DEA guys all over the fucking place."

Danny Ochoa was standing right next to Manny. He was also listening to Ernesto. Danny motioned to Manny to cover the phone.

"Ernesto, hold on a second while I go into the other room."

Danny was always thinking. He saw an opportunity to use Ernesto to get Paco.

"Manny, let him think that Paco was *supposed* to tell him that this operation was a diversion. If he's pissed at Paco, we can use him to our advantage."

Manny thought for a second, but understood what Danny wanted.

"Ernesto, it looks like Customs figured out that Agent Trombley was dirty. We have avoided contacting him. He obviously spilled the beans on the operation, and is probably in custody."

"Shit Danny must be pissed. Manny, you gotta understand, there was nothing I could do—nothing!"

"Ernesto, why did you jump into the water? They couldn't have charged you with anything."

"Are you kidding me? They could have put me away for life with that much coke."

Manny acted surprised.

"Ernesto, didn't Paco tell you that the shipment was bogus? The crates were filled with cheap imitation artifacts. It was a diversion. It was a setup."

"Shit…Paco never said a word. What the I got shot for a fucking load of cheap crap! Why didn't he tell me?"

"I don't know Ernesto. He was supposed to tell you. We haven't been able to talk to him. We don't even know where he is, or who has him. We never figured that Paco would have screwed up that badly. There is a slight possibility that he made a deal to save his sorry ass."

"Manny, I can't believe that Paco would do that. He wouldn't cross us and he sure as hell would never cross Danny."

"Maybe Ernesto. We just don't know."

"What do you want me to do?"

"I'll get Luis Sanchez to pick you up. Where are you?"

"I'm at Monty's."

Manny looked over at Danny. He had a puzzled look on his face. He wasn't sure that he heard Ernesto correctly.

"You're at Monty's? Monty's Crab House?" he asked in a disbelieving tone.

"Yes," said Ernesto matter-of-factly.

"Ernesto…you've got real cohunes. The whole fucking world is looking for you and you're eating crabs! Go home with Luis. Lay low for a couple of days. I'll let Danny know where you are and you're okay. We'll be in touch amigo."

"Thanks Manny. Tell Danny I'm sorry about this. I'm here for him anything he wants…anything!" responded Ernesto with emphasis on the word anything.

"Eat your crabs. I'll call you tomorrow."

Manny ended the conversation, clipped his disposable cell phone back on his belt and looked over at Danny.

"Do you believe this guy? He's eating crabs at Monty's."

"Manny, you can bet that nobody is looking for him at Monty's."

Danny had moved over to the wet bar and was in the process of pouring a couple of shots of 151-proof Ron Rico in a half full glass of Coca Cola. He was facing the bar.

"Manny, I believe he bought your story."

Danny half turned, his head and hand motion suggested that he wanted to know if Manny would like a drink. Manny nodded and Danny made him a rum and coke. Danny clipped the end of a *Montecristo* and ran it back and forth under his nose savoring the aroma of a cigar that took ten years to make. He lit it with the solid gold lighter given to him by his uncle. He took a deep drag. He offered one to Manny as he blew a large smoke ring that moved in a lazy circling motion toward the vaulted ceiling. He paused for a few seconds watching the smoke ring. As the smoke ring dissipated Danny turned and looked seriously at Manny. A look that Manny had seen before.

"We have to get Paco."

Chapter Nine
Virginia Beach, Virginia
October 23, 2010
Saturday
0610 Hours

It was early Saturday morning. The home phone was right next to Rick's side of the bed. Its loud ring woke him from a sound sleep. He glanced at the clock, his eyes were not in focus yet. It appeared to be 0610 hours. It wasn't his golf day and he couldn't make out the caller ID without his reading glasses. Nobody called this early unless it was an emergency or wrong number. His mom was ninety-six and had been recovering from a bout with congestive heart failure. He had just returned from upstate New York. She seemed well and in good spirits when he left. He was hoping it was a wrong number. Rick answered the phone tentatively.

"Hello?"

There was a slight hissing in the phone and an occasional clicking noise. He was about to hang up when he heard a voice.

"Rick—Rick, Carlos here. Didn't wake you, did I? How's it going?"

Rick hadn't heard from Carlos Garcia in over a year, and before that, their conversations were sporadic, far apart and from all parts of the world. Carlos always had a way of picking up a conversation as if last night was the last time they had talked. Real friends are like that. Carlos was a *close* friend.

"Carlos I don't believe it. Great to hear from you. I assume you're not in Dallas?"

"No, I'm not in Dallas. I still have my house there. In fact it's on the market, but I don't expect it to sell. I'm thinking about renting it."

"The market is tough right now. So where are you? Can you tell me?"

"I'm in Kabul. Got a job with the State Department as an independent contractor. I'm leading a team of ex Navy SEALS and Rangers providing security for Hamid Karzai and his entourage."

"Karzai…good luck! That must be a fun assignment. Can you really provide protection for this guy?"

"Probably for the short term. But…you know how these things go. Just a matter of time…just a matter of time before somebody pops him. Besides he's a worthless two-faced son-of-a-bitch anyway. I could care less what happens to him. I prefer that it happens on someone else's watch."

Both Rick and Carlos knew that providing security for a high profile individual was about as effective as protecting your home with an alarm system. You could keep out the neighborhood kids, but not the professionals.

"I haven't talked with you or Lynn in such a long time. Seems like I always think about you guys when I have an…event."

By now Rick was fully awake. His eyes were in focus. The sun was above the horizon. It was 0620. Lynn had not stirred, but was awake enough to know that Rick was talking to Carlos.

"An event?" said Rick.

Event was a political term for, *I got shot…I shot somebody…we blew something up…they killed the guy I was protecting*…basically it means I'm coming home, probably earlier than expected, and I will be looking for a new job.

"I had a close call this afternoon, and it reminded me that I needed to keep in touch with good friends. So, I called to say 'hello'. I kind of forgot about the time difference. Sorry about that. It has been an interesting evening."

Carlos was a former Navy SEAL, if there is such a thing as being a *former* SEAL. SEALs were always employable. Many of them got jobs with the numerous "Black Ops" firms that took up residency just off the beltway around DC. Carlos was one of the toughest guys Rick had ever known. He was five foot nine inches tall, weighed about 160 pounds, and didn't have an ounce of fat on his body. He had a full head of wavy, salt and pepper hair that was complemented by a smooth dark complexion, and surprisingly, a full set of healthy white teeth that were all his. Carlos could hold his own with anyone. A couple of years back, at fifty-three, he had competed in the Double Iron Man competition that was held on the Big Island of Hawaii. He came in third, only to be beaten by the reining World Champion and the guy who had finished second the year before. Navy SEALS were elite and Carlos was certainly one of the best. Rick was looking forward to seeing Carlos again. He knew that Carlos had been all over the world in some government capacity. Carlos had many close calls. Rick also knew that you may only cheat death for just so long. It was time for Carlos to move into an administrative position.

"What happened Carlos?"

Rick asked the question knowing that this wasn't the first time he had asked Carlos, "what happened". Knowing Carlos, it probably wouldn't be the last time.

"I was on the back of my Humvee, and had that little twinge in the back of my mind that told me something was not right…to turn around. When I turned around, there behind me, was a young guy with a handgun aimed at my head. Only his eyes were visible. Anyway, we stared at one another for what seemed like an eternity…you know that feeling Rick…that infinite length of time that slowly passes as you're looking down the barrel of a gun just expecting to see the bullet coming at you in slow motion. It was only a couple of seconds. Then he just turned and ran away. Lucky for me. Rick, I'm getting too old for this field stuff. Been shot once in the head already. Good thing that I'm a *beaner*…no brains, no loss of mental capacity."

"Did you shoot the guy?" asked Rick.

"No…our rules of engagement are pretty strict. Can't shoot anyone with his or her back to you. Can't even shoot *at* them. Can you believe that? Besides, I think he shit his pants."

"Hell Carlos, you could make anybody shit their pants. So you let him get away?" said Rick. It was more of a statement than a question.

"Not exactly. He glanced back just long enough for me to get a shot off."

"Did you hit him?"

"Right between the shoulder blades," responded Carlos.

"So, I take it you'll be coming home?"

"Right after the internal investigation. Seems there is a bit of confusion on what is meant by 'facing you'. Either way, I really don't care. Sooner or later this guy would have mustered enough courage to pull the trigger. Better him than one of our guys."

"How long is…or should I say *was* your assignment?"

"I was scheduled to leave here next Tuesday anyway. Most likely they will let me leave on time. There really isn't much they can or will do to me. I suppose I could get fired. The investigators are—shall we say—sympathetic. Probably get a slap on the wrist in public and a "bonus" when I get home. Hell, I don't know."

"Are you working for a firm, or are you on your own?" asked Rick.

"Actually, I have my own company. That is another reason why I called. I need to talk with you about writing a proposal for a security job in South America. That's if you are interested and still in the business. Also, I am planning on moving to Virginia Beach, and I want my little girl to start looking for a house."

Carlos always referred to Rick and Lynn's daughter, Brooke, as "my little girl". He had known her since she was six years old. She was like a daughter to him.

"I thought you kept your old house in Virginia Beach?"

"Gina ended up with the house. Besides, she deserved it. I'm looking to move up. It's probably a good time to find a good deal. Just don't want to be in the same neighborhood with her."

Carlos and Gina had been married for eight years. She was never cut out to be a Navy SEAL wife. She couldn't deal with the 0300-hour phone calls that would drag Carlos away for unspecified periods of time to places he couldn't tell her about.

"What price range are you looking at?"

"Six to eight hundred thousand," responded Carlos.

"There is a lot in that range. Brooke will know what you will like and the better locations. I will be looking forward to hearing from you. Call me when you get back to Dallas."

"I will. What about the proposal?"

"The proposal—yes. I will do the proposal…just as long as I am not one of the *resumes*. As they say Carlos, been there, done that. My knees won't let me crawl through the bushes anymore."

"This one's a *no brainer* Rick."

"The last time someone told me that 'it's a no brainer', I lost our entire savings," said Rick with a forced laugh. "I will let Brooke know you are coming and want to work with her," he added.

"Great, you know that you guys are special. Hey, say a prayer for me! Better yet, get Lynn to say the prayer. I need to keep all my options open."

"I will, stay safe, love you buddy."

Rick hung up the phone. By now Lynn was in full listening mode. she asked the usual questions. Rick covered everything. Lynn was certainly Rick's anchor. If it weren't for her, there was no telling where Rick would be. Lynn was a prayer warrior. She spoke a fairly lengthy prayer asking for the Lord's protection over Carlos and his team. They also prayed for all the US troops and ended with a special prayer for their daughter, Brooke. Rick got out of bed and went to the bathroom. As he thought about Carlos and the call, he had remembered the clicking noise in the phone. In the old days you could hear a faint clicking noise in the phone…if someone was *eaves dropping*. Maybe it was nothing. Could have been Carlos's satellite phone, might have been the overseas connection. Hell, maybe he was just imagining it. Old habits and fears were hard to break.

Chapter Ten
McClean, Virginia
October 23, 2010
Saturday
1600 Hours

Charlie Dobson and Marcie were on time. The game was just about to start. The Skins were playing the St. Louis Cardinals. Ben was a diehard Skins fan. In fact, he had season tickets but hadn't used them since the guy in the box next to his had way too much to drink and threw up all over his wife, Carol. Ben was not going to get her to another Skins home game—ever! Besides, Carol had gotten use to the McClean country club scene, afternoon teas at the Ritz and her weekly Bridge Club tournaments. She was no longer comfortable with the beer drinking hot dog crowd. Ben would just have to be satisfied watching the Skins on TV, or going to the game with one of his buddies.

Carol liked Marcie, although they had little in common. Most of Marcie's conversation centered on her three children. Ben and Carol were unable to have children. Neither wanted to know which one had the problem. The girls retreated to the kitchen.

Charlie Dobson admired the Anderson household. He wished that he could afford a five thousand square foot house in McClean, Virginia, especially one that was situated at the end of a cul-de-sac on the backside of one of the most prestigious gated communities. He often wondered how Ben could afford such luxurious surroundings. Hell, they were both Deputy US Marshals, although, Ben was the Deputy Director of the Witness Protection Program. Ben's salary was a matter of record. Charlie knew that raising kids was expensive. But somehow Ben always had the extras. He was the only Marshal that Charlie knew that wore a gold Rolex when not in the office. Ben always seemed to have more than his pay grade could support. However, it was no secret that Ben had married well. Carol was from a very well to do Maryland family with a lot of *old* money. It was the only logical explanation.

Ben motioned Charlie to the bar. It spanned an entire side of the family room and was stocked with only the best liquors and wines. As Ben walked around the bar he hit a wall switch that turned on several antique beer signs. His favorite was the Miller High Life Coast to Coast sign that he had found on eBay a few years ago. Without asking, Ben started making Charlie's favorite mid afternoon drink—a frozen margarita. As he was making the drink, Charlie opened the conversation.

"Have you heard anything new on the Spanelli hit?"

"No, the guys downtown are still convinced that it was a mob hit."

"What do you think? You think it was a mob hit?"

"Hell Charlie…I don't know, and quite frankly, at this point, I really don't care. Spanelli is history. In fact, I just got word that we'll be getting a new witness early next week. Some guy out of Miami. I think his name is Ramirez. We are just waiting for the DEA to release him. Couple of our guys are already in Miami waiting to pick him up."

"Are you going to let Lou handle this one?"

"No, it's a little too soon after Spanelli. Besides, Lou put in for a couple of weeks off. He's close to retirement. In fact, I wouldn't be a bit surprised to see him put in his papers. Too bad he couldn't retire on a sweeter note."

"Ben, maybe you and I should take on this new witness," Charlie said eagerly.

Ben finished pouring the drinks from the blender and came around to the other side of the bar. He handed one drink to Charlie and sat down next to him.

"So, you think we should take this guy, Ramirez?"

"Sure, why not? We could use the same logistics we had setup for Spanelli. There's no sense in re-inventing the wheel."

Ben took a drink and leaned forward with both elbows on the bar. He raised an eyebrow and placed the side of his right forefinger on his upper lip. His right thumb resting under his chin. He stroked the corner of his mouth with his forefinger. It was a body gesture that

Charlie Dobson had seen many times before. It was a routine Ben would go through when he was seriously considering what to do. His facial expression indicated that he was comfortable with the suggestion. He was surprised that he hadn't thought about it himself. Actually it wasn't a bad idea at all.

"Let me think about that. As you know, everything is setup and structured uniquely to make a *particular* witness disappear. Until we meet Ramirez in the flesh, we won't know if our current setup will *work* for him. But, you may be right. Hey, the game is about to start."

Charlie yelled to the girls as he and Ben each took one of the leather recliners.

Ben had been with the US Marshals for seventeen years. Not quite the career that you would have expected from a guy, who graduated second in his class at Yale Law School, was a member of "Skull and Crossbones" and editor of the Yale Law Review. Ben was a sure bet to be a partner in one of the top law firms in the country. Certainly from day one his parents thought so. They must have had great expectations for their son when they ceremoniously named him Benjamin Franklyn Anderson.

Prior to graduation, Ben had been interviewed by several of the most prominent law firms in the country. The firms had set up in the Yale University President's personal conference room and conducted private interviews by formal invitation only. The other law students didn't even know they were there. The firms only interviewed students who, at a minimum, were in the top five percent of the graduating class. The fact that they were interviewed was confidential. Benjamin Franklyn Anderson was high on their list. He certainly was a "first round draft choice" on everybody's list. He had also received numerous requests from smaller, less influential firms. The smaller firms could not compete with the larger firms from a prestige or salary standpoint, but they did offer some interesting and impressive perks. However, to Ben, money was paramount. Besides, he knew that it was easy to get lost in a large firm. You had to bide your time and pay your "dues". Although, the best lawyers were like cream, they would always rise to the top no matter where they were. Ben had aspirations of starting his own firm, but needed to gain experience and, more importantly, build his bank account. The only decision that he had made up to this point was to join a firm with strong international law credentials. He had figured out a long time ago during a summer internship that it took the same amount of work to close a million dollar deal as it did to close a one hundred million dollar deal. It was certainly a *no brainer* deciding upon where to spend your effort and your time. He knew that the real money was made doing foreign deals. They seem to have unlimited resources, especially the Arabs and, interestingly enough, the Koreans. Ben knew what he wanted and limited his interviewing to firms located in the New York City and Washington, DC areas. He was leaning more and more toward DC.

Following graduation he headed to Martha's Vineyard for a week of cutoff shorts, tank tops and sandals…not necessarily his. He had spent many weekends there in the past and found it relaxing. The blonde hair, blue eyes and mindless conversation, was *like totally great*. No thinking, just sweating!

Following one of his weekend forays, Ben received a great offer from a prestigious law firm in Washington DC, the Venerable Group. He was close to accepting the offer when he got a call from an old Skull and Crossbones buddy, Gardner Stollie. Gardner was a couple of years senior to Ben, but had seen something in Ben that caught his attention. Moreover, they both had the same aspirations, similar likes, dislikes and political leanings. He remembered the call as if it were yesterday.

"Ben, Gardner here, how are you?"

"Very well. What a surprise; I had heard that you had taken a job in the United Emirates."

"Partially true; I represent a firm that is doing business there. What are you up to?"

"I have been evaluating a few offers, but haven't made a final decision yet. It is turning out to be a little more of a challenge than I had expected."

"Ben, I believe at one time you expressed an interest in international law. Is that an area you are still interested in pursuing?"

"It is. In fact I have narrowed my search and I'm specifically targeting firms that specialize in foreign interests. So far it appears that they all require a lengthy apprenticeship before they will even consider assignment to the foreign investment area. I'm not so sure I want to wait that long."

"Ben, you don't have to wait that long. With my recommendation I can get you into my firm, and you can start from day one with me. I'll have you up to speed in no time. Take a few days to think about it. The firm is Stimson, Mackey, Miller and Tennant. Look them up on the net. They're a real white Anglo-Saxon Protestant company. The Arabs trust them. Give me a call either way. My number is (202) 555-1200 extension 312. Okay Ben?"

"It does sound interesting. Let me think about it. Coming from you I know it must be good. I will call. Good night Gardner."

It really was a surprise hearing from Gardner. Gardner was several years his senior and one of the front-runners at Yale. He had movie star looks, a mellow voice and a captivating personality. Ben looked up to Gardner. The decision process was made even before he went to the Stimson, Mackey, Miller and Tennant website.

That was nearly twenty years ago. After three years at the firm, Gardner and Ben had completed four international deals that netted the company over thirty million in profit. Three of the deals involved the purchase of large metropolitan shopping centers by the Arabs, and the other deal involved the purchase of two thirty-six hole golfing communities by the Koreans. They were halfway through the fifth deal when all hell broke loose. Gardner and Ben were involved in a deal to drive down the cost of oil in order to bankrupt the Iranians. The Iranians were already in trouble financially from their war with Iraq, and any additional pressure on them could break the back of the Ayatollah. All was going well until Ben saw an opportunity to make a small fortune through a side deal with the Kuwaitis unbeknownst to Gardner. Unfortunately for both of them, the Saudi Royal Family got wind of the bribe and notified the State Department. The Feds put pressure on both Ben and Gardner to turn states evidence. Gardner refused to take their bait, but Ben, on the other hand, jumped at the offer and testified against Gardner.

Following the trial, Stimson, Mackey, Miller and Tennant gave Ben two choices. Resign and make a contribution of two million dollars to the their "slush fund", or be prosecuted for a number of charges, the least of which could be espionage. The choice was clear. So after three years, Ben was on the street, and Gardner was in Leavenworth serving a fifteen to twenty-five year sentence.

A job with another law firm was out of the question. Although he was never formally charged, the lack of response or "no comment" to a reference request would be a strong conviction. One day while looking through the classifieds he saw an ad for the US Marshals. He knew that they would be impressed with his law school standing. They wouldn't question his three-year stint with Stimson, Mackey, Miller and Tennant. They wouldn't view him as a "job jumper". He knew that Stimson, Mackey, Miller and Tennant didn't think much of the US Marshals. They looked at them like they did the ATF…as a bunch of "Bubbas". The law firm would undoubtedly give him a strong recommendation, which in fact they did, and here he was at forty-six years old seventeen years later. Somehow he felt that life hadn't been fair to him…it could have been much worse.

Chapter Eleven
Virginia Beach, Virginia
October 26, 2010
Tuesday
1600 Hours

The afternoon thunder bumpers rolled in right on schedule. The forecast was for severe thunderstorms. A tornado watch had been issued for the Tidewater area. It wouldn't expire until 1745. It had been a very long two days for Brooke. Her real estate company's Relocation department had requested her help with a buyer that had been very disappointed with one of the other firms in town. They were desperate to find a house as soon as possible. It was a good opportunity for a quick sale. Although extremely busy, Brooke agreed, and had prepared over thirty properties for review. They had looked at twenty-one of those properties before the brunt of the storm hit. Fortunately, they had narrowed their search down to two houses. The one in Heron Ridge Estates was their first choice, but the listing agent warned Brooke that the seller wouldn't even consider accepting an offer with any contingencies. The house and property had everything that the Kowalski's wanted. It was on the golf course, had a large backyard, and it bordered on a scenic pond. The full length of the backyard was bulkheaded, and the patio offered a spectacular, unobstructed view of the western sky. The kids were already referring to it as *"our house"*. The other house was located in Lagomar. Although it was a bit smaller, and not waterfront, it was over one hundred thousand dollars cheaper, or as Brooke would like to say, "it was a bit more economical". It had all the amenities, and upgrades expected in a quality home including an open attic that could easily be fashioned into a wonderful playroom for the children. The Lagomar home had no restrictions placed on the buyer. Since the weather was getting worse, they decided to finish their search. Brooke dropped them off at their hotel and headed home to prepare the two offers. Hopefully, in a few hours, she would have good news for the Kowalski's. She knew that the amount they were willing to offer was very fair and certainly in the ballpark. However, many sellers hadn't accepted the fact that their houses weren't worth as much as they were the year before. The market had shifted; it was now a buyer's market. The Kowalskis were leaving for Minnesota early the next morning. They were willing to go with either of the properties. However, they really wanted the house on the golf course. Besides, the kids had already laid claim to it.

Brooke made it home just as nickel-size hail began bouncing off the pavement. As she opened the door to the condo, her little white cockatiel, Tawny, announced his excitement with her arrival. Even though his door was open, the storm had caused him to retreat to the security of his cage. He didn't like storms either. He was moving in a rapid staccato motion back and forth in anticipation of seeing Brooke. Before she reached the top step Tawny was on his way to his place of superiority on top of the cage. As soon as she was next to him he lowered his head requesting his afternoon neck rub. Brooke stroked his little neck and talked to him for a few minutes before going into her home office. She needed to get working on the contracts. She planned to fax the Heron Ridge one as soon as she was finished. She picked up her phone and made a call to the agent representing the property. She was on the phone with her when she heard the doorbell ring. The storm was rapidly moving through the area. The sun was breaking through the clouds as little pockets of fog formed over the marshy areas. She peeked out the blinds and peered through the window and saw that a postal truck was parked halfway into her driveway. She didn't think much about it, since the postman would routinely deliver packages to her door, packages that were too big for her mailbox. She went down the living room steps, two at a time, and opened the door while still talking on the phone. The mailman indicated that she had a registered letter that required her signature. As she glanced at the letter she noticed that it was from the Virginian Journal. She could feel her heartbeat increasing each time she looked at the letter in the postman's hand. She had been waiting patiently for a response from the Journal. It had been several weeks since she sent in her entry. She told the agent on the line that she would call back in a few minutes and, by the way, that client was willing to submit a full price contract with only one stipulation. Brooke signed the registration receipt and handed it back to the postman. He could see the anticipation in her eyes, and not knowing what the letter was about, still wished her *good luck*. By now, Brooke was having difficulty containing her excitement. The fact that the Journal had sent a registered letter could only mean good news. They wouldn't spend the money for a rejection…would they? She closed the door while holding the letter close to her chest. She took a deep breath, and looked at it several more times, again breathing deeply. She was really nervous, so nervous that she was actually afraid to open it. She held it up to the light, trying to sneak a peek at the contents. She realized how foolish it was trying to look through the envelope when all that she had to do was tear it open. With a bit of trepidation she carefully opened the letter, making certain not to tear the flap or the letter inside. Her heart was now racing and her palms were sweaty. She hadn't been this nervous since she gave her high school commencement speech. She carefully pulled out the letter, still wanting to just take a peek at it. She unfolded it; the response from The Virginian Journal was brief.

"*October 25, 2010*

Ms. Brooke A. Morgan
812 Marco Court
Virginia Beach, VA
23456

RE: Virginian Journal Writing Contest

Dear Ms. Morgan,
Congratulations! This is to inform you that you have been selected by our editorial staff to write a five-part short story of your choice based upon the US Marshal's Witness Protection Program. A draft of Part One will be due in our office no later than Friday, November 5, 2010.

Ms. Robestein will be your point of contact. She has information concerning the content and structure of the story. Please contact her at (757)-555-7000 ext 16 for guidance or if you have any other questions. We are looking forward to your Serial Adventure.

*Sincerely,
Dwayne Malcolm
Managing Editor
Virginian Journal"*

Brooke read the letter several more times. She couldn't keep from smiling. After reading it for about the fifth time, she pumped her fist a couple of times as if she had just sunk a fifty-foot putt for the win at the Anheuser Bush Classic and yelled…"YES"! She bounded back up the stairs, picked up the phone and called her mom and dad. Rick was standing in the kitchen about to pour a cup of coffee when the phone rang. He looked at the caller ID and answered the phone with the usual *Daddy-Brooke greeting*.

"Hellooooo Brooke."

Brooke had three different greetings. "Hellooooo Pops" meant that she really didn't have anything to say. She just wanted to kill time as she was driving home. "Hellooooo Daddy" meant that she had good news to share. And a not so loud, trailing off "Hey" meant that she had had a lousy day and was not a happy camper; and unfortunately, you answered the phone, so you were going to hear about it!

"Hellooooooooo Daddy!"

The longer the "Hello," the better the news.

"Hellooooo Brooke!"

Their little routine continued a couple more times.

"Dad guess what?"

"You sold a house to your Minnesota people?" responded Rick.

Brooke was one of the top real estate agents in her company, but her real passion was, and always had been, writing. She yearned to be a writer, and wanted to write mystery novels. She loved mysteries.

Her fondest memories as a child were watching Sherlock Holmes and Charlie Chan movies with her dad. She loved the old mysteries, and even now as an adult, she preferred a suspenseful plot instead of the digitally enhanced, action packed, mindless dialog, typical of the modern-day blow em up movies. Give her a Dashiell Hammett or an old Agatha Christi movie, a box of popcorn and a diet coke, and she was glued to the TV set for the rest of the evening.

"No Dad. Is Mom there? I have something to tell both of you."

"She just called, she's on the way home. She ought to be here any minute. What's the news? You can tell me."

"Dad, do you remember the writing contest I entered?"

"Sure I do. The one at the Journal—right?"

"That's the one. Are you ready for this?"

"I'm ready," responded Rick, knowing that her news was obvious.

"You're talking to the winner! The Journal wants me to do a five part Serial Adventure based on the Witness Protection Program!"

"Honey, that's great! Was there ever any doubt? I knew that your input was terrific. You couldn't miss. When do you start? When is it due?"

"I have to submit a draft of Part One by November fifth. That doesn't give me much time. I need to get started. I really need to do some more research. Dad, what I could really use is your help. Will you help me?"

Brooke knew that she could always count on her Dad. He seemed to know a lot…about a lot of things. For years Brooke thought that her dad had been some sort of secret agent…that he had been involved in covert operations. She had also been fascinated by the fact that his former college roommate was the nephew of a well-known Mafioso. She was certain that her dad had *connections*. He would always smile and tell her that he was only part Italian, and to be in the Mafia, you had to be Sicilian—one hundred per cent Sicilian. Brooke loved the stories he would tell her. She could listen to them over and over. As a youngster, she had a million questions for him. However, she couldn't remember any stories prior to his Naval service. She remembered some of the typical college stories, but there were some big holes. His stories were always consistent, but she was certain that he wasn't telling her everything. She even suspected that he had been in the CIA. He never admitted to being in the CIA; however, she couldn't remember him ever denying it either. He would just smile and shake his head in denial. One time she had overheard him talking with his best friend from college about the *trips* to Cuba. He immediately changed the subject when she entered the room. How intriguing she thought there was more to her dad than he let on.

"Let me check my calendar," Rick responded, trying to be serious.

"Dad hello! You're retired!"

"Oh, that's right. In that case, I believe I can find the time. Is this going to be a *once upon a time* story, a *non-fictional* type of story, or may you take some liberties?"

"I believe they will allow me some latitude, but the story needs to be based upon fact. They have also given me a point of contact at the paper."

"Well honey, just let me know. I'll be ready when you are."

Brooke had already published several short stories, but this opportunity could be her big break. It could be the vehicle that would propel her into full time writing. She really enjoyed real estate and loved working with people, but her real passion was to be the next Agatha Christi.

Although The Virginian Journal had selected the topic, the Witness Protection Program fascinated Brooke. She loved doing research. She found it hard to believe that a well-known criminal could literally vanish, become invisible, become someone else and live a new life without ever being recognized. Her dad had given her some very good ideas for the synopsis. She was pleased that the article did not have to stick entirely to fact, but that it could be a novel with little tidbits of fact sprinkled throughout a fictional story. She had already decided upon a title. Brooke's Serial Adventure entitled, *The Last Witness,* was going to be her big break and get her the exposure she needed.

Chapter Twelve
Destin, Florida
November 4, 2010
Thursday
1100 Hours

Nine hundred and fifty-two miles later Rick and Lynn pulled into the Silver Shells complex in Destin, Florida. It was the eighth year they had stayed at Silver Shells. This time it was really special. Matrix Inc. had sold. Rick was retired *again,* although he did agree to do some part-time work for Carl Peterson. This would be the first year that he and Lynn would truly be classified as "snowbirds". They had been coming to Destin on short trips since the early eighties. Destin was a beautiful city; it had a population of about twelve thousand and was located on the Emerald Coast between Panama City and Pensacola. Destin had gone from a quiet little fishing village to a resort city with great accommodations, fine dining, beautiful golf courses, arguably the best beaches in the world and a favorite spot for the snowbirds to winter over.

This time Rick was determined to enjoy Destin, to work out, play golf and attempt a few short walks on the beach with Lynn. Lynn was a real "health nut" and would probably walk him to death if he let her. There was a time that he was in great shape. He was determined to get back into great shape. He had gone to college on a track scholarship and knew how to workout and eat right. On Friday morning, Rick's cell phone rang for the first time in Destin.

"Hello?"

"Mr. Morgan?" said a pleasant sounding voice on the other end of the line.

"Yes, this is Morgan, may I help you?"

"Mr. Morgan, this is Elaine Drew. I am Mr. Peterson's Executive Secretary. He wanted me to tell you that he sent you a package. One of our aircraft will be landing at the Destin-Fort Walton Beach Airport at 1300 hours today. You will need to be there in person with proper ID. Also, there is some biometric ID they will need. He said you would understand. Do you have any questions?"

"That is no problem, I will be there. I do have one question. Has my clearance been upgraded?"

"I will check, please hold."

Rick was looking forward to working part time out of the condo. In 2002 Matrix had developed a proposal for The Peterson Group to support Covert Operations in South America. As part of the proposal effort, Matrix had recruited several former CIA operatives to work as contract personnel for the Southern Command. The kicker was that the operatives had to be able to speak both Spanish and Portuguese fluently and have five years current experience in South American covert operations. Rick had agreed to write the proposal at no cost. The proposal effort had brought Carl and Rick together again.

"Mr. Morgan?"

"Yes."

"Your clearance has been upgraded to Top Secret SCI with full access. Mr. Peterson is in conference and will call you later this week. Do you have any other questions?"

"No, that will do it. Oh, by the way, tell Carl that the sky is blue because of Raleigh Distribution. He'll have no idea what you are talking about, but it will give him something to think about for the next few days. Thank you Ms. Drew."

Rick closed the cover to his cell phone and looked out the large window that extended from the floor to the ten-foot high ceiling. The backside of his penthouse provided an unobstructed view of the Destin-Fort Walton Beach Airport. He would set up office in one of the back bedrooms. From the desk he could look straight down runway thirty-six. The airport had really grown over the years, and now, corporate aircraft could be seen taking off and landing throughout the day and well into the night.

Lynn had already gone for a walk. Rick decided to *sit* this one out. When she got back they would head for the gym. The second series of Supartz shots were beginning to take effect. Rick's knees seemed to go all at once. He picked up his binoculars and went out onto the large balcony that wrapped around the thirty-eight hundred square foot penthouse. He looked up and down the beach. Lynn had headed east, and he could see her bending down looking at something on the beach. There had been a fairly strong wind the night before and she was probably picking up sand dollars. The early walkers would always find the best trophies. Rick continued to pan the beach. He focused on a guy with a fancy metal detector. He had a little digging cup attached to his belt. Rick wondered if the guy had ever found anything of real value. He sure had a fancy rig. Lynn found a wet rolled up twenty-dollar bill the year before.

Lynn made it back at 0900. She had a nice collection of shells, silver dollars and one bewildered starfish. But now, she was ready for a workout.

"Do you want to go to Gold's or work out here?" she asked knowing the answer.

"We can go to Gold's if *you* want to?"

Lynn caught the "if *you* want to" tone in Rick's voice. She could tell that Rick would rather go to the Silver Shell's gym. Actually, it really didn't matter to her. The Silver Shell's gym had a nice array of equipment, it was spotless, and not quite as crowded as Gold's.

"You'd rather go here…so we'll go here."

Rick mused to himself that women had a *gift* of ultimately doing what they wanted to do in the first place, but giving the impression that they were making a sacrifice—just for you. Women were sensitive to *tones*. He thought to himself that they would make good oriental linguists. He hadn't learned how to decipher tones in thirty-eight years of marriage.

Rick was looking at his watch as the Gulfstream C-20D landed at exactly 1300. From its markings, he presumed that the Fleet Logistics Support Wing Detachment at the Naval Air Facility, Andrews Air Force

Base, Washington, DC operated the aircraft. As the aircraft rolled out the noise generated, as the pilot engaged the thrust reversers on the two Rolls-Royce Limited Tay MK611-8 turbofan engines, could be heard up and down the snow-white beaches of Destin. The aircraft turned sharply off the end of the runway and taxied back toward the terminal. It came to a halt just south of the terminal area. A young man in khaki pants, a light green polo shirt and simulated alligator shoes, with no socks, got off the plane. He was carrying two briefcases. By that time Rick had already moved outside to meet the young man.

"You must be Mr. Morgan. I am Roland Carpenter."

Roland Carpenter looked young enough to be Rick's grandson. Rick was feeling old.

"Good afternoon Mr. Carpenter," Rick said as he extended his right hand.

"Please, call me Roland."

Rick and Roland Carpenter exchanged per functionary pleasantries while moving inside the small terminal. Roland Carpenter placed both briefcases, one on top of the other, on a small table that was the resting place for several worn magazines. He opened the top briefcase, which turned out to be a Dell ruggedized laptop. He attached a small scanning devise and turned on the computer. Within seconds, Roland Carpenter was hooked up to the Department of Homeland Security's network.

"Mr. Morgan, will you place your thumb on the scanner?"

"Roland, please call me Rick. I already feel like your grandfather."

Rick placed his thumb on the small screen. Almost immediately a screen appeared with his picture, short biography, job history and vital statistics. Rick couldn't remember the picture or when it was taken, although, it was a current likeness.

"That will do it Mr. Mr. Morgan."

The kid wasn't going to call him Rick. The respect was refreshing. Roland Carpenter disconnected the small biometric scanner and shut down the computer. He then handed the other briefcase and an envelop to Rick. He also took the cell phone from his belt and handed it to Rick.

"These are for you. The envelope contains the Statement of Work. I understand that you will be reporting directly to Mr. Peterson. Do you have any questions for me?"

Rick looked at Roland with a hint of envy. He hoped that the kid didn't pick up on his expression. Roland was all "spit and polish". What a great time of life.

"How old are you?" asked Rick

Roland almost cracked a smile. He fought it back.

"I'm *old enough*."

Good answer Rick thought. He remembered how old he was when he went to Bolivia, and how soon you become *old enough*. Roland Carpenter smiled and left the terminal and boarded the aircraft. The plane was airborne before Rick got out of the parking lot.

Rick drove back to the penthouse. The briefcase turned out to be a brand new Dell Latitude TM XFR D630 fully ruggedized laptop. It had been modified to include an imbedded biometric scanning device. The envelope contained simple instructions for operating the computer and the Statement of Work. Rick opened the computer, turned it on and followed the operating instructions. Within seconds, the desktop had illuminated and a login screen appeared. Rick entered the user name and password from the instructions and placed his thumb on the biometric scanner. The next screen that appeared required an immediate change of user name and password. Rick entered his own user name and password, and then confirmed the password. Almost immediately a screen appeared with the identification "TOP SECRET/SCI" access only. The screen had a Department of Homeland Security logo in the top left corner and a National Security Agency logo in the top right corner. The Peterson Group logo was in the bottom left corner. Between the top two logos was a menu with the names of each continent displayed in a different color. Rick clicked on the blue tab, North America. The next menu listed all the countries in North America. He clicked on "United States". Another menu appeared with numerous headings included. Only one was highlighted. It was simply *Personnel Search*. Rick clicked on it and two other entries appeared—*Male, Female*. For fun he clicked on *Female*. A form appeared with instructions to fill in the form with as much known information as possible. Rick entered his wife Lynn's full name and their address and clicked *Submit*. Lynn's page appeared almost immediately. The picture was recent and the information was correct in all detail. Rick recognized the picture. It was from her Virginia driver's license. Then it dawned on him where they got his picture. It was taken from his current Military ID card. He had just gotten a new ID card at the Little Creek Naval Station. He looked at his ID...it *was* the same picture. The computer was impressive. His new tasking was going to be fun. Just then the cell phone that Roland had given him, made a funny chirping sound. Rick looked at the ID. There was a number—002.

"Hello?" he answered tentatively.

"Rick, Carl here. I see that you got the new phone."

"I have it, it is a bit heavier than mine."

"It is one of our experimental SSPs...sorry about the acronym. Secure Satellite Phone system. The neat thing about it is you can't trace it. In fact I am looking at my screen and it's telling me that you're in Naples, Italy. The phone jumps around the world at random times. Anybody trying to trace your phone will go nuts."

"Then I assume no one can listen in either?"

"That's correct, they can't. Our conversation is scrambled. All they would hear, if they could get that far, is a bunch of gobbly gook."

"I take it your 002? Who is 001?"

"Director of Homeland Security. Hopefully, you will never have to dial 001."

"This is not a *James Bond* thing, is it?"

"Heavens no Rick, just an easy way to speed dial."

"What's my number?"

"Your number is 324. Rick, be sure to use this phone whenever you contact me. By the way, you can also use it in a normal mode. There is a scramble button on the side. Press the button and you will be talking in the plain. The phone will still be untraceable, and no one can eaves drop."

"So, I'm number 324 in the pecking order?"

"Rick, 324 was your aircraft side number. I thought you would like that. Besides, the only pecking order is at the top. That's where all the *peckers* are so to speak. No pun intended. I'll have some tasking for you in a couple of weeks. Say "hi" to Lynn."

"Talk with you later. Thanks for the opportunity Carl."

Rick closed the phone and looked for the scramble button. He still hadn't told Lynn that he was taking a *part-time* job with Carl Peterson.

Chapter Thirteen
Virginia Beach, Virginia
November 15, 2010
Monday
0800 Hours

Part One of *The Last Witness* by Brooke Ashley Morgan appeared in the entertainment section of Sunday's Virginian Journal. The paper's strategy of a weekly Serial Adventure, featuring more fiction than fact, had paid off. The article was an instant hit. By Monday the paper's marketing initiative gained the attention of every major news affiliate across the state and had earned a spot on many of the nightly news channels. Not only was the Serial Adventure touted as a brilliant marketing initiative, but also excerpts from Part One of *The Last Witness* by Brooke Ashley Morgan, were being seen all over Virginia. One very interested viewer was Sidney Bascomb. Sidney was less than amused. He didn't like seeing anything in print about the Witness Protection Program. People had a very bad habit of believing everything they read in print. Sid picked up his cell phone and made a call to Ben Anderson. Ben answered his cell phone on the third ring.

"Hello."

"Ben, Sid here."

"Hey Sid. What's going on?"

"Did you happen to see Channel Seven's news segment on a short story appearing in the Virginian Journal entitled *The Last Witness*?"

"Sid, I just got in and haven't had much time to do much of anything yet. What is it about?"

"It is about a Philadelphia mobster who is being groomed for entry into the Witness Protection Program."

"Yeah Sid, I'm not following you. What's your point?" said Ben, his voice signaling little interest or concern.

"My point is that Dominic Corsetti was from Philadelphia, and although the paper advertises the short story to be fictional, this "Serial Adventure" of theirs is supposed to be based upon factual information and real events."

"Sid, it's a story. You said it yourself…it's fictional. It's merely a coincidence. Don't worry about it. There is no way anyone knows about Corsetti, let alone some short story writer."

"I still don't like it Ben. What if somebody is talking?"

"Sid, nobody is talking, and besides, who would be talking? There are only three guys in the whole world that know what really happened to Corsetti. Even I don't know for sure. I don't even know where he ended up, and you really know nothing. Sid, it's a coincidence."

"Maybe so. I guess I'm a little paranoid. With the Spanelli thing and all the budget stuff that is going on I'm a little stressed out right now."

Ben could hear the stress in Sid's voice.

"Sid, don't worry about it. I'll check it out. There is no way that anyone knows about…our little operation."

"All right Ben. If you say so, I hope you're right. Sorry for the call. See you tomorrow."

Ben hung up. He thought about the call and knew the story could only be a fluke. Sid was worried for nothing. Hell, he was an accountant, and accountants worry about everything. Sid would spend a week looking for a penny. Ben went into the kitchen and grabbed a Killian Red from the refrigerator. Carol would be in any minute. Ben had promised to make veal scaloppini. He loved to cook. It was the only *honest* thing that he did.

Carol had been at the country club most of the day. She started with a nine o'clock tennis lesson followed by a full body massage and then a European facial. She had really become accustomed to the finer things in life. Ben didn't mind. Carol was striking. She was five foot eight inches tall and weighed the same as she did when she had graduated from college. She normally wore her long jet-black hair pulled back and twisted into a spiral that she would let hang down the middle of her back. She had remarkable velvet blue eyes. Carol could certainly be classified as a "trophy wife".

Ben was pounding out the veal when Carol drove up. He could hear the high pitch whine the Jaguar made as she pulled into the garage. He poured a glass of Chateau Montelena Estate Cabernet Sauvignon that had been decanting for the past half hour. It was her favorite wine. Ben met her at the kitchen door, glass in hand.

"Honey, I trust you had a nice day?" he said with a broad smile.

Ben gave her the glass and a kiss on the check.

"I did, except Sven was sick and my tennis lesson turned out to be a waste of time. How was your day?" she said as she put her gym bag on the small yellow step stool next to the garage door.

"Typical Monday. Seems like all the bad things happen during the weekend. Still trying to wrap up the Spanelli episode."

"Ben, have you heard or seen an article that appeared in Sunday's Virginian Journal about the Witness Protection program? A couple of people at the club mentioned it to me. They were wondering what you thought about it?"

"I haven't seen it, but funny that you mention it. Sid just called and asked me the same question. Guess I need to go on line and look it up. What were the people saying?"

"They were just wondering how much was fact and how much was fiction. I had no idea."

"I'll have to take a look after dinner," he responded trying to show no concern.

"Let me go slip into something more comfortable. How long before dinner?"

"About forty-five minutes."

Carol smiled at Ben and headed up the back stairs that led to the master bedroom. Ben watched her as she left. He was a lucky guy to have her. He had met her on one of his forays to Martha's Vineyard. She was there on a long weekend with two of her college roommates. Ben met her in a sandwich shop. She had gone in for lunch but when she went to pay her bill, she discovered she had forgotten her money. Ben overheard the conversation she was having with the fat lady behind the register. The fat lady was less than sympathetic and was beginning to make a scene. Ben offered to pay her bill, and the rest is, as they say, *history*. He and Carol went on their first date that very night. They married two weeks after her graduation. He almost lost her when he was forced to resign from Stimson, Mackey, Miller and Tennant. Carol didn't know, and he never told her the *real* reason. What he did tell her was that Gardner Stollie had done some questionable contracting that resulted in an ethics inquiry. He told her that lawyers often did things in the interest of their clients that bordered on legal gray areas. Their relationship was never quite the same after that.

Chapter Fourteen
Burke, Virginia
November 16, 2010
Tuesday
1900 Hours

Sidney Bascomb was relaxing in his Italian leather recliner watching a Tivo recording of the nightly news when his phone rang. The caller ID said "unavailable". At this time of night he rarely answered any calls, and hardly ever answered a call that was "unavailable". For whatever reason, maybe it was the third Old Fashion he was nursing, he answered the phone.

"Hello?" he said sounding somewhat annoyed.

"Bascomb, how are you there in your comfortable little house in Northern Virginia…Burke I believe?"

"Who is this?" he said as he leaned forward in the chair.

"So soon you forget old friends. Danny says 'hello'."

Fortunately for Sid, he was sitting down. He probably would have fallen if he were standing. A cold clammy feeling came over him. He actually felt faint. He hadn't fainted since high school when his lab partner, Molly Laneski, dissected a frog, pulled out the guts and pretended to eat them. Fat Molly would have eaten anything. For years he had dreams of her sitting across the dinner table with knife and fork in hand looking at him and licking her chops. She probably did eat the guts. The flash back was over, and Manny Dominguez was on the other end of the line.

"Manny Dominguez," responded Sid slowly.

"Yes Bascomb, it is me."

"You mean 'it is I'. How did you get my number? Where are you? Why are you calling me?" responded Sid as he regained his composure.

"I got the number from your ex-wife. She was very cooperative. You know Bascomb, she really don't like you."

Bascomb's marriage was never good, not even from the beginning. He and Karen had nothing in common except his money. He made it, and she spent it. In return he got a few of her perks...when she didn't have one of her many headaches.

"So what is it that you want from me Manny?"

"You remember Paco Ramirez?"

"Sure, I remember him. How could I forget?"

"Paco was picked up by a couple of US Marshals a couple of days ago. We believe that he was flown to DC. We need to know where they are keeping him."

"Manny, I'm an accountant. I don't get involved with field operations. I wouldn't even know whom the hell to call. The guys in the Witness Protection Program are suspicious of everybody, especially since they lost one of their witnesses the other day. They keep close reins on that kind of information."

"Bascomb, I don't give a shit what you have to do, or who you need to talk to, just get the info. Danny wants it by tomorrow. Be a good boy Bascomb, get the info!"

"Manny, I can't do this. Tell Danny he needs to find somebody else. I'm not your *boy* anymore!"

Sid hung up the phone. He was surprised that he mustered enough courage to hang up on Manny Dominguez of all people. He felt sick to his stomach. Manny was nobody to mess with. Manny was not a good guy, he took care of Danny Ochoa's dirty work.

Sid went and made another Old Fashion. He usually limited himself to no more than three in one night. This night would be different. He was not happy to hear from Manny Dominguez. He sat back in the leather recliner and looked toward the ceiling. He lifted the Old Fashion, swirled it around a couple of times and took a long drink, nearly emptying the glass. He sucked in one of the ice cubes and rolled it around in his mouth. The cold felt good, but it wasn't numbing enough. His eyes roamed to the corner of the room on the far side of the bookcase that almost spanned the entire wall. There was a small spider's web strategically placed in order to take advantage of the efficient insect-attracting floor lamp. He hadn't noticed it the night before. This was the first time he noticed the web. He pushed himself out of the chair and walked over to the corner of the room and studied it for several seconds. It was perfectly symmetrical. There was a small flying insect trapped just to the right of the center. It was struggling to free itself. Struggling for its life. A small light brown spider was sitting tucked in the corner of the wall. The spider began moving every so slightly toward the struggling insect. The insect must have seen the spider coming. It was struggling harder, but to no avail. How ironic. The parallel was unnerving. Sidney was trapped in the *Miami web*. It hadn't been there the night before either, but it was there now, and the poor bug was struggling to get free…to save its life, but to no avail.

Sidney was born in Miami. His family had always lived in Miami for as long as he could remember. He had never lived in any other place, or any other house until he got married. He went to Coral Gables High School and had graduated from the University of Miami with a Masters Degree in Financial Accounting. His first job was with a national franchise, Pete Marwick. One of his many clients was a Danny Ochoa. Sidney was very good with numbers. He could manipulate a forecast to achieve whatever result the client wanted. One day Danny Ochoa made Sidney an "offer he couldn't refuse". Danny wanted Sidney to oversee the accounting for all six of his car dealerships. The job paid exceedingly well. After several months, Sidney had heard that Danny Ochoa had other interests…that he owned the dealerships only to legitimize his position in the community…and launder the money that he was making from the drug trade. Sidney chose not to believe the rumors that surrounded Danny Ochoa. Danny paid him well. Then he met Karen. She was young and beautiful and had a golden brown hard body that most girls would die for. She swept him off his feet. He would do anything for Karen…and *anything* to keep her. Why such a beautiful girl married Sidney Bascomb was a mystery to everyone except Danny Ochoa.

As Manny looked at his cell phone he couldn't believe that Sid had hung up on him. The more he thought about it, the angrier it made him.

He started to call Sid back. Then, a little smile came across his face. He ended the call and dialed Danny Ochoa instead.

"Hola Manny," answered Danny.

"Your not going to believe this Hefe, our friend Sidney Bascomb said he wasn't *our boy* anymore."

Danny, expecting to hear more, didn't say anything for a few seconds.

"So, what does that mean?" asked Danny sounding preoccupied.

"It means that he is not going to help us. In fact, he hung up on me. Can you believe that? That pencil neck maricone hung up on me. He hung up on us!"

Danny remained silent for a few more seconds. Then his direction to Manny was very clear.

"Send him a message via Ernesto."

Chapter Fifteen
Washington, DC
November 18, 2010
Thursday
0930 Hours

Sidney Bascomb couldn't sleep all night. He was still having visions of his driveway…and Ernesto Garcia. He knew who Ernesto was and what he did for a living. Ernesto was capable of doing anything Danny Ochoa wanted. Sidney thought that Miami was behind him. The whole reason that he had left Miami was to get away from Danny Ochoa and guys like Manny Dominguez and Ernesto Garcia. Now, here he was in his own driveway, 1050 miles from Miami and face-to-face with Danny Ochoa's hit man. Sidney was in serious trouble and he knew it. He felt lucky to be alive. He got cold and clammy just thinking about it. Thinking about what Ernesto could do to him. He needed to confide in Ben. Ben was smart. Ben would know what to do.

Ben Anderson was sitting at his computer in total concentration when Sidney walked in. Ben didn't seem to notice. Sidney cleared his throat a couple of times. He was almost standing at attention. Ben looked up after Sidney cleared his throat for the third time.

"Hey Sid."

Ben's tone signaled that he really didn't mind being interrupted by Sidney Bascomb. Sid appeared to be looking at Ben, but there was no real eye contact. Ben noticed that Sidney seemed to be detached, but he didn't say anything.

"Ben, how about I buy you a cup of coffee?"

How about I buy you a cup of coffee was their signal that one of them needed to talk in private. Since they both believed that the Patriot Act extended far beyond taping foreign initiated phone calls, they needed to leave the building. Many of the US Marshals suspected that their offices were bugged. True or not, Ben and Sidney knew not to take any unnecessary chances. They would always head to Starbucks for *private* conversations.

"You driving Sid?" asked Ben.

"I'll drive."

"Okay Sid, give me five more minutes and I will meet you at the car."

Ben finished reading the first part of *The Last Witness* by Brooke Ashley Morgan. It was the first time he had read it in its entirety. Ben logged out of his computer and shut it down. He then took the elevator to parking garage three and found Sid's car in the US Marshals reserved spaces. Sid drove them to the Starbucks on Constitution Avenue. They didn't discuss anything in the car other than current events. The usual crowd was there; several people picking up small orders for office personnel, students taking up space with empty cups hooked into Starbuck's Wifi network, several tables occupied with serious coffee drinkers, an older guy in a black trench coat reading the Wall Street Journal and two US Marshals at Ben's *reserved* table next to the window. Ben knew both of the Marshals well. They looked like they were about to finish. Not to raise any suspicion, Ben and Sid went up to them and asked if they minded some company, knowing perfectly well that the Marshals were undoubtedly about to leave. Ben borrowed a chair from the table next to them and he and Sid sat down. As the waiting line finished ordering, Sid got up and ordered two sugar free, low fat caramel macchiatos, after which he went back to the table. By that time the other two agents had finished their coffees and were in the process of saying their good byes. They left, and Sid sat down and scooted his chair a little closer to Ben. Ben opened the conversation.

"Sid, what the hell is going on? Is everything OK? You look a bit stressed. Is it the audit, or…are you having second thoughts about our arrangement?"

"No Ben, nothing at all like that," said Sid as he starred at the table.

"It's not about the article in the paper is it?"

"No no. I've got a I've got a *problem* Ben, and I need your help."

"A problem, what kind of problem? What is it Sid?"

"Ben, there is something in my past that I thought had gone away. Apparently, it hasn't."

Just then the barista yelled that Mr. Sid's order was ready. As Sid walked to get the order, Ben thought to himself, what could be in Sidney Bascomb's past? Sid is such a wimp. He had the appearance and mannerisms of a librarian who had never worked out a day in his life. He wore his gray hair combed straight back, had classic wire rimmed glasses, a pin-striped suite, white shirt and solid blue knit tie. What could possibly be in his past? Certainly, he had no legal problems. Maybe he has a health issue. Actually, Ben liked Sid. He was a whiz with numbers. Sid returned and placed one of the cups in front of Ben. He set the other one down in front of his chair and sat down at the small circular table. He really looked terrible. The stress deepened the lines in Sid's face. He was visibly nervous.

"So what's going on Sid? You look like shit!"

"Ben, when I lived in Key Biscayne, Florida I did some accounting work…actually I did some very creative accounting work for a guy named Danny Ochoa. He owned several car dealerships, but his real business was cocaine. He was *the* Miami drug lord; although no one was ever able to prove it. Long story short, I liked the money, I got used to it, but Danny was getting too much exposure from the DEA, Customs, and the law in general. They knew he was dirty; they were looking hard but couldn't get anything on him. I figured it was only a matter of time before we all ended up in jail. I needed to get out of there; get my family out before the Feds were knocking at my door."

"So you hid away as an accountant with the US Marshals?" Ben smiled.

"Yeah, can you believe that? Anyway, all was going well until Tuesday afternoon. I get this call from Manny Dominguez. He is Danny Ochoa's right hand man. I didn't know that he even knew where the hell I was. He talks to me like it's old times. Tells me Danny needs a favor. I told him that I couldn't help him and, without thinking about the consequences, I hung up the phone. Afterwards I couldn't believe I hung up on him, but I did."

"Did he call you back?"

Sid took a long swallow of his coffee and cleared his throat.

"No he didn't. Then Wednesday night I drive home, get out of my car and run smack dab into Ernesto Garcia. I almost pissed my pants. This guy is a freaking, cold-blooded killer. He kills guys for Danny. Worse yet, he enjoys it. I thought to myself, shit, this is it! Anyway he said that Manny would forget that I hung up on him if I find out where the US Marshals were holding Paco Ramirez. Otherwise he, Ernesto, will be back. He hands me a piece of paper with Danny's phone number. Then he just disappears into the dark like he was never there. When he left, my knees were so weak I almost fell down. I had to lean against the car. I never even heard him drive off."

Sidney stopped talking and lifted the cup to his lips. His hand was shaking ever so slightly. Ben thought about what he had said. Sid was really scared. He had never seen Sidney so distraught. Neither man spoke for a couple of minutes. More pseudo coffee drinkers came into Starbucks and opened their laptops. Ben took another swallow of his caramel macchiato; then a slight smile came across his face. It was as if the heavens opened and he was stricken with a divine revelation.

"Sid, this may not be so bad after all. This just may be a blessing in disguise my friend. Can you get in touch with this guy Manny?"

"Probably, but Ernesto gave me Danny's number. Ben, this is not a guy to mess around with."

"Don't worry Sid, I'm going to save both our asses. This couldn't be better. Is the phone safe?"

"I'm sure it is. These guys only use throw-aways."

Sid reached into his pocket and handed a tightly folded piece of paper to Ben. Ben gave a slight nod as both men finished their coffees. As they rose, Ben put his hand on Sid's shoulder.

"Don't worry Sid, I'll take care of everything." He said with a look of confidence.

They returned to the office. Sid was still visibly upset. Ben tried to reassure him again. By now Ben's mind was working in overdrive. It didn't take him long to come up with a plan. His plan was simple. Charlie Dobson was right, they could take Paco Ramirez on as their next project. He could easily convince the Director of the Witness

Protection Program since so much work and planning had already gone into the Spanelli case. It would be simple and cost effective to use the same scenario—just substituting Paco Ramirez for Spanelli. He was sure he could sell the idea. Then he would get Mickey and Luis to transport Ramirez in the usual manner. No more Paco. Danny Ochoa is happy. However, for this *little* favor, and to keep Danny off their backs, Ben would convince Danny Ochoa that the short story by Ms. Brooke Ashley Morgan could present a problem. She was delving into an area that was too coincidental. A scenario that could trigger an internal investigation that could lead right back to Ben, and eventually to Danny Ochoa. He would ask Danny Ochoa to send Ernesto Garcia to convince Ms. Morgan that it was in her best interest to stop writing the articles. All problems solved. Ben dialed Danny Ochoa.

Chapter Sixteen
McClean, Virginia
November 21, 2010
Sunday
0830 Hours

Ben lay in bed enjoying that phase of sleep where you are partially awake and aware of your surroundings but are still having those little forays into the dream world. Sunday was the only day of the week that Ben and Carol could "sleep in". Both had been raised as Roman Catholics. St. Gregory's was the closest church. However, It had gone charismatic a few years ago. Neither Ben nor Carol liked the singing or jumping around. They were traditional Catholics. The traditional Mass was at seven and eight in the morning. That was to early for them. God would have to wait. They were now members of the group of Catholics who only went to church on Easter and Christmas. There was a term for them, but he couldn't think of it. Christers, or something like that. Somehow the Christers thought that going to church on Easter and Christmas was enough. They were fooling themselves, and so was he. Ben was going to Hell, and he knew it. There was still hope for Carol. She had no idea what Ben was up to.

Carol hadn't quite closed the drapes the night before. A little sliver of sunlight came through into the master bedroom, and all of a sudden, it was morning. He thought about the ray of sunlight. He remembered the nuns saying that Jesus was the *light* of the world. Maybe it was Jesus, and He had come for him. No he was really going to Hell!

Ben glanced over at Carol. She was still in the sleep world. He wondered where she was foraying. She was a beautiful woman, even more beautiful with no makeup. She was two years younger than he, but he looked ten years older than she. He knew he didn't deserve her. She certainly didn't *deserve* him. She represented all that was good in his life. Everything he did, he had done for her. At least that would be his excuse. However, down deep inside he knew that no matter who was laying next to him, money was his true love.

Ben slowly got out of bed trying not to wake Carol. She stirred slightly. He looked over at her. She moved her head to soften the pillow. She let out another little sigh, but didn't awaken. He went into the bathroom and caught a glimpse of himself in the mirror. He stopped. He was starting to look his age. It was getting harder to hold in his belly. When he did let his muscles relax, his waistline was that of the typical middle-aged American male. He put on his robe and went to the kitchen to make coffee. Ben loved coffee and fancied himself as a coffee aficionado. His favorite brand was Gevalia. He was not fond of the Kona brands; he liked a milder flavor that didn't have a burnt taste. He always used natural filters, bottled water, but he never cleaned the coffee pot itself. He believed it enhanced the flavor. Carol loved his coffee. Ben looked forward to that first cup in the morning. He was ready for that cup today and, he was also ready to read the Sunday edition of the Virginian Journal. Ben went to the front door where three different newspapers had been placed neatly in the weatherproof box specifically designed for that purpose. The Financial Times, Washington Post and the Virginian Journal were all asleep in the bin waiting to be retrieved. He had gotten the subscription to the Virginian Journal just for Carol. She was from the Tidewater Virginia area and wanted to keep up with the local news and events. She hardly read the paper. He tried to cancel it, but she had a fit. He went back into the kitchen, poured another cup of coffee and went right to the entertainment section of the Journal where Part Two of *The Last Witness* by Brooke Ashley Morgan occupied a full page.

Part One of *The Last Witness* provided the reader with an overview of the US Marshal's Witness Protection Program. Part One was not only meant to educate the reader, but also to stimulate the reader's imagination through a fictional scenario based upon current events. Part One included factual information such as when the Witness Protection Program was authorized; who makes the final determination that a witness qualifies for the program; the details of the pre-admittance briefing; the benefits that the witness is provided including housing, job training, funding to cover expenses, medical care, to name a few. The article went on to provide statistics on the success of the program mentioning that over sixteen thousand witnesses and family members have been relocated with new identities since the program's inception. The article included all the usual information to provide a comprehensive background for the next article. All the information in Part One was factual. However, Brooke had been very clever to point out *that everything was covered until the witness became self-sufficient.* At the end of Part One, she again emphasized the phrase *self-sufficient.* She left the reader wondering what does self-sufficient really mean? Who makes that decision? How many agents must it take to keep track of over sixteen thousand witnesses and family members? Where does the money come from? Who pays for all of this? And who would know if one or two witnesses disappeared?

Ben took his cup of coffee and the paper and sat down in the den. Part Two of *The Last Witness* really got Ben's attention. There was information in Part Two that was too much of a coincidence as far as Ben was concerned. Brooke had presented a hypothesis that there existed an organization within the Witness Protection Program that specialized in making witnesses disappear really disappear…and for good! Her article contained striking similarities to a fairly recent project that was under Ben's purview. In the scenario she introduces a fictitious mob figure that is killed by his handlers while being transported to his new location. Part two ends with the mobster being buried in the woods. The clincher, and the part that really made Ben uneasy was the single credit referencing an *Anonymous Source*. Ben hated anonymous sources. People always believed articles endorsed by anonymous sources. Part Three was scheduled to appear in next Sunday's paper. It was being advertised by the paper as a must read. Ben sat back in his chair. He stared at the world globe on his bookshelf. He imagined spinning it; stopping it with his finger and being magically whisked away to some tropical island in the Pacific. He could hear his heart beating in his ears. His hands were sweaty, and he could feel little beads of sweat trying to cling to his sides as they ran down from his armpits.

Ben hated not being in control. He wondered about the *Anonymous Source*. He didn't remember seeing reference to an *Anonymous Source* in Part One. He would have remembered that. Why would there be an *Anonymous Source* for a story that was supposed to be fictional? That made no sense. Ben knew all too well that in every lie there is a little bit of truth. He got up from his chair and went into the kitchen and poured a glass of water. He drank it in its entirety and re-filled the glass. His mouth was still a little dry. Carol hadn't come downstairs yet. At this moment he did not want to see her. He knew that he had to find out who the *Anonymous Source* was. Did Brooke Ashley Morgan, in fact, know who the source was? He took another look at the credits. He seemed to remember that she had listed her father in the credits for Part One. He looked again at the credits; her father was not listed for Part Two. Why was reference to her father in Part Two conspicuously absent? Was her father the *Anonymous Source*? How did her father fit into the equation? Maybe the source was someone her father knew. Maybe Brooke forgot to list her father. Could the source be someone Ben knew? Was someone in the US Marshals suspicious of Ben? The questions were racing through Ben's mind. They kept repeating over and over. There were too many questions. Ben had to find out. He was starting to gain composure when the phone rang. The caller ID indicated that it was Sidney Bascomb.

"Yes Sidney, I saw the article," he said knowing that Sid was freaking out.

"Ben, what the hell is going on? This girl knows something."

"Sidney, I don't want to wake Carol, I'll talk to you tomorrow."

"Ben?" responded Sidney sounding desperate.

"Tomorrow Sid! We'll talk about this tomorrow."

Ben hung up. He knew that Sid would be a wreck. This was not the time or place to discuss the article.

On Monday morning Ben decided to check out Brooke Ashley Morgan and her father by accessing the US Marshal's Database. He knew that if asked, he would have no problem explaining why he had accessed the database to check on Brooke Ashley Morgan. Since she was writing an article about his program, he had every right to find out if there was, indeed, any truth that she had received information from a source familiar with the Witness Protection Program. In light of what had happened to Spanelli, it was imperative that he did some investigating. He turned on his computer, typed in his user name and password and immediately gained access to the LAN. He then entered a personnel search and typed in Brooke Ashley Morgan. A page appeared. On the top left corner was a picture of Brooke. It was obviously a picture from the Virginia DMV. The biography indicated that Brooke Ashlee Morgan was born in Virginia Beach on March 21, 1977. She was the daughter of Richard B. Morgan and Lynn A. Morgan. She had attended private school and had graduated Magna Cum Laude from college. She was single. There were no traffic violations, no arrests; there was nothing in her record that indicated anything other than Brooke was a model child and citizen. Ben wrote down her address, telephone number and the address of her employer. He then typed in Richard B. Morgan. The same type of page appeared with Richard Morgan's picture in the top left corner. Morgan had retired from the US Navy and owned a defense-contracting firm that he had recently sold. Everything looked normal except that there were several time periods with no data. There was no information between 1966 and 1972, 1974 through 1976, and 1979 through 1982. Also, there was no birth certificate on file for Richard B. Morgan. It could be an oversight, but the EL Paso Intelligence Center database Ben was accessing was always complete. Morgan had a Social Security Number, an old Military ID number, but no birth certificate. Ben wondered to himself, how did this guy get into the military without a birth certificate? Moreover, how did he ever get a security clearance? Could be nothing. The biography indicated that Morgan was born in Saratoga, New York. Ben went to the New York State database. He accessed Saratoga County records and did a reverse search. There was no record for a Richard B. Morgan ever being born in Saratoga. He did a search for a five-year span either side of 1942. Still no birth certificate. Ben thought to himself that it could be nothing. In those days many children were born with the help of midwives. In many cases, records were lost or the birth was never recorded. It was fairly normal to use a baptismal certificate in lieu of a birth certificate. Even bible records were, in some cases, acceptable. Charles and Jenny Morgan were listed as his parents, but Ben did not find any information on a Charles and Jenny Morgan. Ben wondered… who is this Richard B. Morgan?

Ben leaned back from the desk. He slowly swiveled the chair around and looked out the window. A pigeon was on the windowsill looking back at him. In fact, the pigeon was looking directly at him. Ben didn't like pigeons. Pigeon was a half-word as far as he was concerned. Was this an omen? Who was the stoolpigeon? He thought for a moment, and then decided it was time to give Sidney a call. Sid probably hadn't slept all night.

"Bascomb."

"Sid, how about a cappuccino?"

"Ben, I could use a cappuccino and especially the conversation."

"Sid, I need to make a call. I'll meet you at the Union Station Starbucks in fifteen minutes, okay?"

"See you there Ben," responded Sidney sounding relieved.

Ben left the office and went to his car where he kept a private cell phone. He made a call to Dallas, Texas. The voice on the other end of the phone was that of Luis Escobar.

"Escobar."

"Luis, this is Ben."

"Hey Ben que pasa, how are you doing?"

"As well as can be expected. Luis, we may be getting another witness real soon. Also I may need you and Mickey to make a trip to Virginia Beach to do some detective work."

"How soon Ben, I have a little "Chiquita Banana" here that needs, should I say peeling?"

"Sorry, but it could be fairly soon. Call me on the *number* when you get in, and I will give you the contact's information."

"Okay, you're the boss, we'll be there when you need us. Ben, everything is okay, right?

"It will be," responded Ben. "It will be," he added again.

Luis knew what the "number" meant. No way to trace the call. Ben only used the throwaway cell phones when they were working a project. Luis hadn't talked with Ben since Corsetti.

Chapter Seventeen
Virginia Beach, Virginia
November 23, 2010
Tuesday
1450 Hours

American Flight 434 touched down at Norfolk Airport at 1450 hours. There were eighty-four passengers onboard. One of them was Ernesto Garcia. Ernesto occupied seat 1A in the first class compartment. The flight had been routine. The weather in Virginia Beach was forecast to be in the seventies for the entire week. No rain was in sight. Ernesto had never been to Virginia Beach. He had studied a map of the Tidewater area during the flight. The flight attendant had been very friendly. Her name was Maria. She made it a point to mention that the crew was spending the night. She had mentioned it twice and that she would be having a drink at Catch 31. He told her that he was not familiar with the area. She told him that Catch 31 was located at the new Hilton on Atlantic Avenue toward the north end of the beach. He didn't tell her that he was staying there also. After the flight had fully stopped at the gate, Ernesto retrieved his overnight bag from the storage bin above his seat and was the first passenger to disembark. Maria smiled. He said "maybe later." She smiled again. He rented a Pontiac Grand Am from Budget and was headed west on Norview Avenue just in time to beat the first wave of Norfolk Naval Base traffic on East I-64 as they made their mad-dash for home. As he was driving, he made a call to Ben Anderson. He dialed the number given to him by Manny Dominguez. Ben had taken the afternoon off. He didn't want anyone in earshot as he talked to Ernesto. He was expecting the call.

"Hello, hope you had a nice flight," said Ben matter-of-factly.

"The flight was a little bumpy, but the weather here is nice," responded Ernesto blandly.

"Ernesto, I understand that Manny has filled you in on the *assignment*?"

"He has. Manny did say that you would have some more information for me."

Ben gave Ernesto a rundown on the articles being featured in the newspaper. He spoke very deliberately while emphasizing the scenario that had been put forth by Ms. Brooke Ashley Morgan. Ernesto didn't seem to be very interested. Ben continued.

"If an investigation takes place it could jeopardize my agreement with Danny concerning Paco Ramirez."

The reference to Paco Ramirez got Ernesto's attention. He knew all too well that anything that Paco gave the Feds could affect him also.

"Tell me exactly what you need from me," he said coldly.

"Ernesto, I need you to find out who the *Anonymous Source* is. Quite possibly the *Anonymous Source* is her father."

"How far do you want to take this?"

"Well, there are five parts to the series. She has written two. I would assume, if she does have some damaging information, she would save it for the last part. That gives us nearly three weeks at most. However, to play it safe I need you to find out who the source is as soon as possible. If she should happen to meet with an unfortunate accident, the article will go away, at least in the short term. It might flush out the *Anonymous Source*. If we find out who the *Source* is, and we eliminate him, or her, the problem goes away permanently. So to answer your question, we need to find out who this *Source* is at all costs. I assume you will know how to get that information."

"What can you tell me about her?"

"She's five feet six inches and one hundred twenty-five pounds, blonde hair, blue-green eyes, thirty-three years old, and very attractive. She drives a 2009 white Camry, Virginia Plates JPL-1220. She has a condo in the Strawbridge area of Virginia Beach."

"Good. I assume you have her address?" asked Ernesto still showing no signs of any emotion.

"Yes, and I will also give you her work address and her father's address. All are located in Virginia Beach. Are you ready to write?"

"Let me pull over."

Ernesto pulled over onto the shoulder and retrieved a small notebook from his jacket pocket. It was old and worn.

"Okay, give me the information."

"Brooke's address is 812 Marco Court. Her work address is 6712 Pacific Ave. Her dad's address is 2234 Belvoir Lane. One other thing, I am not sure about her father. There are some gaping holes in his past. I am checking some other sources. It may be nothing, but I don't want you to take any chances. He had a Top Secret clearance, and you don't get that level of clearance by having holes in your resume."

"You think he's company personnel…or maybe NSA?" responded Ernesto showing a little more interest.

"Possibly. I'm going to run a cross check comparing the blank dates in his record against some of the covert operations. If I find a match, I'll let you know. In the meantime, be careful of him; you never know. Where are you staying?"

"I'm going to stay in the new Hilton on the beach. Great rates this time of year. I intend to start my surveillance tonight."

"Ernesto, call me on this phone at ten hundred tomorrow with an update."

"I will call you *when* I have some information," responded Ernesto with emphasis on the word when. He hung up without another word.

Ernesto took I-264 east for Virginia Beach. As he crossed Pacific Avenue he remembered writing down an address with that name. As he was driving, he looked at his pad. Brooke's work address was on Pacific. He was now on Atlantic Avenue, heading north. He made a left and then an immediate right to get back onto Pacific Avenue. He checked the address. He was close. He could see the real estate building ahead on the left. He turned into the parking lot adjacent to the real estate office. There were two parked cars; one was a white Camry license JPL 1220. Ernesto pulled out of the lot onto a back street and parked behind a mud splattered Ford F150 with oversized tires. Redneck, he thought to himself. He decided that he would check-into the hotel a little later. This was a good place to start. Might as well get a visual on his target to see what he was dealing with.

Brooke had just finished showing eleven houses to a newly married couple buying their first home. It had been a long, but good day. She had already informed the listing agent that, on her way home, she would be dropping off an offer.

"Great, I am looking forward to it. We haven't had as much activity on the house as I would have expected. What are the terms?" asked the listing agent.

"Full price with all closing costs paid by the seller. We are also asking to close in sixty days. The buyers are solid have been approved with TowneBank Mortgage," responded Brooke.

"I will present the offer. Hopefully we will have a deal. I will be here until nine tonight. I look forward to meeting you in person," responded a hopeful listing agent.

Brooke hung up the phone and continued to put the paperwork together. Her phone rang again. She looked at the little screen, which displayed a picture of her boyfriend Chris. At first she wasn't going to answer it. She needed to get the contract finished. The phone continued to play Wild Thing. She picked up the phone and made a little face.

"Hey, I'm writing a contract; can I call you back?"

Chris began singing 'La Cucaracha'. It was their way of saying "let's go to Guadalajara for dinner…I need a couple of margaritas."

"Okay, but give me about forty-five minutes. I'll meet you there."

"Great, I'll get a table. Call me on the way and I'll order the drinks."

Brooke finished the contract, took the elevator to the first floor and walked quickly to her car. There was only one other car in the lot. She didn't like being in an empty parking lot alone. The sun had gone down and it was that time of day when everything seemed to blend together. The sea breeze caused the shadows to come alive. Brooke was anxious to get on the road. Driving in Virginia Beach was never a trip, it was an adventure. Brooke started up and turned south on Pacific Avenue. She didn't notice the Pontiac Grand Am following her. Brooke called Chris on her cell phone; she probably wouldn't have noticed a policeman, lights a-blazing, on her tail. Fifteen minutes later she pulled into the Guadalajara Mexican restaurant parking lot just off General Booth Boulevard. She parked her car on the backside of the restaurant in a lonely parking space far away from the other cars in the lot. She couldn't stand door dings, especially on her new car.

Chris saw her as she entered the restaurant. She didn't see him at first. He was sitting in a booth next to the far wall. When she did notice him, he had a big smile on his face and was waving his hands like a receiver all alone in the end zone. Ernesto was close behind Brooke and took a seat at the bar. He ordered nachos and a Modello Especial with lime. As soon as Brooke sat down, the waiter was there taking their orders. Ernesto was halfway through his first beer when the order of nachos arrived. He ate a few bites and decided that it was probably a good time to have a look in her car. Ernesto took another swig of Modello and told the bartender to give him another one—that he would be right back. He went out to the parking lot. She was smart to park away from other cars, but was it safe to park so far away at night? It was easy for him to search her car without raising any suspicion. It was dark, and since it was a Tuesday night there were very few cars in the parking lot. He used a slim jim to gain entry into the car. He knew how to unlock a car without destroying the locking mechanism. It didn't take him long to realize that there was nothing related to the newspaper article, no drafts anywhere in her car. He popped the trunk. Same thing. Everything was related to real estate. The car was a rolling office. Ernesto closed the door and went back into Guadalajara. By then, Brooke and her friend were sipping on another margarita, and looked to be enjoying each other's company. Ernesto ordered another Modello while he polished off the rest of the nachos. Chris and Brooke finished their drinks and left the restaurant. Ernesto soon followed and started the Pontiac Grand Am. He lit an El Rey Del Mundo Choix Suprême and waited for Brooke to drive out. He watched as she hugged her friend and kissed him good-bye. Obviously, he was the boyfriend. Ernesto made note of his truck and license plate number.

Brooke got in and started her car. As she was fastening her seat belt she became very aware of the smell of stale cigar smoke. She was sensitive to smells in general. Maybe it was from outside. There was a cigar store in the shopping center. Probably nothing. She looked around the inside of the car. Everything looked normal for a messy car. She continued on her way. Ernesto stayed a few cars back. He followed her to another real estate office, where she went bounding in, folder in hand. Several minutes later she emerged without the folder and headed south on General Booth Boulevard. She turned into a condo complex. Ernesto recognized the name of the complex. It was the one given to him by Ben Anderson. There was a large parking area and a gated entrance. He waited a few minutes and then drove toward the gate, which opened automatically. It took less than two minutes to located Brooke's condo. He continued on and left by the back gate. He would search her condo during the daytime when he was sure she wouldn't be home. He checked into the Hilton and called Ben Anderson.

"Anderson."

"This is Ernesto. I am at the Hilton. I have already made a visual contact on Ms. Morgan. I intend to take it a little slow at first."

Ben interrupted.

"Not too slow, Ernesto. The next article will be in Sunday's paper."

"Don't worry, I will find out something no later than Friday. I am going to look up her father tomorrow."

"I need you to concentrate on her," responded Ben sternly.

"What if there is nothing to find?"

"Then we need to stop her."

"I thought your main interest was the *Anonymous Source*?"

"That is correct, but one way or the other I can't risk the article being published."

"If I don't find any information in her condo, maybe you should consider her father. If he were to have an *accident* it would disrupt her schedule and give you more time. And, if he is the Source, then you have solved your problem."

Ben paused a bit and realized that Ernesto had come up with a good plan on the spur of the moment. He obviously had some strategic skills.

"That that sounds like a very good option. Let me know what you find out."

"I will call you," responded Ernesto as he ended the call.

Ernesto went down to the bar. He ordered a cafe con leche. The bartender had no idea how to make a cafe con leche. Ernesto tried to explain, but saw that it would be much easier to order a Tangarey on the rocks. He was on the second one when Ms. Maria Gomez, the attractive flight attendant who served him on the plane, sat down on the stool next to him. She smiled; her dark eyes glistened revealing her inner most thoughts. Ernesto took a deep breath. She was striking.

"What will you have?" he asked.

Her answer was a tease.

"What do you think?"

Ernesto woke to the aroma of coffee and perfume. Maria was combing her hair. He glanced over at the clock radio. It was 0615. He raised himself on one elbow. Maria turned.

"Good morning," she said. A large inviting smile crossed her face.

"Good morning to you Ms. Gomez."

"After last night, don't you think 'Maria' is more…suiting?"

Ernesto smiled. He never expected to see Maria again, let alone, spend a wonderful night with her.

"Good morning *Maria*!"

Ernesto emphasized *Maria* as her named rolled off his tongue. He rolled the 'r'.

"When is your flight?" he asked.

"We fly to Atlanta at zero eight fifteen this morning, then on to Miami. I will be off for a couple of days and then I am on a longer run. I was actually filling in on this flight. This is not my regular run."

"Fortunate for me that you were…filling-in."

"Ernesto, last night was it was beautiful. Please understand this is not a normal thing for me. You are the first man that I have been with in over two years. My husband was killed in Afghanistan. It took me over a year to accept the fact that he was never coming home. We were high school sweethearts. You are only the second man that I have ever been with in my life. I have no idea why I did this. For some reason I am extremely attracted to you. You make me feel comfortable…safe."

Ernesto embraced her. She was warm, she smelled wonderful. Her breasts were full and soft against his body. He could sense a slight trembling.

"I have some business here. I will call you in Miami. I promise," he said as he looked into her eyes.

"Please do. My card is on the table. I must go. The airline is very unforgiving if we are late. Time is money," she said apologetically.

Maria kissed Ernesto on the forehead then, with her soft lips, gently pressed her mouth to Ernesto's. She smiled and was out the door. For a moment Ernesto forgot who he was, what he did for a living, why he was here. Reality returned quickly. He poured a cup of coffee and opened the drapes. The sun was surfacing from the Atlantic. There were several people walking on the beach. A pelican dove for breakfast. Two F-18s headed out over the ocean. Morning had come to Virginia Beach. Ernesto showered. He didn't shave. He put on fresh underwear and socks but put on the same shirt and trousers that he had worn the night before. He headed down for breakfast. Ernesto never missed breakfast. The waitress came to take his order.

"And what may I get you this morning?" she asked with a forced smile.

"I would like two eggs over easy, crispy bacon, grits and wheat toast, and burn the toast. I like real toast."

"Would you like a little more coffee?

"Yes, please, and can you show me on this map where Lake James is located?"

The waitress moved in behind Ernesto, and looking over his left shoulder, she pointed to the Kempsville area.

"It's right there. Very easy to get there from here. Just take I-264 west to I-64 east. When you exit onto I-64 east take Indian River Road east. Lake James will be on your right several traffic lights up. If you come to Kempsville road you have gone too far."

"Thank you, that looks to be a very easy trip."

"Twenty minutes at most. I'll be back with your order," she said.

He didn't watch the young waitress as she bounded off. Ernesto lapsed into the night before. Maria was a *real* woman. He knew that he would contact her in Miami.

Ernesto had no trouble finding Lake James and Rick Morgan's house. He stopped in front and walked up the driveway when a voice stopped him.

"Rick is not home. May I help you?"

"Yes, I used to work with Rick and was in town. Thought I would stop by and say hello to him. Do you know what time he will be home?"

"March. Some time in March. He and Lynn are in Florida."

"In Florida? I live in Florida. Would you happen to know where in Florida?"

"Somewhere in the Panhandle close to Pensacola. Ah hell, he told me Destin, yes Destin, Florida. He and Lynn have a condo down there."

"You wouldn't happen to know where in Destin would you?"

"No, sorry, can't help you there," responded the neighbor.

"Thank you for the information."

Ernesto could have pushed it further, but there was no sense in raising this guy's suspicion. He was obviously a busybody neighbor. He had appeared out of nowhere as soon as Ernesto's foot hit the driveway. Ernesto noticed the security sign. Between Scat Security and the nosey neighbor, Rick Morgan's house was safe…at least for now.

Chapter Eighteen
Virginia Beach, Virginia
November 23, 2010
Tuesday
1600 Hours

Ernesto went back to his room at the Hilton. He had hoped to make initial contact with Rick Morgan. His intent was to disguise the real purpose of his visit. He needed to get a layout of the house, the neighborhood, and escape routes, anything that might help him make a clean getaway if necessary. It was probably best that Morgan wasn't home. Morgan's neighbor was a busybody. Actually, the good kind of busybody. He was the kind of neighbor that you wanted to have around when you're out of town. Ernesto went over to the small wet bar and selected a miniature bottle of Jack Daniels Black label. He opened the refrigerator and put three ice cubes into a glass and poured the contents of the bottle slowly over the cubes. As he swirled the dink around in his glass he went out onto the balcony. There were several older folks walking hand-in-hand on the beach. A couple of bicyclers weaved in and out on the boardwalk pretending to be maneuvering around cones that weren't there. The sound of the Atlantic was relatively peaceful—until a flight of four F-18s came out of nowhere. Ernesto ducked as an automatic response to "incoming". He knew that the Naval Air Station was close by. His heart was pounding. Some things never change. He took a drink and his thoughts wondered back to Maria and the pleasures she brought him the night before. He could still see her, the sun illuminating her beauty as it passed through her flight attendant uniform, and the warmness as she kissed him goodbye. He shut his eyes momentarily, and could almost feel her as if she were still in his arms. She was nice. She represented everything good. Ernesto was evil. She had had enough heartbreak in her life. He didn't need to make her a part of his evil world. Ernesto decided that it was a good time to make a call to Ben Anderson. Anderson's anxiety came through loud and clear.

"You were supposed to call me at ten this morning!"

"I had nothing to tell you at ten this morning," responded Ernesto.

Ernesto forgot to add *you asshole*! Ernesto wanted to tell him about Maria just to piss him off. He didn't like Ben Anderson. He couldn't believe that Anderson had gotten through to Danny…talked Danny into doing his dirty work for him.

"So what *do* you have for me?" asked Ben his anxiety waning.

"Her father is in Florida and won't be home for a couple of months. The girl is out of the house. I will give her office a call and pretend to be a prospective buyer. I'll ask if she can show me one of her listings in her father's neighborhood. That should keep her busy while I search her condo."

"Okay Ernesto. Listen to me! This is very important—important for all of us. When do you plan on doing this?"

Ernesto didn't see the urgency, or why Anderson's problem was also his problem.

"This afternoon," responded Ernesto.

With that, Ernesto hung up. No 'goodbye'. No 'see you' later. Ben was listening to dead air. His jaw tightened as he bit down hard. He didn't like Ernesto either.

Ernesto had written down the address of Brooke's listing in Lake James. He knew it would give her another reason to meet him there. She could check on her Dad's house. He made a call to her office.

"Simpson Realty, how may I direct your call?" said the receptionist. The tone of her voice indicated that she had said it too many times.

"Ms. Morgan."

"Please hold."

Ernesto lit an El Rey Del Mundo Choix Suprême. He took a couple of deep drags, blowing several thick smoke rings. How perfect they were circling out in front of him. He was proud of the perfection in those rings. The cigars, sugar and women were Cuba's best exports.

"I'm sorry, but Ms. Morgan is out showing property. She just left. May I take your name and phone number? I will have her call you."

"No thank you. I'll call her back later."

Since she just left, Ernesto knew that he had some time….

Ernesto had called Simpson Realty from a phone booth at the recreation center across the street from Brooke's condo complex. He had been watching, counting the cars going in and out, doing an abbreviated *recon* of the neighborhood. He drove across the street and up to the gate, which rose automatically as he approached. Some *security* he thought to himself. He knew that during the day was the best time to search the condo. He wanted to be in and out within minutes. He parked in the visitor's parking spaces adjacent to Brooke's condo, and then quickly surveyed the neighboring units. There was another condo building across from hers. One unit was obviously empty. There appeared to be no one at home in the other unit. Brooke owned the end unit in her building. The location was perfect for him. Ernesto assumed that most of the residents were young professionals. They would be at work. His assumption was correct. He was hoping there would be a keypad to open the garage door. There was no keypad; however, he noticed a key lock on the side of the doorframe. It was the kind of lock used to electrically open the door when a key is inserted and turned. This was going to be easy. Hopefully the inside garage door was not locked. Ernesto put on a pair of flesh-colored gloves and got out of the car. He used a small pocketknife to pry the cylindrical key lock from the doorframe. It slid out quite easily. He shorted the two terminals with his knife. The garage door went up. He replaced the cylinder and closed the garage door from the inside. The whole process had taken less than twenty seconds. He tried the inside door. It was unlocked. How trusting Ms. Morgan was. He went up the stairs into her condo.

The condo was neat as a pin. There was a cage with a white cockatiel next to a large window. The bird was completely silent. Ernesto approached the cage.

"You don't talk, do you?"

The bird didn't move. Ernesto made a quick surveillance. There was nothing out of place. He chose to concentrate his search in the room that had been converted into an office. There was a large L-shaped desk, two file cabinets, a television, telephone, printer-fax, two small chairs and a desk chair. There was also a docking station for a computer…one that wasn't there. She obviously had a laptop, and it was with her. Ernesto looked through everything, being careful not to change the position of anything. He went through the file cabinet. Nothing. The phone rang. It startled him. It startled the bird also. The fax began printing. It was a real estate contract. He was convinced that whatever information she had, it was with her on the laptop. He went back into the great room. He took one last look around. By now he knew he was wasting time. He went into the kitchen and opened the refrigerator. It was loaded with bottled water. She won't miss one bottle. As he drank the water he checked out the master bedroom and bath. Nothing. He went back down the hallway. Checked out the guest bathroom. He even looked in the toilet tank. Nothing. This was a waste of time, she wasn't a doper, and she wasn't hiding anything in the toilet. He used and flushed the toilet. He went back into the kitchen and threw the empty Fuji bottle into the garbage. There were two other empty bottles in there. He left by the garage door. She would never know that he was there. Ernesto drove back to the recreation center parking lot and called Ben Anderson from his cell phone. Anderson recognized the caller ID. He was still annoyed with Ernesto and it came through in the tone of his voice.

"Well…anything?"

"Her condo is clean. I'm sure that the information you want is on her laptop. It must be with her."

"Can you get her laptop?"

"I can, but…it can cause a confrontation that may not end well. Is that what you want?"

Ben was silent for a moment. He could hear Ernesto's breath through the phone. It was the sound one makes when he is not in agreement.

"I want to know who the *Anonymous Source* is. *That* is what I want!"

Ben placed emphasis on the word *that*. He wanted to add words that were more descriptive, but didn't want to piss off Ernesto. Unfortunately, he needed Ernesto.

"I will see what I can do. Maybe I can use the boyfriend to get the information out of her. I made a note of his license plate the other night.

Get me his address. I will call you back in one hour. Is that enough time for you?" he said sarcastically.

"Yes, what is the number?"

Ernesto gave Ben the license plate number and hung up before Ben could read it back. It was early, and Ernesto decided to go back to the Hilton, freshen up a bit and take an early dinner. The weather was still quite nice. Not as hot as Miami. He didn't even use the car's air conditioner. He enjoyed the fresh air.

Ernesto finished a Cobb salad and a second cup of coffee and called Ben Anderson. He purposely waited over two hours before calling. He loved keeping Anderson on a tight rope.

"It's about time Ernesto. Are you ready to copy?"

"Yes."

Ernesto copied the address and before Ben could say anything, Ernesto hung up. He knew Anderson would be fuming. He really didn't care. The only reason he was there was because Danny Ochoa had sent him. Anderson could go to Hell for all he cared.

At 1730, Ernesto was back in the recreation center parking lot. He had a clear view of Brooke's condo and driveway. It was nearly dark. No one would see him in the car at night. At 1820 Brooke drove in and went into her condo. Ernesto watched as three lights went on in staccato. He lit another El Rey Del Mundo Choix Suprême.

As soon as Brooke walked into her condo, she sensed that something was wrong. There was a faint smell of cigar smoke. She actually liked the smell of cigar smoke as long as it wasn't in her condo. She never let anyone smoke in her condo, and nobody had ever smoked in there; at least not since the construction team built it. She had even swept up all the cigarette butts before any flooring was installed. The scent was unmistakable. It was the same smell she had noticed in her car the previous night. She checked the windows. None were open. No, the smell had originated from inside. She had come through the garage as she always did. She checked the front door. It was locked. She decided to call Chris.

"Hey babe, what's up?"

"Chris, I think someone has been in my condo. I smelled the same cigar smell in my car when I left Guadalajara last night."

"Are you sure it wasn't one of your clients?"

"I'm positive. Can you stop by?"

"Actually, I'm around the corner. I'll be over in a few minutes. What about the lady that lives in the unit below yours? Isn't she a smoker?"

"She smokes cigarettes, but the contractor fixed the vents. Besides, this is definitely cigar smoke."

"Maybe she took up smoking cigars?"

"Don't be funny. Just come over."

Ernesto was about to leave and go looking for Chris, when to his surprise, Chris's truck turned into Brooke's complex. Ernesto turned his car off and sat back watching the condo. Chris was greeted at the front door. Brooke hugged him and they went inside.

"Do you smell that?" she asked making a face as she sniffed the air.

Chris really didn't smell anything, but he knew that Brooke had the nose of a bloodhound. He wasn't going to convince her otherwise.

"Maybe there is a faint smell of smoke. I don't know."

"How can you *not* smell that?" responded Brooke, her voice rising.

"Honey, I really can't. Your sniffer is just too sensitive."

"You're an idiot. This place smells like an ashtray just like my car did, and you
mean to tell me you can't smell it? It's the same aroma."

"Babe, don't you think you're getting a little paranoid?"

The word paranoid didn't set well with Brooke. Her lips tightened, her eyes narrowed, and the little muscles on the sides of her face twitched her displeasure.

"Just go home…you're not helping the situation."

"Honey!"

As she pushed him out the door she told him to,

"Just call me tomorrow."

Chris knew not to argue with Brooke. It was a losing proposition. He backed out of her driveway and left by the western gate. Ernesto slouched in his seat as Chris's headlight swept the recreation center parking lot like a lighthouse on a foggy night. Ernesto fastened his seat belt and followed Chris's truck down Nimmo Parkway. Chris made a right turn on General Booth with Ernesto moving in much closer. By the time Chris reached Princess Anne, Ernesto was right on his bumper. The traffic light turned green just as Chris approached. He continued straight ahead where General Booth turned into Mt. Pleasant. It was very dark; there was an occasional car. Ernesto moved in closer to Chris's truck, backed off and then moved in closer. He was trying to antagonize Chris, but his tactic wasn't quite working according to plan. Chris slowed his truck down to let Ernesto pass. Ernesto pulled out and came along side of Chris. Ernesto rolled down his window.

"Hey asshole! You're an asshole, you know that!"

Chris rolled his window all the way down.

"What the hell's wrong with you man?"

Ernesto needed to get Chris to start chasing him.

"You gringo asshole!"

Ernesto gave Chris the finger and pulled in front of Chris's truck. He then flipped an unopened bottle of beer high into the air that bounced off the hood of Chris's truck, slamming into and cracking the windshield. He was taunting Chris as much as he could. This time, his plan worked. Chris was pissed and was now in hot pursuit. Ernesto had him right where he wanted him. He made a left turn on Indian River Road and pulled into what appeared to be a small parking area that housed a small vegetable stand. By now Chris wanted a piece of him. Ernesto stopped and got out of the car with Chris right behind.

"What's the matter gringo, you don't like being an asshole?"

Chris got in Ernesto's face.

"What the hell is *your* problem?"

"Brooke is my problem asshole!"

The reference to Brooke really caught Chris off guard. He was pissed off and very confused—a recipe for disaster. Before he could respond, Ernesto hit Chris with a crescent kick that he never saw coming. Chris went down, nearly unconscious. Ernesto kicked him in the side of the head. Chris was out cold. Ernesto took a rope from his car and tied Chris's hands and feet together. He then took Chris's cell phone and drove away while dialing Brooke's number.

"I told you to call me tomorrow!"

Ernesto got right to the point.

"Who is the *Anonymous Source*?"

Brooke looked at the caller ID. She was really confused.

"What? Who is this?"

"Ms. Morgan, I want to know *who the Anonymous Source is*?"

"I don't know what you're talking about. Who is this? Where is Chris? Let me speak to Chris!"

"I am afraid he is…tied up right now. I want to know who is giving you information for your story."

"I am not telling you anything until you put Chris on the phone."

"Ms. Morgan you are in no position to tell me what to do. If you don't tell me, and tell me right now, you will never see Chris again… alive! Is that clear?"

Ernesto's voice was very calm and clear. Brooke's heart was now beating in her ears. She knew this had to be the guy who had been in her car and in her condo.

"I don't know who the Source is."

"How does the source communicate with you?" asked Ernesto in a calm clear voice.

"I've gotten one email. I am supposed to get another one this week. That is *all* I know. Please, don't hurt Chris!" she responded, her voice beginning to crack.

"Give me the email address and I will tell you where you can find your friend."

"Is he okay, you didn't…didn't hurt him did you?

"He'll live. He'll be a bit sore, but he'll live—but only if you give me the information that I want. Do you understand?"

"Just a second, I need to start my email."

Ernesto could hear Brooke's keystrokes. He could hear her breathing. He could visualize her panic. He really didn't care.

"Here it is. Tsquare44@TRT.com."

Ernesto repeated the email address. Brooke confirmed that his read back was correct.

"Now where is Chris?" she asked her voice breaking.

"He is at a vegetable stand on Indian River Road just east of Mount Pleasant. Do you know where that is?"

"Yes, I'll find it. Is he okay?"

"He'll be all right, but I suggest you stop writing your article. There are people who will stop at nothing. Do I make myself clear? If you want to stay healthy…and alive stick with real estate."

With that, Ernesto ended the call. Tears were welling up in Brooke's eyes as she called the police and gave them the location where Chris was supposed to be. The full impact of the call hadn't set in yet. Brooke was numb. She prayed that Chris was okay. She jumped in her car wiping away the tears, and raced to the vegetable stand. She knew exactly where it was, it was less than five miles from her condo. The police were there when she arrived. Chris was in and out of consciousness. The rescue squad arrived, and they were on the way to Sentara Hospital within minutes. Once she regained some composure, she went to her car and called her dad. As soon as he answered she couldn't speak slow enough.

"Honey, slow down. I have hardly heard a word that you have said. Just answer my questions. Now, tell me again, what just happened to Chris?"

"Some guy beat him up and then called me," she said her voice quivering.

"How is he? Is he okay?"

"He's on the way to the hospital."

"What did they tell you about his condition?"

"They think his jaw is broken, probably has a concussion, but he should be all right."

"Okay. Did I understand you to say that the guy who beat up Chris called you?"

"Yes, he called me."

"What did he want from you?"

"He wanted to know who my *Anonymous Source* was, and who was feeding me the information for my story. He said if I didn't tell him, I would never see Chris again."

"So what did you tell him?"

"I told him that I didn't know who it was, just that I got an email."

"Did you give him the email address?"

"Yes, and then he told me where I could find Chris. Dad, I was so scared."

"I assume you called the police."

"I did. What should I do. Now I'm sure that this guy was in my car and my condo. I could smell cigar smoke in my car last night and then again tonight in my condo when I got home."

"Honey, where are you right now?"

"I'm out here with the police at the Farmer's market where he left Chris."

"Brooke, I want you to get on the first available flight and come down here."

"What about Chris? I can't just leave him."

"I'll have Carlos keep an eye on Chris. Do you know where they took him?"

"I believe they took him to the new hospital on Princess Anne road."

"Okay. I'll check on Chris. Have one of the Police Officer's escort you home. Just pack the necessities. I will give Carlos a call and have him meet you at your condo. You can probably spend the night in the hospital with Chris. I want Carlos to be with you there. Let me make some calls and then I will call you back. Don't worry honey, we'll figure this out. I love you!"

"Thanks Daddy, I love you too. Call me right back, okay?"

Rick hung up and immediately called Carlos Garcia. Carlos headed out the door to Brooke's while still talking on the phone with Rick. Rick called the airlines and confirmed a seat on Air Tram flight 439 leaving at 0700. He then called Brooke, gave her the flight number and told her that Carlos was on the way. As she was talking with her Dad, Carlos drove up. She signaled to him that she would be out in a couple of minutes. He decided to wait in the car just in case anyone was watching. Within ten minutes Brooke was coming down the steps with a suitcase in hand.

Ernesto headed back to the Hilton. He called Ben Anderson. Ben recognized the caller ID. He was waiting to hear from Ernesto. He didn't say hello.

"Did you get the information?"

"Her source contacts her via email. I have an email address."

"What is it?"

"Tsquare44@TRT.com."

"Did you find out anything else?"

"No. I really don't think she knows anything else."

"Okay. Stay on her until I check this out."

Chapter Nineteen
Pensacola, Florida
November 24, 2010
Wednesday
1320 Hours

The Pensacola airport is just a little over an hour from Destin. That is if you don't get caught up in the Hurlburt Field Base traffic. It was a typical Florida sunny day. The temperature was a comfortable sixty-five degrees. Rick was looking forward to the drive west on Highway 98 and seeing Brooke, but he couldn't get his mind off what had happened to Chris. Chris was young…and he was tough. He grew up in Canada playing hockey and was his team's designated fighter. He was solid as a rock and tough as nails. Whoever did this to him had to be good…a professional.

Brooke was coming in on AirTram flight 439 and scheduled to land at 1302. She would usually come down for a vacation and spend a week to ten days at her parent's condo. She loved Destin, the beaches, the coral blue water, relaxing and lying in the sun. This time, it was not a vacation. She was coming down to escape an enemy that she didn't know. One who had nearly killed her boyfriend. One who was turning her world upside down.

Rick and Lynn had not seen her for nearly two months and were anxious for her arrival. They were a very close family. Brooke was their only child. She received all the perks that were the "right" of only children. She had attended a private school, excelled in sports and was the Valedictorian of her class upon graduation. As an outstanding swimmer, she had been courted by several of the top universities in the country. However, Brooke had "burned-out" as an athlete. She had become more interested in focusing her attention on being a woman, wearing something other than a swim suit and gym clothes, getting her college degree, and pursuing her dream as a mystery writer. Brooke was a parent's dream. You couldn't ask for a better child than Brooke Ashley Morgan. Rick had to stop for a traffic light in front of Wal-Mart. The deceleration woke Lynn.

"Are we there already?"

"No honey we are in Navarre. Did you have a good rest?"

"I did, but I can't stop thinking about Brooke and what happened to Chris. Do you think Chris will be all right?"

"I talked with the hospital just before we left. Chris has a broken jaw and a minor concussion, but he should be okay. He's a tough kid."

"Looks like he wasn't tough enough," responded Lynn. "Who did this to him?" she asked.

"The police are looking into it."

"What about Brooke. Are you sure she'll be safe with us?"

Rick had no idea who was after her, or how far they would go to get the information they wanted, especially considering what had happened to Chris. He really didn't want Lynn to worry.

"Honey, don't worry. I'm sure she'll be safe with us," he responded with a confidence Lynn knew all too well.

"What if she was followed? Do you think anyone followed her?"

Rick knew that once Lynn started asking questions, no answer he could give would be enough. But he knew that no matter what, Brooke would be *much* safer with them in Destin.

"Honey, I can't answer that. But please don't worry, I will take care of it…I promise."

"What about Carl Peterson? You haven't said a word about him. I know that he called you. I'm sure he didn't just give you the computer, or that fancy phone. What does he want from you?"

Rick was hoping to avoid any conversation concerning Carl. Lynn would only worry and have a hard time believing that Rick was just going to be working in an administrative capacity, and not disappearing for several days at a time…and to God knows where.

"Honey, Carl just wants me to do some personnel research. It is something I can do from home, and make a few extra bucks. Keep my mind occupied, nothing more than that."

Lynn didn't say anything for a couple of minutes. She was probably re-visiting her memory of Carl Peterson. The last time she had seen Carl was in Italy. She and Rick had rented a small apartment in Lucrino close to the rail station. One night she was on her way to the bathroom when she heard some moaning sounds. She went into the living room. There was Carl lying on the couch. Rick was wiping away blood as a woman she didn't know was sewing up what appeared to be a wound. Rick never did introduce the woman.

"I can't believe that I'm saying this, but maybe, just maybe it is a blessing in disguise that you took the job with Carl. You know how I feel about him and what he does, or what he used to do. But I suppose he would provide *some help* if need be. But Rick, promise me that you *are* just doing research for him. I just can't stand worrying about you. I don't think I can do it anymore."

"Just research honey…promise," he said diffidently.

Rick crossed the Pensacola bridge and made a right turn onto Seventeenth Street. He approached the underpass. The bridge was covered with graffiti, some of it very cryptic. How times had changed. There was no respect for property. The graffiti reminded him of the New York subway system and all the would-be Picassos. From there, he followed the signs to the Pensacola airport.

Brooke's flight arrived on time. The plane had already taxied up to gate six and was in the process of off loading passengers when Rick and Lynn arrived. They could see the passengers walking up the concourse. Rick checked the arrivals and confirmed that Air Tram Flight 439 from Atlanta had indeed landed and was at the gate. After several minutes, Brooke could be seen in the crowd of arriving passengers as they moved past gate four. She wasn't wearing her usual smile in anticipation of seeing her parents. Rick and Lynn could sense that she still felt threatened. At five foot six inches and one hundred and twenty-five pounds, with long flowing blonde hair and blue-green eyes that seemed to change color with her attire, she easily stood out in any crowd. Brooke would turn heads wherever she went. But this time it appeared that she wanted to be inconspicuous. She actually looked a bit shorter. As she approached, Rick and Lynn could see the pain in her face. She didn't say a word. Her lower lip quivered uncontrollably. Tears punctuated the hugs and kisses. Brooke trembled as she hugged her Mom and Dad. She was hurting, and wanted to talk, but couldn't. She cried all the way to the baggage area. Lynn held her tightly as they waited for her luggage. Although the plane wasn't full, Brooke hadn't noticed the passenger who had occupied the seat four rows back from her the one who had followed her to the airport, and the only one in the baggage area that didn't seem to notice she was visibly distraught. Rick grabbed her black bag with the pink and green ribbon from the baggage carrousel. They loaded the Escalade and drove out of the airport. By Gulf Breeze, Brooke had calmed down. She was in the safety of her Mom and Dad. Rick decided to break the silence.

"Carlos says that Chris is doing well."

"Dad, this guy really did a job on him. He looks terrible."

"Did you talk with the doctor?"

Brooke began to cry. Neither Rick nor Lynn said anything. Lynn handed her a Kleenex.

"The doctor said that he has a concussion and broken jaw. They have him all bandaged up and his jaw is wired shut. He was barely coherent when I was there. The doctor wants to keep him under observation for a several more days."

"Was he able to tell you anything, anything at all about the guy who did this to him?"

"He scribbled on paper that it was an older guy. Hispanic. It was dark."

"How about the car? Did he say anything or remember anything about the car? Any chance he got the license plate number?"

"I didn't ask him. Dad he was going in and out of consciousness. The doctor told me that I needed to let him rest. I really wasn't supposed to be there in the first place, but they made an exception."

"Brooke, Chris is young and strong, he'll be all right."

"Daddy, I hated to leave him," she said as she began to cry.

Rick knew how difficult it was, and how helpless she must have felt. He had been there before…many times, and times where the results were not so good.

"Honey, I'll have Carlos stop by and see him. Carlos will let him know that you are with us and that you are okay. I'm sure that Chris will understand."

"Daddy, what is going on? I don't understand this at all," she said seeming to regain her composure.

"Whatever is going on, it obviously has to do with your story and the *Anonymous Source*. I think you've hit a nerve with someone that fears exposure. It will be interesting to see what information the *Anonymous Source* provides for Part Three."

Lynn had been listening intently and hadn't said a word. She sat in the back with Brooke. Brooke was emotionally drained. The events finally caught up with her. She laid her head on Lynn's lap and was asleep before they were through Gulf Breeze. Lynn spoke quietly.

"Do you think the *Anonymous Source* is a US Marshal?"

Rick thought for a few moments. More than likely it was someone familiar with the Witness Protection Program. It could be someone who is afraid to come forward out of fear of prosecution, or retaliation.

"Probability-wise, I would think so. But from a tactical perspective, it really doesn't matter. Whoever it is, they are not going to stop."

"How can we stop them?" asked Lynn.

"We don't sit back. We take the offensive," responded Rick with a look that meant business.

Chapter Twenty
Virginia Beach, Virginia
November 24, 2010
Wednesday
1130 Hours

Carlos was headed back to Brooke's condo. He was very familiar with the area. Several years earlier, Carlos and his ex wife, Gina, had looked at a house about a mile away. Carlos loved the house, but the day they were there the F-18s out of Oceana Naval Air Station were in the touch-and-go pattern. He could spend all afternoon watching the aircraft. But the look on Gina's face signaled that they would be looking for a home in another neighborhood—a quieter neighborhood. Carlos turned into Brooke's condo complex and went to her unit. Although he had Brooke's permission, he had decided to search the unit during the daytime, since most of the occupants were young professionals and likely at work. He examined the lock carefully, but there were no scratches, no sign of a forced entry. He used his *sledge master key* and had no problem getting in. The first thing he heard was Brooke's cockatiel, Tawny. Tawny started singing away in anticipation of seeing Brooke. The bird stopped singing when he saw Carlos. Carlos made a mental note that he needed to take Tawny to the pet shop to board. The next thing Carlos did was check all the windows; still no sign of a forced entry. He checked the attic access door and the floor below for tale-tale signs of insulation. He also checked the vacuum cleaner bag for insulation. It was clean. Then it hit him. He went back outside and checked the garage door. As soon as he noticed the key lock, he knew exactly how the entry was made. He carefully examined the key lock. There was a tiny indentation in the trim wood at two different positions around the bezel. If anyone came in, they pried out the key lock and shorted the terminals. Carlos went back into the condo.

Everything looked normal. There were no obvious signs of an intruder. Carlos examined the carpet for footprints. He could make out the barefoot prints that, by their size, had to be Brooke's. Several other prints were there. Only one set of prints wore shoes. He went back to the office and stood in the doorway imagining where he would search if he were the intruder. Where would a professional look? More than likely a professional would wear gloves. This could be a waste of time looking for prints. Carlos closed his eyes and tried to visualize the intruder. He went back to the small kitchen. He checked the refrigerator. There were several bottles of water. Maybe this guy took a bottle of water. He checked the trash. There was the usual stuff and three empty Fuji bottles. Two had the tops on, the other had no top. Carlos felt that Brooke would have screwed the top back on the empty bottle. Good place to start. He checked for prints. One bottle had prints that were probably Brooke's. The prints were clear, and they were small. There were no prints on the other bottle. He checked the top of the bottle and found prints that probably would have been made when the bottle was taken out of the packaging and placed into the refrigerator. One of the prints around the top matched the prints on the other bottle. The intruder *did* wear gloves. The gloves left no prints. He took the bottle for a DNA test, but that would take a week or so.

Carlos walked back toward the office. As he walked past the hall bathroom, it occurred to him that the intruder might have used the john. He turned around and looked in through the doorway. He could never remember a time when he took a leak with his gloves on. Not even in the artic. Just maybe this guy took a leak and touched something. Carlos stood over the john pretending to take a leak. He envisioned the process. The seat was down. Most guys leave the seat up. He had assumed the intruder was a man. Maybe the intruder was a woman. No, he had to assume the intruder was a man, it was certainly a man who took down Chris. Just maybe this guy raised the seat. He probably flushed with a knuckle. Probably didn't wash his hands. Carlos stood very still for a minute or two. Then it hit him, the only chance was that this guy lowered the seat without his gloves on. He probably raised the seat with his gloves on, took them off, unzipped, did his business, zipped back up and just maybe lowered the seat with his gloves off. Carlos dusted the entire seat, top and bottom. He found one partial that didn't match any of the other prints in the bathroom. Could be Chris's, but maybe not. Hopefully, it would be enough to get a match. He checked the file cabinet, Brooke's computer, her desk and every other place where a good investigator would expect to find prints. The prints were the same; most likely they were all Brooke's. He kept one of the prints from her office and the partial.

In the car, Carlos made a call to Rick. The caller ID said "Restricted".

"Morgan."

"Rick, Carlos here."

'Hey Carlos, any luck?"

"I'm not sure. I do have a partial print that may be something. I'm sure that someone was in the house. Certainly a professional. Must have come through the garage. There were three empty Fuji bottles in the trash. Two had prints, the other didn't. I kept the bottle for DNA. I will have a friend of mine check out the prints."

"Carlos, can you scan them into your computer?"

"Yeah, I can do that."

"Good, scan and email them to me. I will check them out. By the way, I have a new email address."

"Let me grab a pen. Okay, what is it?"

"Morgan324@TPG.Gov."

"TPG, what does that stand for?" asked Carlos.

"The Peterson Group," responded Rick anticipating Carlos' reaction.

There was a slight delay before Carlos answered.

"Don't tell me that you are working for Carl Peterson," responded Carlos. "So how is ole 'Blue Sky' these days?"

"Same old guy we have always known, just a little older and, hopefully, a bit wiser."

"So what are you doing for him?" asked Carlos.

"I'm doing some consulting work, which provides some great tools and access to just about every law enforcement database that you can imagine. If the print is remotely legible, I can probably identify this guy within a few minutes."

"Good, I'll be home in about thirty minutes. I'll send it right away. Let me know what you find out. Rick, whoever this guy is, he's good, and say hi to Carl for me."

Carlos left Brooke's condo and went south on General Booth Boulevard and then made a right turn on Princess Anne Road. The traffic was starting to pick up. The sun was going down and the high cirrus clouds glistened a golden yellow with hints of bright red. Carlos though to himself that only God could make such a pretty picture. Carlos was going past the municipal center. The speed limit was twenty-five. A very impatient driver in a dodge pickup and oversized tires began tailgating. The guy was revving his engine. The glasspak mufflers punctuated his displeasure with the speed limit that Carlos was obeying. Carlos was now more determined to be a law-abiding citizen. Close to the traffic light the speed increased to thirty-five and then to forty-five Just past the light. The truck left about fifty bucks worth of rubber as it sped past Carlos. The driver was a skinny little redneck with a bulldog hat and a mustache fashioned to make him look tough. The only thing tough about him was his truck. He gave Carlos a New York salute as he passed. What a jerk. Any other time Carlos would have taught this kid a real life lesson, but he was on a more important mission. Besides, he noted the license plate. In a couple of weeks, Carlos would add a little cocktail to this guy's gas tank. He would love to be there right after the engine reached operating temperature. At about twenty-five hundred RPMs, the explosion would take off the front of the truck. Probably happen before he got out of the neighborhood. The little mustached, tattooed, chicken redneck would have a hard time explaining that to his insurance company.

Carlos continued down Princess Anne. He made a left on Providence and the next left onto Sellwood. He pulled into his driveway exactly twenty-three minutes after leaving Brooke's condo. His computer was already on. He scanned both prints into a Power Point file. They looked very good. He opened his email and sent the prints as an attachment to morgan324@TPG.gov. Carlos called Rick on his satellite phone. The caller ID said "Restricted". Rick knew it was Carlos.

"Carlos, that was quick."

"Hey Rick, I just sent you the prints. Bring them up and tell me what you think."

"Bringing them up as we speak," responded Rick as he opened the file.

Rick looked at the screen. The prints were perfect. He just hoped that the partial had enough points to be recognizable.

"They look great Carlos. Let me try the partial first. You want to hold on? I can call you back."

"No, I'll hold on. I'm putting you on speaker."

Rick entered the print into his fingerprint identity software program. The print appeared on the left side of the screen. Several points were identified. Rick pressed the enter button. The speed of prints on the right screen went by so fast they were not discernable. A short message appeared saying that the process could take several minutes while all databases were checked. A ticker at the bottom of the screen indicated that a military database check was in progress. Just as Rick turned to get his cup of coffee the computer signaled that there was a positive match. As Rick looked at the screen, a picture of Ernesto Garcia in an Army uniform appeared.

"Carlos, I got a hit."

"Great, who is it?"

"The guy's name is Ernesto Garcia. He was an Army Ranger, but was given a less than honorable discharge for striking an officer. He was awarded a Bronze Star and Purple Heart for service in Desert Storm. Looks like he got in trouble in Afghanistan. Oh, hold on a second, this is really interesting. It appears he was involved in a drug bust at the Port of Miami and was shot by DEA agents while trying to escape. His body hasn't been found. He is presumed dead."

"Well, it wasn't a dead guy that was in Brooke's apartment, and it certainly wasn't a dead guy that beat the hell out of Chris," said Carlos.

"He has been linked to a Manny Dominguez and Danny Ochoa and ☐ hey wait a minute. Carlos, I have seen this guy. Wait ☐ a ☐ minute. Carlos, I am certain I saw this guy at the airport. He was on the same plane with Brooke. Shit, this guy is probably in Destin. What the hell is going on? Why would a guy like this be after Brooke?"

"Are you sure it's the same guy?

"I'm sure it was him. Says here that he is a lieutenant in Danny Ochoa's organization. Ochoa is a drug king pin."

There was silence on the line. Several scenarios were going through Rick's mind.

"Why would a drug king pin be after Brooke? Hell Rick, maybe somebody hired him?"

"I have no idea, but this must have something to do with Dominguez and Ochoa. I'm sure he was in Pensacola. I can see him right now. Khaki trousers, blue or black sport shirt. Yeah, I'm sure it was him. Carlos, how soon can you be here?"

Carlos didn't have to think for very long before answering.

"I'll fly down in the morning. I needed to put some hours on the plane anyway. Anything else I need to know about this guy?"

"Hold on, let me see."

Carlos waited on the line as Rick went through the information.

"He is an expert in munitions and is a black belt in Tae Kwon Do."

"Great I will go through my little bag of tricks. I'll call you in the morning when I'm airborne."

"Carlos, keep those names in your mind. There has to be a connection."

Carlos hung up. He knew guys like Ernesto Garcia. Ex military, full of machismo, black belt and all the shit that goes with it. However, Carlos knew that there wasn't a black belt in the world faster than his nine-millimeter berretta.

Chapter Twenty-One
Chesapeake, Virginia
November 25, 2010
Thursday
0600 Hours

Carlos finished his preflight and filed a VFR flight plan to the Okaloosa Regional Airport in Fort Walton Beach, Florida. His ETA was 0948 local time. He had already phoned ahead and reserved a room at the Holiday Inn on Santa Rosa Boulevard. He also reserved a Ford Escape from Budget. Carlos was very familiar with the Fort Walton Beach area and the Emerald Coast of Florida. As a Navy SEAL he had flown out of Hurlburt Field in support of special operations in Central and South America. As a civilian working for the CIA he had stayed at that very Holiday Inn on several occasions. He had been there pretending to be a fisherman. His real mission was to identify possible infiltration points along the Emerald Coast.

Carlos took off at 0630. He always enjoyed flying early in the morning. The weather that day was forecast to be CAVU, clear and visibility unlimited, the entire way to Fort Walton Beach. He knew it was smart to get to Florida before the afternoon buildups. The weather could change in a heartbeat. He raised the gear on his Cessna 210 Turbo and contacted Norfolk Departure Control. He was directed to squawk mode 3 code 1200. He "rogered" the controller and requested flight following. He then hit the autopilot and the plane took over. Carlos enjoyed the view and the ride to ten thousand five hundred feet. The new autopilot he had just installed was incredible.

As the plane leveled off, Carlos reached over on the seat next to him, grabbed his satellite phone and called Rick. Rick was expecting the call. He had entered Carlos name and phone number into the phone. No longer did the caller ID say "Restricted". The only other calls he had received on his satellite phone were from Carl Peterson. Carl's caller ID was 002. Rick mused that it should have been *blue sky*.

"Good morning Carlos, I trust that you got off okay?"

"Hi Rick. You should be here. I can see all the way to South Carolina. So smooth I can put my cup of coffee on top of the console and not spill a drop."

"I wish I was there. I need to get back into flying. I used to teach barrel rolls in the T-28, and would put a cup of coffee on the console and not spill a drop during the entire maneuver!"

"Did you put the coffee up there when the student was attempting the barrel roll?"

"One time…never again."

Rick had nearly four thousand flight hours as a Navy pilot, but hadn't flown much in the past couple of years. His company had devoured most of his time.

"Rick, when this is all over, I'm going to get you flying again. So what's the plan?"

"Carlos, the plan is quite simple. I am certain we will have the element of surprise on our side. This guy has no idea that we are on to him, and he certainly won't be expecting you. We can use that to our advantage."

Rick always believed in the *simple plan*. It was too easy to make a *fatal* error when trying to execute a complex plan with many players. There was too much to remember. This was not *Mission Impossible.*

"Carlos, I haven't seen this guy since the airport. I don't want to be looking over my shoulder every place we go. I don't want to alert him in any way either. If he is close by, and I am sure he is, I believe it will be easy to lure him into a trap. He won't be expecting us to be in control of the situation."

"I always liked traps! This is sounding good Rick."

"Since I have no idea when this guy may strike, I want to go on the offensive. In fact, I want to get him tonight at 2200 hours."

"You must have a good plan in mind to be able to pin point the exact time."

"Like I said, the plan is simple. At 2200 hours tonight I plan to be on the Eglin Reservation along highway eighty-seven. The traffic at that time of night, especially on a Thursday, will be minimal. I know you are familiar with that area. Hell, we both went through POW training in those woods. There are numerous turn offs. Just need to agree on the location. I will pretend to have car problems. This will provide our friend with an opportunity to stop and offer assistance. If he does, and I would if I were him, that's when you will overtake him. How does that sound to you so far?"

"Sounds very good to me Rick. If I remember correctly, there is a small lake out there on the left side as you go north. Do you remember that spot?"

"Actually, I do, but wasn't that a favorite parking spot for the locals?"

"Hell, I don't know Rick, I was married to Gina when I went through training. I never had the luxury of sampling the local cuisine," responded Carlos sounding somewhat disappointed. "I'll find another spot and call you with the mileage from the Choctaw field sign, the one that identifies the Navy's outlying field. I assume it is still operational. Will that work?" he added.

"Yes, I know the sign, and it is still there. Carlos, don't forget that this guy is a black belt."

"I know. I would love to test his ability. However, I did bring my little bag of goodies. I'll take him out with a dart. The new stuff we use is instant."

"Carlos, I don't want him dead. We need to question him. I need to know what he is after; and most importantly, I really want to know who sent him."

"Don't worry, the dart will knock him out for a few minutes. I can work him over a bit and soften him up. See how tough he really is. Or, if we don't want to waste a whole lot of time, I do have some drugs that will get him talking. Of course, with the drugs, we'll get truths and lies. We'll just have to sort it out. Hopefully, we'll get enough good info to start putting the pieces together."

"I don't care how it's done. I'll leave that up to you, that's your specialty. I just want to know what he's up to."

"Rick, what are you planning on doing with this guy when we're done?"

"Carlos, he's already presumed dead. I don't want to ever deal with this guy again. He can have an accident in the car or we can make it look like a hit."

"I assume Lynn and Brooke will be with you. Is that a correct assumption?"

"In order to get him to follow I have no choice but to bring the girls with me. If all goes as planned, and we get this guy, they can take the Escalade and go back to the condo. Neither of them will ever have to know what took place after they leave. I'll ride back with you."

"That'll work. What if he doesn't bite?"

"Then we go looking for him. Again, he won't be expecting you. Hell Carlos, since hurricane Ivan there are Mexicans all over the place. You'll fit right in. We find him, find out where he is staying and drop in and say hello with your dart gun."

"Rick, you are a quick study my friend. You always were good thinking on the run. I'm onboard with you. I'll call with the mileage to the rendezvous point. By the way, how is Brooke dealing with all this?"

"She is doing okay, but she is a bit withdrawn. Not herself at all. She is certainly a bit shaken, but Lynn is a great comfort. I haven't said anything to either of them about Ernesto. I told them I didn't want them going out of the condo until I found out what is going on. One other thing, to cover the purpose of your trip take a ride down 30A and look at some of the properties for sale. Be sure to talk with a couple of sight agents. That will establish a purpose for your visit to Destin."

"OK will do. I'll call you by twenty hundred hours with the mileage."

"See you at twenty-two hundred if all goes as planned."

Carlos put his phone in the empty seat next to him. The plan was, indeed, simple. Simple left little to error. He was looking forward to meeting Ernesto Garcia. He didn't like anyone messing with Brooke, his "little girl". Anyone messing with her would also deal with him.

Rick went into the living room. Brooke and Lynn were curled up on the couch with a blanket over their legs hugging cappuccinos and watching Fox and Friends. Rick was not going to tell them that Carlos was on the way. He wouldn't say anything to them about the plan. He would pretend to be taking them to his in-laws in Milton.

Ernesto Garcia had checked into the Holiday Inn on the Emerald Coast Highway. The hotel was located in the center of Destin. He had followed the Escalade to the Silver Shells complex. The road going into Silver Shells was divided. There was only one turn off just prior to the main gate. The turn off serviced the main office, a Ruth's Chris Steak House and a Spa Center. All three were open to the public. Ernesto turned in toward the steak house, then made a right turn and parked in front of the spa. He got out of the car and walked on the sidewalk that went around the spa and surprisingly onto Silver Shells private property. So much for security. He watched as Rick drove from the main gate toward the high-rise condos. There were five of them. Ernesto watched as the Escalade went around a rotary and headed east past the tennis courts. Rick then turned right. From that point Ernesto couldn't see where Rick had gone. It appeared that Rick drove to the building on the left, but he wasn't sure. Ernesto got back in his car and drove out of the Silver Shells complex and made a right turn onto the Emerald Coast Highway. He then made a left turn into Wal-Mart. The parking lot was nearly full. Most of the people appeared to be families enjoying the cooler weather in northern Florida. He drove through the parking lot and took the exit next to Hooter's restaurant. It brought him back to the main highway. He turned right and then made an immediate left onto the perimeter road just west of Silver Shells. Other than beach access, Ernesto determined that there were three gates guarding entrance into the complex. The main gate was up front next to Ruth's Chris. The other two gates allowed access to the perimeter road. They appeared to be the kind of gate that required a Fob or some kind of remote control device to operate. There was a parking lot just off the middle gate that would provide a good surveillance point. The best vantage point was in the parking lot of an old bank that was vacant. However, there was a police car parked in one of the drive-ups. The officer appeared to be catching a nap. Ernesto sat unnoticed in the parking area for a couple of hours. He needed to let Manny know where he was.

"Hola."

"Manny it is me, Ernesto."

"Where are you?"

"I'm in Destin," responded Ernesto.

"Where the hell is Destin?"

"In Florida…in the Panhandle near Pensacola. I followed the girl here. She's with her parents. What do you want me to do?"

"Didn't you get the information that Anderson wanted?"

"I got the email address of the *Anonymous Source*."

"Then why are you still following her?"

"Anderson was going to check it out. He wanted me to stick with her."

Manny didn't say anything. He was obviously thinking about the situation. He didn't like the fact that Anderson was giving orders to Ernesto. He knew the stories about serving two masters.

"Ernesto, hang low. I need to talk with Danny about this. I'll call you back in a few minutes."

Ernesto hung up. His mind wandered to Virginia Beach, the Hilton hotel and Maria Gomez. She was warm and innocent. He hadn't been with a woman that *wanted* to be with him, in years. He reached into his back pocket and pulled out his wallet. Her card was in the billfold section. He looked at it and put it to his nose. He could smell her fragrance. He dialed her number. Her answering system picked up on the first ring. Her voice made his heart beat faster. This had never happened to him before. He started to leave a message when his phone beeped in, letting him know that Manny was on the line. He told Maria's answering system that he had to take a call. He would call back.

"Yes?"

"Ernesto, Danny talked with Anderson. The email is bogus. Danny made a deal with Anderson. He wants you to take them out. You got that?"

"I got it."

Chapter Twenty-Two
Destin, Florida
November 25, 2010
Thursday
1520 Hours

Carlos made the call to Rick at 1520 Thursday afternoon. Rick was in his office going over everything. He always liked to block diagram his plans. The holes would always jump out. Better to see the holes than to fall into one. His satellite phone rang. It was Carlos. He had been expecting the call.

"Hey Carlos, what do you have for me?"

"The best location is two point seven miles on the right side. I'll put out a coke can. There is a dirt road that goes off into the woods. It is hard to see from the highway. Plus, the location will allow us to see a cars coming from either direction for quite a distance. I will call you when I am in position."

"Good. If I'm right, I believe Ernesto will take the bait. If nothing happens after about ten minutes, I will drive off and I will call you tomorrow at zero eight hundred. Don't show yourself unless he stops. No sense in alerting the girls."

"Rick, what if someone else stops?"

"Carlos, if the person who stops even looks remotely like Ernesto Garcia I will say, *man I'm glad you stopped*. That will be your cue to shoot. If I am absolutely sure that it is *not* Ernesto, I will say *thank you for stopping, but I don't need any assistance*. I really don't expect him to be wearing a disguise. I think he will be very bold."

"OK, I'm looking forward to seeing you tonight."

"Same here my friend."

Rick hung up, placed his hands behind his head and relaxed in the chair. A Lear jet was landing at the airport. He held out his right hand, palm down. It was steady as a rock. He was always at his best under pressure. He shut his eyes and began to visualize the plan again. Was it too simple? What if Ernesto put a tracking device on the car? Even if he had, he would still try to maintain visual contact. What if Ernesto has his weapon drawn? Carlos would see the weapon through his night vision scope. A lot of *what ifs* went through his mind. No, the plan was simple, and it was executable. He went over it one last time:

Rick pulls the Escalade over.
Tells the girls that he thinks something is wrong with the right front tire.
Tells them to stay in the car.
Ernesto stops.
Carlos hits him with a tranquilizer dart.
Rick sends the girls home.
Carlos picks up Ernesto and carries him down the dirt road.
Rick drives Ernesto's car behind Carlos.
They get answers.

The whole process to get off the road and out of sight would be less than two minutes. The hardest part will be to get the girls to leave without them asking a million questions. But, he has to keep them in the dark until Ernesto shows up. Once they realize what is happening, Lynn will be upset, most likely she'll be *really* upset, but she will be more than happy to leave. Simple was easy. Simple was always easy. Too many *what ifs* would only confuse the plan. Rick was betting that Ernesto would take the time to make a positive identification. That is all he and Carlos needed.

Rick went into the living room and asked if the girls would like to go to Bone Fish Grill for dinner. Lynn was ready; she was always ready to eat out, and she loved Bone Fish Grill.

"Sure, that sounds good to me," she answered seeing an opportunity to get out of the condo.

Brooke was on the couch reading a book. She was still very quiet. Lynn got up and went over to her.

"Honey, are you ready to get out of the house? Would you like to go out for dinner?"

"I thought we were going to Nana and Paw Paw's tonight," responded Brooke as she placed the book into her lap.

"We are honey, but they won't be home until late, so let's go out and enjoy a nice meal. You will love Bone Fish Grill."

"I need to pack my bag. Should we pack up before we go?"

Rick wanted them to be ready, but needed to come back to the condo, park on the upper deck where the Escalade would be visible, and load the car in plain sight. If Ernesto was watching, and Rick bet that he would be, seeing them loading luggage would force Ernesto to follow them.

"I'll tell you what, why don't you girls pack your things, and we'll come back here since it's on the way, so you can freshen up here while I load the car?"

Rick knew that neither Lynn nor Brooke like using a public restroom. They'd bust a bladder first. He was right. Lynn was first to answer with Brooke nodding her head in approval.

"That sounds good to us," said Lynn as she looked over to Brooke.

Rick called and reserved a table next to the window, where he could see the parking lot. He still had his father-in-law's disabled parking permit over the visor. He would be able to park in the handicap space right in front of the restaurant. He could watch to make sure no one messed with the car.

On the drive to Bone Fish Grill, Rick didn't notice anyone following. The traffic was a little heavy. It's difficult to pick up someone following, especially on short trips. He didn't want to make unnecessary turns. That was a dead give away that he was looking for a tail. He wanted Ernesto to be complacent. He parked in front. The table provided a perfect view of the Escalade. If anyone got close to the car, Rick would see him. Lynn and Brooke did the ordering. Rick and Lynn usually split a meal. They started with coconut-crusted shrimp. The main course was blackened grouper topped off with a fried banana desert. As usual, the meal was wonderful. After dinner, Rick and the girls drove straight back to Silver Shells and parked in front of the condo on the second level. Rick parked in the handicap space. The Escalade was visible from several locations around the complex. He had made sure that it would be. The girls freshened up as Rick loaded the car. They were on the way to Milton by 2100 hours. The fifty-three mile trip to Lynn's parents house normally took about an hour and ten minutes. Rick was hoping that tonight's trip would be much shorter.

There was the usual number of cars on US 98 for a Thursday night. Most had Wisconsin, Michigan and Ontario plates. Rick checked the rearview mirror. There were several cars behind him, but they were too far back to make a positive identification. Entering the town of Mary Ester brought back fond memories of his very first date with Lynn. It was on Valentine's Day in 1971. They had gone to Bacon's by the Sea, had a couple of beers, ate raw oysters and shot pool for a couple of hours. Bacon's was a neat place. It was famous. It was the place where Jimmy Doolittle drew plans on a tablecloth for the bombing of Tokyo. Unfortunately, Bacon's is no longer there. What a shame. Fifteen minutes later he made a right turn on highway 87 north. The stretch of highway close to Navarre was well lit. He could see a couple of cars about a quarter-mile back, but none that he could recognize. Hopefully, one was Ernesto. Rick's satellite phone rang.

"Morgan."

"Rick, I'm in position. Very few cars. Good interval. What is your ETA?"

"About fifteen minutes," he responded as he looked over at Lynn.

"Anybody in tow?"

"Not sure, but I think so," he said trying to sound like it was a casual call.

"Okay, if not I will talk with you in the morning."

Rick hung up. Lynn was curious.

"Was that Carl?" she asked knowing that he was the only one that Rick talked with on the satellite phone.

"Yes it was. You know Carl…always working," responded Rick.

"What did he want?" asked Lynn.

Rick was hoping to avoid answering any questions, but knowing Lynn, he knew he would have to come up with something fast.

"He wanted to know how long it would take me to create a Concept of Operations paper for a close-in support helicopter. Since I have already prepared one for the Navy while at Matrix, it will take about five minutes to find and ten to smooth. I'll get it to him tomorrow."

Lynn was satisfied with Rick's explanation. Brooke had slept through the call. She was still mentally exhausted. The meal was a good sleeping pill. The road narrowed to two lanes. A couple of miles up the road, on the left side, was the sign for Choctaw Field. Rick zeroed is odometer. Brooke was still asleep and Lynn was nodding off. Rick could see a car in his rearview mirror. It was a couple hundred yards back. Rick was doing the speed limit, fifty-five. Only one car had passed him from the other direction. At thirteen miles, Rick began slowing down. The deceleration woke Lynn from her semi-sleep. She looked over at Rick.

"Why are you slowing down? You're not getting pulled over are you?"

She turned to look behind the car.

"No, the car seems to be pulling a little to the right. I just want to check the tires."

"Oh great. There's nobody out here."

"Don't worry, I can add some air if necessary. I have the battery starter in the back of the car, it has an air compressor. Besides, there are a couple of gas stations close to the interstate ten ramp if we need one."

At exactly thirteen point two miles, Rick pulled to the right side of the road and put his flashers on. He was right next to a dirt road going into the woods. He got out of the Escalade, and as he walked around the front of the car, Carlos flashed a red laser light to signal his location.

A car was approaching from behind at about a hundred yards. As it got closer it began to slow down. Rick pretended to be looking at the right front tire. The car stopped about twenty yards in front and proceeded to back up stopping about ten feet from the front of the Escalade. A man got out of the car and walked slowly toward Rick. In the flashing lights Rick recognized the man from the airport. It was Ernesto Garcia. Ernesto's right hand was partially hidden. Before Rick could say the coded greeting Carlos' dart caught Ernesto just under his left ear. Ernesto tried to bring up his weapon but fell face forward as his legs collapsed out from under him. Carlos was there almost as fast as Ernesto hit the dirt. Lynn opened the door. Rick heard the key alarm and yelled:

"Stay in the car. Don't get out of the car!"

Carlos already had Ernesto over his shoulder and was moving toward the dirt road. Rick went to the passenger side; Lynn had already rolled down the window.

"What is going on? Who was that guy, and for goodness sake—what is Carlos doing here?"

"Lynn, listen to me. That guy is after Brooke. I want you to drive back to the condo. I will be home in a couple of hours and will explain everything to you. Now please, don't ask any questions. Drive the speed limit. Don't leave any rubber when you turn around, OK."

"Rick, I don't believe this! Is that guy dead? Did you *use* us to get to him? I can't believe this."

"Lynn, please—*please* no more questions. I will see you back at the condo. Watch a movie. I will answer all your questions later. *Now please*, go back to the condo. You have to trust me on this."

Brooke hadn't said a word. She was in a dream…a nightmare…one that wasn't going away. Lynn slid over, started the car and made a very slow u-turn and drove off. Rick had seen that look on her face before. It was about a two-week look. Rick pulled a pair of gloves from his back pocket. He put them on, jumped into Ernesto's rental car, backed up, and turned down the dirt road. Carols had Ernesto handcuffed to a medium sized Florida pine tree. He was already in the process of administering a hypodermic needle into Ernesto's neck. Rick looked at his watch. The whole process had taken one minute and thirty-five seconds.

Chapter Twenty-Three
Eglin Reservation, Florida
November 25, 2010
Thursday
2215 Hours

Ernesto was still unconscious. Carlos was putting a small syringe into a little leather bag when Rick walked up. This was the first time Rick had seen Carlos in over a year. They initially embraced. Carlos's body was solid. No fat, just lean rock hard muscle. His handshake was firm. Rick had to squeeze back to keep his own hand from hurting. Rick wondered if his body had ever felt that way to someone who had embraced him. Probably did a long time ago. The spot that Carlos had picked was perfect. There were no signs that anyone had been on the dirt road in a long time. The Air Force used it occasionally. The police always set up their speed traps closer to the populated areas.

"Carlos, how long before we can question him?" asked Rick as he got closer to the motionless body of Ernesto Garcia.

Carlos looked at his watch.

"The tranquilizer should wear off in another two minutes, three at the most."

"What was in the needle?" asked Rick.

"It's mostly a KGB cocktail, a little scopolamine, ethanol and SP-17. It will loosen him up quite a bit. He will still try to hide the truth; however, he will unknowingly give us most of the information we need. We will have to pay close attention. We can sort it all out later," responded Carlos.

"Have you used this stuff before?" asked Rick as he again got closer to Ernesto.

"Yes, in Afghanistan, although it was probably not needed, since it was hard to stop the rag-heads from talking. They'd give up their grandmother to save their ass. We would get a hard case every once in a while. The stuff is good, but not perfect. However, we were always able to determine the truth. Looks like Ernesto is coming around."

"Carlos, don't forget that he is a black belt. Might still be able to do some damage with his feet."

"I'll keep clear. Besides, the drug will really slow him down. You going to take some notes?"

"I've brought a small recorder," responded Rick.

"Great."

Ernesto moved his head and wanted to touch his neck when he realized that he was hugging a tree. He was confused. He looked around and saw Carlos and Rick.

"What the hell? Who are you guys? What's going on here?"

"Mr. Garcia. My name is Garcia also. Maybe we are related?"

Carlos's laugh was more of a smirk.

"I don't think so. You look like a *maricone* to me. Who the fuck is he?"

"He is the father of the person you have been following. Why are you here Ernesto?"

"I I don't follow her. I don't know this girl at all. How do you know my name?"

"I didn't say the person was a girl. But you know her don't you. Manny asked you to follow her—isn't that correct?" asked Carlos.

"I don't know what you are talking about. I don't know no Manny. Who's Manny?"

"Manny knows you. He set you up, and he gets his orders from Danny Ochoa," offered Rick.

"Danny would never set me up. He's my cousin. We grew up together in Cuba. Danny wouldn't set me up."

"Then why are you making love to a tree?" asked Carlos.

"Fuck you, I don't know…you tell me."

"You're handcuffed to a tree because you pissed off Danny. You didn't succeed in your mission. Danny wanted the girl dead, and you fucked up!" said Carlos.

"No No, Danny just wanted me to find out who the *source* was. He needed the *source*."

Ernesto tested his handcuffs. He realized he wasn't going anywhere. He had no idea that Rick and Carlos had gotten all the personal information about him off the DEA's database. The tone of Ernesto's voice suggested that he was starting to believe that Danny really had sent these guys after him.

"Why is he interested in the *source* then?" asked Carlos.

"I don't know. Why is her father here?"

"Ernesto, you are in no position to ask questions. Look at me! I will ask the questions. Why would Danny want to know who the *source* is?" asked Carlos in a louder voice.

"Hell, I don't know. Probably the guy in DC knows."

"What guy in DC?" asked Rick.

"The guy I went to see for Danny. I need some water."

Carlos motioned to Rick in the direction of the Ford Escape. Rick went over and found a couple of unopened bottles of water. He handed one to Carlos. Carlos opened the bottle, put the cap in his pocket and moved a little closer to Ernesto.

"You want some water, tell me the name of the guy in DC."

Ernesto squinted his eyes. Hey, I'm not feeling so good. I need a drink. Give me a drink and I will tell you his name."

"Tell me his name and the bottle is yours," said Carlos.

"It's it's Reynolds, yeah it's Reynolds," responded Ernesto. He wasn't convincing.

"Ernesto, you need to tell me the truth. There is no Reynolds," snapped Carlos.

"I need some water."

"What is his name? I can't help you with Danny unless you tell me his name," said Carlos.

"What are you talking about? What do you mean, help me with Danny? Danny is the one who sent me to see him."

"Why did Danny send you to see him?" asked Rick.

"Danny needed to know where Paco is being held."

"Who's Paco?" asked Carlos.

Rick went and whispered to Carlos.

"Carlos, try the Witness Protection Program on him. That seems to be the connection to Brooke."

"Is Paco being held by the US Marshals?"

"Of course, that's why I went to Bascomb. You know all this stuff, why you asking me stuff you already know?" responded Ernesto as he shook the handcuffs.

"Ernesto, I will ask the questions," said Carlos firmly.

"What the hell is with Danny? At first he didn't want this girl dead. He just wanted me to find out who was giving her information."

"So why are you here? What do you mean by *at first*?"

"I didn't find out anything in her apartment. I figured she had the information with her. I was waiting for the right opportunity. When I got the info, I would give it to Danny."

"Then what?" asked Rick.

"There's no then what. Then I give the info to Danny, and that's it."

"Who else knows about this Ernesto?" asked Carlos.

"Nobody. That's all I know. I need a drink. You're going to let me go, right?"

"Sure Ernesto, I got no use for you," responded Carlos with as much sincerity that he could muster.

Carlos handed the bottle of water to Ernesto. He and Rick moved a few feet away. They both agreed that Ernesto probably didn't know any more information that would help them. They basically had what they needed. They had been there long enough. It was time to go. The drugged water was rapidly taking effect. The last conscious thought Ernesto ever had was of Maria Gomez. Carlos took the bottle and screwed on the cap that he had put in his pocket.

"Rick, do you have his weapon?"

"Sure, right here."

Carlos took the Berretta. It had a silencer on it. Carlos looked over at Rick. Clearly, Ernesto meant business. When he got the information he wanted, he probably would have killed all three of them. Carlos was about to shoot Ernesto in the head when Rick put his hand on Carlo's shoulder.

"Hold on a second. Since we are on the Eglin Reservation the Feds will get involved. If we move him we could leave some trace evidence. Let's put him in the car. We'll go back to our original plan of a fiery accident. The fire trucks will make a mess of the area. It will take weeks for the forensic guys to figure out who this guy is. He probably used an alias to rent the car. Either way, the Feds won't release his identity until they're sure they know who he is."

"Okay, I had prepared for the accident. I'll dowse the inside of the car with gasoline. I have a nice little IED that will do the job quite well. Hell, they will probably think this guy was a terrorist and his device went off prematurely. That's if there is enough evidence left at the scene. Rick, drive out to the road and go up a couple of miles, turn around come back and pick me up. Let me check to make sure no cars are coming."

Carlos went to the edge of the woods. No lights were visible. He motioned to Rick to drive forward. Rick drove with the lights out.

"I will meet you at the road in precisely five minutes. Let's sink watches."

Five minutes later Carlos and Rick were on the way back to Destin.

"Carlos, I think the law will have a field day when they finally identify the remains. Especially since they believe Ernesto Garcia drowned in the Miami River."

Carlos let out a little laugh and added,

"I bet the weapon will yield some interesting ballistics information, that's if there is enough left of it. You know that this guy was a hitter," said Rick.

"Well, no matter what, he won't be bothering Brooke, or us for that matter. Any thoughts on the information he gave us?" asked Carlos

"Carlos, I am sure that Danny Ochoa sent him. My initial thoughts are that Ochoa wanted to find this guy Paco. Paco probably has information about Ochoa's operation, and Ochoa wants to get him before he has a chance to make any deals. Maybe Ochoa thought that Brooke's *source* would know. I do believe that Ochoa tasked Ernesto to find out. Ernesto used the phrase *at first*. That is a bit troubling. The only thing that is not totally clear to me is Bascomb's role. Why did

Ernesto go to Bascomb? Ernesto is a Lieutenant he takes and follows orders. I need to review the tape; I don't remember if Ernesto actually said that Danny sent him, or said, "that's why I went to Bascomb". The only logical conclusion is that Bascomb is a US Marshal."

"Sounds like you did a lot of thinking in that short turn around," said Carlos.

"I need to play the tape a couple of times," said Rick as he looked into the rearview mirror.

"Rick, do you think Ochoa is a threat?"

"He's certainly a threat. It will be interesting to see how he responds to Ernesto's death. If he decides to screw with Brooke, we'll take him out."

"Maybe we should take him out now, eliminate the threat, and diffuse the situation," said Carlos.

"Carlos, I tend to agree with you, but first we have to determine where Bascomb fits into the equation. The Feds won't be able to identify Ernesto's remains for several days. That will give us some time and a bit of an edge. I will check this guy Bascomb out tonight."

"You really think you will have the time?" said Carlos as he smiled at Rick. "You're going to have fun explaining this to Lynn. Do you want me to go in with you?" he added.

"No, I'll be all right. I'm sure she and Brooke will have a million questions. It will be a little rough at first, especially with Lynn. When I explain the situation, they'll be okay."

"Are you going to tell them what happened to Ernesto?" asked Carlos. It was actually a rhetorical question.

"No, I'll tell them that we let him go. They rarely watch the local news. If they find out, I'll worry about it then."

By now they were halfway between Fort Walton Beach and Destin. A Florida State Police car raced past heading west on US 98, his blue lights flashing. Two minutes later a fire truck went by in its entire splendor. The truck was heading west also. Less than a minute later two more police cars went by. Rick looked at Carlos

"I hope the fire doesn't destroy too many acres. I understand it has been pretty dry around here," said Rick.

The fog was beginning to roll in. The large condo complex on the other side of the Destin bridge was hardly visible. On the left side, the lights from McGuire's created little green ghosts that danced away in the fog. Destin was shroud in fog. There were only two cars on the street between the bridge and Silver Shells. Rick turned right at the light just after the Grand Mariner and a couple of blocks before the Silver Shells complex. He stopped the car at the stop sign.

"Carlos, I'll walk in from here since you don't have a condo sticker. It will be better if we are not seen together. I'll call you at zero eight hundred tomorrow. By the way, why don't you take another ride down 30A and look at some more properties. Sign a few Realtor logs. It will give you an alibi for coming to Destin just in case someone decides to check the airport logs."

"Good idea. Talk with you tomorrow."

Rick got out of the vehicle and headed for the *Lynn Inquisition*!

Chapter Twenty-Four
Destin, Florida
November 26, 2010
Friday
0800 Hours

Rick answered all of Lynn's questions...at least to her partial satisfaction. She was not very happy and still a bit miffed that Rick and Carlos had used her and Brooke as decoys. Rick assured her that it was the only way to get Ernesto out in the open, and that they were never in any *real* danger. They had to get him on their terms, not his. The excitement of the night before had renewed Brooke's spirits. She was more excited about the next phase of her dad's plan; and was now more convinced than ever that her dad was, indeed, *connected*. Rick *was* connected, but not to the people that Brooke had secretly wished for all these years. She was no longer scared. Her adrenaline was pumping. In fact, she was ready to participate in the next phase, as she put it. Lynn wasn't as adventurous, and still mulling over Rick's statement that they were never in any *real* danger. Rick had no difficulty convincing Brooke that her part would come into play later. Rick looked over at Lynn. She still had the *look* on her face.

Rick had played the tapes over several times, making notes as he listened to Ernesto's answers. He was convinced that the key to solving the problem was Bascomb. He developed a scenario that he would bounce off Carlos. Carlos was not only an experienced field operative, but he was also a good tactical operations guy. Carlos was a quick study. He had the rare quality of being able to adapt to a rapidly changing environment while still meeting the mission objective with the resources at hand. Rick called Carlos on his secure satellite cell phone. Carlos conscience was clear. He had a good night's rest and was in the process of making coffee when his phone rang. He saw that it was Rick.

"Good morning Rick. I see you made it through the night. Any battle scars?"

Clearly, Carlos knew that Lynn could be a handful…in more ways than one.

"She's okay. She accepted my explanation with, uh, *reservations* so to speak. However, she did leave the door open for a cross-examination. I believe she will continue to revisit the discussion for the next several days."

"I bet she will. Rick, you have made a good life for her and Brooke. She is comfortable in the safety of the world you built around her. I'm sure she has created a very large security bubble."

"She is a good woman, I hated to keep her in the dark, but she is not good at acting," said Rick as he changed the subject. "Carlos, I went over the tape last night and I believe I have identified a scenario that is probably very close to what is going on. First of all, and pardon my colorful metaphor, the shit hit the fan when Brooke's second article on *The Last Witness* was published. Have you read the two articles?"

"Rick, I hate to admit that I haven't, but I will. How many are there altogether?"

"There are to be five in the series, with the last one already being advertised as a 'real shocker'. The key point in the second article clearly stated that there was an organization within the US Marshals that was making some of the witnesses disappear and disappear for good! Also, at the end of the second article, her credits listed an *Anonymous Source*. Carlos, what we know is this: Ernesto works for Danny Ochoa. Ochoa is looking for a guy named Paco. The computer database lists one of the "Known Associates" as Paco Ramirez. Now according to my database search, Paco Ramirez was recently picked up during a drug bust in Miami and placed in US Marshal custody. Ernesto said that a guy named Bascomb sent him, and that Danny had ordered it. I did a database search on Bascomb and found a Sidney Bascomb in the US Marshals. Several years ago Sidney Bascomb lived in Key Biscayne,

Florida and worked as an accountant for several car dealerships. Guess who owns the dealerships?"

"Danny Ochoa, right?" responded Carlos.

"Right! So Carlos, this is what I believe is going on. I believe that this whole episode with Brooke is a *quid pro quo*. Brooke's article, thanks to the *Anonymous Source*, contains information that is right on the mark. It is scaring the hell out of Bascomb. Danny Ochoa didn't need to go after Brooke; he had Bascomb on the inside. There is only one plausible reason for Danny Ochoa going after Brooke; it is payback for Bascomb taking care of Paco Ramirez. I don't believe for a minute that Bascomb is in this alone, but he is the key to finding out who the real boss is. Unfortunately, since Ernesto didn't succeed in his mission, Brooke is still in danger."

Rick paused. He didn't like the thought of Brooke and Lynn being in danger, especially from an unidentified individual.

"Carlos, does this make any sense to you?"

"It makes perfectly good sense to me. How much time do you think we have until someone else shows up?"

"When they identify Ernesto's body, I believe we'll have about twenty-four hours. Part Three of *The Last Witness* is supposed to be published in this Sunday's paper. We might be able to buy some time if the paper will agree to slip a week. Hell, if they play it up right, they could get some great publicity from a delay."

"Rick, I'm sure you have a plan."

"Carlos, how long will you be available to help?"

"For you, for Brooke hell, as long as it takes. I'm in between jobs at the moment."

"Carlos, I can't thank you enough. I really need you to go to DC. I would go myself, but I need to be here for Brooke and Lynn. I don't want to link you and Brooke together here in Destin. Besides, for what I am thinking, your Hispanic heritage will work better to scare Bascomb. I need to get in touch with Carl Peterson."

"You mean...*blue sky*?"

Rick laughed.

"You know Carlos, Carl still can't figure it out. Anyway, his company The Peterson Group does quite a bit of Black Ops work. I am going to call him and see if he will fly you to DC. Once I find out, I will call you back. Also, I will let you know how to proceed with Bascomb. I still need a few more hours to plan this."

"I'll be waiting to hear from you. You know Rick, I could fly my plane to DC."

"I thought about that, but I think it would be better if you leave your plane here just in case they find out who Ernesto is, and are smart enough to check the airfields. As you know, hit men tend to fly in and fly out the same day."

"You just keep thinking Butch!" laughed Carlos referring to a line in one of his favorite movies, *Butch Cassidy and The Sundance Kid*.

Rick hung up and wasted no time dialing Carl Peterson's private number. Elaine Drew answered half way through the first ring.

"The Peterson Group, Elaine Drew, how may I help you?"

"Hello Ms. Drew, Rick Morgan here. Is Carl available? I hate to disturb him, but I really need to speak with him."

"Hold on Mr. Morgan, I will check."

Rick was certain that no matter how busy Carl was, he would always make time for him. They went back a long way.

"Rick, what's going on? I've been meaning to call you. I will have some tasking shortly."

"Thanks Carl, actually I wasn't calling about the tasking. I have a…favor to ask."

"What's up Rick?"

Rick gave Carl an abbreviated version of what he had told Carlos. Carl was happy to hear that Carlos was "still alive".

"Rick, the Gulfstream is in Jacksonville. I can have the plane there in forty-five minutes. They were getting ready to head back to DC in about an hour anyway. Your *new buddy* Roland Carpenter is aboard. Will that work for you?"

"Carl, that will work splendidly. I will owe you one actually, if my memory serves me, I will owe you another one."

"You owe me nothing my friend. When this is all over let me know how it went down. I'm looking forward to seeing Carlos. Is he available for some work?"

"You know, I believe he may be. He said that he was between jobs. I think he was working as a contractor for the State Department. You couldn't ask for a better asset! He'll be at the Destin-Fort Walton Beach Airport when the plane lands. Thanks again Carl. Oh Carl—I'll be briefing him on our task. Could you provide ID if he needs it?"

"Sure, no problem. In fact we can do it on the plane. I'll tell Roland to cooperate fully with Carlos. Roland can make any ID he needs. Rick, I need to show you what we have on that plane. I think you'll be amazed. We have come a long ways since the old days."

"Thanks Carl...when this is over."

Rick immediately called Carlos. Carlos said he had already packed and could be at the airport within twenty minutes. He would keep the room and the rental car. Rick told Carlos to call him when he was airborne. At 0910 the Gulfstream landed and taxied to the small building that masqueraded as the field's Operations Center. Carlos went outside, bag in hand, and was greeted by Roland Carpenter. At 0920 they were airborne, and at 0935 Rick's cell phone rang. Carlos was strapped in and drinking a freshly made cup of coffee.

"Carlos, that was quick."

"Hey this is some set up. I had heard about this equipment, but I didn't know it was operational."

"Yeah, Carl wants to give me the grand tour. By the way, he was happy to know that you are still alive!" said Rick.

"What was it that Samuel Clemens said, *reports of my death have been greatly exaggerated*?" responded Carlos.

"I thought you only read Tactical Operations Manuals? By the way, I think that Carl would like to hire you."

"I could live like this, at least for a while," responded Carlos as he looked around the plane. "Tell me what you are planning for Bascomb."

Rick didn't have as much time to think this one through. He would have liked a little more time. But, he favored simple plans. He had reviewed Sidney Bascomb's biography and was convinced that he couldn't possibly be the brains behind the Witness Protection Program scheme. He had downloaded Sidney Bascomb's picture and biography to his cell phone.

"Carlos, I'm convinced that there is *at least* one more US Marshal involved in the DC area. I will send you Bascomb's picture and a short biography. If looks are descriptive, he's no powerbroker. I believe if you play the role of one of Danny Ochoa's Lieutenants, you will be able to scare this guy enough that he will either mention his partner's name or lead you to him. The info that I am sending includes his work location, telephone number, email and even his parking space assignment. I will leave it to your discretion how you decide to make contact. When you make initial contact I suggest that you tell him Danny is very upset that he, Bascomb, has not followed through with the agreement concerning Paco Ramirez or Brooke Morgan. Also you tell him that Danny wants to know, *where did you send Ernesto*? Since you will be accusing Bascomb of these things, he may give you a name."

"I will probably need access to the building," said Carlos.

"I'm sure that Roland Carpenter can fix you up with whatever identification you may need. He can also provide you with a 'bug' that you can attach to Bascomb."

"Who's Roland Carpenter?" asked Carlos.

"He's the young guy with the whitewall haircut that looks like he's on a high school tour. Carl said that he was aboard the flight and would instruct him to provide whatever you needed."

"I see him at a computer station," said Carlos as he looked Roland over. "Rick, we are getting old my friend," he added.

"He is young, but he must be good to be working for Carl Peterson. Carlos, if you have any questions give me a call."

"Will do. Have you thought any more about…Ochoa?"

"I have."

Chapter Twenty-Five
Washington, DC
November 26, 2010
Friday
1100 Hours

The Gulfstream landed at Dulles International Airport at 1240. It was an unseasonably warm day in the DC area. The wind was out of the south and the pilot made a smooth landing touching down right at the threshold numbers on runway 19R. He reversed the engines and was able to make the first turn off. The Peterson Group had a long-term contract with Jet Blue that allowed them access to the B-Gates. The Gulfstream taxied to gate 6. The team was disembarking within 15 minutes of landing, and took the concourse to the parking area where The Peterson Group had assigned parking. They also had several cars available for personal use and surveillance. Carlos selected a Ford SUV with Georgia license plates. He thanked the crew and gave Roland Carpenter a sincere *thank you* and firm handshake. Carlos was impressed by Roland's enthusiasm. He really liked the kid, and down deep inside he knew that their paths would cross again.

Carlos put his duffle bag on the back seat of the Ford and was heading east on the Dulles access road within thirty minutes of landing. Roland Carpenter had been extremely helpful. He was able to access the Virginia DMV records where he found the title and registration to Sidney Bascomb's 2008 Buick LaSaber. Using the car's VIN, Roland was able to make both a key and key Fob for Carlos. Carlos was very impressed by Roland's resourcefulness and the suite of equipment installed aboard the Gulfstream. It was a field operative's flying candy store. He could have shopped there all day. Approaching the beltway, Carlos called Rick.

"Good afternoon Carlos. I hope you had a nice flight."

"I did. Rick, that aircraft is unbelievable, and Roland Carpenter is a trip. The kid is smart as a whip, and he loves what he is doing. He was probably the video king growing up."

"I'm sure you are right about that. The kid is certainly mature beyond his years."

"Rick, hopefully they'll keep him on the technical side of business. He's good. He's real good!"

"I'm sure Carl Peterson recognizes his talent," responded Rick. "How long before you will be downtown?" asked Rick.

"Weather is good. Traffic's not bad. Still some lunch-hour people weaving in and out of traffic making their way back to work. Should be there in about twenty to thirty minutes," responded Carlos.

"Did Roland take care of you?" asked Rick.

"Yes, he set me up with a smart card ID as a Peterson Group employee. Seems they have a contract with the US Marshals. The ID will allow access to both locations in DC," added Carlos.

Before Rick could respond Carlos continued.

"I understand from the material you sent that Bascomb's office is located at 500 Indiana Avenue. Roland has already updated the US Marshal's database with my new ID and fingerprints. By the way, he also made me a set of keys and a key Fob to Bascomb's car. I just need to determine how this guy usually gets to work. Car-pooling could present a slight problem. The Metro would be an ideal place to make contact. If the car is there, I will bug it and put on a tracking device. If he is car-pooling I'll catch him at home."

"Sounds like you were busy on that flight."

"I was, unfortunately, it made the flight go by too fast."

"Too fast," responded Rick.

"Yeah, I was enjoying seeing all the toys they have, and the capability to produce just about any ID you would ever need, responded Carlos.

"I do need to take a tour of the plane," said Rick.

Rick changed the subject.

"Carlos, I completely trust your judgment. I do believe that a face-to-face will be the most effective way to get to Bascomb. We need to scare him, shake him enough so that he will go to his partner, or partners as the case may be. You said that Roland made you an ID card that will give you access to the US Marshal's office?"

"Yes he did."

"In that case why not approach Bascomb on his own territory? He will certainly be at ease in his own environment; at least until you mention that Danny Ochoa sent you. That should take him by surprise, especially since it was so easy for you to gain access to his office. He'll probably be speechless for a few seconds. I would think that his body language would speak volumes. If you ask him about Paco, you will certainly establish undeniable credibility. You know how to interrogate. Hopefully, you can get him out of his office and to some place neutral."

"I agree. I will keep you updated. Hey Rick, guess what kind of car Bascomb drives?"

"A Buick," responded Rick with confidence.

"How the hell did you know that?"

"He's an accountant!" responded Rick. Buick is a good deal.

"You're amazing. So you think that all accountants drive Buicks?"

"Not all of them, most of them do, Bascomb does for sure. Besides, it was listed on his personnel sheet," laughed Rick. "Talk with you later."

Rick wished they had had more time to come up with a better plan, but time was of the essence. He had total confidence in Carlos. Carlos was an experienced operative. He was the best that Rick had ever seen. He was certain that Carlos would soon be calling back with the name of Bascomb's partner, or partners. Rick went to the living room where Brooke was typing on her computer.

"Hey honey, how is the article coming?"

"Slow, I can't finish until I receive the next packet of information from my...*Anonymous Source*."

Brooke made a little face and squeezed out the words, "anonymous source".

Rick hadn't seen the original material that was emailed to Brooke. He only knew that the *Anonymous Source* was supposed to email more material by the end of the week. This whole DC scenario with Carlos may end up being a moot point if the *Anonymous Source* could, indeed, identify the supposed ring leader within the US Marshal's Witness

Protection Program. Regardless, the current situation being what it was, he knew that Brooke was still in danger. It was only a matter of time before there would be someone else trying to find out who the *Anonymous Source* was. Worse yet, it was highly probable that someone would try to stop her from finishing the article altogether. He and Carlos needed to beat them to the punch.

At 1420, Carlos parked The Peterson Group SUV in one of the US Marshal's visitor parking spaces. He could see Bascomb's Buick. Carlos easily passed through the initial building security check. He took the stairs and headed for room C250. He had played his character over and over in his mind. He knew how he wanted to handle Bascomb. Both he and Rick believed that there was someone over Bascomb pulling the strings. Carlos entered the US Marshal's office. A female secretary, in a tailored blue suit that was at least two sizes to small turned the login sheet in his direction. She handed him a pen and asked for his ID card. She swiped the ID card through a card reader that was on an Italian credenza behind her. The card reader was attached to a Toshiba laptop. There was also a flat screen on the counter next to the login sheet. Carlos's picture appeared on both the laptop screen and the flat screen on the counter. Carlos's mug was staring back at him. It was the picture that Roland had taken earlier, however, the clothes were different. Roland was, indeed, a sharp kid. His new name appeared under the picture. The secretary handed back the ID, and Alberto Cruz was cleared to enter. He requested to see Sidney Bascomb.

"Do you have an appointment with Mr. Bascomb?"

"No, but I have some important information for him from Miami," he responded. Please tell him, I can assure you that he will want to see me," Carlos added.

Sidney Bascomb was going through a pile of receipts when his phone buzzed.

"Bascomb," he answered sounding a bit annoyed.

"Mr. Bascomb, there is a gentleman here to see you. He has a valid contractor identification card".

Bascomb knew that several contractors provided surveillance support in the field. He had no idea why a contractor would need to see him.

"Ms. Jacobs, who is this gentleman?"

"His name is Alberto Cruz. He said that he has some important information for you...from Miami."

Bascomb's heart sank a little. His only ties in Miami were an ex-wife and Danny Ochoa. His hesitation in responding was all that Carlos needed. Ms. Jacobs seemed to be impatient. She raised her eyebrows a bit and pursed her lips waiting for a response.

"Send him in Ms. Jacobs."

"Down the hall, second door on the left," she said without making eye contact with Carlos.

"Thank you."

Ms. Jacobs pressed a button under her desk, the door buzzed, and Carlos entered the hallway. There were pictures in the hallway of Deputy Marshals killed in the line of duty. By their looks, many of them had missed out on a lot of life. All the doors were closed. There was an eerie silence. Nobody in that office was having any fun. Carlos knocked on the second door on the left. Bascomb got up and opened the door.

"Mr. Cruz, come in, please, sit down," he said trying not to show any emotion.

Bascomb motioned to one of two chairs that were positioned at slight angles in front of his desk.

"I understand that you have some information for me from Miami?"

"I do, but it is more of a personal nature. Maybe you would feel more comfortable over a cup of coffee?"

Carlos wanted to get Bascomb out of the office. He had prepared a note that simply stated that he was there as a representative of Mr. Ochoa's interests. He handed the note to Bascomb as they were talking. Sidney Bascomb looked at the note. His mouth slackened a bit. He wet lips a couple of times and looked up at Carlos. He didn't say a word. First it was Ernesto and now another one of Danny's Lieutenants, one that was able to get through security. It was almost as if he knew that this day was coming. The blood had drained from his face; his color was ashen. He was visibly shaken. Carlos motioned toward the door. Bascomb nodded in agreement, put on his coat, and they left the office.

"Mr. Bascomb, do you have any preference for coffee?" asked Carlos calmly.

"Yes, let's walk over to Union Station. I need the fresh air. There is a very nice Starbucks there with *enough* privacy."

Carlos could use the walk also. It was a brilliant day on the mall. The joggers were out in force, several tours were being conducted and there were the usual homeless individuals who seemed, for some reason, to fit in. Carlos figured that they were probably the only honest people in DC. There were very few people in Starbucks.

"So tell me Bascomb, are we going to have to worry about Paco?"

"As far as I know, Ben's guys are going to pick him up in Dallas. Other than that, there is nothing else I can tell you."

"Danny does not want him testifying. Can you guarantee that he will not testify?"

"Once he's in the guys' custody you can assure Ochoa that Paco will not testify."

"For your sake I hope you're right. By the way, we haven't heard from Ernesto. Has he made contact with the girl in Virginia Beach?"

"I have no idea. That is Ben's department. He talked directly with Ochoa about that."

"Maybe I need to talk with Ben myself. Shall we go see him?"

"Ben and Carol are out of town. He isn't due back into the office until Monday. Will you be here Monday?" asked Bascomb.

Bascomb was hoping that the answer to his question was no. He really didn't like this guy at all. It brought back bad memories of Miami and fears of Danny Ochoa, and what Ochoa would do.

"No, I will be in Miami. Tell Ben about our conversation and that I will be contacting him very soon."

With that, Carlos got up and left Sidney Bascomb to ponder the empty table and chair in from of him. Sidney didn't even see Carlos, a.k.a. Alberto Cruz go out the door. Sidney's mind was a million miles away. How did he ever let Ben Anderson talk him into the witness scheme? He was free when he got away from Miami. Now it's all back...and more.

Carlos was convinced that he had learned enough information from Bascomb to determine who was running the show. However, just for insurance he bugged Sid's car and hid a tracking device underneath the rear bumper. At 1600, he opened the driver's side door of The Peterson Group SUV, jumped in and started up. He took a pad and pencil from the console and wrote down all the information he learned. The main points were Ben and wife Carol, and the guys in Texas. Bascomb said that the guys in Texas were picking up Paco. That strongly suggested that the guys in Texas were probably Deputy US Marshals. He knew that Rick would figure it out.

By 1700 Carlos was on the beltway heading back towards Dulles. The traffic was terrible. Carlos dialed Rick's secure cell phone.

"Carlos, so soon? It's either really good news or really bad news."

"The news is good. Bascomb bought my charade. I got a couple of names. He said that it was Ben who talked with Ochoa about Ernesto. He never mentioned Ben's last name and I didn't want to push it. However, I do know that Ben works in the same office and that his wife's name is Carol. Also, there are at least two guys in Dallas that are supposed to 'pick up' Paco. The fact that Bascomb said, 'pick up' suggests to me that they are most likely Deputy US Marshals. I did bug his car and placed a tracking device on it."

"Carlos, you get a gold cigar. I will go into the database and find this guy. And if the guys in Dallas are deputies, then I might be able to find them through Ben's phone records. I'll let you know as soon as I find out."

"Sounds like a winner. What do you want me to do?"

"I need you back here. Keep your cover by looking for property. I just need a little time to go over everything. What about the bug? Is it one of yours or Carl's?"

"It's one of Carl's. I got it from Roland. Both the bug and tracker upload to a satellite. Everything is recorded, so we can monitor it all through our satellite phones and download to the computer. Roland said that you have the access code on your computer under satellite tracking mode 3. I'll call you when I'm back. I'll use my new ID. Just call me Alberto."

Carlos hung up and headed west on the Dulles access road. Rick went to his computer and gained access to the US Marshal database program. He was able to identify Benjamin Franklyn Anderson and wife Carol within two minutes. There was no other individual with the name Ben at the Indiana Avenue location. Just for confirmation, he checked the US Marshal roster at the US Courthouse on Constitution Avenue. There was a Ben Spitzer listed, but his wife's name was Maryann. No, Rick was sure that he had the right Ben. Lynn came to the door.

"Rick, you have to see the news. They found a car burned out on the Eglin Reservation," she said. The look was back.

Chapter Twenty-Six
US Marshals, Washington, DC
November 26, 2010
Friday
1600 Hours

Paco Ramirez had arrived at one of the US Marshal safe houses in Fairfax, Virginia. He was being very cooperative. He had agreed to testify against Manny Dominguez and Danny Ochoa in return for immunity from prosecution, including a guarantee of entry in to the Federal Witness Protection Program. The Attorney General was more than agreeable, considering they estimated Danny Ochoa's operation to be in the hundreds of millions of dollars a year for at least the last four years, and that was a conservative estimate at best. Giving Paco immunity from prosecution was certainly worth his testimony. Paco was a gold mine of information. Not only did Paco know the ins and outs of Ochoa's operation, but he also had information about Ochoa's many rivals. Paco Ramirez was a bonanza! This could be one of the biggest busts in DEA history.

Ben's suggestion to use the same logistics that he had set up and were in place for Spanelli had paid off. The Director notified Ben that his team would be taking on Paco Ramirez as his next project. Ben had also convinced the Director to move Ramirez out of Northern Virginia as soon as possible. Corporate wisdom suggested that the more they moved a witness, the safer he would be. They had lingered one day too long in the case of Spanelli. It proved to be a fatal mistake. Ben made a call to the US Marshal's field office in Plano, Texas.

"Escobar."

"Luis, Ben here."

"Que pasa amigo? I was hoping to hear from you."

"Looks like we are back in business. I need you and Mickey to make a witness pick up. He will be arriving at Love Field at 1930 your time. His name is Paco Ramirez. Presently, he's scheduled for the December session of the Grand Jury. However, there is a slight change in plans that I will explain later. I need you to *put him on ice*."

Put him on ice was Ben's signal that meant exactly that; Luis and Mickey would be making a late night relocation. The old cross and flowers would mark the spot!

"No problem Ben, Mickey and I will be there to pick him up. Anything else we should know about this guy?"

"I will put all the information that you will need on the network. Deputy Marshals Williamson and Justice will escort him. I will give you a call later."

At 1630 Sidney Bascomb caught Ben in the parking garage. Ben had just unlocked his car and was about to get in. He didn't hear Sidney's steps as he approached. Sidney grabbed Ben's arm. His usual limp grip was uncharacteristically strong enough to startle Ben.

"Sid, you scared the hell out of me!"

"Sorry Ben, but I had to see you before you left. I just had a conversation with another one of Ochoa's guys."

"Where did you see him?" asked Ben looking surprised.

"He came to my office. He had ID that got him past the front desk."

"What did *he* want?"

"He wanted to know the status of Paco Ramirez."

"What the hell is their problem? I told Ochoa I would take care of Paco, and I will."

"Ben, he also asked about Ernesto Garcia. He said that they haven't heard from him. Have *you* heard from Ernesto?"

"As a matter of fact I haven't, but Sid, it's only been a couple of days. This guy only calls when he has something to say. He doesn't tell me much. He would probably go through Ochoa anyway. I'll give Ochoa a call. What was the guy's name?"

"Alberto Cruz. His name is Alberto Cruz. He wanted to talk with you, but I said you were out of town."

"Sid, you look like shit! Don't worry about this. Get a hold of yourself, I will take care of this."

"Ben, be careful, Ochoa is a very dangerous guy. He is not a guy to fuck with. We don't want to piss him off."

Ben could see the apprehension and fear in Sidney's face. Sidney was beginning to fall apart. He had never heard Sid using foul language. Ben had enough on his mind dealing with the stories by Ms. Brooke Morgan. He didn't need a meltdown by Sidney Bascomb.

"Sid, I'll call him on the way home. Everything is going to be okay. Look at me Sid. Look at me! Everything is going to be okay. You got that? Don't go paranoid on me. Everything is going to be all right."

Sidney pursed his lips and looked away from Ben. His head began a repetitive nod that was meant to signal affirmation but continued on as a nervous twitch as Sidney walked away. Ben had never seen Sidney Bascomb so out of control. Ben got into his car and sat there for a few minutes thinking about his conversation with Sidney. The name Alberto Cruz went through his mind. Did Ochoa have another Deputy Marshal in his pocket? He started the car and headed for home. By 1730 he was in heavy traffic on the George Washington Parkway. The Friday night commute was no fun at all. Commuting in DC was never fun at any time. A slight drizzle began. That would add another thirty minutes to the commute. Ben got out his private phone and dialed Danny Ochoa on the number he was given by Sidney, a number that was supposedly untraceable. Ben still didn't take any chances on the phone. He didn't want to use names if at all possible.

"Hola."

"Mr. Ochoa, Do you recognize my voice?"

"What is this a fucking game? Yes I recognize your voice. Are you worried that my phone is bugged? Hell, you of all people should know if it is bugged or not."

"You can't be too cautious these days. We both have a lot at stake here." Said Ben.

"So why are you taking a chance on calling me…Mr. Benjamin Anderson?"

So much for anonymity. If anyone were listening in on the conversation there would be no doubt who was on the line.

"Why did you send one of your Lieutenants up here today?"

"I have no idea what you are talking about. I didn't send anyone there…*today*."

Ben understood Ochoa's inflection on *today*. It was an unmistakable warning.

"Your telling me that you didn't send anyone to put pressure on Sidney Bascomb and our arrangement?"

"You are not listening to me! I sent no one."

"So the name Alberto Cruz means nothing to you?"

"Alberto Cruz? I don't know any Alberto Cruz. Someone is fucking with you, and it is not me."

"What about your man in Virginia Beach? I need that information, and I need it real soon."

"I haven't heard from Ernesto since he followed the girl to Florida. I expect to hear from him soon. Don't worry. He will get the information."

"And when he does, I will complete our arrangement." Responded Ben.

"I *know* that you will complete our arrangement. I have no doubt about that."

With that Danny Ochoa hung up. Ben didn't realize how important the arrangement was to Danny Ochoa. He had nothing to threaten Paco with. Paco Ramirez was an orphan. He had no idea who his parents were. His family was the gangs in Havana. Danny had nothing to hold over Paco's head. There was no wife, no kids and no family to ransom. He didn't even have a steady girlfriend. Danny would have to kill half the prostitutes in Miami just to get Paco's attention. And then, there was the other half to deal with. No, he needed Paco to disappear for good!

Ben had only moved about a mile during the entire conversation. From above, the traffic must have looked like a giant inchworm going and stopping, going and stopping. He didn't even remember driving the mile. Ben was convinced that someone was on to him, but who was it? Who could it be? It couldn't be Sid; Sid was afraid of his own shadow. Sid wouldn't make waves, waves that could wash over him, drown him. Certainly not Taylor Reese. He and Taylor had hatched the plan to start with. That made no sense at all. Couldn't be Luis or Mickey. They were directly involved in the killings. They certainly had the most to lose, even if one of them made a deal. Murder is still murder! That left only Charlie Dobson. Ben made another call to Dallas.

"Escobar."

"Luis, slight change of plans on Ramirez. I need you to pay particular attention to this guy. Call me back in *ten minutes*."

Luis understood that Ben was telling him to hold off on Ramirez. He wanted Luis to call him back on a disposable cell phone. They would put Ramirez *on ice* at a later date.

"Ben, I understand. Anything else?"

"By chance, have you heard of or seen the stories about the Witness Protection Program entitled *The Last Witness* that are being published in the Virginian Journal?"

"No, I haven't. I believe I heard a couple of the guys talking about it. Is it something I need to read?"

"Unfortunately, it is. At first I didn't give it much attention. The stories are supposed to be fictional but include a fair amount of factual information to stir reader interest. Last week's article included a scenario that caught my attention. It will interest you and Mickey. Has anyone from DC contacted you guys lately? Asked any questions about me?"

"Nobody has contacted me. I can't say for sure about Mickey, but if they had, I'm sure he would have said something."

Ben trusted Luis. He could tell that Luis was sincere and telling him the truth. He and Mickey were young and had a lot to lose if someone found out what was going on.

"Luis, the second part of *The Last Witness* contained information that was just too much of a coincidence. Are you familiar with the name Danny Ochoa?"

"Yes, I have heard his name a few times. He's the number one drug kingpin in Miami. Bad guy! Was the article about him?"

"No, nothing like that. I wish it were that simple. Unfortunately, Sid used to work for him."

"Our Sid? Sidney Bascomb worked for Danny Ochoa? Are you shitting me!"

"I wish I were. Sid did some creative accounting work for Ochoa. Now Ochoa is using their former relationship to put pressure on Sid to find out where we have stashed Ramirez. Part Two of *The Last Witness* I mentioned, refers to an *Anonymous Source*. I need to find out who the *Anonymous Source* is. I have made an arrangement with Ochoa. I take care of Ramirez, and in return, he will find out who the *Anonymous Source* is. Until he provides me with that information, I want to keep Ramirez alive and well. I need a chip in this game. Ramirez is my chip."

"Be careful Ben. From what I know about Ochoa, he owns all the chips…and the house!"

"I'll be careful. I may need you and Mickey to come here and take care of some business."

"Let me know."

"I'll give you a call in a couple of days."

As Ben hung up, he was going by the exit to Langley. It reminded him that he still didn't know who Brooke Morgan's father was. The holes in his record were obvious, even to the casual observer. He still had no idea where Richard Morgan was born, or even if his name was really Richard Morgan. His database search led nowhere. It was as if Rick Morgan didn't exist during those time frames. He was convinced that Richard Morgan was an alias or that he was born in some other part of the country, or in some other part of the world for that matter. He had to be CIA or NSA. Hell, he could have been KGB for that matter. English may have been Richard Morgan's second language. Anything was possible.

Chapter Twenty-Seven
US Marshals, Washington, DC
November 26, 2010
Friday
1700 Hours

Lynn had turned on the local Pensacola channel to hear the weather forecast for Saturday. She was peeling potatoes and wasn't paying much attention when the Channel Three news anchor reported about a car fire on the Eglin Reservation north of Navarre on highway 87.

"It appears that the car had exploded, touching off a two acre fire. There was a body inside that was burned beyond recognition. The FBI and US Air Force officials are conducting an investigation. We will report any news as the investigation proceeds. In other news"

Rick came into the living room. Lynn had an *I want an explanation look on her face.* Rick had seen that look before…many times before.

"What is it that you wanted me to see?"

"They just reported that a car blew up on the Eglin Reservation last night, and there was a body inside."

"Okay."

"*Okay*? Just *okay*? So it *is* just a coincidence that they found the car in the vicinity where we stopped last night? Where Carlos popped out of the bushes and did whatever Carlos does. Please tell me you're not doing *contract work* again?"

"Honey, I swear to you, I am not doing *that kind* of contract work."

"Then how do you explain Carlos just popping out of the woods? A car with a body in it that is probably the guy who Carlos dragged off into the woods."

Rick knew that he would have to let Lynn know what was going on, at least some of what was going on. She knew that he had been involved with *government contract operations* in the past, even when he was an officer in the Navy. The Navy had provided terrific cover for the little excursions that Rick had gone on while in some foreign ports. The Navy Brass had no idea of Rick's other career. The government would disavow any connection to Rick. Lynn had known ever since 1983 when the aircraft carrier he was on had pulled into Greenock, Scotland. The Navy had put together a dependent's cruise, and at the last moment, Lynn had decided to *surprise* Rick. Rick had taken leave and was in Belfast. When he got back to the ship, he heard that Lynn was staying at the George Hotel in Edinburg. To save his marriage he had to tell her the *truth*, a novel idea for a married man on leave in the British Isles…without his wife. She knew he was a storyteller. This time his story was even too bazaar for her. She wanted to believe him, but she also wanted to go home. He convinced her to stay at least another day. She finally believed him the next day. The headlines in the local paper had a half page spread on an Irish Republic terrorist, Padrig O'Toole, who was found shot to death in Belfast. She never questioned Rick again…until now.

"Lynn, somebody is still after Brooke, and they mean business!"

Rick's directness hit Lynn right between the eyes. No trying to make excuses. No sweet talk. No trying to side step the issue. Rick got right to the heart of the matter. She wasn't expecting that the episode the night before was, in any way, connected to Brooke. She had been prepared to confront him. But the fact that Brooke was somehow at the center of this shook her to the core.

"What? What are you saying? Why would they follow Brooke to Florida? What is going on?

Rick raised his hands in the air in a gesture of surrendering and pursed his lips while titling his head slightly to the left. She stopped asking questions and was now back into listening mode. Rick motioned toward the dining room table. He poured them both a glass of Pinot Noir. They sat, glass in hand, sipping wine. Lynn had that little puppy dog look that said, 'tell me something that will turn out good in the end'. Lynn never could stand suspense; she wanted to know the ending right up front. It was never fun watching any kind of mystery movie with her.

"You know the article that Brooke is writing for the newspaper?"

"Yes…about the US Marshals…*The Last Witness*."

"Well it appears that the information she received from her *Anonymous Source* has turned out to be a lot more truth than fiction. *Somebody* doesn't want her finishing the article. That same *somebody* sent our *burn* victim, Mr. Ernesto Garcia, to get information out of Brooke. Mr. Garcia was not a very nice man. In fact, the DEA thought they had killed him a few days ago. Supposedly he was shot during a drug bust at the Port of Miami."

"Then, what was he doing here? How did you know he was here?"

"I had Carlos go through Brooke's condo. He sent me a couple of fingerprints. I ran the prints, and one of the partial prints belonged to our friend, Ernesto."

"But how did he know Brooke was here?"

"Honey, he followed Brooke. When I ran the print his picture came up on the screen. I remember seeing him at the airport. He was on Brooke's flight. He followed her here. That is when I decided to call Carlos. We set a trap for him."

"Is it over? "It's not over is it?"

Rick would love to tell Lynn that it was over, but he knew it had only just begun.

"Probably not, but we obtained some very good information from him. We know his Washington contact, and we also know the guy he works for in Miami. Carlos is on his way back from DC as we speak."

Rick was hoping that Lynn didn't ask him about the guy in Miami.

"I can't believe this. Does Brooke know any of this? How long were you going to keep me in the dark?"

"Honey, you know more than she does. I didn't want to scare you or Brooke. I didn't want to say anything until I knew that we were in control. I believe we have them on the defense. By the way, I am getting help from Carl Peterson."

"Carl Peterson? I thought you were just doing administration work for him. Please, don't tell me your back full time with Carl?"

"He *is* The Peterson Group. Lynn, to do this, and do it right, we need his help. He has…resources."

Lynn got up from the chair and looked out through the sliding glass door. Destin represented everything good. Her family, friends, a reward for many years of following Rick around the world. She sipped her wine as she took in the sunset. The sunset agreed with the weather forecast. It was going to be a nice day on Saturday. She was quiet. Rick new that in Lynn's case, quiet was good. She was thinking about everything that Rick had said.

"Honey, Carl has mellowed. It is a different job. I'm just doing security checks on people for the Department of Homeland Security."

"So why did Carlos go to DC?"

"Ernesto gave us a name. Carlos went to see him. We are certain there is another individual involved. We need to know who that individual is."

"What if you don't find out?"

"Carlos found out. We already know who he is."

"So what next?"

Rick didn't want to tell Lynn much more. There wasn't much more to tell at this point. She would want to know the outcome…right now. This wasn't a movie. He and Carlos needed to sit down, analyze what they had, and come up with an aggressive plan. They still had the element of surprise on their side. Rick knew that Lynn would really be worried if he continued on with a lengthy discussion of what was next.

"Honey, trust me. Carlos and I will take care of this."

"Like this guy…Ernesto?" she asked.

"Yes! If it becomes necessary…just like Ernesto Garcia. Honey, I will *never* let anyone touch you or Brooke!"

Lynn poured another glass of Pinot Noir. Rick couldn't remember a time when she had more than one glass of wine…except in Scotland. All that was happening understandably troubled her. Her world had been very organized, very comfortable…up until now. However, down deep inside Lynn knew that Rick would take care of them. Rick was not a "wait and see" kind of guy. He was an operator, and she knew it.

Rick and Carlos had made a conscious decision to leave Ernesto Garcia on the Eglin Reservation. They knew that the FBI would get involved. The car, the body and whatever evidence they could find would be sent off to Washington or Quantico for forensic analysis.

The FBI lab would identify him. They would probably have a field day with his gun. It would be at least ten days before any information was released to the public. Ten days was enough time for Rick and Carlos to put all the pieces of the puzzle together. His main concern at this point was Danny Ochoa. Drug lords tend to get really pissed off when one of their own is taken out. At 2215, Rick's satellite phone rang. It was Carlos.

"Carlos, welcome home, how are you doing?"

"Doing well Rick, any luck with the name I gave you?"

"Yes, I believe the guy we are looking for is Benjamin F. Anderson. He fits the profile and is one of the team leaders for the Federal Witness Protection Program. It has to be him. We could follow up with Bascomb and confirm that Anderson is the guy."

"I might give Bascomb a call. I'm sure by now he's talked with Anderson. I'll call as soon as I hang up. No sense giving them time to think about it. How long before Ochoa gets wind of what has happened?"

"Probably won't be too long. If Bascomb or Anderson calls him about your meeting with Bascomb, he'll start getting real suspicious."

"Rick, we need to take care of this guy before he gets on to us."

"I know…I'm working on that. You will probably need to make a trip to Miami. I'm going to give Carl a call. We may be able to piggyback on a trip down there and do some reconnaissance."

"Are you thinking about just taking him out or talking with him?"

"Maybe both. There is a part of me that wants him to know that he shouldn't have messed with Brooke. He's not invincible, he's accountable. But, I don't want to play games with him either. Plan for one of your IEDs. We need to get him in an area where there will be no collateral damage. I don't want to fire up the locals. The ideal thing would be to hit him at his house, in his driveway. You can make that decision after you do your recon."

"Sounds like you been doing more than just thinking about it."

"I checked out his address on Google Earth. He lives in Coconut Grove on one of the canals. He has a large yacht tied up along the bulkhead. There is a large wall and a security gate. The info is probably dated, but not too old."

"Rick, if he has a boat that would be an easy target."

"Probably, but just our luck to kill a manatee. I can stand the US Marshals, drug lords…but not PETA!"

The PETA comment reminded Carlos that their headquarters was located in Virginia Beach.

"Rick, they're your neighbor. So, when can we get together?"

"Not yet. Let's make sure no one else is here looking for Brooke. You can look over our shoulder and see if you pick up anyone watching us. I'll get back to you as soon as I talk with Carl."

Rick could hear Carlos singing, *"Blue skies from above, baby I'm in love…"*. With that, Rick hung up and called Carl Peterson.

Chapter Twenty-Eight
Pensacola, Florida
November 26, 2010
Friday
1900 Hours

Carl Peterson had just finished three eggs over easy, two strips of bacon, hash browns, wheat toast, orange juice and coffee. It was a bachelor's delight. Carl loved eggs, and on many occasions had them for both breakfast and dinner. Surprisingly, his cholesterol had never been over 140. He finished dinner, rinsed off the dishes and placed them in the dishwasher. Three days of dishes were stacked neatly at attention waiting to be cleaned. Carl went into the den and turned on the TV. It was already tuned to the Fox News channel. He was looking forward to Bill O'Reilly. He threw the remote onto the seat of his leather recliner, went to the wet bar and poured a twelve year old Viella Reserve into a snifter. He rolled the snifter in his hands and was about to take a sip when the phone rang. He looked at the caller ID. It was Rick Morgan. He answered it before the second ring.

"Rick, you must have ESP. I was just thinking about calling you."

"Hey Carl. How's it going?"

"Going well my friend. Just had dinner and now I'm warming up a brandy. By the way, Roland is going to send a few names for you to review. Have you had a chance to check out the computer?"

"I have. It is really a terrific tool," responded Rick as he changed the subject. "Carl…I need to talk with you."

"You have my undivided attention."

"I would prefer to talk to you in person…and as soon as possible."

Carl sensed the urgency in Rick's voice.

"Is this business related?"

"No, not with *our* arrangement. I have a personal situation that I have been dealing with that is escalating. I need your…support. I can come to DC at your earliest convenience."

"Rick, that won't be necessary. All I need is an excuse to go to Pensacola. In fact, why don't I fly in tomorrow? We can have dinner and a few beers at McGuire's? You can bring me up to date on your… *situation*."

"Carl, tomorrow would be great. I will pick you up at the airport. What time will you be landing?"

"I can be there at 1600. Plan on picking me up at Sherman field. We have an arrangement with the Navy."

"I'll be there, and Carl, I'll be alone. This isn't for Lynn's ears."

"Sounds good. I can fill you in on some of the things that we are doing that you may find interesting…and possibly quite helpful."

"Thanks Carl. I am really looking forward to seeing you."

Carl hung up and pondered the phone call for several seconds before letting it go and relaxing in his favorite chair. As he sipped the port, his mind wandered to Cuba, Costa Rico, Guatemala, Panama, Nicgurauga, Bolivia, Sigonella and several other unspeakable places; he smiled, whatever Rick needed, Carl would be there for him!

The Gulfstrean landed exactly at 1600. Military related flights were always on time. Rick hated to fly commercial. Commercial flights were rarely on time; and it was a real surprise if your baggage made it on the same flight. Security is really a joke. The last two times that Rick flew across country, he and Lynn were on one flight and their luggage ended up on another. The airlines needed to come up with a method that would ensure the passenger would be on the same flight as their baggage. The TSA people always seem to have a chip on their shoulder. Some were helpful, but for the most part many of their employees were one step ahead of the welfare line, and most of them needed to be on a diet.

Rick was waiting outside the terminal as Carl came down the ladder. He hadn't seen Carl in over twenty years. From a distance, Carl looked to be in good shape. As he approached, Rick could see that he was indeed in good shape and had aged very well. His hair was silver grey.

He still walked ramrod straight. Carl was heavily tanned, and at six feet two inches he was an impressive figure of a man who had been in nearly all the jungles of the world. He had survived malaria, scorpion stings, numerous spider bites, three snake bites and had an almost fatal encounter with a really pissed off prostitute in San Jose, Costa Rico. And those were just a few of the things that Rick knew about. They had been there together. Carl's handshake told Rick that he was still working out. His hug confirmed that Carl was, most definitely working out. He hoped that he looked half as good to Carl.

"Rick, great to see you. You son of a gun, you haven't changed at all. A little grey around the temples, but life is obviously treating you well. How's Lynn. She still pissed at me?"

"Lynn is doing great, and yes, she's still pissed," responded Rick punctuated by a genuine laugh.

"Rick, I have completely forgotten why she is mad at me."

"You remember the night we took the embassy personnel to the restaurant in the Viking Hotel in Bergen, Norway? Somehow my wallet slipped out of my pocket and onto the floor, and you just happened to pay the bill with my American Express credit card."

"That was rather good wasn't it?"

"Well, to this day she has not completely accepted my explanation of *what* I spent twenty-two hundred and fifty kroners on in the Viking Hotel."

"Maybe I to talk to her."

"I would recommend letting that dog sleep. Did you really find my wallet on the floor?"

"Well, actually I picked your pocket. However, I was never any good at putting wallets back. Besides, if you caught me, it would have spoiled everything."

"Carl, it certainly made for a good story. Do you have any luggage?"

"No. My company has a condo on Pensacola Beach. I have everything that I need there. Sure saves me time packing," said Carl as he patted his wallet pocket. "Do you mind dropping me off on your way back to Destin?" he asked.

"Of course not. My car is out front."

NAS Pensacola and Sherman field had taken quite a hit from Hurricane Ivan. If it weren't for the Blue Angels and the Naval Air Museum, NAS Pensacola might have been closed for good. It had been strongly considered.

As Rick and Carl proceeded down Palifox Avenue, Carl reached over and touched Rick's right forearm.

"Is everything okay my friend?"

"Carl, can we talk…strictly off the record?"

"Of course Rick. You are the only reason that I'm here. I assume this also has something to do with our friend Carlos?"

Rick thought for a few seconds before continuing.

"Carl, someone is after Brooke."

"What do you mean, *after* Brooke?"

"She has been commissioned by the Virginian Journal to write a short story. It appears that someone does not want her to finish. Someone with…connections.

"What is the story about?" asked Carl.

"The US Marshal's Witness Protection Program."

Rick looked over at Carl. Carl had the kind of look on his face that told Rick he was already in analysis mode.

"The Witness Protection Program. And why would that cause someone to go after Brooke?"

"After the first article, Brooke received some information from an *Anonymous Source* that she incorporated into the second article. After Part Two was published, all hell broke loose. A guy named Ernesto Garcia searched her car and condo and nearly killed her fiancée. He also followed her to Destin."

Carl was rapidly getting the picture.

"And…where is the guy now?" asked Carl. It was a rhetorical question. Carl knew the answer.

"He, or I should say his body is at the FBI forensic lab at Quantico."

"Ah…enter Carlos." Nodded Carl.

Just then Rick turned into McGuire's parking lot. Even for a Sunday night the lot was nearly full. Carl hadn't been in McGuire's for several years. There was now over one million two hundred thousand dollars on the walls and ceiling. Most certainly it was a unique décor for a restaurant. Rick and Carl were seated in a booth where someone from Anchorage, Alaska had signed a dollar bill the night before. They ordered New York strips and two Killian Reds.

"Rick, so you know who the guy was? Tell me his name again?"

"His name was Ernesto Garcia."

"That name sounds familiar. What else can you tell me?"

"From what I can piece together there are a couple of players involved here. I know for sure that Garcia was sent to DC by a guy in Miami by the name of Danny Ochoa."

Carl perked up at the name Danny Ochoa.

"Whoa amigo, hold on a second. Danny Ochoa is not just 'a guy' he is a drug lord, and not a very nice fellow. Why in the world would he be after Brooke?"

"Well, it appears that he sent Ernesto Garcia to DC to meet with a guy named Bascomb who is with the US Marshals. It seems that Ochoa wanted to put pressure on Bascomb to find out where the US Marshals were holding one of his guys, a guy named Paco Ramirez. At least I believe that is his last name. Then, for some reason, Danny sends Ernesto Garcia to Virginia Beach to try to find out who Brooke's *Anonymous Source* is."

"So Rick, the question is, why would Ochoa send Ernesto after Brooke. He would have to know that Brooke would have no idea where this guy Paco is being held."

"Exactly. That told me that it was either Bascomb, or someone he works with who got Ochoa to send Ernesto to find out who the *Anonymous Source* is in return for telling him where Paco is being held."

"A quid pro quo." Responded Carl.

"Correct. So I sent Carlos to have a little talk with Bascomb. Carlos pretended to be one of Ochoa's Lieutenants. From that conversation we learned that the other player is a Deputy Marshal named Ben Anderson. I believe that it is Anderson who is sweating bullets over Brooke's article and what she might learn from the *Anonymous Source*."

Rick took a healthy swig of beer. Carl was in deep thought about what Rick had just told him. Before Rick could continue, Carl spoke up.

"Have you considered the possibility that Bascomb might have gone straight to Anderson?"

"Yes, in fact, for credibility purposes, Carlos told Bascomb to tell Anderson that he was going to call him."

"And, what about when Anderson calls Ochoa asking about… Lieutenant Carlos?"

"I have considered that, and before you ask, I have also considered what Ochoa will do when he finds out that Ernesto has been, shall we say, *killed* in Florida."

"I assume you have a plan?"

"Carl, I am fighting a two-front war here. I need to diffuse the situation and concentrate on one front. The bottom line is that I need to terminate Ochoa. Make it look like a drug war. Then I can concentrate on Anderson without having to look over my shoulder towards Miami."

The waiter brought two of the finest New York strips in Florida. They were steaming hot. Rick was still covering his with butter as Carl was into his third bite. Carl took a drink and without looking up said,

"Drug Interdiction is one of my Government projects. I have a whole file on Danny Ochoa and his operation. You're welcome to whatever I have."

"Carl, I don't want to jeopardize your contract in any way."

"No problem. My company just provides surveillance and analysis."

Carl stopped and pulled out his cell phone and made a speed dial call. Roland Carpenter answered the call.

"Roland, Carl here."

"Mr. Peterson. How are you?"

"Doing well Roland. I am here with Rick Morgan. He is going to be helping us with the Drug Interdiction program. I need you to provide him with computer access and also the live satellite feed."

"No problem sir, he will have access in about ten minutes."

"Thanks Roland."

Carl took another bite of steak without giving a second thought to the fact that he just signed Danny Ochoa's death warrant. Both men finished dinner and ordered another couple of bottles of Killian Red.

"Thanks Carl. I need to act soon and I certainly don't want any collateral damage."

"Rick, I think you will find the satellite feed quite interesting. Are you familiar with thermavision?"

"Yes, basically I am."

"Well, we have been experimenting with it to create a thermavision profile. We believe it is as accurate as a fingerprint. It appears that everyone's thermavision profile is unique. In other words, we have created a thermavision database of persons of interest. You can zoom in with the satellite, in real time, and make a positive identification of any person of interest in our database. For your information Rick, Mr. Ochoa is in our database."

"Carl, you're a good friend."

"You were always there for me. Have you decided how you're going to make the, shall we say…hit?"

"Well, as you know, Carlos is the best ordnance man I have ever met. It will be one of his IEDs. Since the bomb will have the same signature that led to Ernesto's fate, the FBI will conclude that the hit is most likely drug related. In fact, I believe it will create a power struggle in Miami that will lead to a real drug war. At that point they will certainly have no time or interest in Brooke. Then I can concentrate on Anderson."

Carl finished the Killian Red and looked at the dollars framing the booth.

"What do you think Rick? Is Ochoa worth a buck?"

Chapter Twenty-Nine
Miami, Florida
November 26, 2010
Friday
2100 Hours

Danny Ochoa wasn't happy about the call from Ben Anderson. He didn't care one bit what happened to Anderson. His only concern was with the whereabouts of Paco Ramirez. He made a call to Ernesto Garcia. There was no ring. In fact, the call went straight into Ernesto's voice mail. He tried it again with the same result. Danny checked his own phone. It indicated full service with four bars. Danny found it hard to believe that Ernesto had turned off his phone. Ernesto would never turn off his phone, and if he did, he would let Manny know that he would be off line for a little while. Ernesto was always punctual and very good about keeping in touch. Danny hadn't heard from him in over twenty hours. He decided to call Manny Dominguez.

"Hola."

"Manny, have you heard from Ernesto?"

"No Hefe…not yet. I will give him a call."

"No point. I just tried to call him. I don't think his phone is on. Manny, something is not right. Ernesto would have checked in with one of us by now. Come over, we need to talk."

"Okay Hefe."

Manny hesitated a bit. He thought Danny might be overreacting, but he knew not to question him.

"I'll be there in about thirty minutes."

Manny lived in a four-bedroom condo on Key Biscayne overlooking the Atlantic. He was normally alone except for the occasional weekend with Elana Pedroso. This was one of those lovely weekends. He did not want to leave her. She did not want him to go. However, Manny knew that when Danny used the phrase, "we need to talk", no excuse would be good enough. Elana would just have to wait. Manny put on a clean pair of khaki slacks, a new Tommy Bahama shirt and Versachi sandals and took the elevator to the garage where his white Mercedes 420 was parked. He had an end space that was marked Reserved B1401. Nobody ever parked in Manny Dominguez's space, not even by accident. Manny drove north on Crandon Boulevard, across the Rickenbacker Causeway and made a left turn on South Dixie highway. He continued south and made a left turn on LeJeune Road. He turned into Danny's driveway twenty-five minutes after Danny's call. He pressed the call button. The lens on a camera over the gate made a little noise as it zoomed in on him. The fisheye lens reminded him of a lizard's squint just before the bite. Danny's voice came over the speaker loud and clear.

"Hey Manny, you're right on time as usual."

As if Manny would ever be late when summoned by Danny Ochoa. They were close, but Manny would never be cavalier in his actions around Danny. There was barely an audible click and then a low humming noise as the gate began to swing open. Manny proceeded slowly up the driveway. He didn't see any of the roving patrols. He never saw them, but he knew that the grounds were under constant watch. Danny's house was not far from the street, but it was well hidden behind a twelve foot, eighteen-inch thick wall that was reinforced with three quarter inch rhebarb. There was crushed glass cemented on top of the wall. The glass wasn't visible from the street. There were cameras along the driveway as well as numerous cameras located at strategic points on the grounds. There was a camera at each corner of the house. It was the most protected and fortified house in Coconut Grove. Manny parked in one of the five spaces just to the right side of the three-car detached garage. There were burglar bars on all of the doors and windows. No burglar in his right mind would have tried to break into Danny Ochoa's house. Danny could have left the house wide-open if he wanted. Danny met Manny at the door. There was a youthful spring in his step as he skipped down the stairs, arms were outstretched in a friendly gesture of welcome.

"Manny my friend. Was it hard for you to leave Ms. Pedroso? Or, is it actually *Mrs*. Pedroso?"

"It is Mrs., and yes it was *hard* when I left her."

Danny had a good laugh.

"Poor Mr. Wiggly! So you are just as bad as me…ey Chico?"

"Yeah, yeah…we'll both be shot by jealous husbands."

"If you have to die, it might as well be over something worth while. I've seen her. You could get shot for a lot worse. Would you like a drink?"

"Sure, I'll have what you're having."

The bar in Danny's house covered the entire western wall of the game room. His liquor collection would be the envy of any renowned liquor connoisseur in the country. He poured a 1971 Delamain Cognac for Manny. Manny took a sip. One of the pleasures in life was sharing the bar with Danny Ochoa. They moved over to an Italian glove leather couch that faced a fifty-two-inch Sony Plasma TV that was mounted on the wall over a black marble-topped credenza. On top of the credenza were two black boxes. One controlled the Bose surround sound system, and the other provided video feed from the various cameras that comprised the security system. On the screen were two rows of what appeared to be still shots of the grounds around Danny's house. All eight frames were, in fact, live feeds from the selected cameras. The input would shift to other cameras on a random basis. Danny could select any camera at will, at any time, and use a small joystick to reposition the view. On one screen Manny caught a glimpse of a passing figure with and Oozy over his shoulder. Danny Ochoa was never alone.

"So Manny, what do you think is going on with Ernesto? Could it be that he was recognized and captured?"

"I don't think so Hefe. He is too good to get caught. Besides, he wouldn't go down without a fight. We would have heard about it by now."

Danny took another sip of his 80 proof Cognac. He appeared to be in deep concentration trying to conjure up an image of Ernesto. Danny tried hard to figure out what he was doing in the Pensacola area and why he hadn't called.

"Do you think he is with some woman?"

So much for deep thought. Danny's mind always reverted to the basic primal needs of the male animal. One of his favorite sayings was, "the power of the pussy!" It was a phrase that had to be said in English. Spanish just didn't capture the essence of the meaning.

"Danny, I would doubt that strongly. He is not with anyone. Ernesto has always put our business first. Maybe there is something wrong with his phone and he just doesn't realize it."

"But he would have tried to call us by now and would have realized that he had a problem with it. There are pay phones all over the place. No Manny, something is wrong."

They both sipped the Cognac. Manny looked up at the screen. Another shadow moved in front of the three-car garage. Two of the inputs changed to a different location on the property.

"Manny, I want you to go to Pensacola. See what you can find out. Ernesto rented a car there and followed the girl to Destin. He is staying at the Destin Holiday Inn on the Emerald Coast Highway. He used the name Roberto Soto."

"Maybe we should just call the Holiday Inn?"

"No, no, I don't want to alert the authorities, especially if he *has* indeed been captured."

Manny knew that he had to go to Destin.

"If I go snooping around I'll need a cover."

"You could certainly pass for a DEA agent. Hell, you know all the lingo. Probably better if you go as a Private Investigator."

"I'll need ID."

"I'll call Sanchez. Let me get my camera; he'll want a digital picture. Take a look in that closet over there and pick out a white shirt. There should also be a couple of ties in there. A blue one would be good. Make you look official."

Danny left the game room and returned just as Manny was pulling the tie through a loop that he was holding open with the tip of his left thumb. He pulled it tight. He was never able to get that neat little dimple in the tie. It had always frustrated him. The tie was a little long, but it wouldn't matter for the picture. Danny removed a painting of the Civil War by Salvatore Dali from the wall and had Manny stand where the picture had hung. He snapped a couple of frames. He and Manny reviewed them in the playback mode. They both agreed that the first one was, by far, the best. Manny had the look of a really bored Government employee that couldn't wait for three thirty to arrive.

"I'll take this one to Sanchez."

"Why not email it?" asked Manny.

"I don't trust the email. I never send anything that I wouldn't expect to share with the law. Besides, too many young kids hacking away and stealing identities."

"Danny do you really think anyone would have the nerve to steal *your* identity?"

"Manny, the kids these days have no respect. Most of them don't even know who I am."

Manny found that quite amusing. He had trouble suppressing a laugh.

"They know who you are. Most of them want to be you!"

Danny Ochoa loved the attention. Everyone did know who he was, and the law knew what he did for a living. They just never had enough hard evidence to get a conviction.

"Pour us another drink while I give Sanchez a call."

Danny opened a photo pack and thumbed through the pictures. He threw a couple on the bar and picked up one of his disposable cell phones and made a call to Rafael Sanchez.

"Rafael, Danny here."

"Mr. Ochoa, how are you?"

"Rafael, you have known me since we were kids, call me Danny."

Rafael Sanchez had, indeed, known Danny Ochoa since they were kids, but he still had a hard time calling him by his first name.

"Okay…Danny, what can I do for you?"

"I need you to put together a package for Manny. All the usual stuff. Is it okay if I stop over in the next half hour?"

"No problem, the wife is at her mother's in Tampa. I could use some company."

"Good, I'll see you in a bit."

Even though Danny used several disposable phones, he was still very careful not to say anything incriminating on the phone. He knew there was always a possibility that his acquaintance's phones could be tapped. It was always better to deal in person and to talk with the television, radio, or even the water running. Serious business was always conducted at a new location, and he never used the same location twice.

"Manny, here's a couple recent pictures of Ernesto. I'm going to take your picture over to Rafael's and get your ID package. Do you have any preference for a name?"

Manny thought for a few seconds.

"Armando Mila," he answered.

"I like that. Do you want to pick the ID up here, or on the way to the airport?"

"It would be easier for me to pick it up here."

"I will have it tonight. I would like you to take an early flight to Pensacola. Ernesto got in to Pensacola in the early afternoon. Hopefully the same shift will be on duty at the car rentals. I don't know which one he rented from. It will be a good place for you to start. Say hello to *Mrs.* Pedroso for me."

"I will say more than hello to her. See you tomorrow morning."

Chapter Thirty
Miami, Florida
November 27, 2010
Saturday
1030 Hours

Manny was booked on Delta flight 1580 leaving Miami at 0935, arriving in Pensacola at 1346. The flight had a layover in Atlanta. Danny had left Manny's new ID in a Bank of Bermuda leather zip pouch along with six Montecristos next to one of the large marble lions that guarded the front door. It took Manny thirty-two minutes to drive the eight and a half miles to the Miami International airport. The traffic in Miami seemed to get worse by the day. The number of illegal drivers was staggering, and almost all of them had trouble reading and obeying the road signs. However, the airport functioned well. Manny had booked his flight under the name of Armando Mila. He picked up his electronic ticket at one of the many computer stations and checked in at gate 9B at 0845. At 0910 he was the first passenger to be seated in first class. His seat number was 3C. Manny never understood why the airlines would board the first class passengers before the rest of the passengers, especially if they loaded everyone through the forward door. He didn't enjoy sitting there with his hot cup of freshly brewed coffee and being bumped by oversized passengers with oversized carry-ons, all in a rush to find their seats in the back of the plane. At least he would be allowed to disembark before the stampede began. The flight to Pensacola, including the layover in Atlanta, was uneventful. The airplane almost arrived on time.

Manny had been to Pensacola on many occasions. Not only did he enjoy the dog track, but also he was becoming a Pensacola Pilots fan. Maybe if Jai Alia had a little fighting once in a while, he would enjoy it even more. Hockey was much faster, especially in person. He went down the escalator, turned to his right and into the baggage claim area where the car rental agents were standing at attention in expectation of a client. Since the rest of the passengers hadn't arrived, he had his choice. He started with Hertz. The agent greeted him with a broad smile. Her teeth looked as if they wanted to jump out of her mouth and bite him. Her nametag rested high on what were obviously over-sized silicon breast implants. They were too perfect. He was beginning to feel like a deer frozen in the headlights. Her name was Molly.

"Welcome to Pensacola, may I help you?"

"I hope so Molly. My name is Armando Mila."

As he was talking he took out his new wallet and presented his Private Investigator identification.

"I am trying to locate a missing person. His name is Roberto Soto. Can you tell me if he rented a car from you?"

"Do you know the date?"

"Yes, it would have been Wednesday the twenty first. Probably around two o'clock."

Molly moved over to her computer and made several keystrokes. She looked inquisitively at the screen as if it were playing a show that she didn't recognize. She made a few more keystrokes and a slight smile exposed little white lines that broke the smoothness of her tan face.

"I am sorry, but I do not show a Roberto Soto in our system."

Manny would have been surprised to find Ernesto on the first try.

"Thank you for your help. I will check with the other agents."

"You're welcome. If you need a car, we are here."

Manny went to the National Car Rental and had no luck there either. By now Molly was busy with three people in line. Budget was next. Manny edged out one of the buffarillos that had messed up his hair with her right hip as she waddled through first class on her way to the corral.

"Welcome to Pensacola, may I help you?"

Manny mused that they all went to the same training class. Probably exchanged uniforms for the next day's business. What did he expect?

"Yes, my name is Armando Mila. I am a Private Investigator from Miami, and I have been hired to find a missing man by the name of Roberto Soto."

Manny presented his ID. The agent, an African American girl with a name he couldn't figure out, asked him,

"What day would he have rented the car?"

"I believe he rented it this past Wednesday around two o'clock."

She went to her computer and punched in the name Roberto Soto. Whatever appeared on the screen got her attention. Her left eyebrow rose, and she appeared to be chewing on the inside of her left lower lip.

"Mr. Soto rented a Pontiac Grand Am on Wednesday at two twelve PM. However, there is a note here that says the car was involved in an accident and won't be returned."

"Does it say anything about Mr. Soto? Where he is, or where the car is located?"

"No, it doesn't. I can call our home office if you like?"

"Would you please? This is an emergency situation."

Manny waited as the agent went into the small office and made a call. Another Budget Agent, a young man named Leonard, showed up with two coffees and a couple of sweet rolls. Manny noticed that Leonard walked funny...*maricone* he thought. He went into the office and put down one of the coffees and a sweet roll in front of Ms. Whatever Her Name Was. He then approached Manny and asked,

"Welcome to Pensacola, may I help you?"

"No thank you, the young lady is checking something for me."

A couple from Manny's flight came over and told the young man behind the counter that they had reserved a car. They gave their name as Mr. and Mrs. Jones. Mr. Jones was at least seventy. Mrs. Jones was about thirty-six, in more ways than one. Manny's thoughts wandered to Elena Pedroso. Ms. Whatever her name broke Manny's thoughts with,

"Mr....ah, I'm sorry, what was your name?"

"My name is Armando Mila."

Manny rolled the name *Armando* off his tongue as if he were talking to a deaf person.

"Mr. Mila, I may have some bad news for you. It appears that the car was in some sort of accident, burned up, and the driver was killed. I'm sorry to have to tell you that."

"You are sure?" he asked.

"Yes, unfortunately, I am."

"Are you also sure that Mr. Soto was the driver?"

"Well…no, I can only assume he was the driver. He was alone, and indicated that he would be the only driver."

"Where did this happen. Where is the car?"

"Over near Fort Walton Beach. According to the computer it has been impounded by the FBI."

Just then Leonard interrupted.

"I couldn't help over hearing your conversation. There was an article in the paper about that the other day. I'll bet it was *our* car that blew up over on the Eglin Reservation."

"Is that the Air Force Base?"

"The Reservation is their property. It happened up on highway eighty-seven. Oh hell, we may still have the newspaper. Let me look, it may be in the office."

Leonard returned with a badly crumpled paper. He thumbed threw it and found the article he was looking for in the local news section.

"Here it is right here. Just a short blurb."

He handed the paper to Manny. Manny scanned it very briefly. It was a short article.

"Sorry about the condition of the paper, but it was in the trash can. I'm surprised it was still here."

"Thanks, may I keep it?"

"Sure, no problem," responded Leonard trying to gain eye contact. He was unsuccessful.

Manny took the paper and went back up the escalator to the restaurant and ordered a coffee and a blueberry muffin. He folded the paper accordion style with the article on top. He took a bite of the muffin and began reading.

"Fort Walton Beach. Units of the Florida State Highway Police and Sheriff's Department, including fire trucks from Fort Walton, Navarre and Holley responded to a car fire on the Eglin Reservation. The incident occurred at approximately 10:30 PM Wednesday night, thirteen miles north of highway 98 on highway 87. Preliminary results indicate that the car may have exploded from an incendiary device that

was being transported in the car. There was also a weapon with silencer found at the scene. Authorities removed a body from the vehicle. The body was burned beyond recognition. The FBI has impounded the car and transferred all evidence to their lab at Quantico Virginia for further analysis. The resulting fire consumed two and one half acres of pine forest. We will provide further information when it becomes available."

Manny sat back and looked out at a plane turning into one of the gates. Next to the window a young baby was working hard at vocalizing her desire for lunch. Her mother was preparing to accommodate her. Life went on…but not for Ernesto. Manny was sure that the unidentified body was that of Ernesto Garcia. Manny made a call to Danny Ochoa.

"Danny."

"How is it going Manny?"

"Not good. There appears to have been an accident. I believe it was Ernesto."

"How is he? Where is he?"

"I believe he is dead."

Danny didn't say anything for several seconds, which seemed like a very long time.

"Manny, are you sure about this?"

"It was the car that he rented from Budget. They also found a weapon with a silencer."

"Where did this happen? When did it happen?"

"On the Eglin Reservation night before last."

"What is the Eglin Reservation?" asked Danny.

"It is property owned by Eglin Air Force Base."

"What the hell was he doing there?"

"I don't know. It is along a highway that is north of highway 98."

Again there was a long silence on the line.

"Danny, there is something else that makes no sense to me. Their preliminary investigation indicates that there may have been an incendiary devise in the car. That is not Ernesto's style. The gun, yes, but not a bomb. He wouldn't use a bomb. The FBI has impounded everything. What do you want me to do?" asked Manny.

"Just stay where you are. I'm going to give Anderson a call. There is something here that is not right. Anderson hasn't told us everything. This was no accident. Somebody took Ernesto out. I want to know how that somebody knew. How did they find out? I don't like this Manny. I don't like this one bit. I'll call you back."

Danny hung up the phone and went to the kitchen and got a bottle of spring water. His mouth was dry. He didn't like being on the other end of the stick. Ernesto was good. He was a black belt. He never went into a situation that he couldn't control. His target was a girl! A girl and her parents. But now Ernesto was dead. Danny finished the bottle of water and made a call to Ben Anderson on Anderson's private cell phone.

"Anderson."

"You prick, you haven't told me everything," yelled Danny into the phone.

"I will call you back in five minutes," responded Ben.

Ben Anderson recognized Danny Ochoa's voice. He didn't want to get into a discussion in his office. He was convinced that the walls had ears. Ben went down to the garage and called Danny from his car. Danny picked up on the first ring.

"Can you talk now you prick?"

"Yes. What the hell is with you? What haven't I told you?"

"You tell me Anderson. Ernesto has been killed. I believe it was made to look like he's some kind of terrorist or something. Somebody took him out. Somebody who knew what they were doing. What don't I know about this girl?"

Anderson didn't say anything. Danny could hear him breathing rather deeply on the other end of the line. Anderson's thoughts went back to Brooke's father, Rick Morgan. The holes in Morgan's resume were shouting…covert operative, CIA maybe. someone who has done *wet work*. Morgan was a guy with experience, *and* connections.

"Anderson? Are you there?"

"I'm here," responded Ben rather sheeplessly.

"Tell me Anderson, how could a girl and her *elderly* father overpower Ernesto? He was a black belt, and he was armed! He was an *Army Ranger* for heaven's sake! What haven't you told me Anderson?"

"I checked them both out when the article came out. She was clean as a whistle. The father had a few holes in his resume."

"A few holes, what the hell does that mean?" snapped Danny.

"It means just that…a few holes. Maybe I should have checked him out further. Problem was that I kept running into blank walls."

"So who is this guy?"

"I'm not sure, but all the holes correspond with some dates of interest."

"Speak in a language I can understand."

Ben really didn't want to get into this with Ochoa. But Ochoa wasn't in any mood to be put off. He kept pushing.

"Well, he was conspicuously absent in October nineteen sixty-seven for example. I cross-checked the dates and Bolivia pops up. Che Guevara was killed in Bolivia during that time frame. It was a combined CIA-Ranger operation. Another one was nineteen seventy during the time Noriega was taking action in Panama. Another gaping hole in nineteen eighty-six and seven during the Iran-Contra arms deal. The list goes on. Could be a coincidence."

"So what you're telling me is her father is some kind of fucking secret agent?"

"I wouldn't go that far."

"You wouldn't go that far? You prick! Ernesto is dead! He didn't fucking commit suicide!"

"I'll do some more checking. I just don't want to raise any flags. If he is former CIA, bells and whistles will go off that could lead right back to me. I'll do some snooping around and see if anyone knows what happened at Eglin. Maybe it isn't Ernesto."

"Don't waste your time. It was Ernesto. You do what you have to do. I will take care of the girl and her father. What about Paco? We have a deal!"

"Don't worry. You take care of the girl, and Paco will be history."

"I'm not worried. You're the one who needs to worry if Paco goes to the Grand Jury."

With that, Danny hung up and dialed Manny.

"Manny, I want you to finish Ernesto's job. Be careful, her father could be ex CIA. That fucker Anderson never said a word, and he had suspicions. No amateur could have taken out Ernesto."

"Did Ernesto give you any indication where they were?"

"In Destin at the Silver Shells complex. Use your PI status to find them. Let me know when the job is done. If Anderson doesn't do something about Paco, Bascomb will be next. That will send a message loud and clear to Anderson."

"I'll call when I locate them."

Manny rented a Ford Escape from Molly. She asked him if he had located the car rental agency that had serviced the guy he was looking for. He told her that he had and that he needed to do some follow up work for his client. His ID easily passed her inspection. She handed him the keys, and he was on his way to Destin…and a meeting with Rick Morgan.

Chapter Thirty-One
Destin, Florida
November 27, 2010
Saturday
2200 Hours

Lynn and Brooke had gone to bed early. The TV was still on. Brooke was on Rick's side of the bed. They were both facing in the same direction. Rick could see them clearly in the flickering light of the TV. They looked more like sisters than mother and daughter. The sound was turned so low that Rick could hardly hear what Bill O'Reilly was saying to Al Sharpton. Bill had a "you have to be kidding me" expression on his face. Rick had suffered a substantial hearing loss over the years. He had a lot of trouble with words containing S's and L's. All the prime time TV shows were an hour earlier in Destin. Once you got used to it, going to bed at ten at night quickly became the norm. Rick turned off the TV and went into the kitchen and poured a cup of day old Jamaican Blue Mountain coffee that Lynn had brewed that morning. The coffee was robust to say the least, but it was still good. There was a note from Lynn telling him that she missed him and loved him, and that there was some tiramisu in the refrigerator. There was also a postscript that told him that Carl had called at 2145 and needed Rick to call him back as soon as he got in. He went back into the bedroom that doubled as his Destin office, lifted the lid of his Dell Latitude TM XFR D630 and turned it on. As the computer was came out of the standby mode, he dialed Carl's cell phone.

"Peterson."

"Carl, you called?"

"Rick, yes I did. It was really great seeing you after all these years. I enjoyed our time together."

"Same here Carl. You have always been there for me, and more importantly, you are a good friend."

Rick knew that real friends could be counted on a single hand. Carl was in the top three.

"Rick, when I got back to the condo I checked the daily activity log. Our surveillance of Ochoa's operation revealed that Manny Dominguez flew to Pensacola early this afternoon. From what you told me tonight, I can only assume that Dominguez is looking for Ernesto Garcia. He is no dummy. He probably knows where Ernesto was staying. It would be easy for him to trace the license plate back to the rental agency. By now the rental agency knows the car has been involved in an accident. For sure the FBI has questioned them to find out the identity of the driver."

Rick's mind began developing scenarios. All of them led to he, Lynn and Brooke.

"Carl, it is time to bite the octopus between the eyes."

Carl knew exactly what Rick meant. Many years before, Rick and Carl were involved in an operation out of Sigonela, Sicily. As part of their cover they posed as Italian fisherman. Not an easy assignment since neither of them spoke Italian very well. The two weeks at the Defense Language Institute in Monterey, California prepared them to find the bathroom and order a cappuccino, but not much more. On one of the trips, the catch of the day was octopus. The tentacles would wrap around the fisherman's arms, his neck, whatever was close by. The fisherman would simply bite the octopus between the eyes. The tentacles went limp.

"Be careful Rick, Dominguez didn't get to be Ochoa's right hand man by being a diplomat. Let me know if I can be of help."

"Thanks Carl. I'll give you a call tomorrow. I need to think about this."

Rick put the phone down and watched a small single engine plane land at the Destin airport. He wasn't expecting another one of Danny's goons so soon. He figured that he had at least a couple more days. He looked through the collection of CD's and placed one of his favorites into the stereo. The first composition was Concerto Grosso by Handel. Classical music was soothing, calming, it was the catalyst

Rick needed to concentrate on the problem at hand. Rick always loved classical music. He couldn't understand why the gym insisted on playing rap music. After a workout at the gym he felt like donning on a sweatshirt and watch cap and robbing a Seven Eleven. He sat down at the computer and double-clicked The Peterson Group icon. The screen that appeared had several new menu items thanks to Roland Carpenter. He clicked on the Counter-Narcotics icon. Rick followed the prompts, and within a few seconds, a complete dossier of Danny Ochoa appeared on the screen. The screen included several menu items. Rick was particularly interested in known associates. There were two names that were prominent, Manny Dominguez and Paco Ramirez. Another item that interested Rick was titled "Lieutenants". One name jumped out immediately, Ernesto Garcia. There were several other Lieutenants listed. Rick knew that *Lieutenant* was another name for enforcer. He read the entire dossier and decided that it was time that he and Carlos got together. There would be no *talking* with Danny Ochoa. It was nearly midnight. Carlos never went to bed early. He opened his satellite phone, hit button number 3 and then pressed the send button. Carlos picked up before the second ring. He recognized the restricted ID.

"Hey Butch, you must be thinking."

"I am Carlos. It is time we get together. How about coming over here tomorrow morning for breakfast?"

"Is Lynn making it?" asked Carlos. There was excitement in his voice.

"Is that the only way to get you here? Don't you like my eggs and grits?"

"I do, I really do, but I like her biscuits and tomato gravy a lot more."

"I'm sure she'll oblige. How does eight thirty sound?"

"Fine with me. Do I need a pass or something to get in?"

"I will call the gate guard and give him your name. He will give you a yellow pass for the day. We are staying in St. Barth. As you come in, it is the building on the far left. After the guardhouse make a left at the first rotary. That will put St Barth in front of you. Drive straight back and you will see the under ground garage on the left. I'll meet you there and show you where to park."

"Is it okay to use my real name?"

"Sure it is, and what *is* your real name this time?"

"Carlos will do just fine. I will see you in the morning. By the way, is Lynn okay with everything? Is she okay with me?"

"Relatively speaking, she is. You know Carlos, she has always liked you. She's just not sure what you do for a living."

As Rick made that statement he was painfully aware that Lynn really had no idea who she had married, what he was capable of, or what he would do to protect his family.

"I'm looking forward to seeing her, and especially my little girl."

Rick put the phone down and went back into the living room. The only light that was on was the small light under the microwave. It was enough. He walked over to the sliding glass door and went out onto the balcony. The Gulf of Mexico was very calm. The moon was one day short of being full. Its reflection created an inviting pathway to the horizon. The pure white sand had the appearance of a fresh snowfall. The Emerald Coast of Florida was truly a paradise. He had been all over the Hawaiian islands, but it didn't compare with Florida's Emerald Coast. Destin was no longer that sleepy little fishing village that was named by Dewey Destin so many years ago.

Carlos drove into the Silver Shells complex. He passed Ruth's Chris Steakhouse and stopped at the guardhouse.

"Good morning, I'm here to see Mr. Morgan."

"And your name sir?"

"Carlos Garcia."

"Please wait a second."

The guard went back into the guardhouse and returned with a yellow pass that was to be placed on the rearview mirror.

"Here is your pass. You have Mr. Morgan's address?"

"Yes, thank you."

The gate went up and Carlos followed Rick's directions. The grounds of the Silver Shells complex were manicured to perfection. Several landscape people were shaping bushes and sweeping the area. They all looked like Carlos. Three young house keeping ladies were pushing their carts toward a building with the name of another Caribbean island. As Carlos pulled up to the entrance of the underground parking garage, he noticed very few cars. Most of the spaces were empty. Rick appeared from an area to the left of the driveway. He signaled Carlos to a space that was next to Rick's Escalade.

"Good morning my friend", said Rick as he embraced Carlos.

"Good morning Rick. I'm really looking forward to Lynn's biscuits and gravy.

"I'm sure you will be pleased. Lynn has already started the process. Brooke is excited about seeing you. She has grown into quite the women since you saw her last."

The breakfast exceeded all of Carlo's expectations. Lynn had always liked Carlos, and Brooke had always looked up to him. Both of them had been competitive swimmers. When she was twenty-four years old, Carlos entered her in the 24-hour Navy SEAL Challenge that was sponsored by Blackwater Ops. She was the only woman among fifty-six *macho* guys, fourteen of which had to drop out and receive medical attention during the simulated *hell week*. The instructors thought it would be fun to single out and pick on the only female present, so they picked Brooke as one of the two platoon leaders. She ended up surprising everyone. Carlos was so proud that he pinned his Trident on her at the end of the award ceremony. Carlos always had respect for Brooke's resolve. She was the daughter he never had. None of them mentioned the night on highway 87. After breakfast, Rick and Carlos went to the office to "discuss business".

"This is a nice setup Rick. Have you been coming here a lot?"

"We have been coming to Destin since about nineteen eighty-five. Mostly short trips. The last three years we have been staying for three months. This is the first year in this building."

Carlos looked out at the airport. He picked up a small pair of binoculars and scanned the ramp area. He found his plane. He handed the binoculars to Rick.

"It is a great view. Do you see that blue and white Cessna 210, just eight spaces from the trailer?"

Rick focused the binoculars and found the aircraft.

"I do, is that one yours?" he said giving Carlos a surprised look.

"It is. It is a great little plane. Cruises at 180. I'll take you up. So where are we Rick?"

"I got a call last night from Carl. Another one of Ochoa's guys is in town. We think he is looking for Ernesto, but there is a good chance he will come after Brooke. It wouldn't be hard for him to find us."

Carlos picked up the CD by Handel. He gestured with it toward Rick.

"I assume you came up with a good plan?"

"I thought about this most of the night. I strongly believe we still have the element of surprise though Ochoa and his guys may be a little more cautious since the Ernesto situation. Regardless, Dominguez has no idea that we know who he is or what he looks like. Ochoa has no idea that *he* is a target. And, none of them know who you are."

Carlos was listening intently. Rick was making sense, he was the strategic planner. Carlos could execute the tactical side.

"Carlos, we have to assume that Dominguez is after Brooke. Therefore, I need to

get she and Lynn out of here.

"Exactly what I was thinking!

"A friend of mine has a house in Miami. You can fly them there and as a *slight* side adventure, take care of our friend Ochoa."

"Slight? I'm beginning to like this plan."

"Carl said that he would provide whatever help we need. Let me show you something here on the computer."

Rick brought up the satellite surveillance feed on Danny Ochoa's house in Coconut Grove. It appeared to be a live feed.

"That looks like real time. Is it?" asked Carlos.

"Within a second. As you can see, Ochoa's car is still in the driveway. I can switch to a thermavision view. Look there to the right of the garage, there is a roving patrol. There is another one out by the front gate."

Carlos looked intently at the screen. "Amazing," he said.

"Why don't we hit him as he leaves the property?" Carlos added.

"We will. But I want to ensure that you are far enough away to make a clean get-away. And most importantly, I don't want to risk any friendly casualties."

Rick got up and asked Carlos if he wanted another coffee. He went into the kitchen and came back with two cups and a couple of sweet rolls.

"You have figured this out haven't you Rick?"

"I have. There are only two directions that he can go when he exits the property. From a shortest distance aspect he would turn right. From a shortest time aspect he would go left. I want him to go left. As you can see, there is a stop sign on that corner and what appears to be a cable box. A well-placed IED could easily take him out with minimal collateral damage."

"So how do you get him to turn left?"

"I'm working on that. Hopefully Carl can help us there. Maybe create a diversion at Ochoa's car dealership. Anything to get him to leave the house when we want him to…and turn left."

"So, I will be close by and you will let me know when to trigger the IED?"

"Correct. If there are any civilians in the area, we will abort. From what I can see, there is very little traffic between 0900 and 1030. A few cars, but no walkers."

"Sounds like a good plan to me. What about Lynn and Brooke?"

"I'll get them ready. Lynn likes Miami. Brooke has never been."

"What if this guy is watching the condo?" asked Carlos.

"I'll drive out first. Most likely he will follow me and do a personal evaluation to determine what he may, or may not be up against. Once I leave, give me some time to figure out if he is trailing me. Once I know, I'll call you and then you and the girls can head for the airport. If you need some overnight stuff, Lynn can fix you up. What about the material for the IED?"

"I have some in the car, and the rest is in the plane."

"Is that safe?"

"It is until I put it together."

"Carlos, do you see any tactical flaws?"

"No. We just need to get him moving right after I place the IED. I'll probably make it look like an addition to the cable box. I'll take a ride over there tonight and make that decision. If I see a problem I'll let you know. When do you want this to go down?"

"Tomorrow morning about 0915. From the surveillance information, he never leaves before 0930."

"Let's do it," said Carlos.

Rick and Carlos shook hands and embraced. Just then two Blackhawk helicopters flew in formation down the beach at about one thousand feet. They were special ops helicopters out of Hurlbert Field. Carlos smiled at Rick.

"Like old times, eh Carlos?"

The adrenalin was pumping. Rick headed into the living room to prepare Lynn and Brooke.

Chapter Thirty-Two
Destin, Florida
November 28, 2010
Sunday
0900 Hours

As Rick and Carlos were having breakfast, Manny Dominguez was on the phone with Danny Ochoa. Time was getting short. The Grand Jury was scheduled to be in session on December first. Paco Ramirez was first on the list.

"Danny, I will check with the front desk at Silver Shells, but if Morgan rented the condo from a private owner, he will be a little harder to find. The Post Office would know, but they wouldn't give that info to me. I think that Anderson would be our best bet."

"I will give him a call. I need to shake him up a bit anyway. He probably won't be able to get that information until Monday."

"He could probably find out what kind of car Morgan drives. That would at least narrow my search."

"Manny, Morgan drives a 2010 white Escalade with Virginia plates. I remember Ernesto telling me that when he called while following them to Destin. I don't remember the plate number, but it was one of those specialty or vanity plates."

"Good. I'll start with Silver Shells. I'll pick him up sooner or later. Let me know when you get his address. I'll call you later."

Manny hung up and decided to try an old trick that many real PIs would use to find out which unit their mark was staying in. He went to the front desk of the Silver Shells complex. There were two young ladies behind the counter. One was Hispanic, the other Anglo. He purposely selected the Hispanic girl. Her name was Gabriella.

"Hola Gabriella, my name is Armando Mila. I have an envelope for Mr. Morgan. I don't remember his unit. Could you let him know that I am here?"

"I know the Morgans, but Mr. Morgan doesn't rent from us. He rents from a private owner, but I don't have his number. Hold on a second, I think there is a UPS package for Mrs. Morgan. Let me look."

"Thank you, you are so kind."

Gabriella went into the back. She fumbled through some packages and stopped looking when she found a small box with blue lettering. She came back out with the box.

"Here is the address. The Morgan's are in St. Barth, unit B403."

Manny wrote the address on the envelope, handed it to Gabriella, and asked her to put it with the box. There was just an advertisement in the envelope with a note to a Mr. Jordan. When Morgan got it, he would think that the front desk had made a mistake.

"Thank you so much."

He walked out and thought to himself, *Jim Rockford* would have been proud. He new everything he needed to know. Manny went out the main gate and turned left. He made the next left that was the old beach road. It paralleled Silver Shell's property. There were two more gates that allowed an exit. They were electronic gates. He drove up to one, it didn't open. They were owner gates that required a fob to open. Three ways in, three ways out. He turned around and pulled into the small parking lot next to the first electronic gate. From his vantage point he could see the road going up to St. Barth. If Morgan drove out, Manny would see him. He was in a position to follow no matter which way Morgan went.

Rick didn't have a hard time convincing Lynn and Brooke to go with Carlos to Miami. He didn't want to scare them but did tell them that he believed another individual was in town looking for Brooke. It would be easier for him to find out who the guy was if he didn't have to worry about their safety. Besides they could do some long overdue shopping. No one would be looking for them in Miami. At 1040 Rick drove out of the garage and out the main entrance. He didn't notice the

Ford Escape that pulled out of the parking lot by the first electronic gate. Rick turned right on the Emerald Coast Highway heading east. As he was driving he made a call to Carl Peterson.

"Hey Rick, how's it going?"

"I need a favor. Can you find out what kind of car Dominguez rented?"

"Sure, no problem. I'll check his known aliases against the rental database. He doesn't know we're on to him so he probably used one of his standards. I'll call you back in about ten minutes. By the way, I can probably find out where he's staying. The swipe cards contain personal information that is entered into the hotel's computer system. I'll get Roland on that."

"Thanks Carl."

Rick pulled in to the Exxon station and proceeded to fill his tank. He noticed a white Ford Escape that pulled into the Aveda parking lot next door. Rick could see the car in the reflection of the gas pump. The driver didn't get out. The windows had enough of a tint that Rick couldn't see into the vehicle. He didn't look directly at the car. He did not want to alert the driver in the event it was Dominguez. It took twelve gallons to top off the tank. Rick pulled his receipt and headed out through the back exit, turned left, and got into the right lane to continue down the Emerald Coast Highway. As he was going past the entrance to the Regatta Bay Country Club, he caught a glimpse of the white Ford Escape in his rearview mirror. Just then his phone rang. It was Carl.

"Don't tell me Carl, he's driving a white Ford Escape."

"He's that bad, huh?"

"Well, he *is* at a disadvantage. He has no idea we are on to him."

"Do you want the license number?"

"Sure, what is it?"

"It's Florida plate KGB seven, seven, four, two."

"KGB…you *are* kidding?"

"No, I'm serious. Can you believe that? Like old times…huh?"

"Thanks Carl. I'll be in touch."

"Rick, be careful of this guy. He's not a fighter. His weapon of choice is a Glock three eighty. He'll want to be up close and personal for the hit."

"Yeah…so do I!" responded Rick his voice clear as a bell.

"Rick, Roland just handed me his room number. He's staying at the Holiday Inn, ten twenty highway ninety-eight. You can view the layout on their website. Good hunting!"

Rick continued down the Emerald Coast Highway and made a left into a golf driving range. Manny continued going east and made a u-turn at the next cross over. He came back and parked on the far side of the parking area. Rick called Carlos.

"Carlos, Manny is following me. He parked several cars away. Have a good flight. I'll call you later."

"Okay Rick. Be careful."

"I will."

Carlos hung up, and he, Lynn and Brooke headed for the Destin airport. Rick got a large bucket of balls, and before he was finished hitting them, Carlos and the girls were at ninety-five hundred feet on their way to Miami. As Rick walked to the putting green, Manny reached into the glove compartment and retrieved his Glock three eighty. He fitted a silencer to the barrel and placed the gun into a folded newspaper. He got out of the Escape. Rick was working on his putting grip as Manny walked slowly looking for a firing position. When he was sure no one was looking, he slipped into the bushes next to the clubhouse. He had a clear view of the putting green. He knelt on one knee and took aim at Rick. There were three other people on the green. Just as he was about to pull the trigger, two jabbering older women stepped off the clubhouse porch and stopped right in front of the bushes completely blocking his view. He had no shot. He didn't move. They talked for what seemed like an eternity before moving on. Rick was no longer on the putting green. He didn't even see Rick leave. Manny put the gun back into the paper and slipped out of the bushes. He looked around for Rick. Rick was already in the Escalade and backing out of the parking space. Manny headed back to his car and followed Rick as he headed back toward Silver Shells. It was 1145.

Rick could see the white Escape several cars back. He went through the main gate, and instead of going to the underground garage, he purposely parked on the second level in front of St. Barth. Manny could see the Escalade as Rick placed his key fob in front of the security lock and entered the building through the front door. It was exactly 1210. Rick went up to B403. It was very quiet…too quiet. He missed Lynn and Brooke. He went into his office and hit the play button on the stereo. A CD by Handel was still loaded. He poured a cup of coffee and looked out at the parking area. He saw Manny drive past the entrance to Silver Shells and turn down the old beach road. He knew where Manny would park to have the best vantage point. He also knew that Manny could see the Escalade. Rick went into the closet and pulled a leather gun pouch from his suitcase. He went back into the office, put on surgical gloves and opened the pouch. He placed the 9mm Beretta on a towel that he had put on the desk. He reached back into the pouch and pulled out a black silencer. Handel's *Messiah* was playing as he broke the weapon down. Lynn had put that CD in before she left. It was her way of leaving him a message. He put the gun back together, carefully wiping each part in the process and oiling the moving parts. He took all the bullets out of the clip and wiped it down. He thoroughly wiped each bullet and put them back into the fifteen round clip one by one. He would only need two rounds, but would take no chances. He thoroughly wiped the silencer and twisted it onto the barrel. He put masked tape around the stock and trigger. The serial number had not only been ground down but also removed with acid. The gun was untraceable. It had belonged to an Irish Republican Army terrorist…a very long time ago.

Danny Ochoa was getting impatient. He had called Ben Anderson, but Anderson didn't answer his call. It was less than a week before the Grand Jury hearing. He couldn't afford them questioning Paco. He knew Paco would cave under any sort of pressure. The more he thought about it, the madder it made him. He knew that Anderson was avoiding him. No one in his or her right mind would blow off Danny Ochoa. He decided to call Sidney Bascomb. Danny knew that Bascomb was a real wimp. Bascomb would get in touch with Anderson. Sid answered on the fourth ring.

"Hello?"

It was a very weak hello.

"Hello Sid. You guys are trying my patience. Anderson won't answer my calls. I am not fucking with you guys anymore. Paco is dead tomorrow or you guys are. Your choice. Manny is already there just waiting to put you out of your fucking misery."

Bascomb was speechless. He thought that everything was in place to take care of Ramirez. He couldn't muster enough energy to say anything.

"Fine Bascomb, you can remain silent, but I better hear from Anderson, or you can kiss your ass goodbye. I might not even wait until tomorrow. I might just make an example of you. I bet that will get Anderson's attention."

Before Bascomb could respond he heard the phone click. He was sure that Danny had slammed the receiver. He was still speechless. His heart was pounding. He knew that Danny didn't make idle threats.

Sidney immediately called Anderson. Sidney's fear of the situation came through loud and clear. Ben told Sid that he would call Ochoa.

"Ben, this guy will kill the both of us. Please…*please* call him right away. He's really pissed. I've had the misfortune of seeing a Columbian necktie. I don't want to be wearing one!"

"Sid, get hold of yourself. I'll call him. I'll call him right now. Don't worry."

Ben hung up. This whole thing was falling apart. He still had no idea who the *Anonymous Source* was, and to complicate matters, he had Danny Ochoa breathing down his back. He had seen the call from Ochoa, but he didn't want to take care of Paco Ramirez until Ochoa had delivered on his promise. He had no choice but to call Ochoa.

"Anderson, it's about time you called me. I want Paco dead. I want him dead now. Do you hear me?"

"You were supposed to find out some information for me. We had a deal."

"We gave you the email address of the *Anonymous Source*. That is all there was. What do you want? You want me to drive you to the guy's front door?"

"The email was no good. It belonged to a Systems Engineer with Northrop Grumman."

"Maybe he's the guy?"

"We checked him out. He's not the guy. His email was spoofed by the real source."

"Spoofed? What the hell are you talking about?"

"It's complicated. We could eventually find him, but it will take too long. I, no *we,* can't afford to wait."

"Anderson, as far as I am concerned, I delivered. You take care of Paco—today! I have a guy in Destin. He will take care of the girl and her father tonight. No more screwing around. *Today* Anderson!"

Ochoa hung up. Anderson knew that he was between the proverbial rock and a hard place. He knew that the death of Ramirez so soon after Spanelli would trigger a stand down at the very least, and most likely, an intense internal investigation that he didn't need. But he had no choice but to give Luis and Mickey the go ahead.

Rick went into the living room. The condo was very quiet without Lynn and Brooke. The three of them loved to eat chocolate covered strawberries and play card games. He looked down at the pool. Several young girls were taking advantage of the afternoon sun. They were probably down for a long weekend. They looked good from a distance. Five pelicans flew by in right echelon, gracefully maneuvering on the afternoon thermals. There were high cirrus clouds in the western sky. It would be a beautiful sunset. Just then, his regular cell phone rang. It was Lynn.

"Hi honey. How was the trip?"

"It was a beautiful flight. Didn't take as long as I had expected. Carlos's plane is really nice. He let me fly it, Brooke also. Carlos rented a car, and we are at Angel's house. He has done a lot of renovations. The kitchen is brand new. Are you okay?"

"I am. Please don't worry, maybe I will fly down in a couple of days."

"Be careful. I'm sure that you haven't told me everything, but I trust your judgment."

"Don't worry babe, I'll be okay."

"Your not as young as you used to be," she reminded him.

"Well that's encouraging."

"Love you. Brooke says she loves and misses you. We are looking forward to seeing you."

"Is Carlos there?" asked Rick.

"He's gone to get something at Home Depot."

"Tell him 'hello' for me. I love you honey. I'll call you tomorrow."

Rick hung up the phone. He took a bottle of water from the refrigerator and went out on the balcony. The Gulf of Mexico was calm and inviting, but cold this time of year. The sun was below the horizon. The sunset was just as he expected. It was spectacular. One of them would not see the sunrise. He went back into the office. The CD had cycled through and Handel's *Messiah* was playing again. Rick looked over at the stereo. He had a plan. It was time.

Chapter Thirty-Three
Destin, Florida
November 28, 2010
Sunday
2030 Hours

Rick put on his fishing jeans and an old faded sweatshirt. He took the oldest ball cap that he had and smeared dirt from one of the houseplants on the bill and top. He did the same with a pair of deck shoes. He also smeared some of the dirt on his forehead and the right side of his face. He fashioned an arm sling from one of Lynn's cleaning rags. He went to the refrigerator and opened a bottle of water and drank over half the bottle before putting it down. He looked in the mirror at a ghost from the past. A ghost he thought was at rest. But, by definition, ghosts never rest. He took one last look around the condo. He said a short prayer to himself. Such hypocrisy he thought. He remembered a sermon from long ago where the guest preacher said that God always answers prayer. God's answer is *yes*, *no* or *you've got to be kidding me*! In this case, Rick knew God's answer. He put the gun into the sling and took the elevator to the garage level. He slipped out the back door of the garage, looked around, and moved deliberately across the patio to the gate leading down to the pool level. The high cirrus clouds had moved in. There was a halo around the moon that looked like a giant smoke ring. He grabbed a broom that was by one of the cabanas and exited through the gate on the western side of the pool area. If anyone were out walking he would start sweeping. He walked down the short path to the road that went between St. Lucia and St. Thomas. The road led to the back exit leading out of Silver Shells and onto the old beach road across from an Italian restaurant. There were no cars on the road, and just a few cars at the restaurant. No one had seen Rick; if anyone had, they would pay him no attention. Most of the residents this time of year were retired. Most were already in bed. He left the broom on the other side of the gate and walked a block to the parking lot where Manny Dominguez sat in his white Ford Escape. He was smoking a cigar; his eyes were fixed on Rick's Escalade. Rick put the sling on his arm, the Beretta firmly in his right hand. He pretended to be drunk and trying to find an unlocked car to spend the night in. When he got to the white Ford Escape, Manny rolled down the window. Manny must have caught a glimpse of *the bum* in the side mirror.

"Get the fuck away from here," he said sharply. There wasn't a compassionate bone in his body.

Rick turned his head away so that Manny wouldn't recognize him or become suspicious. He pretended to have the shakes. Rick bobbed his head up and down like a cork in the water. He talked as if he were somewhere in outer space, somewhere other than Destin.

"Sorry man. You gotta smoke. I need a smoke. Please man…just a smoke," he mumbled.

"Yeah, smoke this asshole!"

Manny threw out what was left of his montecristo. Rick had already determined that there was no one else in the parking lot. There was no one in sight. He reached down with his left hand and picked up what was left of Manny's cigar; the Beretta in his right hand aimed at the side of Manny's head. Rick put his right knee against the door. In a very clear voice Rick spoke the last words that Manny Dominguez would ever hear, at least in this life.

"You should have stayed in Miami. Stayed away from my daughter!"

Manny turned. The look on his face told Rick that he knew he was a dead man. Before Manny could reach the gun he had resting on the seat next to him, or push the door open, or even blink, Rick's bullet entered Manny's left temple. Blood spattered on the passenger's seat and door. Manny slowly slid over on his right side. His eyes had the look of a pigeon that just bounced off the windshield of a semi truck. They saw nothing. His body twitched slightly and then stopped. Rick looked around the parking lot. There was no one in sight. He threw the Beretta into the car, removed his hat and arm sling, wiped the dirt from his face and causally walked back to the condo by the same route.

2030 Hours, McLean, Virginia

Ben Anderson really didn't want to call Luis. Paco Ramirez was his ace in the hole. With Paco gone there would be no guarantee that Danny Ochoa would follow through with his part of the bargain. However, Ben had no choice. Sidney was scared to death. The fear in his voice was more than convincing. Ben reluctantly picked up his cell phone and made the call.

"Escobar," answered Luis still sounding like he was on duty.

"Luis, Ben here. How's it going?"

"Going well Ben. We are getting ready to move Ramirez again. Any new instructions?"

"No, but the schedule has changed a bit. Just *put him on ice*."

Luis knew what that meant. He also knew that it probably meant that the problem in Virginia Beach had been taken care of. No more worries, they all would be in the clear.

"I'll call you Ben when we make the next stop. Do you want me to call Taylor?"

"Yes, that will save me a little time. Talk with you later."

2120 Hours, Silver Shells

Rick went back into the condo. Handel's *Messiah* was still playing, probably on its third time through. He could certainly use the Messiah in his life right about now. He poured a Jack Daniels on the rocks, went back to the bathroom and took a hot shower. Killing Manny Dominguez really didn't bother him. Dominguez was a bad guy. He probably caused the ruin of many young adults, kids, even children. He deserved what he got. Besides, Manny Dominguez should never have come after Brooke. A big mistake on his part, and a bigger one for Danny Ochoa. Ochoa was next. The shower was refreshing. It easily washed the dirt of Manny Dominguez from Rick's body, and soul. Rick felt clean inside and out. It was time to call Carlos.

"Hey Rick. It is good to hear from you. I assume that everything went well."

"It did. We are clear at this end. Is everything set for tomorrow?"

"It will be. Just putting on some finishing touches."

"Good. Call me when you are ready for my input."

"Will do Rick. I'm glad you're back in the game. Talk with you tomorrow morning. By the way, you need to give Lynn a call. I know she is really concerned. She tries not to let on, but she really is."

"Thanks Carlos, I'll give her a call."

Rick had never considered what they did…*a game*. It was business. It was always business with a purpose. By tomorrow this time, if everything went as planned, he could concentrate on Anderson. It still wouldn't be over until Anderson was out of the picture. Rick thought about Sigonella and the octopus. He called Lynn on Angel's home phone. She answered on the first ring. She must be worried. Lynn would normally let the phone ring at least four times before she would answer.

"Rick, I was hoping you would call."

"Hi honey. Are you doing okay? Did you and Brooke have fun shopping?"

"We did, but we both want you to come on down. Is everything okay back there?

Rick could tell by her voice that she was very concerned. He needed to reassure her that everything was, indeed, okay…that they were all safe.

"Honey, everything is fine here. It turned out to be a false alarm. Guess I'm getting paranoid in my old age. I intend to fly down there tomorrow. Maybe we'll take a couple of days off and fly over to Paradise Island. Would you like that?"

"Would I like that? Of course, that would be great. Is that a promise?"

"That is a promise. Go ahead and make the reservations. Be sure to use Carlos's credit card. I still don't want anyone knowing where you are. Tell him I'll reimburse him later."

"I will. Call me tomorrow. By the way, Brooke got another input for her story."

Rick thought about that for a few seconds before answering. It was *The Last Witness* that started this whole mess, and it wasn't over yet.

"Has she started working on the next part?"

"She has. She says the material is quite revealing. She is keeping it a secret. She's working on it as we speak. Do you want to talk to her?"

"I won't disturb her. You know how she is when she's in the writing mode. Tell her I said 'hi' and that I will see you both tomorrow. Love you honey."

Rick hung up and went into the office. The one thing he hadn't thought about was the computer. Brooke didn't use a wifi network on the road. She must have used Angel's home computer and accessed her account from his line. That could be traced, but by that time he and Carlos would be in full control. He looked out at the parking lot. No police cars yet. It wouldn't be much longer. He turned on the computer and brought up the satellite feed. He zoomed in on Danny Ochoa's house in Coconut Grove. He could see the house and Danny's Mercedes Benz parked on the circular driveway right in front of the house. The resolution was impressive. The system was nearly good enough to make out the license plate number. He switched to thermavision. There were two figures between the garage and the house. One of them went toward the front gate while the other one went around the garage and proceeded to the back of the property. The hood of the car indicated that it had been driven recently. There probably was a way to calculate the exact time the car was parked just from the heat signature. Roland Carpenter was probably working on the algorithm. The system was good. Rick went and poured another Jack Daniels on the rocks. As he took his first sip he heard sirens. He looked out the window. Someone had found Manny Dominguez.

Chapter Thirty-Four
Destin, Florida
November 29, 2010
Monday
0730 Hours

The traffic in Miami was worse than he had expected. Mondays and Fridays were always the worst. Fortunately, Carlos had completed his reconnaissance of Danny Ochoa's neighborhood the day before. He had calculated the distance and blast radius and determined that the IED would be most effective if placed in the sewer drainage pipe that was right next to the road. It would easily take out Ochoa and minimize any collateral damage. However, the blast would most likely take out power and water to the neighborhood. He and Rick had decided that if anyone were within a half block of the target site, they would abort the mission. The key was to get Danny out of the house at a time they knew traffic would be at a minimum. Monday morning between 0930 and 1000 should be good. If they had to abort, Carlos was prepared to take Danny out at his place of business.

As Carlos was driving to his trigger point, Rick was on the phone with Carl Peterson.

"So I assume you took care of business last night?"

"I did. Sadly to say, it was merely routine."

"Rick, this guy was no good. I'm sure you did many people a big favor."

"Carl, as I get older I realize that life is precious. It should be valued, but unfortunately, it isn't. There is no respect for life. It never changes. I guess what they say is true, God will sort it out."

"Are you becoming a philosopher?"

"No…no way. I just know how much I love Lynn and Brooke. How much enjoyment it was to watch Brooke grow up. Watch her go through those little phases of life. Some not so little. I just wonder what happens to the kids you see, playing and having fun, then growing up and becoming callused, having no conscience. When does it happen? Why the change? What is the tipping point? Carl, how do kids turn into guys like Ernesto, Manny and Danny Ochoa?"

"Rick, they start by killing cats and dogs…and they enjoy it! It progresses from there. You are right when you say that God will sort it out. We are just giving him a little bit of help."

"I hope you are right. I hope *we* are right."

"Rick, we are on the right side."

"Carl, I'm sure the FBI will get involved with Manny Dominguez. I left the weapon. When they make the connection between Dominguez and Ernesto Garcia they probably will come to an initial conclusion that they are in the throws of a drug war. The coup de grace will be Ochoa."

"What about the gun's ballistics?"

"No problem. It's a barrel I had made by a friend of mine many years ago. He has been dead since the early nineties. This was the first time a bullet has been through it. I guess in the back of my mind I knew I would have a need for it. I just never dreamed it would involve Brooke."

"You seem to have all bases covered," said Carl.

"Probably. Remember our training, nothing is ever perfect. There is always something overlooked. Some little piece of evidence left behind just waiting for some CSI wanna-be to connect the dots. That is why I like to keep things real simple. No mission impossible. Less things to go wrong."

"A couple down, and how many to go?" asked Carl.

"That's the real question. I just want to do battle on one front. Brooke had no idea what she was getting into."

"Still no idea who the *Anonymous Source* is?" asked Carl.

"No. But, I am convinced that he, or *she* as the case may be, had no interest in hurting Brooke. However, our *Anonymous Source* had to know that this whole thing could blow up and put Brooke in the cross hairs. That doesn't set very well with me."

"Is Carlos in position?"

"He is. I just need you to create a situation that will cause Ochoa to leave his house on or as close to zero nine thirty as possible. I noticed from the surveillance log that he usually leaves by ten hundred. I would rather see him out at zero nine thirty. From what I can gather from the surveillance tapes that seems to be a low traffic period in his neighborhood. Very few cars go down his street anyway."

"Rick, I'll have one of my guys go over to one of his dealerships and let them know he has information about Ernesto. It is common knowledge that the DEA is still looking for him in Miami."

"Carl, will you have your guy go to his dealership in the Kendal area? That should guarantee that he'll go left out of his driveway. I need him to take that route."

"Sure, that will work well. We have an office down where Homestead Air Force Base used to be. I'll have him at the dealership about zero nine fifteen. Will that work?"

"It will. I will call you when this is over."

"You won't have to. I'll see it on the screen!"

It was a nice day in the Miami area. A few clouds, but clear. No haze. Ochoa's neighborhood was peaceful and coming in clearly from the satellite feed. Rick zoomed in to where he could see both Ochoa's driveway and the corner where the IED was waiting to do its damage. He zoomed back out and counted a total of four cars moving in the entire neighborhood. None were moving on Ochoa's street. There were two bike riders that were causally riding two blocks to the northwest. Hopefully, they would stay away from Ochoa's immediate neighborhood. If this were a *Company* operation, a crew of workers would be in place. There would be utility trucks, barricades and all the necessary signs and people to ensure that no friendlies entered the target area. For this operation it was just Rick and Carlos. Rick would have to rely on the satellite system. Rick had decided that if anyone other than Ochoa was in the target area, they would abort. Rick's satellite phone rang. It was Carlos.

"Hi Carlos. Are we a go?"

"We are. I placed the IED last night. Just drove by it and I could see the antennae. I can trigger it from over a mile away. There is a neat little coffee shop that will do just nicely. Is our target time still around zero nine thirty?"

"Yes. I'll call you back at zero nine twenty-five."

As Carlos was talking, the waitress approached for his order. He left the phone in place.

"I'll have an espresso please and a blueberry scone," he said smiling at the waitress.

He then continued talking to Rick.

"Looking forward to hearing from you. This will go well."

At 0915 Danny Ochoa received a call from one of his day managers, a short stocky ex-marine by the name of Ernie Fernandez.

"Hola."

"Good morning Mr. Ochoa, this is Ernie."

"Que pasa Ernie?"

"Mr. Ochoa, there is a guy here from the DEA. He says he has information about Ernesto Garcia."

"Put him on the phone."

Danny could hear Ernie talking with the agent.

"Mr. Ochoa, he says for security reasons, he must talk with you in person."

"Did you check his identification?"

"I did. It's authentic."

Danny was silent for a moment. He had full confidence in Ernie Fernandez. Ernie shrugged his shoulders as the agent looked on.

"Okay. I'll be right down," responded Danny. He hung up the phone and starred at it for a few seconds.

"He is coming down. Would you like a coffee?" Ernie asked.

"Yes, that would be nice. How long before Mr. Ochoa will be here?"

Ernie looked at his watch.

"At this time of day…about thirty minutes."

Ernie poured the coffee and also offered the agent a donut. The agent took the coffee but turned down the donut.

"I need to make a couple of calls. I'll be in my car. What is Mr. Ochoa driving?"

"He has a new black Mercedes Sedan with gold trim. You can't miss it."

"Okay, I'll watch for him. I'll be outside."

Danny Ochoa was nearly dressed when he received the call. He finished dressing and poured a cup of fresh coffee into a Starbuck's stainless coffee mug. He screwed the top on tightly and went out the front door. Rick could see him as he exited the house. He already had Carlos on his satellite phone.

"Standby Carlos we got a target. He's alone."

Danny Ochoa started his car and drove slowly down the driveway. The gate opened automatically. Ochoa turned left as expected.

"Standby Carlos, about ten seconds. Target site is clear."

Danny Ochoa approached the stop sign. He always stopped. The police loved to harass him. He wasn't going to give them any more ammunition. Rick continued the count down.

"Five…four…three…two…one…*bingo!*"

The blast could be heard for several miles. Some of the patrons sitting close to Carlos spilled their coffee. All looked up at each other with quizzical expressions. A large plume of black smoke lifted into the sky over Coconut Grove. It looked like a mini mushroom cloud. Suddenly the power went out and people seemed to be everywhere. Carlos tried to look as surprised as everyone else. He was one of the first to speak.

"What the *hell* was that?"

One of the older patrons was quick to answer.

"Probably one of those terrorist guys. I've seen some suspicious characters living over there in a house by the park. Must be a dozen of them. They always seem to be at home. Probably dealing drugs too. I'll bet they were making bombs. One of them probably blew up in their face."

By now Carlos could hear a number of sirens. A fire truck went racing by with several firemen in full regalia. Two Miami police cars went racing by with blue lights flashing. Everyone in the restaurant was now outside looking in the direction of the smoke. Carlos finished his espresso, slipped away and headed back to his motel. No one saw him leave.

Rick had seen the blast on his satellite feed. It made an interesting pattern on his computer screen. He zoomed out to check the collateral damage. He could see the flames engulfing Ochoa's car in a staccato dance. All four tires were blazing away, putting out thick clouds of black smoke. There was a large stream of water from a broken water main shooting across the highway. To someone on the ground, it must have looked like an out of place rainbow. There were several police cars approaching from the direction of Danny's house. Another came in on the road to the north of the intersection. Within ten minutes there were three fire trucks and a couple of rescue vehicles on scene. It didn't take them long to get there. There was no activity around the rescue vehicles. That was a good sign. There was a high probability that there were no friendly casualties. The blast had put a gaping hole in the street. Ochoa's car had slid part way into the hole. One fire truck was spraying foam on the car. The fire was nearly out. A privacy wall next to the sidewalk had blown inward. It appeared that the only casualty was Danny Ochoa.

Rick decided that he had seen enough. The mission had gone well. He opened his brief case and retrieved a passport that was secured to the top underneath the lining. He brought up the Delta Airlines site on his computer and booked a flight under the name, Richard Miller. He was confirmed on Delta flight 4653 leaving Fort Walton Beach at 1540 arriving in Miami at 2046. The flight had a one hour and three minute layover in Atlanta. Rick would have a small carry-on, so the short layover wouldn't be a problem. He gave Lynn a call. She sounded winded when she answered the call.

"Hey honey, you must be working out?"

"We are. Just finished a walk and are doing some push ups."

Lynn was in great shape. Rick wished he had half the discipline that she had when it came to food and exercise. Rick had burned out from the gym a long time ago. He only worked out to be with Lynn.

"Honey, I'm flying in tonight. Can you pick me up? I will be on Delta forty-six fifty-three arriving at twenty forty-six."

"Twenty forty-six…so what time is that really?"

"Honey—pick me up at eight forty-six PM. Okay?" Lynn never did get used to, or like twenty-four hour time.

"Oh good, that's great. Brooke and I will be there. Also, I booked us at the Atlantis on Paradise Island. We leave on Wednesday and return on Sunday. Is that okay?"

"That is just fine. Brooke *is* going with us isn't she?" asked Rick.

"You really think she would stay back?"

"That was a foolish question. Can I say hi to her?"

Rick could hear Brooke in the background. They had some exercise tape on the TV.

"Hellooooo Daddy."

That meant she was happy to hear from him and had something good to say. After what they all had been through he really didn't want to hear, "Hey".

"Hellooooo Brooke," he responded.

They repeated the usual amount of times.

"I hear you got another input for your article. Is it good information?"

"It is. There are some locations listed. Whoever my *Anonymous Source* is, I believe he knows what is really going on."

"When did you tell the paper you would give them the next installment?"

"I've promised a draft to them by Friday afternoon and the smooth no later than noon on Saturday. I have most of it done now. I'm in the editing phase. It's looking good."

"I'm anxious to read it. Are you looking forward to the Bahamas?"

"What do you think? Can't wait to wear my new thong!"

Brooke loved to tease.

"Yeah…RIGHT! Your new thong…I'm looking forward to seeing you both. It will be nice to have some down time. Love you honey."

"Love you Daddy."

Brooke handed the phone back to Lynn. She and Rick said their goodbyes. Rick put the phone down and took a deep breath. A lot had happened in the past twenty-four hours. Hell, a lot had happened just in the last twelve hours. As he hung up the phone the Destin police had already cordoned off the area to the west of Silver Shells. Danny Ochoa's car was still emitting little puffs of smoke. Luis and Mickey were planning their trip to New Mexico. Sidney Bascomb hadn't shown up for work. Taylor Reese was cleaning the mud off his cowboy boots. The FBI made a positive identification on Ernesto Garcia's remains, and Ben Anderson was still trying to figure out who was on to him.

Chapter Thirty-Five
Washington DC
November 29, 2010
Monday
1100 Hours

Ben Anderson was sitting at his desk when an audible alert on his computer signaled that he had a priority message. He clicked on the email icon and his email inbox appeared on his desktop. The priority message was flagged and blinking. It was from the DEA in Miami. He opened it to find out that Danny Ochoa had been killed in a roadside bombing approximately a block from his home in Coconut Grove. The email stated that the bombing was similar to the roadside techniques used by al Qaida in Iraq. Ben read the email again. He checked the header. It was indeed from DEA, Miami. His initial reaction was a feeling of relief. Danny Ochoa had become a real pain in the ass. Ben didn't like dealing with him. Arrangements with guys like Danny Ochoa never seemed to end very well. But now as fate would have it, Ochoa was no longer a threat to him or for that matter to Sidney Bascomb. Ben's euphoria didn't last very long. He soon realized that he still had a serious problem in Virginia Beach. A problem that was now back in his court. A problem that he would have to deal with…and one that he would have to deal with *soon*. At least Sid would be relieved. It was at that very moment that he also realized he hadn't seen Sid all morning. Sid always came around during coffee break time. Sid loved his carmel macchiato and blueberry scone. They would usually head for the Starbucks at Union Station. He buzzed Sid's office. Sid's secretary, Ms. Jacobs, answered with her usual "my pants are too tight and my blouse won't button" voice.

"Mr. Bascomb's office. How may I *help* you?"

She over emphasized *help*. She would have been good back in the days of Sam Spade, especially if all you saw were her legs.

"Ms. Jacobs, Ben Anderson here. May I speak with Sid?"

"I'm sorry Mr. Anderson, but Mr. Bascomb is not in. Do you want me to take a message, or would you prefer his voice mail?"

"No. Just tell him that I called."

Sid was always on time and hardly ever took any time off, except for Christmas and New Year's. This was not like Sidney Bascomb—not at all.

"What time do you expect him?"

"I really don't know. He never said anything about taking the day off."

"Have you called him?"

"Well…no I haven't," she responded defensively.

Ben couldn't believe that she just sat there all morning without calling Sid to see if he were all right. Ask if he were sick. Ask when he was coming in. These were normal secretary concerns. But, Ms. Jacobs was not your normal everyday attention-to-detail secretary. She probably spent the morning retouching her pumped up red lips and filing her fingernails. What a bimbo. Ben couldn't understand why Sid had hired her, why he tolerated her. She wasn't even his type, and she was dumber than dirt.

"Thank you Ms. Jacobs. I'll try him at home."

As he hung up he imagined her reaching into her mouth with those long red fingernails, pulling out her gum in a long thin band, twirling it around and then sucking it back into her mouth like one long piece of spaghetti. He shook his head. Ms. Jacobs was a real piece of work.

Ben thought more about Ochoa. Ochoa had sent Ernesto Garcia to find out who the *Anonymous Source* was. Ernesto hadn't been seen since, and now Danny Ochoa was dead. Manny was supposed to be in DC, but he hadn't seen or heard from him either. Something was fishy. This whole mess started with *The Last Witness* by Ms. Brooke Ashley Morgan. Ben called Sidney Bascomb. The phone rang about six times before Sidney's answering machine came on.

"You have reached Sidney Bascomb. I am unable to come to the phone. Please leave your name, number, the date and a short message and I will call you back as soon as possible. Speak clearly after the beep."

The phone beeped at least a dozen times before the single tone. Obviously, Sidney hadn't answered his phone in quite a while. Something was not right. Ben decided to take a ride over to Sid's house.

At 1230 the traffic was not too bad. Most of the commuters were at lunch, or just ending lunch. They hadn't made the mad dash back to work yet, as if they were that excited to be back at work. It was all about being in front of the other guy. Ben headed down 395 south toward the beltway. The more he thought about Sid, the more it bothered him. The last time they had talked, Sid was such a wreck and on the brink of falling apart. The call from Danny Ochoa nearly put him over the edge. Ben headed west on 495 towards Tysons Corners. His cell phone rang. The traffic was just heavy enough that he didn't look at the caller ID.

"Ben Anderson."

"Ben, Charlie Dobson here."

"Hey Charlie, what's going on?"

"I haven't talked with you in a couple of days. I wanted to touch base with you. Is everything on schedule with Ramirez?" asked an anxious Charlie Dobson.

"I believe so. Luis and Mickey are scheduled to move him tonight. We just need to be prepared to transport him back in time for the Grand Jury."

"Is there anything I can do?"

"No. I think everything is in place."

"Ben, did you see the email on Ochoa?"

"I did."

"Will that change anything with Ramirez?"

"I don't think so, at least not from our side. As for Ramirez I suppose that's up to the Attorney General. I'm sure Ramirez knows enough about Miami drug operations, and who the other players are, to keep the Attorney General interested. Unfortunately for Ramirez, he may not end up with as sweet a deal as he may have gotten by ratting out Ochoa."

"Ben, do you think there is a drug war going on in Miami?"

"No, what makes you think there is?"

"Well, it looks like somebody took out two of Ochoa's Lieutenants."

"Ochoa's Lieutenants? What Lieutenants? What are you talking about?"

"Didn't you read it, it was in the second email?"

"No, I didn't know there was a second email. Charlie, I'm not in the office. I'm on my way out to Sidney Bascomb's. What did it say?"

"It seems that there were two guys killed in the Fort Walton Beach-Destin area that were also part of his organization. One was a guy named Ernesto Garcia, and the other one was Manny Dominguez. Hold on a second, let me bring up the email."

Ben's mind was racing. Ochoa dead. Garcia and Dominguez dead? Ben didn't like what he was thinking. Everything was pointing back to *The Last Witness* and Rick Morgan. Who the *hell* was Rick Morgan?

"Okay, here it is. Let me see. I'll paraphrase this, unless you want me to read the entire email?"

"Just give me the salient points Charlie."

Charlie Dobson read the important points in a rhythmic melody.

"Okay. They have identified a body in a car on the Eglin Reservation as that of Ernesto Garcia, a known Lieutenant of Danny Ochoa. Before positive identification was made, the FBI had been working on a theory that the body was that of a terrorist attempting to bomb Eglin Air Force Base. However, after forensic analysis, the FBI is now convinced that Garcia was, in fact, the victim of a drug related hit. Their conclusion was reinforced when it was learned that another associate of Garcia's, Manny Dominguez, had been found shot to death in a rental car in Destin, Florida. Ben, it sure looks like somebody wants to take over Ochoa's drug operation."

Ben was silent for a few seconds. He and Sid were probably the only law enforcement guys who knew that this was *not* a drug-related gang war. But he couldn't tell anyone.

"Thanks Charlie. I'll call you later."

Ben exited on Braddock Road and headed for Burke, Virginia. He tried to call Sid. He got Sid's answering machine again. Twenty minutes later he pulled into Sid's driveway and parked next to the Buick. He felt the hood. It was cold. There were leaves on the hood; a few were wedged in the windshield wipers. It was obvious that Sid hadn't driven the car at all that day. As Ben got out of his car he began to get that little sinking feeling that tells you that this is not going to turn out very well. He rang the bell. No answer. He rang it a couple more times and also knocked firmly on the door. Still no answer. He cupped his hands, put them on either side of his head and tried looking through the door's side panels. He couldn't see anything. The blinds had been drawn and there was very little light inside. Ben walked around the house to the back yard. He went through the gate and walked around the pool area to the patio sliding glass door. He looked through the door into the den. He was about to leave when he thought that he noticed something in a high wingback chair. The chair's back was toward the sliding glass door. It was in a slight angle. He looked again but couldn't make it out through the bamboo shades that were lowered, covering the entire sliding glass door. He knocked on the door. Still no answer. He tried to open it, but it was locked. He suspected that Sid had a security system, but he didn't know for sure. He was convinced that all was not well in Sid's house. Sid really sounded distraught during their last conversation. What if he did something stupid? Worse yet, what if he left a note! Ben went around the house and back to the front door. He rang the bell again. He moved back from the door and looked around by the walkway at the front of the house for those little security system signs warning a would-be burglar. There were none. It dawned on him that he hadn't even tried the front door. He knew that Sid would never leave the door unlocked. Unless, he wanted someone to have easy access…didn't want anyone breaking down the door. Ben tried the door. Down deep inside he was hoping that it was locked. Maybe Sid had a date. One that picked him up. One that was good enough to spend the night with. The door wasn't locked. He opened the door slowly and leaned inside.

"Sid? Sid, are you in there? Sid, it's Ben."

Ben raised his voice louder.

"Sid? Hello Sid?"

Ben knew this was not going to be good. He walked straight to the den. He looked over toward the high wingback chair. He could just make out part of an arm and hand on the left armrest.

"Sid?" he said cautiously. He really didn't want to look.

The wingback chair faced a large bookcase. Everything on the bookcase was neatly placed. All the taller books were positioned to the left. A stereo was on, but the music had ended. Ben moved slowly around to the front of the chair. By now he knew exactly what he was going to find. Sid had the look of a misplaced mannequin. He was slumped back in the chair, his head resting uncomfortably against the left side of the high wingback. His feet were up on an ottoman. He had on a robe and slippers. His eyes were partially open, staring at nothing. His mouth was opened just enough to give the impression that by the time he realized what he had done, it was way too late. There was an empty pill bottle on the stand next to the chair keeping company with a half empty bottle of Grey Goose. The glass next to the bottle was empty. Ben didn't have to check Sid's pulse. The blood had drained from his face. Sid had been at room temperature for a long time. He had taken the easy way out, or was it a coward's way? Either way, Sid's earthly problems were over. Ben looked around the room. There was a pen and a folded piece of paper on the coffee table. Ben's heart seemed to skip a beat. He picked up the paper. It was folded once. He opened it carefully, as if expecting something to jump out at him. He was the first to read the last words of Sidney Bascomb.

"I'm sorry for what I have done. I made some very bad choices. Choices that have consequences. I am not a strong person. I am not strong enough to spend the rest of my life in prison. To my friends, please forgive me. To my enemies, I'm sure we'll meet again. I hope God has mercy on my soul."

The note was signed Sidney A. Bascomb.

Ben was relieved that he wasn't mentioned in the note. The note would certainly raise a lot of questions. Questions that could lead back to him. Since Sid was an attention to detail kind of guy, there is no way he would have committed suicide without leaving a note.

If Ben destroyed the note, it would undoubtedly get the attention of any detective worth his salt. The DC area was loaded with talented detectives. There was no sense in creating more questions and an internal investigation that would certainly throw suspicion on the entire division. Surely there would be an internal investigation. It was bad enough that Sid had mentioned that he had made "very bad choices". Of course "bad choices" could mean almost anything. No, he had to leave the note. If anything, Ben knew to never mess with a crime scene. Ben went back outside and got into his car and called 911.

While he was waiting for the police, he called Luis Escobar. With the death of Danny Ochoa, there was now certainly no pressure to kill Paco Ramirez. In fact, there was a high probability that the US Attorney General would rescind his authorization to provide Ramirez with witness protection. Luis had already heard about Ochoa and his Lieutenants.

"Ben, I was just thinking about you. I was expecting your call."

"I take it that you have heard about Ochoa?"

"I heard about him during the morning briefing. It looks like a drug war is going on in Miami. I assume you will be transferring Ramirez to DC?"

Ben knew that if a drug war was in progress, Rick Morgan was the instigator.

"I believe, when the decision is made, DC will be Ramirez's next stop. I suppose there is a possibility that the Miami authorities will want jurisdiction. Local DAs love to grandstand. However, that decision will be made above my pay grade."

"So Ben, how long do you think we will be baby sitting this guy?"

"Probably a day or two. I'll try to find out. Maybe I can influence the process."

Ben hesitated a bit and then decided he needed to tell Luis about Sid before Luis heard it through other channels.

"Luis, there is something else I need to tell you. It looks like Sidney Bascomb committed suicide."

"Say what?" Come again."

"Sidney Bascomb committed suicide."

There was silence on the line. Neither man spoke for nearly a minute or so. Ben knew that Luis was contemplating the news, probably wondering how Bascomb's death would affect their operation. More specifically, how it would affect him personally. What were his options? Ben was the first one to break the silence.

"Luis, I will be out of the office most of the afternoon. Just so you know, I was the one who found Sid and reported the suicide. I am waiting for the police as we speak."

"Ben, did he…did he…"

Ben finished Luis's sentence.

"Leave a note? Yes, but it was benign. We will discuss that issue the next time we get together. When I receive word concerning Ramirez, you will be the first to know. I do expect the Attorney General will want him brought back to DC. My intent will be to request that you and Mickey accompany him. It will give us an opportunity to go over a few important issues."

Luis wanted to ask more questions about Sidney Bascomb. He knew that one question would lead to another, and then another. With the police on the way, he didn't want to be left hanging in mid sentence. He trusted Ben's judgment.

"Okay Ben, call me as soon as you know something."

Ben hung up just in time to hear approaching sirens. His initial thought was that it was entirely too late for sirens. Cops were like little kids. They loved to use their sirens. They were getting closer. No matter how soon they got to Sidney Bascomb's house, he was in another world…a world that was *not* a better place.

Chapter Thirty-Six
Destin, Florida
November 29, 2010
Monday
1445 Hours

In normal fall traffic it was about a twenty-minute drive to the Fort Walton Beach-Destin airport from the Silver Shells complex. The afternoon thunder bumpers were beginning to build to the west. There were already storms visible out over the Gulf of Mexico. At the moment, Rick's only thoughts were on Lynn and Brooke. He knew they were most likely enjoying the shopping in Coral Gables. There were several traffic lights on the way through Niceville. Rick was making good time. He had hit every light on green except the one coming up in front of the new Gold's Gym. As he waited for the light to change, he noticed a young man on the sidewalk. He was dressed in all black. His hair was spiked like the dorsal fin of a sailfish, and from Rick's view, he could make out several demonic tattoos that were mild compared to the numerous facial piercings. The young whatever-he-was gazed aimlessly at something on the edge of the sidewalk. The "thing" on the sidewalk must have been doing a frontal attack on demon boy's engineer boots. Demon boy danced around a little bit and then must have gotten tired of the little thing. He stomped it into oblivion with an awkward hop step. Life meant nothing to demon boy. The light changed. Rick drove on realizing that demon boy was *our* future. The American system was failing miserably, or maybe there really was a conspiracy to dumb down America. If indeed there was, it was working. Where were the parents? Who were the parents? They were probably older versions of demon boy...a balding head replacing the spikes. Within another generation, the United States would be a Third World Nation. America was certainly well on its way and the Department of

Education was making the path to Third World Nation membership inevitable. Rick made it to the airport with time to spare. He parked in the commuter's parking lot and entered the terminal.

As Rick waited to board the plane, he made a call to Carl Peterson. Carl was in his office at the old Homestead Air Force Base complex. The Gulfstream was parked on the tarmac less than one hundred yards away. Several Peterson Group employees were busy watching surveillance screens. Roland Carpenter was typing on his keyboard as he watched a Coast Guard Cutter approaching a small fishing trawler somewhere in the Gulf of Mexico. All the information was real time. Carl immediately recognized the ID from Rick's satellite phone. It was the phone that he had given to Rick.

"Hi Rick. How are you doing? I see that you have been a busy boy."

"I am doing well, and yes, Carlos and I have been very busy."

"What is next?" asked Carl sounding like a young boy experiencing his first real adventure.

Rick didn't have a formal next step. The first phase of his plan had gone without a hitch. It went so well and fast that he hadn't had time to work on phase two. He was getting mentally prepared to do just that.

"Actually, I am working on it as we speak. Are you in DC?"

"No, I'm in our South Miami office. The little war you precipitated has everybody jumping through hoops. Hell, I've got additional tasking as a result. I can keep you working for at least another three years!"

"No thanks my friend. I am happy doing the security checks. Actually I am heading your way. I'm at the Fort Walton Beach-Destin airport and will be arriving in Miami around twenty-one hundred. Maybe we can get together tomorrow?"

"That would be nice. They got the best stone crab in the world down here. Fresh each day."

It had been years since Rick had stone crab. It just wasn't the same any other place. Miami had the best. There were more one-armed stone crabs off the coast of Florida than any other place in the world.

"Carl, Brooke got another email from her *Anonymous Source*. Could your guys do an analysis of it?"

"Sure, what are you looking for?"

"Ideally, I would like to know who the *Source* is. The two emails she has received appear to be from the same individual. However, they have very different *from* addresses."

"Rick, a lot of people have more than one address. Hell, I've got a dozen or so myself."

"I understand that, but she has replied to the emails, and in both cases, she made contact with individuals that had no idea who she was or what she was talking about."

"Sounds like your *Anonymous Source* has some computer savvy. Probably spoofing someone else's email. Those things can be hard to track down, especially if your *Anonymous Source* knows someone who will provide him with company access. I'll put Roland on it."

"Thanks Carl. I need to focus on DC."

"Do you have any leads yet?" asked Carl.

"Did I mention Sidney Bascomb? I believe he will be able to provide some valuable information."

"Bascomb? Hold on a second Rick. Seems like I just saw something on someone named Bascomb.

Rick's flight began boarding. He would need to hurry since there were only about thirty passengers.

"Rick, I knew I saw something. Bascomb committed suicide."

The news of Bascomb's suicide caught Rick off guard.

"Are you sure about that? Are you sure it was Sidney Bascomb?"

"I'm sure. He was an accountant with the US Marshals. I think you will find this interesting, guess who found him?"

"Don't tell me...Ben Anderson?"

"Right on Rick. Looks like Anderson's operation had its *first* casualty, that is if you don't count Ochoa and company."

"Carl, I have to board my flight. I need to think this through. I really want Anderson to fall on his own sword, so to speak. If it's okay with you, I will call you later tonight?"

"Anytime Rick."

Rick turned off the satellite phone and boarded Delta Flight 4653.

Although Rick hadn't started to develop the second phase of his plan, in the back of his mind he knew that Bascomb would have played a prominent role. Bascomb knew all the players, and from Carlos's impression of Bascomb's intestinal fortitude, Rick knew that he and Carlos would have no trouble getting information out of him. Bascomb's suicide presented a *minor inconvenience*. As he thought about Bascomb's suicide, the flight to Atlanta went by very quickly. The weather in Atlanta was good. A slight haze hung over the city. Rick counted eleven planes in the airport traffic pattern, and those were the ones that he could see. The landing was smooth; probably an old time Air Force pilot at the controls. Rick was the third passenger to disembark. He wasted no time taking the tram to Concourse B. He stopped at Starbucks and got a regular coffee with half and half. Then he stopped at one of the newsstands and picked up a small note pad and pencil. As he arrived at his new gate, they were already boarding first class passengers. There were twelve first class seats. Rick was in seat 2B. His coffee was still hot.

With Bascomb out of the picture, Rick would have to focus on Ben Anderson. Brooke had told her dad that the *Anonymous Source* provided information that pointed to a connection in Dallas, Texas and Scottsdale, Arizona. That meant at least two more individuals were involved in Anderson's Witness Protection scheme. Rick assumed that at least one had to be a Deputy US Marshal. Up to this point he had not considered taking out a US Marshal, even one that was dirty. Nobody would care about Garcia, Dominguez or Ochoa, but the law took a dim view of one of their own being killed, even a dirty one. They would definitely send a signal that you can't kill law enforcement individuals and get away with it. However, when it came to the safety of Lynn and Brooke, no one would receive immunity from Rick Morgan. Rick thought about demon boy. Rick was different. He never was a hunter. He couldn't kill an animal. He released all his fish. He even put spiders outside the house…and he hated spiders. But people, they should know better. Rick had no remorse when it came to eliminating garbage from the top of the food chain.

The flight to Miami took off right on time. First class wasn't what it used to be, but it was still significantly better than being trapped in the middle seat in the tourist section. The flight attendant, a young man in his early thirties, was very attentive. He kept Rick supplied with well made Old Fashions. Rick wasn't used to drinking this early in the day, but he felt the necessity to make a farewell toast to the ghost of Sidney Bascomb. Bascomb was just a pencil neck geek who wanted to be accepted. His fate was most likely determined from the beginning by a doting mother who dressed him in tight little pants, suspenders and a bow tie. The kid was doomed from day one. It would have been easier with Bascomb in the picture. Rick opened the pad and began to block diagram the things he knew. He made lots of little squares, rectangles and decision blocks. He connected them with arrows that defined relationships, direction of flow, asked yes or no questions that led to different paths. No matter how he diagramed the scenario, all paths led to Brooke, and surprisingly to Rick himself. He hadn't thought of himself as a target, but realized that Ben Anderson might reach a conclusion that Rick was, in fact, the *Anonymous Source*. That put a new twist in the scenario. With Rick out of the picture, Lynn and Brooke were vulnerable. If he were Anderson, that was exactly the course of action he would take. Eliminate Rick Morgan. With that in mind, Rick began looking at a DC scenario. He would take the fight right to Ben Anderson's door.

The flight landed twelve minutes early. Rick was the first passenger off the plan. As he walked out through the gate, he immediately saw Lynn and Brooke. They were excited to see Rick and quickly joined him as he cleared the gate. The waiting passengers paid them little attention. Within fifteen minutes they were in the Cadillac that Carlos had rented for them and heading west on the Miami expressway. The traffic was heavy for that time of night. Lynn was excited about her new purse; Brooke wanted to talk about Part Three, and Rick needed to tell them that he needed to go to DC for a couple of days.

"So, how do you both like Miami?"

Lynn was first to answer

"It's a lot more crowded than the last time we were here, and everyone speaks Spanish."

"Honey, they probably speak English also."

"No they don't. You have to look for someone to speak English. Look at the signs. There are more in Spanish than English."

Brooke entered into the conversation.

"Dad, what was it you always said about destroying your enemy?"

"Divide and conquer," he responded. He didn't have to think about it.

"Well, doesn't it look like America is going down that road?"

"It does." Rick answered sadly.

Rick wanted to change the subject. He knew down deep inside that America was headed down a path of inner destruction. He could talk about the subject for hours.

"So how is your article coming?" he asked changing the subject.

"Great. The draft is complete. I talked with the paper today, and they are not only thrilled with the attention the article has gotten, but also with the increase in circulation."

"Have you heard any more from the *Anonymous Source*?"

"No, but I'm sure that I will. The paper loves the mystery that the article has created. I can't wait for the next email myself!"

Rick couldn't wait either. If the *Source's* information was accurate, he could possibly learn who the other players were. All he would need is their initials. He would then tie the initials to the locations. Tying them to Anderson and the former Mr. Bascomb would be a piece of cake.

"Honey, have you heard from Carlos?"

"He called this morning. He's seeing one of his old girlfriends. Wants you to call him when we get in."

"How's the house?"

"It's really nice. Angel has remodeled the kitchen, put in all new bathroom appliances, and travertine marble flooring throughout. It even looks like all the mattresses are new. It's really nice."

Rick exited onto Bird Road and arrived at the house thirty-six minutes after they left the airport. The house was as nice as Lynn said it was. Lynn went into the kitchen and opened the refrigerator.

"How about some dessert?"

"That would be nice."

"What would you like?"

"Surprise me. Preferably, something without caffeine. Let me give Carlos a call before it's too late."

Brooke walked into the kitchen with a draft of Part Three in her hand. She had that look on her face that said she was pleased with how it turned out.

"Dad, will you take a look at this?"

"I will, but I need to call Carlos before it's too late. I will read it with dessert, okay?"

Brooke nodded in agreement and Rick dialed Carlos. Carlos was in no position to answer the call, but he did. He was breathing heavy and it wasn't from doing push-ups, not real ones anyway.

"Rick, your timing is terrible."

"Am I interrupting something?"

"Not anymore!"

"Sorry pal. Call me tomorrow morning. I can use your tactical expertise."

"I'll call you about zero nine hundred, okay?"

"That will be fine. Which old girlfriend are you with?"

"Consuelo," he responded as he tried to catch his breath.

"I thought she was married?"

Carlos looked over at Consuelo and then turned toward the window and spoke in a low voice.

"Her husband passed away last year. She is still a beauty...and still likes me."

"Consuelo. If memory serves me, she was the career student, the one who thought *Moby Dick* was a venereal disease."

"You could forget that you know."

"Never Carlos. It is one of those little faux pas that makes life worth living. Have fun Ahab!"

Chapter Thirty-Seven
Miami, Florida
November 30, 2010
Tuesday
0900 Hours

Rick was spending the morning with Lynn and Brooke. The weather in November was usually quite nice. This November was no exception. The hurricane season was over. There was a Bermuda high stalled off the coast, which was providing a welcomed relief to the hot and humid weather of late summer. College football was in full swing. The news featured articles about the escalating price of oil, the loss of jobs, the rebuilding of the University's football program, and one particularly disturbing story about a looming drug war in Miami. There seemed to be no heir-apparent to the Ochoa drug empire. Rick was happy that neither Lynn nor Brooke spent much time reading the local section of the newspaper. They had just finished having their own cereal creation at "The Cereal Bowl" on South Dixie Highway when Rick's phone played the theme from James Bond.

"Morgan."

"Hey Rick, Captain Ahab at your service."

"Yeah right! I'm sure you have done enough *servicing* for the week."

"Not quite. Rick, I had forgotten how much I missed her. I should have married her years ago. She would have been good for me."

"Carlos, you would have been bored silly once the honeymoon ended. You do remember what happened to Captain Ahab?" asked Rick.

"Not really, but you're probably right. So where are we?"

Rick really needed to talk with Carlos in private. He didn't want to say anything that might worry Lynn and Brooke.

"We are just finishing up breakfast. I talked with Carl Peterson yesterday afternoon. He has some work for you—that's if you are interested. He sent a Statement of Work, I just happen to have it with me. Rick put his hand over the mouthpiece of the phone, and looked over at Lynn who had just finished her last spoonful of high grain cereal. Brooke was fascinated with a little two-year old that appeared to have discovered her belly button for the first time.

"Honey, is it okay if I take you guys back to Angel's, I need to drop off some papers to Carlos?"

"I have a better idea, why don't you drop us off on the Miracle Mile. You can pick us up in a couple of hours."

Shopping was always Lynn's way of expressing her displeasure, especially when she knew that Rick wasn't being totally up front with her. She knew he was hiding something but wouldn't ask him questions in front of Brooke.

"Thanks honey."

"Carlos, where is a good place for us to meet?"

"There is a coffee shop here at the Hyatt. I'll meet you there at eleven hundred. Will that work for you?"

"Are you at the Hyatt on Alhambra Plaza?"

"I am," responded Carlos.

"That will work. See you then."

Rick hung up the phone. The girls were ready. The idea of going shopping on Miracle Mile had perked them up considerably. Rick picked up the receipt as Lynn and Brooke headed to the ladies room to freshen up a bit. Rick paid the bill with cash and went back to the table and left a nice tip for the waitress. As Rick was waiting for the girls, he scanned the newspaper racks. The headlines were similar except there was a short clip on the front page of the Miami Herald about a drug war. The banner indicated that the entire article could be found in the local section starting on page B5. He searched his pockets for some change, but before he could come up with a couple of quarters, the girls were out of the ladies room and heading in his direction. They were all smiles and talking only as a mother and daughter can. It was probably best that he didn't get the paper.

"Are you ladies ready?"

"We are indeed," responded Lynn with a forced smile.

It was only a fifteen-minute drive to Miracle Mile. The strip was loaded with enough fine shops to keep Lynn and Brooke occupied for the next several hours.

"Honey, remember, cash only. Please, no credit cards! If you need to call me, use one of the pay phones. You did leave your cell phones at Angel's?"

Actually, Rick knew exactly where the cell phones were. Not only were they back at Angel's, but he had also removed the batteries. He didn't want to take any chances. He knew how easy it was to trace a cell phone.

"Don't worry, by now we know the drill."

It bothered Rick that Lynn's tone was a bit cavalier.

"Honey, I just want to make sure that no one knows that we are in Miami."

"How much longer do we have to play this game?" asked Lynn.

Rick wished that it were just a *game*. It wasn't.

"Not much longer. We are in the home stretch. By the time we get back from the Bahamas everything will be back to normal."

"I hope so."

At least Rick hoped that everything would be back to normal. Brooke jumped into the conversation. She was normally very talkative, but she hadn't been quite herself since she arrived in Destin.

"Dad, have you talked to Chris?"

"Honey, I have. He's home and is doing very well. It's still really hard for him to talk with his jaw wired shut, but he should be back to normal in a couple more weeks."

"Does he know where we are?"

"No. I told him that it would be better if he didn't know, and that I expect this whole thing will be resolved very soon."

"Dad, when this is all over will you fill us in on what you and Carlos have been doing?"

Rick knew that he would never tell she or Lynn everything.

"Sure honey, just don't worry about anything. I'll meet you guys here in a couple of hours. Call me at one—okay?"

"Okay. I love you Dad, say hi to Carlos."

Rick made a left turn heading west on Coral Way. He remembered a time when there was nothing but empty fields along the stretch of road with the exception of a few auto junk yards and a peripheral business or two that didn't meet the zoning requirements of the business areas. The last time he was on Coral Way was back in the nineteen sixties. He had spent an interesting night at the Coral Way drive-in watching "Godzilla meets Rodan". The only thing he remembered about the movie was its name. In those early days you could shoot a canon down Coral Way without fear of hitting anything. Miami had changed…really changed. Rick wasn't sure that it had changed for the best. He was less than a mile from the Hyatt Regency. He pulled in at 1052 and parked next to the dumpster. Carlos was sitting out front at a wrought-iron table with a coral top that was shaded by a large Banyan tree. He was nursing an espresso as he checked out the local beauties. He hadn't noticed Rick.

"Looking for a new crew, Captain?"

"Funny man. I *am* very happy with my First Mate, thank you. I assume things went well in Destin?"

"They did. Now it is time to focus on Anderson."

"Have you got a plan?" asked Carlos as he leaned in closer to Rick.

"Not quite. I did have a good starting point, but unfortunately there is a new wrinkle. Sidney Bascomb committed suicide. At least that is the preliminary conclusion."

"Seriously? Bascomb's dead? Did I scare him that badly?"

"I think we can safely conclude it was a combination of your visit compounded by his overwhelming fear of Danny Ochoa."

Carlos finished his espresso and signaled the waiter for two more.

"Rick, Bascomb was weak. I should have taken the opportunity to press him for more information. I probably could have found out who the other players were."

"Carlos, I think he would have become very suspicious. Anyway, it's too late now. Bascomb is history. The flight here gave me an opportunity to think about another course of action. I still believe we have the upper hand, and as long as we stay on the offensive, we can maintain control of the situation."

"So if I am reading you correctly, we are going to take the battle to Anderson!"

"Almost to him. I think we should make our stand in Virginia Beach. We get him or his people there…on our territory. They will need to find some place to stage from. Once we mark them, they become the prey and we are the hunters."

"How are you going to get them to Virginia Beach?"

"By making Anderson think that Brooke is back there."

"What if he sends a couple of goons?"

"I thought about that. I think if he sends anyone, it will be one of his own guys. He would be foolish to hire someone, bring in a stranger, possibly someone he would have to deal with later. He's no dummy. No, I think he'll send the guy or guys that do his dirty work."

"Rick, since he doesn't know where Brooke is, how will he know that she is back in Virginia Beach?"

"If I were him, I'd be watching the airlines, checking her credit card transactions and monitoring her cell phone calls. Remember, he has no idea that you flew her to Miami. For all he knows she's still in Destin…keeping a low profile. I made sure that neither she nor Lynn used their credit cards or cell phones since leaving Destin."

"Rick, why don't we just take out Anderson? You always said that if you kill the head, the arms would die. Wouldn't that solve the whole problem?"

"I don't believe it would in this case. I think we would lose our tactical advantage. Our strength still lies in the fact that we are certain Anderson is the leader. He's in charge. He's the brain behind the witness scheme. I suspect that he is one arrogant son-of-a-bitch who will put his own survival and reputation above any of his gang members. To save his own skin, he will sacrifice them in a New York second. No Carlos, I think he will send his guys as soon as he believes Brooke is back in Virginia Beach. Once we take them out, he will be alone. He'll have nowhere to go and nowhere to hide. He'll be ours."

Carlos thought about Rick's strategy. He finished the espresso and took a long look around the restaurant. It had filled to capacity without him even noticing. He normally noticed everything.

"So you want me to go to Virginia Beach?"

"Both of us will go to Virginia Beach. We can fly up there early tomorrow morning and get everything set up. Do you know a female we can use to impersonate Brooke?"

Carlos thought for a moment. A slight smile came over his face.

"I do. Do you remember Ann Peters?"

"Anya, the little blonde that beat the crap out of you in Sigonella?

"I see you remember her! responded Carlos shaking his head. "Let me make a call. I believe she's living in Northern Virginia. Last I heard she left the *company* and started a security consulting business. She's making a bundle of bucks teaching corporate executives how to stay alive overseas. Might have to give her a few dollars," he added.

"How old is she?" asked Rick.

"She's in her early fifties. She used to be in great shape. She could easily pass for mid forties. With a blonde wig, and a little distance, she could pass for Brooke."

"Why did she beat the crap out of you?"

Carlos shook his head again.

"Let me see if I can locate her. Maybe Carl is still in contact with her," responded Carlos. He didn't answer Rick's question.

"You try your sources and I will give Carl a call. When we get to Virginia Beach and feel comfortable with everything, I'll use Brooke's credit card at one of the grocery stores. Hopefully, Anderson will get a hit on her transaction and fall into our trap."

"Hopefully? Rick, you always told me that *hope* wasn't a strategy."

"It isn't Carlos, but at this point, Anderson has got to be sweating bullets. He can't afford to let Brooke publish the next installment of *The Last Witness*. I am counting on the fact that he has to be desperate. He's got to buy time, and the only way to do that is to go after Brooke. He knows that if he can stop her, he stops the articles."

"But Rick, what about the *Anonymous Source*? If Anderson is as smart as you think he is won't he realize that even with Brooke out of the picture…he's still got a real problem with the *Anonymous Source*?"

"That is true. But he has to take things one-step at a time. And Carlos, I am not going to take any chances with Brooke's life. Besides, there is a strong possibility he may think I am the *Anonymous Source*. At this point, he's probably figuring on taking us both out."

The waiter came over and asked if they would like lunch. It was nearly 1300. Rick told him that they were about to leave.

"Rick, we could fly up this afternoon. The weather is good."

"I better spend the rest of the day with Lynn and Brooke. I'll get Carl to give me a call later and request that I attend a meeting for him in DC. Lynn won't like it since I'm supposed to be retired. But, she won't argue. I'll take a cab and meet you at the airport. What time do you want to take off?"

"Let's shoot for zero six hundred. That will get us in Virginia Beach around 1130."

"Okay my friend. Say 'hello' to Consuelo."

As Rick was walking toward the car, his phone rang.

Chapter Thirty-Eight
Washington, DC
November 30, 2010
Tuesday
1230 Hours

As Rick Morgan was meeting with Carlos Garcia, Ben Anderson was reading a priority message on his computer from the Attorney General's office that instructed him to move Paco Ramirez to the Federal Court House in Washington, DC. The message came at a good time. Ben really needed to talk with Luis and Mickey. Escorting Ramirez provided an ideal opportunity for them to get together under normal working conditions, plus it would be on the government's nickel. Ben had spent most of Monday afternoon with various law enforcement officers and the Burke Medical Examiner and Coroner. An Internal Affairs representative from the US Marshals came out to ensure that proper police procedures were observed. The preliminary investigation did not find any evidence suggesting that Sidney Bascomb's death was anything but a suicide.

Ben had known Sidney for nearly twelve years. As he reflected on their relationship, Ben realized that he had never done anything with Sid on a social level. Sid kept to himself. He enjoyed his books, classical music and nightly solitude. Sid was a frail individual who was never the same since the telephone call from Ernesto Garcia. The only good news in all of this was that Ms. Jacobs would be reassigned. She was a major waste of air. Hopefully he wouldn't have to see her waddling up and down the hallways. Ben re-read the priority email and forwarded it to Luis Escobar. Ten minutes later he followed up the email with a phone call.

"Ben, I'm reading your email as we speak."

"Good. I need you to schedule the transfer as soon as possible. I would like to see you and Mickey in the air later today."

"I'll check the flight schedules. Are we still limited to commercial flights?"

"Yes, from a budget perspective we can charge Homeland Security under the Air Marshal Program. I'll alert the safe house just in case they decide to put him there first. I'll give you directions where to go when you are leaving the airport. I'm not a hundred percent sure what the Attorney General's office plans to do with Ramirez, but I'd bet a month's pay that Miami is lobbying real hard to take him back to their jurisdiction. Until we hear something, we'll follow normal protocol."

Ben didn't give a rat's ass what happened to Paco Ramirez. It was because of Ramirez that Sidney Bascomb was dead. It was also because of Paco Ramirez that Ernesto Garcia, Manny Dominguez and Danny Ochoa were dead, although no one but he and Rick Morgan knew that.

Coral Gables, Florida, Hyatt Regency 1330 Hours

Carlos Garcia went back up to his room in the Hyatt Regency and looked through his duffle bag for his address book. The entire book was in a code that Carlos had used as a kid. It consisted of symbols created from two tic-tac-toe grids and two large X's. One of the tic-tac-toe grids had a dot in each of the spaces, and one of the large X's also had a dot in each of the four spaces. There were a total of twenty-six spaces, one for each letter of the alphabet. Only Carlos knew the method he used to place the letters on the grids, and only he knew how many times he changed the code. His address book looked like a strange language. For example if the letter M were in the center of the tic-tac-toe the letter M would be represented by a square. As Carlos looked for Ann Peter's number, he decided that one day he would hand his address book to Roland Carpenter and see just how good the kid was. Carlos dialed the number he had recorded several years earlier for Ann Peters. The phone rang at least six times. Carlos was about to hang up when she answered the phone.

"I can't believe you are still alive. Where the hell are you Garcia?" she answered as if it were just yesterday that they had talked.

"Nice to hear from you too Ms. Peters. It is still Peters?" Carlos asked.

"It is and it always will be!" So what are you up to?"

Carlos was surprised to hear that she was still single. She was a very attractive woman with light brown hair and baby blue eyes. She had great discipline and always found time to workout at least four times a week.

"Do you remember Rick Morgan?" Carlos asked.

"Of course I do. How could I forget Sigonella and the time I whipped your butt. If he hadn't intervened, you'd still be sitting down to pee."

"I hope that wasn't the only highlight in your career."

"I know you didn't call for a rematch. What's up Garcia?"

Carlos gave Ann a rundown starting with *The Last Witness*, the *Anonymous Source*, Danny Ochoa and his guys, Ben Anderson, the suicide and the attempted attacks on Brooke. He then briefly outlined Rick's plan to trap Anderson and his men, and use her to impersonate Brooke.

"Alright count me in. I have one thing to finish here. I can drive down tomorrow afternoon."

"Thanks Ann. I'll owe you one."

"No you won't. My company will bill you. My fee is four hundred dollars an hour. Friends are friends, and business is business. When I have to wear a gun, it's business."

"No problem Ms. Peters. I'll call you when we get in and let you know where to meet us. Drive carefully," he said sounding like he really didn't mean it.

"One other thing, can you have Rick send a picture of his daughter? He can send it to this phone number."

"I'll let him know. I am sure he can and will."

"Tomorrow Garcia."

Carlos was relieved that Ann was available and willing to help. He had worked with her on several covert operations in Europe. Her real name was Anya Petrov. She was born in Russia. English was her second language, although there was no hint of an accent. She was an expert in small arms, and at five foot five inches tall and somewhere around one hundred and twenty-five pounds, she could take down a two hundred pound man in about five seconds. She knew all the pressure points and had no problem grabbing a guy by the balls and squeezing until he passed out. Carlos knew that first hand…literally. If it weren't for Rick, Carlos would indeed, still be walking funny. After Sigonella, Carlos had a new found respect for Anya Petrov. After Rick rescued him, Rick reminded him that the name Anya meant "Grace of God". You wouldn't have known it from her grip! Just then he remembered that Rick was going to give Carl Peterson a call. He dialed Rick and told him that Ann was on board.

"Rick, can you phone her a picture of Brooke?"

"Sure, what is her number?"

Carlos gave Rick the number and told him that he would see him at the airport at 0600.

South Miami, Le Boudoir Restaurant, 1315 hours

At 1315 Rick met Lynn and Brooke at Le Boudoir on Miracle Mile. They had already ordered Hi Tea for three. Trophy wives, who were enjoying a day out on the town while their sugar daddies were busy making millions trading commodities, occupied most of the tables. They sounded like a flock of geese. There were very few men, and those that were there had long since retired. They wore gold Rolex's and Patek Philippe watches. All the men wore cotton trousers and silk shirts opened down to the third button, including Rick who was feeling out of place with his paltry Rolex Submariner, except Rick always wore an undershirt. The tea was excellent and the French pastries were, as one would expect from a French pastry chef. Even the French waiters were unusually hospitable, and they were actually French. Rick gave Lynn an *I love and miss you kiss* that lingered on her lips. Even after thirty-nine years of marriage there was still that little spark. They would always have that spark. He hugged and placed a light kiss on Brooke's forehead.

"So how are my beautiful ladies? How are the shops on Miracle Mile?"

"They are very nice…and very expensive," responded Lynn as she purposely moved the medium-sized bag with her foot.

Both Lynn and Brooke were good shoppers. Lynn never bought anything to impress other people. She could care less about brand names. She bought things because she needed them and liked them, and she never bought anything that wasn't on sale.

"Only one? If you need more cash, I have more cash."

"This is fine right here. We really don't need much of anything. It was just fun walking down the strip and watching the shoppers. How was your meeting with Carlos?"

"It was good, I think that he is going to go to work for Carl Peterson."

Brooke finished a silver dollar sized cream puff. She wiped a little bit of cream from the corner of her mouth and placed the napkin back in her lap. She smiled at her dad. Although she seemed to be detached, she wasn't.

"Dad, I have been thinking, maybe I should back off from *The Last Witness*."

"Honey, why would you want to do that? This could be the big break that you have been waiting for."

"Big break? Dad, it's not worth it if something were to happen, especially to you or Mom."

"Nothing's going to happen to me or Mom…or to *you*," said Rick reassuringly.

Rick placed special emphasis on *you*.

"That is a promise, and you know I have always kept my promises," he added.

"I know Dad. Please don't take offense, but you're not as young as you used to be."

"Honey, believe me, I can take care of myself. Don't be fooled by the movies. There are guys out there a lot older than me doing covert operations, and doing it quite well."

"Dad I hope so. Mom and I know what you and Carlos are doing. We saw the news and what happened to that guy on the Eglin Reservation.

We also saw a report about another guy killed in a parking lot next to the Silver Shells complex. And I remember Carl Peterson."

Kids are always a lot smarter than parents realize. And, they are certainly a lot more observant.

"Dad, I can remember Mom crying. I used to get in bed with her and we would just cuddle together, wondering if you were coming home. She never knew where you were or what you were doing, but I knew. I knew that you were more than a Naval Officer. I've known it from the time I was twelve years old."

Rick took a healthy swallow of tea. He looked fondly at both Lynn and Brooke. He knew that someday he would be having this conversation. He had hoped it wouldn't be this soon. However, this was not the time or the place.

"I want you both to know that when this is all over, and it will be soon, we will sit down and have a long family talk. A talk that must remain our secret. So please, trust my judgment this one last time… okay?"

Both Lynn and Brooke gave a reluctant nod of approval. Lynn had tears in her eyes, tears that Rick had seen before. Tears that he knew he would be wiping away in just a few days.

"Brooke, promise me that you will keep working on *The Last Witness*."

"I will, but please be careful."

Rick smiled.

"Honey, maybe someday you can write several novels on *The Adventures of Rick Morgan*," he responded holding up both arms and making a muscle.

"Those are the stories I have always wanted to hear. You tell them Dad, and I'll write them," she said with a big smile.

Rick looked over at Lynn. From the look on her face he could see that she was somewhat content. However, he knew that long ago she had resolved herself to the fact that she couldn't change his mind once it was made up.

"Lynn, Carlos and I need to fly to DC tomorrow and meet with Carl."

"Do you have to go tomorrow?" she asked her face showing disappointment.

"I do if we want to keep our vacation plans."

"What time are you leaving?"

"Early, I'll take a cab. I don't want you to have to drive in the morning traffic. Honey, this will be the last time. I promise."

Lynn wasn't sure where Rick was going. Maybe he *was* going to DC, but likely it was someplace else. If he did tell her where he was really going, it would probably be the first time. Even after bearing all, she knew Rick was back into character. She just had to trust him.

"Honey, I'm going to give you some more cash. The cell phones are at Angel's. I took the batteries out. If you need to get in touch with me, call my satellite phone from Angel's home phone. Otherwise, just have fun. No one knows that you guys are here, and I don't want them to know."

"Okay, but call me each day at Angel's."

"I will. Are you both ready to head out of here, or do you want to look around some more?"

"Dad, lets go back and play some Nines."

"That sounds like a winner to me."

They left Le Boudoir at 1445 and headed back to Angel's. Although they had gotten a lot out in the open, Rick could feel the trepidation in the air.

Chapter Thirty-Nine
Washington, DC
November 30, 2010
Tuesday
1730 Hours

Ben Anderson was moving at a snail's pace in heavy traffic on the George Washington Turnpike. He was certain that there had to be an accident up ahead for traffic to be moving this slowly. Tuesdays weren't usually this bad, but the Washington area rubber neckers were notorious. Ben had endured a particularly long day involving a myriad of police interviews. The questions were mundane.

"Was Mr. Bascomb having any personal problems?"

"Did he gamble?"

"Was he dating anyone?"

"Have you noticed any changes in his personality?"

Ben found himself mouthing the next question before it was asked. These people must use a correspondence handbook that they ordered off the back of a matchbook. The real question:

"Was he doing anything illegal that you know about that would make him take his life?"

And, if you answer that question with a 'yes' you can kiss you career and ass goodbye. How infantile. The only worse questions were from those moronic onsite news reporters who ask some poor guy who has just lost his entire family in a house fire:

"How do you feel?"

The entire floor seemed to be in mourning except for Ms. Jacobs. She had no problem expressing her *professional* view that Sidney Bascomb was a time bomb waiting to explode. She was obviously an armchair psychologist who had been educated by Ann Landers, Oprah Winfrey and Dr. Phil. Sidney's office was shut up tighter than a drum.

There was yellow crime tape across the top, middle and bottom of the door. There was also a seal across the doorjamb that was signed by the Director. Ms. Jacobs was working out of an adjacent office until all of Sidney Bascomb's files could be reviewed and released. He would be glad when she and her cheap perfume were gone. Ben was going over everything in his mind when his cell phone rang. It was Luis Escobar.

"Luis, did you schedule a flight?" he asked without a greeting.

"Ben, we're already on the ground in Chicago. In fact our flight is about to board. We'll be on American Airlines flight twenty-three fifty-two arriving Dulles at twenty forty-five."

"Great. I'm going to have a couple of our guys meet you and take Ramirez to Fairfax. I'll pick you and Mickey up. Did you happen to make a reservation?"

"No, we didn't have time. We expected to stay at the safe house."

"No, don't do that. I'll get you both a reservation at the Marriott at Tysons Corner. The Attorney General's Office is still dicking around with the Miami authorities. However, I expect that Miami will win this one. Does Ramirez know what is going on? Did you tell him anything about Ochoa?"

"We told him on the way to the airport. I'm not sure if he was relieved or scared shitless. He was quiet the rest of the way. He hasn't said much at all."

"I'm betting that a couple of Dade County officers are already on their way to DC."

"Ben, do you really think the Feds will give him up that easily?"

"It's a matter of who can get the biggest bang out of this guy. Right now there is not a whole lot he can give the Feds. They'll sit back and wait for the fallout. I don't think they want to spend another dime on him. I'm sure we'll lose him to Miami."

"You are probably right about that. We'll see you about twenty-one hundred."

Ben put his cell phone on the seat and thought about Ramirez. He was the only top Ochoa Lieutenant left. He still had a lot of information that he could bargain with. Miami probably wanted him back, so they could use him as bait. Somebody needed to let Ramirez know what his options were before he was dangled like a worm on a hook. Ramirez's life expectancy was less than that of a mayfly.

There was an accident, but it had been removed well off the highway. There was still one police car on the side of the road with his light on that was the focus of the rubber neckers. Ben was convinced that these local cops parked their cars close to the highway on purpose. If they had to work the commute crowd, the commuters would pay the price. For Ben, there was no rush to get home. Tuesday was Carol's bridge night. She was having dinner with the girls at the country club. Ben had answered enough questions; he needed a couple of hour's solitude and a stiff drink before picking up Luis and Mickey.

Flight 2352 boarded on time. Although Paco Ramirez had his coat placed neatly over his handcuffs, most of the passengers were very much aware that a prisoner was on board. The trio was assigned to row fifteen seats D, E and F. Mickey took the window seat. Luis had the aisle seat. A little girl in row fourteen stood up on her seat and smiled at Paco. Her mother pulled her down and told her to mind her manners. Paco said his first words since he was told that Ochoa was dead.

"How did Danny die?"

Luis really didn't want to strike up a conversation. But, what the hell, he probably wouldn't see Ramirez again.

"He was killed by a roadside bomb."

"A roadside bomb. You are serious?" asked Ramirez a puzzled look on his face.

"Yes."

"What about Ernesto Garcia and Manny Dominguez?"

"Ernesto's car blew up with him in it, and Dominguez was shot in the head by an unknown assailant in Destin."

"So you guys really think this is drug related?"

"You tell me Paco?"

Ramirez was silent for several minutes. Luis glanced at him out of the corner of his eye. Mickey seemed to pay no attention at all. He was locked onto something outside the plane. Paco's face indicated that he was contemplating the hits on his friends. The flight attendant began going over the emergency procedures as the plane was pushed back from the gate. Ramirez spoke without looking at either Luis or Mickey.

"I don't think this is drug related."

"What makes you think it isn't?"

"Our only real competition, or you might say *fear*, was from the Jamaican Posse. But a roadside bomb is not their method. They would rather chop off your head and leave it on a pole; make an example for others to see. They are brutal. They wouldn't take the time to use a roadside bomb. Besides, they wouldn't know how. A machete is much cheaper."

Luis didn't answer Ramirez. He suspected that the Miami authorities probably came to the same conclusion, but, since there was no collateral damage, they wouldn't waste any resources looking for the party who was responsible. Paco never said another word during the flight. The plane landed five minutes early. Luis, Paco and Mickey were allowed to disembark before the rest of the passengers. Ben Anderson and two Deputy Marshals, Williamson and Justice, met them in the boarding area. The Deputies signed for Paco. As he left, he turned and gave a slight smile in Luis's direction. It was a *goodbye* smile.

Ben, Luis and Mickey headed East on the Dulles Access Road. It was a short drive to the Tysons Corner Marriott. The traffic at 2130 was minimal.

"So how was your flight? Did Paco give you any trouble?"

Luis answered before Mickey had a chance to say anything.

"It was a quick flight. Paco didn't say much, only that he thought the hits on Ochoa, Garcia and Dominguez were not drug related."

"Not drug related huh. What makes him think that?"

"Mainly the roadside bomb," responded Luis.

"Well, he's probably right about that."

"Ben, what about the note that Sidney left? Are we in the clear?"

The mention of a note got Mickey's attention. Luis had said nothing to Mickey about the suicide note. He knew that Mickey would have a million questions. None of Luis's answers would have satisfied Mickey's concerns.

"The note was basically generic. Sid didn't mention any names, he just indicated that he had made some bad choices, choices that could land him in jail."

Mickey was paying very close attention and spoke before Luis had a chance.

"That was it? I don't like the part about jail. That will make a stronger investigation. They will be looking at all his contacts, his records. Do you think he left a paper trail?"

"Mickey, calm down. They have just started the investigation. Besides, bad choices could mean anything. He may have had his faults, but he was a good accountant. All his records will look the same."

"But what about *our* witnesses?"

"Mickey, don't worry. Witnesses come and go. Once they become self-sufficient they're out of the program. Some of ours just went out a little earlier. That's all."

"Ben, I hope you're right," responded Mickey.

Ben knew that it would be almost impossible for anyone to find anything out of the ordinary with Sidney's records. He was meticulous.

"I'm right about Sidney Bascomb. Unfortunately, we have bigger problems than that. This thing with *The last Witness* is about to bite us in the ass if we don't do something, and do it real soon. The next article is scheduled to come out this Sunday, and if Ms. Morgan is true to form she is going to provide initials with the locations."

Luis started to speak, but Ben interrupted him.

"Hold your thought. We're here. Let's get you guys checked in and we can finish this conversation in the lounge. I'm sure at this point we could all use a drink."

The check-in was routine. Mickey went up to the room and Ben and Luis went into the lounge and took a booth in the corner. There were several couples and one foursome at the tables. Three guys were at the bar watching replays on ESPN. Ben and Luis ordered two bottles of Samuel Adams while they waited for Mickey.

"Ben, are we going to have trouble with this thing?"

"I *don't* think so."

Ben's response was diffident, and Luis knew it.

"I think we need to follow protocol to the letter. Answer all questions to the best of our knowledge, and do our job. Don't forget, witnesses are leaving the program all the time."

Just then, Mickey entered the room and was looking everywhere but in Ben and Luis's direction. Ben stood up and Mickey gave a little shrug and joined them. The waiter came over.

"I'll have what they're having," said Mickey.

The waiter didn't say anything and headed back toward the bar. Mickey entered the conversation.

"Ben, you were saying something about the next article."

"Yes I was. If the next article contains initials, it wouldn't take a whole lot of police-work to cross-check those initials with the two locations she provided in her second article. Taking that a step further, I don't think it would be too difficult to tie that information to a particular Witness Protection team."

"So what do we do?" asked Luis.

Ben took a long swallow of beer. He put the bottle on the table. His expression was telling. It was a "what the hell do you think we have to do" kind of look.

"We have to stop Ms. Morgan from delivering the next article."

Both Mickey and Luis took long drinks. They also knew what had to be done. Ben signaled the waiter for another round.

"Ben, doesn't this just delay the inevitable? What about this so called *Anonymous Source*? How do we find him…or her for that matter? Do you have any idea who the source is?" asked Luis.

"It could be her father, although I'm not one hundred percent sure."

"Ben, if not him, who could it be? You know it's not me or Mickey. We have too much to lose. Hell, we've committed capital crimes. Could it have been Sid?"

Ben had thought about Sid, but Sid wouldn't have brought suspicion on his own head. He would never have taken that chance. No, Sid fell apart when Danny Ochoa entered the picture. Sid was scared to death of what Ochoa was capable of doing.

"Anything is possible, but I am certain he is not the *Anonymous Source*."

Luis had a pensive look on his face.

"What about Reese?" he asked.

"Reese is a possibility, but what reason would he have. He makes a lot of money for digging holes. He helped me come up with this scheme to start with."

"Ben, there's nobody left. What about Charlie Dobson?" asked Luis.

"I thought about Charlie. He's always wondered how I could afford a home in McClean. He's a bit envious. But, how would he know anything. He'd be guessing at best, and nobody is that good. I have never given him any reason to suspect anything."

All three took a drink of their beers as if being choreographed by a hidden director. The three guys at the bar were cheering a three-year-old Baltimore Orioles game. Mickey finished his bottle and confirmed what all were silently thinking.

"It has to be her father…but how did he happen onto that kind of information?"

Chapter Forty
Tyson's Corner
December 1, 2010
Wednesday
0800 Hours

Ben Anderson, Luis Escobar and Mickey McGuire met for breakfast at the restaurant inside the Marriott. All three had the night to think about what had to be done. All three knew *exactly* what *had* to be done. Time was of the essence. As they dined on eggs over easy, pancakes, home fries, bacon, toast, jelly and freshly brewed coffee, Ben clearly addressed their situation.

"Listen guys, if we don't stop Ms. Morgan from publishing the next article our asses will be in a major sling. There is no clever way to do this, but to go in, take her out, and make the scene look like a robbery that went terribly wrong."

"Ben, have you thought about hiring someone to do this?" asked Luis.

"I thought about it, but then we have *someone else* to deal with."

Without looking up or lifting an eyebrow, Mickey spoke through a half-full mouth of pancakes that made him sound like a punch drunk fighter.

"We could just waste the guy when he's done."

The veins in Ben's forehead signaled his inner struggle with Mickey's unsophisticated solution to what Ben perceived as a much greater problem. There were times Ben wondered how Mickey had ever qualified to be a Deputy Marshal. Luis and Mickey continued to eat breakfast. Mickey's head was still down close to his plate as if he were watching to make sure that nothing escaped. Ben decided that he owed Mickey an answer.

"I believe we would be taking an unnecessary chance if we try to hire someone to do our dirty work. And besides that, we could walk into a sting operation. Hell, we set up those kind of stings ourselves. No, we need to take care of this on our own."

Luis moved around in his chair. His body language suggested that he was somewhat uncomfortable. He took a bite of toast and jelly and then chased it down with a pretty good slug of coffee. He put his cup down and lightly wiped his mouth before he spoke.

"Ben, I have no trouble knocking off these witness bums, but an innocent girl…that doesn't set very well with me."

Ben may have agreed in principle with Luis, but it was a moot point. Their butts were on the line. Deputy US Marshals didn't do well in prison.

"Guys, it's simple, it's them or us; and who the hell do you think killed Ochoa, Garcia and Dominguez?"

With that comment, Ben got their attention. It was obvious from their expression that Ben had made a salient point. One that shed new light on the situation.

"Okay, you make a good point Ben. I will go along with this, but I prefer that Mickey takes out the girl. I have no problem eliminating her father."

Ben looked at Mickey who was on his last giant forkful of pancake. Nothing had escaped his plate.

"Mickey, are you okay with that?"

"I got no problem with that. Let's do it and get it over with!" he answered showing no emotion.

With that, all three had finished breakfast. A waiter came over and began clearing the table. Ben held out his left hand, palm up, and pretended to write on his hand signaling that he was ready for, and wanted, the check.

"She and her dad are staying in Destin, Florida. I have their address. I need you guys to get on the next available flight to either Pensacola or Fort Walton Beach. We really don't have a lot of time here."

Ben purposely didn't say anything about Brooke's mother. Luis already expressed the fact that he didn't like taking out innocent civilians. However, Mickey had no conscience. He could have taken out Mother Teresa, and had no remorse.

"Why don't you guys get your things and check out while I look up the flights?"

As the waiter approached the table with the bill, Luis and Mickey got up and headed for their rooms. Ben signed the bill, took his credit card and went to the information desk where he asked for the telephone numbers of Delta, American, Southwest and Trans AM. He started with Delta.

Chesapeake Regional Airport, Chesapeake, VA 1050 Hours

Carlos rolled in on his final approach to the Chesapeake Regional Airport. The flight from Miami was uneventful and refreshing. It gave he and Rick time to revisit the events of the past couple of weeks. Turning on base leg, Rick read off the landing checklist.

"Fuel Selector."
"Landing Gear Level."
"Landing Gear Light."
"Mixture."
"Propeller."
"Wing Flaps."
"Airspeed."
"Elevator Trim."

It was the first time in a long time that somebody had actually gone through the landing checklist item by item. In fact, Carlos couldn't remember when he had put his flaps down in increments. They touched down at exactly 1050. The weather had been excellent for flying. A strong Bermuda high was stalled well off the coast. It provided a strong tailwind for the entire flight. The weather in the Tidewater area was quite typical of early December. It was cool with only forty-five percent humidity. Carlos touched down right at the numbers. He used aerodynamic breaking to slow the aircraft. He was easily able to pull off at midfield. They could see a crowd of people waiting their turn to go skydiving. It certainly was a clear day for it. Carlos taxied the plane into the space next to a Cessna 310. One of the linemen, a well-tanned Norwegian with a name patch that identified him as Olaf, was eager to chock the wheels. He recognized Carlos. Rick and Carlos got out of the plane and retrieved the overnight bags that Carlos had strapped firmly into the empty passenger seats. Rick gave a generous tip to Olaf who was already in the process of cleaning bugs off the leading edge of the wings. Olaf seemed out of place. Rick wondered what had brought him to Chesapeake. He didn't ask. They got into Carlos's SUV and headed out of the airport. Carlos made a right turn onto West Road heading toward Route 17. Once on 17 North, it was a short drive to the ramp for 64 West toward Richmond. They had made it there in less than fifteen minutes. There was hardly any traffic. As Rick and Carlos turned onto 64 West, Carlos's cell phone rang. At first he didn't recognize the caller ID, and then realized it was Anya, or as she liked to be called, Ann Peters.

"Carlos here."

"Hello Garcia. I was able to get on the road early this morning, I'm just three miles west of the Hampton tunnel. Where do you want to meet?"

"Are you ready for lunch, or just a snack?"

She didn't have to think about it for very long. Her response was almost immediate.

"I'm hungry. I could eat a big juicy steak."

"Raw or cooked?" asked Carlos.

"Funny, Garcia."

"You know Ann, after all these years, you could call me Carlos."

"Garcia is more…condescending don't you think?"

"Okay, have it your own way. We'll meet you at Ruth's Chris Steak House."

Carlos looked over at Rick as he mentioned the name of the restaurant. Rick nodded in agreement and gave quick thumbs up. Both he and Carlos were ready for a substantial meal. The coffee and lemon biscotti breakfast didn't go very far. It had worn off a couple of hours earlier.

"Ann, do you remember how to get to Pembroke Mall?"

"I do, but just in case, refresh my memory."

"Stay on 64 East until you come to 264. Take 264 East toward the beach. Take the second Pembroke exit. That will head you in the direction of the mall area. After you go across the railroad tracks, turn right at the light. Dick's Sports will be on your right. Take the second left and you will see Ruth's Chris Steak House ahead on your left. Park anywhere you find a space. There is a parking garage if you need it. We should be there in about thirty minutes. You're probably the same distance away as we are. Did you get all that?"

"I recorded it Garcia. Is Rick with you, or is he going to meet us there?"

"He's with me. We just flew in from Florida."

"Say 'hi' to Rick. See you in thirty Garcia, and by the way, I drive better than you!" she said as she hung up.

Carlos turned to Rick.

"She says, 'say hi to Rick'. She calls you by your first name. She calls me Garcia. She's a fucking trip!"

Ruth's Chris Steak House, Virginia Beach, VA 1145 Hours

Rick and Carlos were sitting at the bar when Anya Petrov, a.k.a. Ann Peters, walked into the foyer. Neither of them had seen her in many years. With the sunlight as a backdrop, she had an angelic glow outlining her as she entered the restaurant. She was obviously still in very good shape. As she got closer, Rick was amazed at how much she resembled Brooke. Rick had sent her a current picture of Brooke, and Anya had captured her overall look to a tee. She really could pass for Brooke. Even close-up. She immediately recognized Rick and Carlos. She walked up, pulled out a stool, threw her bag on the bar and gave Rick a warm hug and cheery hello. Carlos looked on wondering if she would hug him or punch him in the gut. Just in case, he began tightening his stomach muscles, and squeezed his thighs together. He looked like he was holding his breath. Carlos still had no idea what had come between the two of them in Sigonella.

"Rick, you haven't changed much at all. How long has it been?"

"Fifteen…maybe twenty years?"

"You are looking good. How is Lynn?"

"You must need glasses Ms. Peters. Lynn is doing very well. Thank you for asking."

"Please, call me Ann."

She looked over in Carlos's direction. Carlos tightened his stomach muscles again. He was bracing for the punch. Rick couldn't tell if she were looking at him or through him.

"Garcia, I know *you* haven't changed one bit…have you?"

"I guess not Ann."

"Ms. Peters to you Garcia," she said and it was obvious that she meant it.

She signaled the bar tender and requested a Sam Adams Dark.

"I need to use the ladies room. Please excuse me."

She looked around and spotted the Restroom sign. As she walked away Rick leaned over to Carlos, who had relaxed a little and was in the process of lifting a bud light. He whispered in Carlos's ear.

"I think she likes you."

Carlos's expression changed from one of relief to you gotta be shitting me.

"Yeah, she likes me. What she would really *like* is to squeeze my balls until I turn blue. She's a trip, I'll bet right now she's standing facing the commode with one hand on the wall taking a leak."

"You *really* do like her don't you?" said Rick. It was a rhetorical question.

Carlos's lack of a response told Rick that there was more to Carlos's feelings toward Anya than he was willing to admit. Anya was back in less than two minutes. Carlos wanted to ask her if she had washed her hands, but he was tired of holding in his stomach. She sat down and drank nearly three fourths of the bottle before putting it down. Rick signaled the hostess and indicated that they were ready to be seated. The hostess led them to a table near the back of the room. There weren't too many patrons for lunch. It was tough for Ruth's Chris Steak House to compete for the PF Changs and the Cheesecake Factory crowd. The waiter came over and wanted to recite the luncheon specials. Rick held up his hand and told the waiter that they all wanted New York Strips and baked potatoes. Surprisingly, Anya wanted hers well done. Carlos looked somewhat relieved when she didn't order it blood rare.

"So what's the plan Rick?" she asked.

The flight had given Rick a lot of time to devise a plan. While flying over Georgia he remembered a movie with Ray Miland called *Daughter of the Mind*. In the movie supernatural things were happening involving Ray Miland's dead daughter. Miland thought he was losing his mind. Down deep inside he knew the images he was seeing could not be real. He knew it had to be a hoax. He went to a magician, played by John Carradine, and told Carradine what was happening, what he was seeing. Carradine said,

"You show me a spook, and I'll show you an operator."

"But how are they creating the illusion?" asked Miland.

"Don't try to figure out how they are doing it, but how *you* would do it. Then you will be able to solve your problem."

Rick decided to use the same logic, but in reverse. He would put himself into Ben's shoes, pretend to be Ben and determine how he would approach the problem. Rick knew that Ben Anderson had to act quickly. The next article would be in Sunday's paper. Anderson had to believe that a draft of the article would be in by Friday, certainly no later than Saturday. Rick was convinced that he probably had someone in Destin looking for Brooke. Rick had to stay on the offensive. He would set the trap in Virginia Beach at Brooke's condo.

"Since we left Destin, Lynn and Brooke have not used their credit cards or cell phones. I intend to pay this bill with Brooke's credit card. When we leave here, I will buy a couple of weeks of groceries at the Farm Fresh by her condo and also charge that to her card. If my strategy is correct, Anderson will be monitoring her credit card transactions. He will get a hit on the transaction and assume she is back in Virginia Beach. I think he will waste no time coming after her."

Anya was first to speak.

"Do you think *he* will come?"

"No, frankly I don't. But if I were him I would send someone I trusted, and someone who has a vested interest in his witness scheme."

Anya's and Carlos's expressions indicated that Rick's observation was plausible. They were in agreement…so far. At that point, the waiter placed Caesar salads in front of Rick and Carlos and placed a house salad in front of Anya.

"Rick, do you have any idea how many are involved in the scheme?"

"As I have told Carlos, I believe at least four and possibly five. One has committed suicide."

"So what is our assignment Rick?" asked Carlos.

"Ann, I want you to become Brooke. Do the normal in-house things. But, be ready for an intruder. I would expect him to come in and try to over power you, and see if he can find out any information that could lead them to the *Anonymous Source*. He won't know you are expecting him. Carlos, I need you to recon the area. If you were doing the surveillance, where would you set up? Where is the best place to watch the condo? If there is more than one location, select the top two. You take one location; I'll take the other. Any questions so far?"

Ann spoke up.

"Rick, what about a camera on the house, a way of giving me a heads-up?"

"I intend to put one on the condo across the street. It's vacant and will provide a clear view of the front door and garage. Since her living area is basically on the second floor, I am sure we will have the access covered."

"Do you want me to question him?" asked Ann.

"If you get the opportunity, but I don't want you to take any unnecessary chances. I have no idea who will be coming or what his capabilities are."

"Or hers," responded Ann.

Rick hadn't considered that a woman could be part of the scheme, although it was unlikely. He thought about it for a few seconds and then dismissed the thought.

The waiter came with a tray of steaks that had been cooked at sixteen hundred degrees. They were still sizzling. The plates were very hot. Rick and Carlos covered theirs in butter. Ann had hers already covered in mushrooms and onions. All three took a bite and had already begun making artwork out of their baked potatoes.

"Ann, seriously. Nothing risky. I want this guy to leave in a body bag."

Ann was in the process of cutting another piece of steak and never looked up from her plate.

"I have no problem with that, right Carlos?" she responded without looking at Carlos.

Carlos instinctively tightened his stomach muscles and drew his knees closer together.

"Carlos, if there is another guy, one of us will take him out," said Rick.

"What if they don't take the bait—just watch?" responded Carlos.

"Then I will follow them back to where they are staying and take them out in their motel room. As far as I am concerned, that would be ideal. Any other questions?

Carlos was in his tactical mode.

"What if Anderson has a contact here?"

"He could have, but I don't think so. The *Anonymous Source* indicated that the ones involved in the scheme were located in DC, Texas and Arizona. To make this work, I had to make assumptions, and before you say it, I understand what *assume* stands for. However, my instinct tells me that whoever is coming will be here late today, tomorrow at the latest. Since I have already used Brooke's credit card at the bar, we need to get into position. Are there any other questions? Things I may have missed?"

Anya and Carlos studied the remaining food on the table. There probably were other questions, but only ones that would delay the inevitable. Rick signaled the waiter and without asking for the check, handed him Brooke's credit card. As they waited for the bill, Rick went through some last minute directions.

"Carlos, lets swap vehicles. Ann will go with me in your SUV to the grocery store. Then I'll drop Ann at Brooke's."

Rick looked over at Ann who had just sneaked a peek at Carlos.

"I assume you brought hardware?"

She pulled her lips together tightly and tilted her head to the side revealing a dimple on her left check.

"I'll take that as a 'yes'. Carlos, do you have a small spy camera?"

"I have exactly what we need. It would probably be best if I set it up. If anyone is already watching, they'll just think I'm looking at the condo that is for sale. The transmitter has a two-mile radius. It will be perfect."

"Good. Call me as soon as you have mapped the area. Is there anything else?"

"What if Anderson doesn't bite?" asked Carlos.

Rick looked at Carlos and then at Ann and back to Carlos.

"Then I will take care of Anderson."

Chapter Forty-One
Atlanta, GA
December 1, 2010
Wednesday
1300 Hours

Luis and Mickey had a three-hour lay over in Atlanta. Luis had just finished a cinnabon and coffee. Mickey had gone to the men's room. Luis was enjoying the parade of pretty young women in the terminal area when his cell phone vibrated, interrupting one of his mile-high airline fantasies. He took the cell phone from his belt and saw that he had a voicemail. It was from Ben. The message was short and direct. Stay where you are. Call me! Luis got up from his chair next to the terminal walkway and moved over by a large window that looked out over the gate area. He dialed Ben. Ben had been in his office for the past couple of hours. He was on another line with a detective from Burke, Virginia when his cell phone rang. As soon as he saw it was Luis, he told the detective that he had an urgent call and would get back to him. Ben grabbed for the phone as if it were alive and about to jump off the table and run away.

"Luis, I have been trying to get in touch with you."

"Ben, we just landed a few minutes ago. I had my phone off. What's up?"

"About an hour ago I received two hits on Ms. Morgan's Master Card; and then about fifteen minutes ago I got another hit from a Farm Fresh. She must be back in Virginia Beach, and I would assume on her way home with groceries as we speak. I have already changed your flight. Do you have a pen? Are you ready to copy?"

"Yes, just a second." Said Luis reaching into hi pocket.

Although they had plenty of time, the anxiety in Ben's voice came through loud and clear.

"Okay, shoot."

"You and Mickey have confirmed reservations on Delta Flight five three zero four departing Atlanta at fourteen forty-four and arriving Norfolk at sixteen twenty-two. Did you get that?"

"Got it."

"Luis, it is a commuter aircraft in a different terminal. I suggest that you check in right away. If I remember, you both had carry-ons?"

"That's right. We will have no problem with the bags."

"Call me when you're on the ground."

Ben was relieved that he got in touch with Luis. One problem down, one to go. He dialed Detective Barlow. He really wasn't in the mood to talk with him, but he needed to be cooperative. Of all the police that showed up at Sidney Bascomb's house, Martin Barlow was a real professional. He was head and shoulders above the rest. Ben had noticed how easily Detective Barlow took charge of the scene. Barlow had been with the police department for over twenty years. This was his second career. He was a retired Marine Corps Master Sergeant. He was proud of his service and still wore a military haircut. At sixty-three years old, he looked like he worked out quite regularly with heavy weights and probably ran three miles a day. He was not your typical veteran detective.

"Barlow," he answered sounding official.

"Detective Barlow, this is Ben Anderson. Sorry, but I had to take that other call. How may I help you?"

"Thanks, this shouldn't take too long. I understand that you and Mr. Bascomb were good friends. Is that true?"

"It is. We have been *very good* friends for a number of years."

Detective Barlow caught the Tom Clancy response and made a note on his pad.

"Very good friends...in that case, were you aware of his connection to Danny Ochoa?"

Actually, Ben hadn't been aware until a couple of weeks ago when Sidney came to him and told him that he had received a call from Manny Dominguez.

"I didn't until a couple of days ago."

"A couple of days ago. Do you remember how many days ago?"

"I don't remember exactly…Actually, I believe it has been a couple of weeks."

"Why do you suppose he told *you*?"

"Because we *are* friends, and I believe he needed to talk with someone he trusted. He had gotten a call from someone who worked for Ochoa. He was obviously distraught over the call.

"Did he tell you what the call was about?"

Ben knew that Detective Barlow was good. He needed to stay as close to the truth as possible without involving himself.

"He said that Ochoa wanted him to find out where we were keeping one of his Lieutenants."

Ben knew to keep his answers short and to the point. There was no sense in offering information that wasn't requested.

"Do you remember the Lieutenant's name?" asked Detective Barlow.

"Yes, his name was Paco Ramirez."

"Did you report this fact to your superiors?"

Detective Barlow was good. Ben didn't like where this was going.

"Unfortunately, I chose not to."

"Why?"

Ben hadn't been on this side of an interrogation in a long time. He was starting to wish that he were the one asking the questions. He wasn't quite sure where Detective Barlow was going with this line of questioning.

"Sidney had created a new life. He asked for my help. I needed time to evaluate the situation. Initially, I thought if we just ignored Ochoa, events would take care of themselves."

"Did he tell you what his involvement was with Danny Ochoa?"

"He said that he had worked for him as an accountant. He did the books for several of Ochoa's car dealerships."

"Did he tell you that he also did the books for Ochoa's drug operation?"

Although Ben was expecting the question, it still made him uncomfortable. He hoped that Detective Barlow did not sense his emotion.

"No he didn't. Detective Barlow, I'm not sure that I'm following you. Where are you going with this?"

"Deputy, there appears to be a connection with the deaths of Danny Ochoa, Ernesto Garcia, Manny Dominguez and Sidney Bascomb. Do you not see that?" responded Detective Barlow.

Ben knew the connection, and it was far from any scenario that Detective Barlow could ever have imagined.

"Detective Barlow, do you actually think that Sidney was still involved with Ochoa, and that his death may not be a suicide?"

"I think that is a distinct possibility."

"With all due respect, I think you are way off base. Sidney Bascomb was a good man who left Miami behind. I can only believe that Ochoa was using Sidney's past to blackmail him. It was too much for Sidney to handle. In fact, when I learned that Ochoa had been killed I called Sidney to give him, what I considered to be, *good news*. I firmly believe that if Sidney had known that Ochoa was dead, you and I would not be having this conversation."

"You may be right about that, but I will be looking further into Bascomb's records. Who knows what may turn up? Thank you for returning my call Deputy Anderson. I will stay in touch."

With that, Detective Barlow hung up. Ben slowly put the phone back into the cradle. He sat back in his chair staring at the phone. He could hear his heartbeat pounding in his ears. He hoped that his trepidation wasn't obvious to detective Barlow. He knew that Detective Barlow was heading down the wrong road. But all roads lead somewhere, and Barlow's road could lead right back to him and the witness scheme. For the first time, Ben wished he knew more about Sidney's record keeping process. He got up from his chair and looked out the window at the after-lunch crowd scurrying back into the buildings like army ants. He thought about Ms. Brooke Morgan. This whole mess started with her and *The Last Witness*.

Brooke Morgan's Condo, Virginia Beach, 1345 Hours

Rick and Anya arrived at Brooke's condo at 1345. Rick unlocked the door. Both he and Anya went in to check out the condo. Anya led the way with a Beretta nine millimeter in hand. There was staleness in the air. A staleness that pervades every home that lies dormant. The condo was empty and it didn't appear that anyone had been there. Rick checked the condo for *bugs*. None were found in any of the obvious places. He checked for hidden cameras. Both he and Anya agreed that the condo was clean. However, just in case, from that point on Rick began calling her Brooke.

"Brooke, I'll get the groceries. Why don't you give Chris a call when you get a chance?"

"I will, when I get settled."

She even sounded like Brooke. It took Rick five trips to unload the groceries. He spent another fifteen minutes with Anya making small talk.

"Honey, call me if you need anything. Love you."

"Love you too Daddy."

They hugged, and Rick left. The charade had begun. As he left, he saw Carlos across the street looking at the condo that was for sale. He pretended not to notice and drove out of the neighborhood. He turned into the Seven Eleven just off General Booth Boulevard and called Carlos.

"Hey Rick. I'm just pulling out. The camera is in position and working well."

"Good. Have you finished the recon?"

"I have. I'll take position one, which is over in the Rec Center parking lot. You can take position two, which is by the Konikoff building. The Rec Center would be the best location because of the traffic. We can keep in touch via cell phone."

"Sounds good Carlos. I'll call Anya and let her know that you will give her a heads up."

"Okay."

Anya was making herself at home. It was easy for her. She liked Brooke's décor. She was surprised that they had certain similarities. She put the groceries away and turned on the TV to CNN. Whenever she was in front of the windows she kept moving just in case someone was watching. She heard her cell phone and realized she had left it in the master bathroom. She saw that it was Rick.

"Hey Pops."

Rick hadn't realized how much he had told Anya about Brooke.

"I just wanted to let you know that Carlos has everything in place. He will call you if someone approaches the condo. I suggest that you leave the door unlocked. Lets make it easy for him to enter. He won't know that you are expecting him."

Anya knew that no one could be listening to their satellite phones, but she kept up the charade just in case there was a bug in the house.

"Yes, I have everything put away. Thanks for being there for me. I'll give you a call later. Love you."

Rick hung up and opened his computer. He went into web mail and entered Brooke's email address and password. She had over forty-five emails. Rick recognized all but three that were an AOL account. The subject line on the second AOL message simply said "Initials". He knew it was from the *Anonymous Source*. The message was short.

"Ms. Morgan. The following are involved in the witness protection scheme:

Dallas Texas—LE and MM, Phoenix, Arizona—TR"

Rick wrote down the information and decided to call Carl Peterson. Carl must have been sitting on his phone. He answered on the first ring.

"Hey Rick, how's it going?"

"Very well Carl. Are you busy?'

"No more than usual. However, for you, I'm never busy. How may I help you?"

"I have initials to go along with the locations in Brooke's article. I was hoping you could put some names with the initials?"

"No problem. Give me the info," said Carl as he prepared to write.

"Dallas is LE and MM Phoenix is TR"

"Okay, LE and MM for Dallas and TR for Phoenix. Anything else if we make an identification?"

"Carl, if my strategy is correct I believe one or two of these guys are on their way to Virginia Beach. It would be nice to know if that is the case."

"I'll put Roland on it. It won't take long if the info you have is correct. Give me about thirty minutes."

"Thanks Carl."

Rick double clicked his satellite surveillance icon. He entered his password and the system initialized. He typed in Brooke's address. The satellite system zoomed in on her condo complex and then zoomed in on her condo. It was real time. He moved the scene over to the recreation parking lot and found Carlos. He zoomed in and could actually tell that the car was occupied. The resolution was amazing. They really didn't need the camera. However, he knew that there was a few seconds delay. A few seconds could be fatal. Just then his satellite phone rang. It was Carl.

"Carl, that was quick."

"It was pretty easy. The deputies in Dallas are Luis Escobar and Mickey McGuire. Roland is still working on the Arizona contact. He's convinced that TR is not a Deputy US Marshal. You're going to love this; yesterday Escobar and McGuire escorted Paco Ramirez to DC. Then this morning they booked a flight to Pensacola. Does that ring any bells?"

"It sure does, especially with Destin only an hour away."

"Rick, it gets better. A little while ago they changed flights in Atlanta and are now on their way to Norfolk. Their flight is scheduled to land at sixteen twenty-two."

"Seems like my plan is working. Can you let me know when they rent a car?"

"Not only can I let you know, I will give you the make and license number."

Rick checked his watch. It was 1605.

"Great. I can't thank you enough Carl."

"Like old times Rick. Makes me feel young again."

Rick called Carlos and passed on the information. Carlos was a bit relieved and decided to grab a power nap. Rick also called Anya and told her the same information. Anya was drinking a bottle of Perrier and watching the news. Rick continued to check out the satellite image. He decided to focus on his own vehicle and make a determination of the time delay. He scanned to the Konikoff building and easily located the SUV. He rolled down the window and stuck his arm out. It took about two seconds to show up on the screen. That was nearly real time, but not good enough when it came to a tactical situation. He moved the view back to Brooke's condo. The cell phone rang and interrupted Rick's concentration. It was Carl Peterson.

"Hey Carl."

"They just rented a dark blue Camry, Virginia plate LAT nine three seven four. I'm watching them right now on satellite. Looks like they are turning east on two sixty-four."

As Carl was passing the information, Rick was searching the intersection of 64 and 264. He picked them up behind a small truck.

"I think I have them. Are they behind a small truck?" he asked.

"You got them. Rick, go to tools, your system will allow you to put a *marker* on them. Then you can just follow their movement."

"Got it. That is really something."

"Let me know how things work out. Is Carlos at Brooke's?"

"Do you remember Anya Petrov?"

"Of course I do. I thought she started a company and was in DC."

"She did, but she is helping me with this one."

"How is Carlos handling seeing her again?"

"I haven't figured out their relationship. He seems to flinch every time she gets near him."

"Ah…Sigonella."

"You know what happened in Sigonella?"

"Sure, remember we were sitting at the bar…"

Just then Carl was signaled that he had a call from Homeland Security.

"Hey Rick, I have to take a call. Just call me later when you get a chance."

All the time Rick was talking, he was watching the computer screen. The Camry had just taken the NAS Oceana exit. Rick called Anya and told her that there were two of Ben Anderson's guys on the way. She continued to watch the news. At 1650 the Camry made a right turn onto General Booth Boulevard. Rick called Carlos.

"Carlos, if they don't stop, they are about five minutes from your location."

"Okay, let me know when they turn down Nimmo Parkway. Is Anya ready?"

"She sure seems to be," responded Rick.

"They just crossed over Dam Neck Road. Looks like they're pulling into the Seven-Eleven."

Mickey jumped out of the car and went into the Seven Eleven. Luis waited in the car. He had been unusually quiet during the flight to Norfolk, although Mickey never noticed. Mickey rarely started a conversation, and was just as happy to avoid a lengthy discussion. He returned with two sodas, several packs of cheese crackers and two hot dogs. He handed one of the sodas to Luis. Luis was in another world. Mickey had to shake him to get his attention.

"What's the matter with you? You haven't said a word since we left Atlanta."

Luis had a serious look on his face as he took the cup.

"Mickey, something is not right. I can't quite put my finger on it, but I think we are being set up."

"You think Ben is setting us up?"

"No…not Ben. It just doesn't feel right to me."

"What doesn't feel right?"

"I just have a feeling that we are dealing with a professional who is one step ahead of us. I used to know a guy named Morgan, and if it is the same guy, he's a step ahead of us…you can bet on it!"

"Yeah, but there's two of us Luis."

Luis looked over at Mickey in disbelief. Mickey's cheeks were puffed out with crackers. He was trying to wash them down with soda. It was dripping on his shirt. Mickey had never faced an opponent on equal footing, and most certainly not one with Rick Morgan's capability.

"What if he has some help? The kind of help that could take out guys like Garcia, Dominguez and Danny Ochoa."

"You really think so—huh?"

"We need to be real careful," said Luis as he looked over at Mickey. "Real careful," he said again, his voice a bit louder.

As Mickey continued to wolf down the crackers, Luis open the doors and placed toothpicks into the push button on the door jams so that the interior lights wouldn't come on when the doors were opened. He started the car and turned right on General Booth. Rick could see the car moving on his satellite system.

"Okay they are heading out of the parking lot. Nimmo is coming up. They just made the turn. You should just about see them coming."

"Got them."

Chapter Forty-Two
Virginia Beach, VA
December 1, 2010
Wednesday
1800 Hours

Luis and Mickey drove down Nimmo Parkway and made a left turn into Brooke's condo complex. The gate was not there for security reasons; it was there to slow down the residents. It was triggered by an electric eye that opened to any car as it approached. It let Luis and Mickey enter unchallenged. Carlos immediately made a call to Anya.
"Yes."
"Two guys in a dark blue Camry just entered the complex. They are driving slowly. I believe they are checking addresses."
Carlos continued to watch the vehicle. It was actually going slow enough for someone to jump out and move into the shadows without being noticed. Rick was also watching the satellite image, but was unable to distinguish anything with enough certainty to make an informed decision."
"Okay Ann…Ms. Peters, they have turned around and are heading in my direction. I'll keep you informed."
"Thanks."
Anya didn't talk much with Carlos, even when it was extremely necessary. She didn't like being dependent upon him one bit. However, this time she really needed to trust him. Trust that he would notify her as soon as anyone was about to enter the condo. It was imperative that the element of surprise was on her side. Anya had already made up her mind that if both men entered the condo, she would shoot the first one and then deal with the second one on her terms. If she could get him to talk that would be a plus, but she would shoot him in a heartbeat if necessary. Luis and Mickey drove into the Rec Center parking lot

and parked facing the condo complex. They parked a few feet from the exact spot that Carlos had identified as tactical position one. After they turned the lights off, Carlos called Rick to give him an update.

"Hey Carlos."

"Rick, they are in position. I assume they will wait until the evening traffic dies down. They are several rows in front of me. I have a clear view of their vehicle and a clear shot if needed."

"Good, hold your position. Carlos, I can relieve you if necessary. Just let me know."

"I'll be okay. I have a thermos of coffee, water and some protein bars. I also have a piddle pack with me. When do you think they will strike?"

"I believe it won't be too long. These guys have been on the road for the last couple of days. They came straight here from the airport. I'm sure they consider Brooke an easy target. They probably just want to get it over with and head out of town."

"Rick, do you think they are planning on coming after you next?"

"I would think that is their plan. I'm sure that Anderson knows I wouldn't let Brooke return alone. And there certainly is a strong possibility that Anderson thinks I'm the *Anonymous Source*."

"Well, it won't matter what their plan is, they'll never get that far anyway. Rick, I haven't seen a car go into the complex in the last fifteen minutes."

"Carlos, can you see movement in Brooke's condo?"

"Yes, Anya is doing a good job. Everything looks very natural."

"How about the camera…now that it is dark?"

"It's fine. The streetlight provides enough illumination. I have a clear view of the front door and garage."

"Okay, looks like we just have to wait. I'm going to move from this position and go into the condo complex from the other end. I can park down the street at one of the condos that is for sale. If you see any movement, call me right after you call Anya."

"Will do," responded Carlos.

Luis and Mickey finished the hot dogs that they got at the Seven-Eleven. Mickey gulped the soda he was drinking then let out a loud belch that Luis felt vibrating through his seat. Mickey said nothing. He hardly talked at all, and he was never apologetic. Although they had been partners for nearly twelve years, Luis didn't really *know* Mickey. Mickey was a *Yankee*. He had grown up in Glens Falls, New York in a small house on Haskell Avenue. Although born in America, Mickey always considered himself to be Irish first and foremost. His claim to fame was that he was tougher than nails and had a jaw of iron. Little Mickey could hold his own with anybody, and unfortunately, he always wanted to prove it. At five feet eight inches and one hundred and sixty-five pounds, he didn't present a formidable appearance… from a distance. But up close it was obvious that "Little Mickey" had his share of bouts. He had thick hands, fleshy knuckles and a flat nose that was classic. As a teenager he had fought as a middleweight in the Golden Gloves. He probably could have become a contender but didn't have the discipline or patience to "pay his dues". Mickey wanted to make a quick buck. Ben Anderson provided that opportunity. At 2130 Luis looked over at Mickey. Mickey had dozed off.

"Mickey…Mickey wake up!" he said.

Luis shook Mickey. Mickey was in a deep sleep. Luis thought to himself that people with a clear conscience could sleep well. Mickey had no conscience, he could sleep *very* well.

"What's up? We ready?"

"You're ready. Go take care of business and then we will head out to her father's place…and Mickey, if the door is unlocked, there may be more in that house than you can handle. We can abort and look for another opportunity."

Mickey checked his weapon, making sure that there was one in the chamber. He screwed on a silencer and got out of the car without even looking over at Luis. Mickey never showed an iota of emotion or remorse. Luis watched him head across the street, and almost said out loud that Mickey was one dumb son-of-a-bitch.

As Mickey was heading across the road, Carlos called Anya and gave her a heads-up. He then called Rick.

"We're on Rick."

"I'll give you thirty seconds and then I am moving in to give Anya some backup. On my count—thirty and—*counting*!"

Carlos got out of his truck and was at the door of the Camry within fifteen seconds. He then crouched down and moved to a position in front of the Camry.

Mickey went up the steps to Brooke's front door. He slowly turned the doorknob. It turned easily. He slowly leaned against the door and opened it without making a sound. As he was going in, he thought about what Luis had told him. He didn't think about it too long. He was in and he was going to take care of business. He locked the door behind him. He went down to the door leading into the garage and locked that door also. He then moved up the stairs, staying close to the railing to avoid making any sound. He could hear the TV. It was fairly loud. As he got to the top step he could see that the TV was coming from a room in the back of the condo unit. With gun in hand he stood very still and looked around the great room. There was one light on in the corner next to the bookcase.

As Mickey was surveying Brooke's great room, Rick was approaching the steps that led up to the front door. Luis had been laying back in the car with his head on the headrest when he spotted Rick moving slowly up the steps to Brooke's condo. He had no idea who it was, but from their guarded movement, Luis knew that it had to be someone who had spotted Mickey. It could be a cop, a neighbor; in fact it could be Rick Morgan. Luis had no way of signaling Mickey. He couldn't call him because he left his phone in the car. He could flash the headlights, but the odds of Mickey seeing them were slim to none. The only other option was for him to go over and help Mickey. Luis got out of the car, and as he moved forward, Carlos quickly moved from his position and took Luis down.

Mickey moved along the wall behind the dining room table. He could see the flicker of the TV. The kitchen was to the right at the mid point of the great room. The light was off. He looked down the hallway to the right. There were two rooms, both doors were shut. He started down the hallway toward the rear of the condo. Since there was a large screen TV in the great room, Mickey assumed that Brooke was in the master bedroom watching TV. As he started down the hall Anya stood up from behind the kitchen counter with her Beretta pointing at Mickey's back. She could see the weapon in his right hand.

"Don't turn around, don't even move or you're a dead man." She said very deliberately.

Mickey froze in his tracks. He was unprepared to be on the business end of a gun. Somewhere in the back of his mind he didn't believe that Brooke Morgan was the gun wielding type. He thought about just turning and firing.

"How do I know you have a gun?"

"You don't know, but this might help."

Anya slowly pulled back the hammer. Even with the TV, the sound of the Beretta being cocked was unmistakable. Mickey hadn't moved. He was weighing his options. Anya moved out from behind the counter and now was about ten feet behind Mickey.

"I don't think you want to shoot me. I'm a Deputy US Marshal."

"Then you should have knocked. I assume you have a search warrant?"

"I don't need a warrant, I have probable cause."

"You have nothing. Drop your weapon!"

"You're not going to shoot me sweetie," responded Mickey confidently.

Luis looked up at Carlos Garcia. He was looking into the barrel of a silencer.

"Take it easy pal, I'm a Deputy US Marshal."

"I know who, and *what* you are."

As Carlos looked down at Luis he realized that he had seen him before. It was dark, but he knew he had seen Luis before. He slowly let him up.

"I know you—don't I?" said Carlos not expecting an answer.

Luis had recognized Carlos right away. He remembered Carlos from training when Carlos taught Judo to incoming classes at Camp Perry.

"I was one of your students many years ago Mr. Garcia, or may I call you Carlos?"

Carlos recognized Luis. Luis was one of the best young CIA agents in the class. He was smart, quick and eager.

Mickey still hadn't moved hardly at all. His heartbeat was normal and he was breathing slowly.

"No, I don't think you are going to shoot me, are you sweetie?" he said again.

"You call me sweetie one more time and I'll blow your balls off—one at a time."

Mickey still wasn't fazed. She really didn't scare him.

"Last chance asshole. Drop the weapon," she demanded.

Mickey whirled around and fired his weapon toward Anya. As Mickey whirled around Anya had moved to the left and dropped down into a squatting position. She fired right after Mickey took his shot. Anya's bullet hit Mickey squarely between the eyes right in the middle of his flat nose. He was dead before he hit the floor. Upon hearing the shots, Rick used his key to open the front door. He went cautiously up the stairs. Anya got up slowly and walked over to where Mickey had fallen over backwards. He was spread eagle on the floor. Blood was staining the hallway carpet. His eyes said that Mickey's story had ended. Anya caught a glimpse of Rick out of the corner of her eye. They both holstered their weapons. Rick was first to speak.

"I take it that you didn't get any information out of him?"

"Sorry Rick, but there was no way this guy was going to tell me anything."

Carlos motioned to Luis to get up. He didn't know that Luis was no longer with the CIA. A lot of agents find out that the covert world is not for them. Hopefully they find it out before it's too late.

"Luis, what happened to you? Why are *you* here?"

"No choice Carlos. It was either this or…

Luis didn't finish the sentence.

"Carlos, how did you get involved?"

"I've known Brooke since she was eight years old. Her father is one of my best friends. "Why Luis, why you?"

"Carlos, I just got tired of risking my life capturing these low lifes and within minutes they're walking down the street before I get the paperwork done. I've seen too many guys die, and for what? So, we help get rid of the trash and make a few bucks to boot."

"It's wrong Luis."

"What about Mickey? Asked Luis.

"I don't know, but it wasn't Brooke in the condo. We had another former operative helping. I imagine Mickey didn't succeed in his objective."

"So what now Carlos?"

"We take you in, you tell the authorities what you know and hopefully you get a break. You know the game, you can ask for immunity."

"It isn't that easy Carlos. There is no way that I can do prison time. You know what they do to cops in prison."

Carlos didn't like where this was going. Luis probably had another weapon and was going to try to use it.

"Luis, it doesn't have to end this way."

"Sorry Carlos. Can't do it."

Luis moved to his left while reaching behind his back. He pulled a Glock 380 from his belt. He fired the first shot hitting Carlos just under the right collarbone. The bullet went clean through. Carlos went down on one knee. His right arm went numb and he dropped his weapon. He was trying to get his breath while reaching for his weapon with his left hand. Luis quickly moved in front of Carlos, stepped on his hand and aimed his gun at Carlos's head.

"Sorry pal, but I can't go to prison."

Carlos never heard the shot…the bullet entered Luis's left ear. Luis wouldn't have to go to prison. Carlos looked to his right, Rick was moving slowly toward Luis. He kicked the Glock away from Luis's hand. Luis wouldn't need it anymore.

"Carlos, is it a bad hit?"

"Bad enough. I can't believe I let him get the drop on me."

Rick put Luis's body in the back seat of the Camry and called Anya.

"Rick, are you guys okay?"

"I'm okay, but Carlos has been hit."

"Is he going to be all right?"

"Yes, but you need to take care of him. Looks like a through and through."

"If you move Brooke's car out of the garage I will put the Camry in there. We can load up McGuire."

"Rick, what are you planning to do with them?" asked Anya.

"I'll give Carl a call. I'm sure he can hook us up with a couple of cleaners."

Chapter Forty-Three
McClean, VA
December 2, 2010
Thursday
0900 Hours

The day didn't start well at all. Carol was feeling under the weather, and Ben couldn't get the coffee maker to work. He searched for the owner's manual to no avail. He found manuals for everything else, including things that he and Carol had sold in garage sales years ago. The one he needed was nowhere to be found. He fooled around with the coffee maker for about fifteen minutes, got frustrated, and decided that he was wasting valuable time. It would be much easier to stop by the Seven Eleven and pick up a cup of coffee and a cake doughnut. It made no sense; the coffee maker had worked perfectly the day before. What was so different about this morning? Maybe Carol had cleaned it. Ben never cleaned the coffee maker. He felt that cleaning it messed up the flavor of the coffee. Ben left Carol a short note, picked up his cell phone and briefcase and headed out the kitchen door. The car was a mess from the previous night's thunderstorm that didn't end until 0422. Ben remembered the time because he looked at the clock. He had looked at the clock about every twenty minutes. The rest of the dead leaves were plastered everywhere. The sky was still overcast. It was a winter sky. Ben hoped that this morning was not a forecast of things to come. He hadn't slept all night. He had expected to hear *good news* from Luis. He should have heard from him by now. He should have heard from him last night. Luis had called to tell him that they had landed and were renting a car. That was before 1700. Where the hell were they? Why hadn't Luis called?

The drive to work was about as good as the coffee maker. Traffic seemed to be moving at a snail's pace. It probably wasn't any worse than usual, but Ben's rush to get to work made each little delay monumental. When he finally made it to his office, he immediately checked his phone and email; still no word from Luis. He called the receptionist. She told him that there were,

"No messages for Mr. Anderson."

He dialed Luis's cell phone…again. Still nothing. This was not good. Luis was disciplined, he was punctual, and he always provided timely updates. Ben hadn't heard a word from him since they started the stakeout. Ben sat back in his chair and let out a long sigh. The ghosts of Ernesto Garcia, Manny Dominguez and Danny Ochoa began dancing around in his head. They told him that Luis and Mickey had suffered a similar fate. Ben felt a cold sweat overtaking him. Sweat rolled down from his armpits. He rarely showed emotion, and he never broke a sweat. Ben had always been in control. But this wasn't looking good at all. He slowly pushed away from his desk, got up and walked down to Sidney Bascomb's office. The yellow tape was still in place. Ben stood very still and looked at it surprisingly, as if this was the first time he had seen it. If anyone had seen the look on his face they would have signed him up for a trip to the company shrink. Ben shut his eyes, let his head drop and felt a slight tremor run unchallenged through his body. The ghosts were laughing at him. They let him know that his coffee partner, Sidney Bascomb, was with them. For the first time in his life, Ben thought he was losing it. He was not in control. The ghosts danced around and told him that Rick Morgan was in control.

Virginia Beach, Carlos Garcia's House, 1030 Hours

Rick, Carlos and Anya just finished having pancakes with Vermont maple syrup. They were nursing cappuccinos, and reviewing the events of the previous week. Anya had done a good job cleaning Carlos's wound. He was well on the way to a complete recovery. Anya was in the processes of ribbing him when Rick's cell phone interrupted her frontal attack. Rick picked it up and looked at the caller ID. It was Carl Peterson.

"Good Morning Carl."

"It *is* a good morning. I have some information concerning the person in Phoenix. His name is Taylor Reece. He is a land developer and real estate broker who has sold properties to the US Marshals. Roland put together a profile on Reece. Looks like he and Ben Anderson met about eight years ago. No criminal record, a few speeding tickets, but that's it."

"Taylor Reece. Will you email his address and telephone number?" asked Rick.

"Sure. By the way, your other thing has been *cleaned* up."

"Carl…I…I don't know what to say?"

"Just say 'thanks' and that you will continue to work for me."

"Thanks Carl, but actually I haven't done anything for you yet!"

"Hey Rick, if you see Anya, I need to tell her something," said Carl, the tone of his voice changing.

"Carl, she's here, I'll put her on."

Rick handed the phone to Anya. Carlos couldn't hide his astonishment. Down deep inside he would have thought Carl would have wanted to talk with him. At least to say 'hi'.

"Hello Carl. It's been a long time," she answered.

"It has, and if memory serves me right, the last time was Sigonella."

Anya looked over at Carlos. Her face suggested that Carl had resurrected a very bad memory. Carlos's muscles tightened out of instinct. He was beginning to understand the concept behind Pavlov's dog.

"Carl, I believe you're right. It was ,indeed, Sigonella."

"Anya, there is something I need to tell you…something I should have told you in Sigonella, but for some reason unknown to me—probably a little jealousy—I purposely let you believe something that wasn't true."

Anya's mind began moving at warp speed. She tried to visualize the bar in Sigonella.

"And *what* was that?" she asked tentatively.

Carl took a deep breath. Anya could feel Carl's nervousness on the other end of the line. She listened intently.

"You had gone to the ladies room and as you returned, I knew that you heard Carlos say *Carl, she's a dyke*."

Anya's heart began to pound. She really didn't want to relive Sigonella.

"Anya," Carl said as he hesitated. "Carlos wasn't talking about you. He was talking about the female bartender. I knew you misunderstood. I also knew that Carlos really cared for you. Quite frankly I was happy when you stopped paying him attention," he added.

Anya was speechless for a few seconds. Her mind was racing. She wasn't expecting Carl's *confession*. She thought about Sigonella and the relationship between the four of them. She had sensed that Carl liked her, but she wasn't interested in him that way. The more she thought about she realized that she could respond with some tough things, but too much time had gone by. Sigonella was a long time ago…a very long time ago.

"Thanks Carl. Thanks for clearing that up. Here's Rick."

Anya got up from the table and took a cold bottle of water out of the refrigerator. Her throat and lips had suddenly become very dry. Carlos could see that she was a bit uneasy. He wondered what Carl could have said to her. He wanted to say something, but his history with Anya had been strained at best. Anya stared out of the kitchen window. She saw nothing except the night in Sigonella. She was in love with Carlos but had never revealed her true feelings. There was no place for true love in their business.

"Carl," said Rick. "Lynn, Brooke and I are going to spend the weekend in the Bahamas. I'll be ready for tasking next Monday."

"I'll have something for you."

"Would you *like* to say *hi* to Carlos?"

Rick's voice and inflection suggested that Carlos's feelings would be hurt if Carl talked with Anya and not to him.

"You are right, I should."

Rick handed the phone to Carlos and walked over toward Anya. She looked at Rick. There was a slight hint that she was fighting back tears. Rick put his arm around her shoulder and gave her a hug. Whatever Carl had told her; Rick knew that it softened her heart. He had never seen Anya cry. He suspected it had everything to do with Carlos and Sigonella.

"Hey Carl. How is everything with The Peterson Group?"

"It will be that much better when you're aboard. I hope you consider a position with us."

"I am strongly considering a position. I just need a few days off."

"I'm looking forward to it Carlos. By the way, I really owe you an apology, one that I will understand if you do not accept. Do you remember telling me that you thought the barmaid in Sigonella was a dyke?"

Carlos thought for a few seconds.

"I sort of remember that," he responded.

"Well Anya overheard you and thought you meant her. That is why she has treated you the way she has all these years. She was hurt deeply, and I knew it. I can't change the past, but I hope you will find it in your heart to forgive me."

Carlos was stunned. At first he didn't understand why Carl would have done that. But they were young and competitive.

"Carl, it was a long time ago my friend. I *will* call you in a few days."

"Thanks Carlos."

Carlos hung up and handed the phone to Rick. He looked over at Anya. She had already turned and was walking toward him. The tears on her cheeks were real. They embraced without saying a word. Carlos's muscles were finally relaxed.

Chapter Forty-Four
Washington DC
December 2, 2010
Thursday
1400 Hours

The Ghosts of Ernesto Garcia, Manny Dominguez and Danny Ochoa were fighting with the ghosts of Luis Escobar and Mickey McGuire. They were all speaking Spanish except for Mickey who was now only a foot tall and dressed like a little green leprechaun with bright orange hair. Mickey was running around with a newspaper in his hand trying to get each one to look at it. They would kick him through the air like a soccer ball. He would bounce several times and then return waiving the newspaper at them yelling *The Last Witness…The last Witness*! Ben could hear a phone ringing in the distance; it was getting closer and closer. It was getting louder. He wanted to answer it, but he couldn't find it. The ghost of Mickey hit him with the newspaper. Ben jumped back and opened his eyes. The phone was still ringing. It was the phone on his desk. He looked at it for a few more seconds, took a deep breath and cleared his throat. His hands were sweaty. He looked around the room for the ghosts.

"Anderson," said a voice he didn't recognize. "Meet me at Starbucks."

Ben didn't say anything for several long seconds.

"Who is this?" he asked tentatively. "Hello? Hello…who *is* this?" he demanded.

The caller had hung up. The dial tone returned. Ben checked the caller ID. The call had come from the Starbucks at Union Station. It was the Starbucks that he and Sidney Bascomb had gone to on a regular basis. The phone had scared away the ghosts. Ben's mind was clear. The caller had to be Rick Morgan. Morgan was the only one left that could have pulled this off. The only other guy *alive* that knew anything at all about the witness scheme was Taylor Reece, but there was absolutely no reason for Taylor Reece to make waves. Taylor had nothing to gain and everything to lose. Somehow, it was Rick Morgan. It had to be Rick Morgan. He had found out about the scheme; and to help his daughter's career, he was the one feeding her the information. The *Anonymous Source* thing was a nice touch. Rick Morgan just had to be the *Anonymous Source.* Ben knew that he had to go to Starbucks.

The usual crowd was there. Several students had their computers open and were grilling each other in preparation for an upcoming exam. A young couple was holding hands and leaning in toward one another having a very private conversation. The stains on their coffee cups were dry. The guy with the black trench coat was back in his customary place. He was sitting in the large cloth covered easy chair and reading one of the free newspapers. An elderly lady was working the New York Times crossword puzzle. She was in a race with herself. She appeared to be winning. Ben continued to look around the room; there were no other men. Ben ordered a cappuccino and blueberry scone, grabbed the remaining Wall Street Journal and took a seat at his regular table. Maybe Morgan was across the street checking him out. Ben noticed several people at the entrance to the Metro. None seemed to fit Rick Morgan's description. As Ben was looking out through the window he didn't notice that the guy in the black trench coat had gotten up from his chair and was approaching his table. The sound of the chair being pulled back and dragged across the floor startled Ben. Ben turned as the guy in the trench coat sat down across from him. Ben didn't recognize him, but he was positive that it wasn't Rick Morgan. The guy in the black trench coat had shoulder length hair that was graying. He wore tinted glasses and a small gold loop earring in his left ear. His hands were rough looking. There were letters tattooed on each of his fingers. Ben had seen similar tattoos. They were the kind that guys got in prison. Who the hell was this guy?

"Can I help you? Do I know you?" asked Ben wondering why this guy pulled out the chair and was now starring at him.

"You don't recognize me do you Ben?"

"I'm afraid you have me at a disadvantage," responded the stranger.

"I *know* that I have you at a disadvantage. Do the names Stimson, Mackey, Miller and Tennant ring any bells?"

Ben got a sinking feeling in his stomach. It rang a chorus of bells. He hadn't heard those names in over fifteen years. Another ghost from the past. The guy in the trench coat removed his glasses and the longhaired wig he was wearing. Ben's heart pounded.

"G a r d n e r S t o l l i e."

Ben said the name very slowly.

"Never thought you would see me again…did you Ben?"

Ben didn't say anything. He hadn't seen Gardner in what felt like a lifetime.

"No, frankly I didn't."

"You just couldn't keep your nose clean, could you Ben?"

"What do you *want* Gardner?"

"What I want, you can't give me. I want fifteen years of my life back. I want my dignity back. I want my virginity back. I want my fucking life back. Can you do that for me Ben? Can you do that…give me my life back?"

Ben didn't really care to look at Gardner. He looked back out the window. He didn't expect to see Gardner Stollie again—ever again. He never wanted to see him again. That chapter of his life had ended a long time ago.

"You're the one who set this whole thing up? You're the *Anonymous Source*?"

A wry smile crossed Gardner's face. It didn't linger very long.

"Ben, you'd be surprised what you can learn in prison. I learned all about computers from the guy who hacked into the Department of Defense mainframe. You must have read about him. I learned how to spoof an account. I learned about *bugs* from a well-known democratic strategist. I even found *you* through the IRS database, and I did that while sitting in the prison library."

Ben's mind was racing, grabbing for anything that would seem to justify his actions to Stollie.

"Gardner, I thought that you were on the take. The Feds told me that you were."

Ben was lying, but at this point, it was worth the try. Gardner wasn't buying it.

"Ben, we had such a good deal. We were making big money, but you, you son-of-a-bitch, you had to get greedy. The Kuwaitis would have taken care of us...and legally!"

Ben remembered everything as if it had happened yesterday. Gardner was right. It was a good deal. The plan hatched by the State Department was so simple. The Iranians were already in financial trouble. Their war with Iraq was draining them. The State Department would provide an oil subsidy to either the Kuwaitis or the Saudis. It didn't really matter which one, there just had to be a paper trail. The operation was being financed using monies obtained through a tax increase on oil company profits. The money would be used to reduce the *apparent* cost of a barrel of oil being sold to the US. It certainly was a great deal for the Arabs. They still sold their oil for the same price but got subsidized in the process to make it look like they were selling at a lower price. The American public was happy, because they thought they were getting cheaper oil. Besides, there was grass roots pressure on the Government to add a windfall tax on oil company profits. The Iranians wouldn't be able to compete. They would lose oil revenues and go further in debt, putting additional pressure on the Ayatollah. It was a good plan from the Government perspective. However, what the public never seems to understand is that the additional tax on profits is passed along to them at the pump. The little guy never gets ahead. Stimson, Mackey, Miller and Tennant were the ideal firm, since they were relatively small and did not appear to be politically connected. The deal had been going on for nearly ten months. Everything was going fine until Ben got greedy... real greedy. He made a secret deal with the Kuwaitis. Gardner had no idea what Ben had done, and if he had known, he would never have gone along with it. Somehow the Saudi Royal Family found out and accused both Gardner and Ben of taking a bribe from the Kuwaitis. The State Department was swift to act. Ben, in order to save his ass, agreed to be a witness for the prosecution and pin the entire thing on

Gardner Stollie in return for immunity. He was forced to resign and make a contribution of two million dollars to the Stimson, Mackey, Miller and Tennant "slush fund". Gardner wasn't so lucky. He didn't see it coming. Not only did he have to donate the two million dollars, but also he was sentenced to fifteen to twenty-five years in prison. Gardner Stollie ended up being the fall guy, although he was straight as the proverbial arrow. He had been planning his revenge ever since.

"How did you find out what was going on?" asked Ben.

"Ben, I knew you wouldn't stay clean. You'd be on the take somehow. So I decided to follow you. I bugged your car. There's more than just gum stuck to the bottom of this table. I started coming here almost on a weekly basis. I listened to conversations between you and the *late* Sidney Bascomb. Then I got a brilliant idea. I pretended to be a marketer. I approached several newspapers with a marketing scheme to increase their circulation. It was a simple plan. They would run a contest, and the winner would write a serial adventure. I even suggested the subject matter…the US Marshal's Witness Protection Program. Then when the Virginian Journal selected Brooke Ashley Morgan, the daughter of Richard B. Morgan, to write the series, *The Last Witness*… it was a gift from heaven, in more ways than one."

"So what now Gardner? Where do we go from here?"

"Ben, we go nowhere. I'm going to get on with my life. You've got your own problems. From my calculations, it's just you and Taylor Reece left. I'm sure you know who hit your team and took out the Miami drug guys. The beauty of this is I haven't even had to lift a finger."

Ben found himself without words.

"You know, I did some research on Richard B. Morgan…he's certainly nobody to screw with. I'm sure he is not very happy with how you treated his *only* daughter."

Gardner's smile revealed a set of yellow teeth stained by years of prison cigarettes.

"I'd be looking over my shoulder if I were you!" he added emphatically.

With that Gardner got up from the table. His looks had suffered from prison life. He had several facial scars that he would carry to his grave.

He wasn't the same tall handsome Gardner Stollie that Ben knew from college. However, he had a look of satisfaction. As he turned to leave, he slowly glanced back, the wry smile returning.

"Well Ben, I guess Karma really is a bitch!"

Gardner continued to smile as he walked away. He never said another word as he disappeared into the DC afternoon, leaving Benjamin Franklin Anderson staring blankly at the empty chair.

Epilogue
Atlantis Hotel, Paradise Island, Bahamas
December 3, 2010
Friday

On Friday Morning Ben Anderson kissed Carol and told her he would call her later. She was still a bit under the weather. He hadn't said much the night before. She could tell that he wasn't himself. There was something on his mind that really bothered him. However, she knew that Ben would tell her what it was when the time was right. The coffee maker still wasn't working. He would stop at the Seven Eleven. Ben left by the kitchen door and got into his car. He sat there for a few minutes wondering what this day would bring. It definitely hadn't been a very good week. At least it was a beautiful morning. The sky was clear, the leaves had dried up and blown away by a slight breeze out of the west. Ben turned the key and started his car…for the last time. The explosion could be heard for several miles. The blast blew out all the windows in the front and side of the house, and caught the large birch tree next to the garage on fire. The police would later conclude that Ben Anderson's death was somehow connected to Danny Ochoa and Miami's drug war.

Off the coast of Puerto Rico a crew member on a Greek freighter removed a worn canvas cover from a dark blue Camry. He put a cable around the car. The crane operator hoisted the Camry off the deck and swung it out over the Atlantic. He dropped the Camry into the Puerto Rico Trench. On the bridge, the water depth measured twenty-five thousand one hundred and seventeen feet. The car rapidly went out of sight and sunk into the abyss with the bodies of Luis Escobar and Mickey McGuire in the trunk. The trunk had been welded shut.

Paco Ramirez was returned to Miami authorities. He tried to hire Arthur Silverman to represent him. Silverman told Paco that his docket was full and he couldn't help him at this time. Paco was assigned a public defender that was unable to secure bail. He was confined to the Dade County Jail, and two days later was stabbed to death in a jail yard melee. No one has been charged with his murder.

Taylor Reece was on the dance floor with *the* large bosomed cowgirl when Federal agents entered the bar. Taylor had signed up for the Giants Fantasy Camp in January. He wouldn't be there…and he wouldn't be digging any more graves in the desert.

Roland Carpenter cracked Carlos's secret code in twenty-two minutes and forty-seven seconds. It probably would have been more difficult if Carlos hadn't listed the coded names under the corresponding alphabetical tab.

In an unrelated incident, the Virginia State Police stopped Senior Chief Michael Lucas for driving erratically on highway 3 outside of Fredericksburg, Virginia. A random search of the vehicle revealed a MK11 Sniper's rifle and a box of 7.62 mm rounds. One round was missing. It was later learned that Lucas's Father-in-Law was a Superior Court Judge who was on Nicky Carbone's payroll. The ballistics matched the bullet that killed Anthony Spanelli.

Anya Petrov, a.k.a., Ann Peters and Carlos went out on their first date. Carlos forgot all about Consuelo. Rick was right, he would have been bored silly. Anya would never let Carlos get bored. She let him call her Ann. His stomach muscles never tightened again.

Lou Mallory retired after thirty-six years of exemplary service. There was no gold watch, no service medal, just the customary wooden plaque and thank you letter from the Attorney General. He and his wife moved to Panama City, Florida. He is presently writing a novel entitled *The Unprotected*.

Detective Barlow still believes that Sidney Bascomb's suicide was somehow tied to Ben Anderson, and he is not at all convinced that Ben Anderson's death was purely drug related. Although the case has been closed, he is continuing the investigation on his own time and nickel.

Carol Anderson received one million six hundred thousand dollars from Ben's life insurance policy. After a short stint in Phoenix, she moved back to Chesapeake, Virginia, took back her maiden name and has been seen about town with a young man by the name of Sven Johannson. She never was a very good tennis player.

The FBI, DEA, US Customs, US Marshals and Miami Police were not solely convinced that the deaths of Danny Ochoa, Manny Dominguez, Ernesto Garcia and Ben Anderson were at the hands of the Jamaican Posse. However…they really didn't care. They are still searching for Luis Escobar and Mickey McGuire. Hertz took a write off on the Camry.

Gardner Stollie had his name changed and moved to Portland, Oregon. He took a job as a legal assistant with an environmental firm. The company soon recognized that their new employee, Gregory Stanton was very talented. They offered to send him to Law School. Gregory accepted.

Chris fully recovered from his injuries. His had a million questions. He and Brooke are planning a June wedding. They both signed up for a Martial Arts class.

Rick Morgan finally told Carl Peterson why they call him *blue sky*. Rick, Carlos, Anya and Carl were in the Viking Hotel in Bergen, Norway. Carl had met a tall blonde blue-eyed Norwegian gal that was all over him. As she led him off toward the elevator, Carl started singing *Blue skies from above, baby I'm in love*…as the elevator doors closed. That was his theme song, especially when he thought he was going to *get some*. The bartender couldn't stop smiling. He said that he hoped Carl had enough to drink and was the adventurous type. It seems that the tall blonde was actually a *he*. When Carl returned, he said that he had had a *great time*. They worried about him for years. They never told Carl that they knew…until now.

Current—Paradise Island, Bahamas 1800 Hours

American Flight 4991 had landed in Nassau as scheduled. The one hour and fourteen minute flight from Miami hardly gave Rick, Lynn and Brooke time to take their shoes off and enjoy the flight. Brooke had sent Part III of *The Last Witness* from the FedEx office at the airport.

It was the first write the editor would see, but she had no intention of changing anything. They enjoyed the four-day three-night vacation.

Virginia Beach, December 10, 1600 Hours

Brooke Morgan's article on *The Last Witness* was a monumental success. The Virginian Journal's circulation had increased by eight percent. Sony Pictures had called Brooke to set up a meeting. It appeared that they were interested in buying the movie rights to *The Last Witness*.

On December 12th the managing editor for the Virginian Journal, Mr. Dwayne Malcolm called Brooke to tell her that they would like her to do a five part series on the ATF. Brooke was thrilled. The first thing she did was call her dad.

She greeted in the usual *I got great news* manner:

"Hellooooooo Daddy."

Rick responded in kind.

"Hellooooooo Brooke."

Their greeting went on a couple more times as usual.

"Guess what Dad? The Journal has commissioned me to do a story on the ATF. I can take liberties. Just has to have some truths. I'll need your help."

There was silence on the line. Brooke looked at her phone to make sure she was still connected.

"Dad?...Dad?...hello Dad...come on, I know you're there...you're retired!"

Would you like to see your manuscript become a book?

If you are interested in becoming a PublishAmerica author, please submit your manuscript for possible publication to us at:

acquisitions@publishamerica.com

You may also mail in your manuscript to:

**PublishAmerica
PO Box 151
Frederick, MD 21705**

www.publishamerica.com

PublishAmerica

Manufactured By: RR Donnelley
Momence, IL USA
February, 2011